THE
GREAT ARK

THE
GREAT ARK

T.C. DRIVER

authorHOUSE®

AuthorHouse™
1663 Liberty Drive
Bloomington, IN 47403
www.authorhouse.com
Phone: 1-800-839-8640

Published by AuthorHouse   07/11/2012

ISBN: 978-1-4772-4380-0 (sc)
ISBN: 978-1-4772-4379-4 (e)

Library of Congress Control Number: 2012912507

CONTENTS

This book is dedicated to my fellow Virginians who don't matter, who don't count, no matter what race or sex they may be. Many men are held in jail without a trial, or bond, having not been convicted of anything. I know what I'm talking about I was in jail serving a just sentence myself with them. Other men were being held without charge for years after their lawfully court appointed sentence was over. This power has been and will always be abused. The doctors and lawyers who run the civil commitment system in Virginia are lazy no good blood-suckers on the taxpayers and should be cut off of the state gravy train. It does not cost $100,000 plus per prisoner to lock up these pitiful men. To call most of them dangerous to the public safety is so silly as to be insane in and of itself. Most of these pitiful men pose no danger to your wife and kids what so ever and their crimes are tracked and registered. They are not worth giving up our rights for. Just like modern medicine the new pill often does more harm than the disease or sickness did in the first place.

T.C. DRIVER

Jesus is Lord

Jesus will be our Judge

All illustrations in this book were done by my friend and fellow inmate a WVRJ Mike Fitch. Mike is from Christiansburg Virginia. Thank you Mike, I hope we can work together again in the future.

CHAPTER ONE

The Water Desert of Brazil

I boarded my shuttle craft, an older model thirty-five foot cabin cruiser, before four am that morning. Now daylight, I was awakened by nonstop captain bells and horns. The sea was choppy; with two foot, windblown white caps. Aching and stiff, I balanced to my feet. My sea legs sure were getting old. I cursed the ache under my breath and glanced starboard. *Was my new assignment a damn aircraft carrier?* While scanning the sea for another vessel, my eyes gazed upon the most beautiful sailboat I had ever laid sight upon. Her graceful lines were enchanting as of a woman. *Snap out of it, Cornelius!* I quickly speed dialed Rosie while walking up port deck. Rosie was the nerve center and only employee of my small employment company back in St. Augustine.

The grand ole carrier was steady underway making about eight knots. We pulled through its wake as if giving chase. Climbing onto our boats bridge just as Rosie picked up, I watched straight ahead and said nothing. We drove at one third throttle right into the back, or stern, of the ship. This boat ate us like a big fish! The mouth, or back door, did not shut behind us and we docked inside.

A gangplank came down and two crew members boarded us from port. Over the radio, someone shouted: "Good job, Sarah! Welcome aboard!"

Having lost cell with Rosie, I turned toward the captain as long strawberry blond hair spilled from her cap. With few words, she directed our quick steps, giving me a silent, warm smile as the elevator doors closed. In less than two minutes of docking, we walked out of that elevator straight onto the ship's bridge. I thought, Star Trek (ha-ha). Looking like an airport tower, the bridge bustled with activity and commands. Nine

1

young men stared into computer screens. Three older men stood behind them as if instructors. Five others stood around a mockup of the ship's hangar, main and flight decks in clear plastic. From behind me, the same loud voice bellowed. "Welcome aboard, Cornelius!"

It was Captain Coe himself in Navy dress whites just like Sarah's. I was stunned that he knew my name and saluted. "Good morning, Captain!"

"Stand down, Cornelius" replied Captain Coe. "None of that on this bridge, no time for formalities. Welcome to the Ark. We officers do dress for dinner; 1900 sharp. We will talk about old times then. Officer Booth will now take you to your quarters"

Booth and I walked across the ship not talking much.

"Who are these people" I thought to myself. The Ark was not an American Navy warship. The U.S. Navy had gone out of business two years before. It would be months before I received a proper tour of the ship; sixty-eight months before my tour ended. Not in food service, but as a flight instructor to college and post graduate age kids. This ship, named simply, The Ark, and owned by God only knows who (or what), was commanded by one Joe Coe. He was a one-time school acquaintance of mine. My stay aboard The Ark is the strange story I tell you in this book. Little did I imagine that the next six years of my life would be spent aboard her or that my life and vision of the world would be changed forever?

That night we did dress for dinner, as we have every evening since. I met a staff of four hundred sixty-two other officers. Thirty-six were old Navy pilots like me. We pilots sat at the head table in the Officer's Mess with Captain Coe, two of his daughters (Sarah and Haley), four other women and Captain Coe's six disciples who never left his side. His daughters, who were twelve years apart in age, and of two different Mothers, were the Captains crowning jewels and the object of much attention in our group.

The next day, I met one thousand nine hundred plus veteran seamen that made up the ship's crew. For the next nine weeks we had the ship to ourselves. Then we were joined by fifty-eight professors, two thousand two hundred students, two hundred fourteen associate professors, one hundred twenty-four elderly passengers and thirty-six mysterious military commando types. Yes, it was in Brazil that the big empty ship came to life. For now, officers and crew alike went about the job of training, learning the ship and their various duties. The crew was hard-working, very professional and well paid. We worked twelve-on/twelve-off for three days with the fourth day off. Most officers and senior crew worked overtime, making for long days and sound sleep. Down time was plentiful and our work not very stressful. The cruise was enjoyable; a labor of love for most. Our quarters were comfortable; almost cruise ship luxury. We had barely enough crew to run this size ship. The Ark had a department for everything. She was a floating city. Her officers and crew were assigned to A, B and C duties as needed. Food service did a great job. That being my focus the last nine years, it was taken notice of closely by me. I could find no complaint with them. Truly, they amazed me. Laundry, Brig, Ship Maintenance, parts, Aircraft and Vehicle Maintenance, Flight Deck, Main Deck, Medical, Supply, Pharmacy, Dentistry, Water Plant, Sewage Plant, Safety, college, Purchasing, Weapons, Fire, Police, Commissary, Library, Bridge, Damage Assessment, Communications. Each group did drills and training including us pilots, even though as yet, we had no planes on our main or flight decks, except for an old mail plane. We did have shells of planes in the garage for parts.

Our ship anchored and moored at a long beautiful dock in Brazil. We would stay longer than I expected, over nine months. This was a full year of study for our students. We old guard pilots started training in Boeing B44s at our own local airstrip. Both dock and airstrip were non-military and private. They were very close to, but not right in, any major city or town. Our operations were not secret; but rather mysterious.

The Boeing B44 planes were light-weight, Australian designed, one seat, high performance fighters with a large bubble canopy. They could turn right or left without banking. These planes had long wings that could pivot and sweep back; connected to a short, straight wing coming from the bottom of the fuselage by two vertical stabilizer fins. Both wings joined at this pivot point. The long wings that pivoted, and the tail fins, could flex their skin and shape during flight. Our B44 planes were powered one high bypass turbo fan jet engine right behind the cockpit. They were a joy to fly, with a maximum cruise speed set at 585mph. Coe was a fuel efficiency nut, so we often cruised at the plane's fuel sweet spot of 465mph with wings ¾ swept back. These planes could dive with full-swept wings like a bird of prey, gaining speeds of over 600mph. Each pilot put in at least two hundred hours in the B44s before landing on ship. Our training included gunnery and bombing practice using electronic and laser simulators built into our planes on board computers. I assumed correctly that arms did exist, but that we could not afford the cost of live fire practice. It also appeared that these planes could fly themselves. Or be flown from remote control and had very little, if any, radar image with the safety beacon off. These assumptions would be proven correct, but now I had not yet been briefed on these subjects.

Landing on the ship was a breeze. These planes could take-off and land in a short distance. When landing, we would spread our long wings out straight, slowing us to glider speeds before touchdown. That's when powerful thrust reverse and the plane's brakes would stop us in our tracks. Our flight deck used much less personnel than the former U.S. Navy. During takeoff, our computer governed engines were set for two minutes of extra fuel burn and higher rpm, which produced a three to one thrust to weight ratio with "cannons only." By this I mean that no bombs or missiles or extra fuel tanks were loaded. None of the catapults or restraining cable systems found on old Navy aircraft carrier flight decks was needed with our light-weight planes, but a cable system was on deck; but not used or trained for. We had twenty B44s, but we only used twelve. Eight planes were held in reserve. Four others were for parts only and not flight ready. During this time, twelve singe-engine sea planes started using the ship's big door at its stern to taxi out into the harbor and up river, flying grad students and professors on constant "save the planet" trips to nowhere. Many students were flying these simple sea planes, but as yet, only staff flew B44s on and off ship. A wide variety of water craft also started using our big back door to come and go from the ship. The students used many jet-skis and air boats; and of course, there was Sarah Coe and her cabin cruiser' one of two aboard the Great Ark.

I had daily access to shore leave during this time, over nine months in all. The ship lingered here so long, I wondered if we might ever put to sea again.

I met my girl Josie during this stay, but could never convince her to join me aboard ship. Josie would stay behind when our sail date did finally come. She was "all girl" and not ashamed of it. Not conflicted as are so many western women. We spent many good times together; a needed break and sanity check from life aboard The Ark. A store in town named "Kelly's" sold great cuts of meat. Kelly's and grilling out was my constant path. We often went bowling or lizard hunting in a local stream near Josie's place. What they did with the lizards I could not figure. Sometimes you just don't know.

For a fourteen week summer season, the ship's flight deck was taken over by students in open-air, ultra-light, one man flying crafts. They would buzz the long beaches toward the city; where "the action" was! Their brightly colored wings filled the bright sky. Our beautiful dock was near, but not in, a town that was a suburb of Atkins, Brazil. Even the ultra-light planes could make landings to one other town. It sounded like Sao-Luis. I always pronounced the name as Saint Louis just to aggravate Josie and her family. My Portuguese language skills were close to zero and I simply did not care. People should speak the Queen's English or nothing (ha-ha). Our ship was out of sight of most locals and tourists alike.

I had always thought Brazil was covered with thick tropical rain forest or farm land; there was none of that here. This area of Brazil was covered with sand dunes, just like the Sahara desert; only wet, with puddles everywhere. If this sounds crazy, a big wet desert, I apologize, but truth is, Brazil is sand dunes as far as the eye can see. Some students would land on these sand dunes and have trouble getting back into the air. Like the Outer Banks at Kitty Hawk, this sand was a good place for foolish horseplay and dare-devil flying. Sarah and I would take off with the other men from our crew, but not with the students. Our small group would stay to ourselves, and soon started playing with large, brightly colored beach balls. Dropping the balls and catching them with the wing-struts of our plane before they hit the sand below. This game of catch became so popular that there was a local shortage of beach balls. The endless sea of sand hills, often with water puddles, was a strange and eerie sight. Some students, each day needed rescue, but most found their way back to the ship with stories of valor to last them a lifetime; all without serious injury.

One funny day I remember well, Sarah landed on a moist, hard section of sand to pick up beach balls, and a herd of wild goats moved in front of her plane, blocking take-off. These animals took a liking to Sarah and would not leave, even when she tried her mean face and screaming, she was stuck.

The other four ultra-lights in our group flew around her laughing so hard that we ran out of fuel before getting back. Running out of fuel was frowned upon and "against the rules". Refueling by another ultra-light was a fairly common practice and easy to do. We used five gallon fuel plastic fuel jugs and had plenty of places to land in the hard, wet sand next to the surf.

One particular hot summer day that season, a loud mouth, goofball, showoff student named Anthony Strange got slaphappy and splashed down his ultra-light in the harbor on take-off. His little open-air, ultra-light was over loaded with party ice bombs. He was famous for buzzing friends on campus and on the beach, often hitting an open cooler with ice. Joe and Chief of Staff Friday would raise hell and lock him in the brig; all to no avail. This tall, thin, likable, "mule stubborn", loud, young, black man was uncontrollable and a constant entertainment. Haley, the younger and slightly better looking of the Coe sisters, dove off the flight deck into the harbor, getting to the young man, Anthony, and unbuckling him quickly before his plane sank. She was credited with saving his life. Joe Coe scolded Haley for her daring technique, but hey, it worked! Why fuss?

"Don't expect this old man to dive off this ship's flight deck! That dive is over fifty-five feet" I called out to young Haley.

Haley was a rare combination of beauty, strength, brains and humor, a pleasure to know. She was an Army officer from the now closed West Point, a part-time model and a combat hero in Afghanistan before the Chinese moved in. Haley, still in her twenties, had been through a lot in life, but was still Joe Coe's baby girl. Sarah; twelve years older and by Joe's first wife Gloria, I was always closer to. Sarah often felt upstaged by her perfect little sister. Joe had a middle daughter back home named Blair and both a younger and older son. The older son was also from his first wife, Gloria. I learned quickly that their sissy, older brother was a family disgrace and was not to be mentioned around Captain Coe.

That summer, I often joined up with Sarah's boat for a ride into town. Sarah would buy clothes, and I would see Josie and buy beer. We often waited for the others in her taxi run. That's when Sarah and I started sharing time together on the huge, white sand beaches.

Those beautiful beaches were endless. There were people everywhere, but the beach was way to majestic to become crowded. When we sat on the beach, we could watch the slow, colorful ultra-light planes coming and going from the ship on the far horizon, but we could not quite make out the ship with the naked eye. College students loved buzzing up and down the beach and landing in a grass field by the college in town. Illegal sound systems were often put on these little craft, and tickets by the local police had become a common embarrassment to the Great Ark and Captain Coe. Our spoiled little college brats were "going wild" and having the time of their lives. A sign-up list kept all one hundred forty-four of these open-air, one seat fold up flying crafts in use. They were a graceful, ever present, beautiful sight. Their colorful wings and the drone of their little motors filled the blue sky.

Sarah Coe, one hot summer day, in her only slightly modest, two piece swimsuit was just about all this old Granddad of two could suffer. I wondered how foolish I was to sit in the sand, enjoying her company, us both flirting back and forth. *Don't play the old fool*, I kept telling myself. She seemed to light up around me. Often I stayed clear of her just to keep my sanity.

The Great Ark started taking on supplies at an increased rate. I knew setting sail was coming soon. I had worked B time in the purchasing office. Over ten million dollars of supplies came aboard that last month, plus four and a half million dollars in aviation fuel alone. The ship made fresh water and also hydrogen fuel, none of this fuel we had yet used. This large volume of cold hydrogen fuel would make sense as time played out.

The ship was powered by a U. S. Navy nuclear power plant by B & W, but Indian Navy, Israeli, French, Italian, Russian, German, American and Japanese "nukes" were in and out of our "dungeon" power plant at different times, rotating in four groups of six each time. Always one group from VPI in Blacksburg, Va. VPI and the VPI of India seemed to be both experts on the power plant. They could have their ole dungeon; I loved the high perch of my cabin (and fresh air.)

That evening, on my high deck railing outside my cabin door, I was relaxing before going to bed and sipping three fingers of red wine. (It's good for the digestion) I was looking down the length of our beautiful cement pier. I always enjoyed its hundreds of lights reflecting on the sea. This evening was a treat; for oh what a tranquil sight. The most beautiful sailing yacht I had ever seen! This yacht was parked between the Great Ark and the beach. The majestic contours of this yacht anchored just below me brought to mind the open sea. Wow, I thought about having my own boat; being my own Captain. Hanging over the bow of this large sailboat was a pig; like the ones some barbeque places have.

"Hello, sailboat," said I, "God speed!" I stood on my deck railing dreaming of just sailing away.

"Time for bed, Cornelius" a voice said, for I had started to doze. The next night we did leave Brazil. Our departure was uneventful; without fanfare. At sea the next day, a spirit of adventure filled the big ship. Our two helicopters, that I had never seen fly (too fuelish), were both pressed into hard service. All females had been tested and all pregnant girls were being shuttled to shore by, I suppose, Friday and Edison Oiler, the only two men I knew who flew the birds. Haley's friend Lisa St. Stevens was on

the list. Captain Joe stood firm on his orders; no favorites; no exceptions. Haley and Sarah put ole' Coe through hell. Their screaming was heard throughout the ship. This was a humiliating embarrassment to Joe. Five or six gals would go on each chopper trip depending on how much junk each girl had. Eighteen or nineteen trips were made, so at least one hundred of our nine hundred coeds had gotten knocked up in Brazil. The girls in dorms A, B and C were different, or special. These ABC girls were very "popular" and "friendly" with both staff and crew. Not much like real college girls at all. These gals were much too sleazy for the college girl natural law of averages. I suspected that many were "pros" or that a "girl's gone wild" video was being made on ship, but I never did ask about it. Our older staff and the young bucks alike were as "fed horses in the morning" with these girls. They seemed to enjoy their work; or study (ha-ha). Someone in personnel knew how to pick em and was evidently trying to keep the mostly male crew happy. These girls were not picked for brains or serious college study. Most did not even attend class. The sick, torrid display of immorality was constant and overbearing. Often my comrades did not bother to "get a room" and would take their dates to secluded parts of the ship, not caring if you walked up on them or not. This ungodly behavior was so open that I often wondered if the poor young women were not being drugged.

I had my girl Josie back in Brazil. We had grown close. I had paid her rent ahead for a year thinking she might come with me on the Ark, but alas, I was on my own once again. Another "ex" to send Christmas cards to, I guess. No woman in her right mind longs to be a lonely sailor's wife and no one can blame them. Ask my lovely ex-wife Patty, back in Virginia. She has always been the true love of my life. I missed her so much. I called Patty that night, a few days away from or first port of call in South Africa. We talked our usual fifteen minutes. I was close to being late with my monthly payment to her. She seemed glad to hear my voice. *Patty and I back together again one day?* I wondered if that could be. It's odd; often in this life one just doesn't know! Most people who do claim to know are fakers. Really, they're just as dumb as the rest of us. You and I, my friend, you and I!

The South Atlantic Ocean was unusually calm and cool for this time of year and land was on the far horizon. I sat in on a college lecture lured by the title, "The Cost of Freedom". This professor quoted Bill Ayers often and talked about "the good of the many outweighing the rights of the few". The greater good for mankind, he called it. I got so mad that my greater good was to leave early. I stormed out and the anti-professor was born. The ship's young college students listened closely. They were content to soak up the poison poetry and the abject stupidity of their idiot teacher's classroom remarks. *Someone has to tell these kids the truth. Tell them the truth of God's word. Shut up, Cornelius,* I heard myself say. *Mind your own business.* But no, I would not listen. God was calling me to act. Why would God use a person like me? Why not a minister? Sometimes you just don't know.

CHAPTER TWO

Gumbo Station The bombing of Africa

In South Africa we docked again and took on even more supplies. Some change in personnel also; about two hundred men added. They looked like military types, but without the uniforms. The ship's top six student pilots finished up their first two hundred hours of flight training in B44s at an airstrip nearby with very poor conditions; not like our beautiful base in Brazil. We instructors got more flight hours also and our first live firing range practice. Our cannons were very impressive. These new, larger caliber cannons were very destructive and affective weapons; tiny smart bombs really. I judged the cannons to be triple effective and triple range compared to the old U.S. Navy. Shore leave was rare during this stay at port. We pilots took advantage of our B44 training to grab some R&R, but official shore leave was cut off. So was all horseplay out of the back of the ship; no jet skis, swamp boats, etc. Our twelve single engine sea planes did operate in heavy service taking grad students into the interior of Africa. Two professors had mapping projects which included the dropping of sensors; this was all funded by a US government grant. Very odd; America had shut down her military bases and operations. Washington was broke. The old U.S. Navy was shut down. These professors must have top priority; this "save Africa from the world" pipe dream. One trip, which required camping and refueling on a remote fresh water Lake was much talked about by our energetic and excited students to anyone on ship who would listen. And of course, all of us "old timers" wanted to tell stories of "back in the day".

All pilots had five long weeks of training in South Africa. This was now thirteen months on the Ark for me and soon to be my second Christmas;

only six students had qualified to do solo ship landing and takeoff. One of these six students named Michael Lang, a "quiet type" (he looked like Harry Potter), fell to his death off a catwalk in the interior of the ship. There was no real funeral or investigation. All the boy got was a quick burial at sea very near the harbor. "This is wrong" I said out loud. "No flight home for the body!" Somebody, or some country, was paying his college tuition aboard the Ark, plus flight training. But this one didn't count. After a short, cold ceremony on the starboard flight deck, splash! Lang was gone. Michael Lang had been a suitor, or close friend to both the Coe sisters and was soon to be a son-in-law I had thought. I watched the Lang service from the railing outside of Medical. At this cold, windy, five minute service, none of the Coe family attended. I slept uneasy late into the next day. The ship was "on hold" for days just outside the port in South Africa.

Early the next afternoon, I got a rare call from Rosie back in St. Augustine.

"What time is it there?" Rosie said shouting in her rough, Cajun smoker's voice. (Rosie is no spring chicken)

"You can call me anytime, Rosie. What's up at the office?" I shouted back, even though the phone connection was clear. She said I had financial "exit" paperwork that had to be turned into the IRS. Two men wearing "ACORN" pins had stopped by the office asking questions. Rosie then asked if I was Mexican or maybe part black as she was. Rosie said that both my Mother and Grandmother were named Juanita and that I had family on the Mississippi Delta just like her.

"Rosie, are you serious? This all sounds crazy. We've only got twenty-six people placed; mostly in food-service aboard ships. We are too small for the feds or Osoma to worry about." *Exit paperwork?*

"No, Corneliwus. Wee's got over two hundreds peoples now" said Rosie. "I dooes better without you, Cornelius (ha-ha). What about your Mother's maiden name? It sounds Jewish, Cornelius."

"Yes, I suppose it does, Rosie. We're Baptist, you know that! Rosie, just fill in something before the financial freeze thing goes into effect. What difference could it possibly make? Ok, Rosie? Yes, I will text you each week! I promise! Goodbye. Miss you, too."

Wow, it sounds like things are getting a little weird back in the states. Rosie said a lot had changed. That police were searching people everywhere they went. Some of my relatives did look kind of dark in those old metal photos taken at the turn of the century. Wouldn't it be funny if I was black and didn't even know it? Dad didn't say? But my brother is darker than me. So often in life we don't even know the basics. Yes, one often just does not know.

The next afternoon, the Great Ark was still marking time. We were parked just outside the harbor. I was in the ship's big snack bar with an old Navy friend named Gary Litton. Gary was the manager and sometimes bartender. He only worked the bar himself at slow times and when he did not have any help. Gary had his dozen TV screens which were usually on sports, set to "Ice Road Truckers" while two professors' wives were all about putting up the snack bar Christmas decorations. These wives wanted to "give back" to students for being good and caring about Mother Nature, for "going green" and all of that B.S. Both were wearing "First Lady" t-shirts. Gary poured me some red wine. He was smiling and saying nothing, as was his nature; just nodding his head. Gary pretended to be listening to the women as they stacked boxes around the room. Both women were pumped up and fired up with "estrogen filled energy"; much needed while making all those complicated decorating decisions that only female "do-gooders" can.

Oh, yes, these will look great over here" Linda said in a high-pitched tone. This "cow talk" was mind numbing. We two old bulls looked on in amazement, thanking God we didn't have to mess with all that crap. Of course, the two old cows tried to sucker us into breaking ranks and joining their decorating madness by needing a ladder or asking "Can you hold this for a minute?" We two men, being wise old bulls, didn't bite. Gary and I just looked at each other and grinned. These two women both wore out and frustrated, sat down near us men to discuss the all important position of their tree. We were told which tables had to be moved; which ones to take out. These gals soon figured out that we two men were worthless as male beasts of burden and started looking around for younger saps to do the "heavy lifting". Jean, also called Peanut, listened to Linda as Julie, their friend from housekeeping, walked in to help. All three of these women also volunteered at The Gospel Cafe only one hundred feet across the breezeway deck.

"The Gospel Cafe is not putting up a tree this year" said Julie.

"That's awful" said Peanut. "Where's their Christmas spirit?"

"The Christmas spirit will be in here" said Linda as she held up the small, very top piece of the tree high over her head.

"People forget the real meaning of Christmas" Peanut said as she pulled a giant Coca Cola Santa from a box.

"Maybe the people in the Cafe are just Christians" I said. "Maybe they believe in the Bible. Try to live by Bible teachings and that's why they don't put up a tree."

Linda rolled her eyes at me.

"Yes, Christians." Those who live by God's Holy Word would never in a million years put up a 'Christmas Tree', because the Word of God speaks clearly and directly against doing so. In fact, one of the main reasons people settled in America was for Godly Christian believers to escape the then new, evil holiday of Christmas. Christmas was being forced upon them. They considered it pagan, an abomination to God. Neither the Puritans or the Quakers celebrated this pagan Christmas"

"Cornelius, that story sounds crazy" cried Linda. "If America was founded by Christians, why would they be against Christmas?"

"Beware, my good friends" I spoke up, "worldly and/or conventional wisdom is always the opposite of God's truth. Most people are always fooled. The Bible tells us so. Wide is the way to destruction; narrow is the way to God. The Angel is very good at deceiving. A pro at what he does. Popular culture, worldliness or mainstream is often backward to God."

"Look at that television show" I said. "It's all about Ice Road Truckers. Those trucks run only this time of year. That's where Santa Claus and the Christmas tree both come from. My ancestors are from Northern Europe; we made this Christmas stuff up. Christmas is our tribal history. Now, sit down and listen"

"So, it's truckers, Cornelius? Give me a break" snarled Peanut.

"For thousands of years, long before the time of Christ's birth, older men would travel far and wide during this, the coldest, part of the year. They were the Grandfathers of family groups. These older men often trained the youngest boys, or 'elves' (ha-ha). This time of year is when travel was easy or even possible. Also, men didn't have crop work to do. Nothing has changed much in the great north. Our travel season goes on the same today"

The ladies took a break to listen to my Christmas story only because my old friend Gary made them all hot chocolate, his famous Katrina drink, made with Chocolate kisses, marshmallows, chunks of banana, and coco mix. The banana chunks are flooded school buses of course.

"Just like today, muddy, soft ground made travel difficult. As soon as the ground, rivers and lakes froze over, the older men were off and running. Yes, on their way. Men would tie up wild and domestic reindeer to big sleighs, because their little wagons couldn't hold very much. These mature men were off to visit and trade with family and friends. Often this was the only time of year they could make the trip. The vast Euro-Asia landmass was huge, seemingly endless. Men traveled as far as they dared. Back home, his wife put candles in the windows, she kept candles burning all night. All the other women did also. These trips were dangerous; also very important for trading purposes. This was a life and death matter to many families. These candles were the only beacon old winter travelers had. The heavens or stars were changing during this time; the longest night was now over. A celebration of the New Year; another earth cycle was here."

"For many centuries, many ancient years, men built houses with one wall against a natural, or cut, rock face. Often even a small cave, if possible. This was used for a wind break, a sturdy wall and a place for his fireplace. Often travelers could park on top of a rock face cliff and come down a ladder into the dwelling. This was convenient in heavy snow. Their chimney was most often a big hole in the roof lined with skins and fur. Mushrooms were hung and dried on a string in front of the fireplace. They were worth a lot of money in trade. These mushrooms were bright red or white balls with red spots. They were used in medicine or to 'get high' or in the winter spirit."

"These old men would, prior to leaving and during their trip, look for small evergreen trees and scrape out the snow and pine needles from around its roots looking for mushrooms. These mushrooms have a symbiotic relationship with pine trees. This means simply that they need and like each other. The smaller pine trees, with branches close to the ground, helped protect the mushrooms from being eaten by reindeer. These mushrooms were very powerful; even deadly. When given to reindeer, they would pull the sleigh faster and faster; even to the point of death by exhaustion, if given enough. Yes, they would fly! Families often drank reindeer urine to get a safe dose of the drug instead of making tea directly. To many, this watered-down urine method was more agreeable. Often, urine was put in eggnog. This is also where the gold chord and the name Goldwater came from (ha-ha). Men would place furs and animal hides around a good mushroom producing pine and hang wind chimes on it with gold colored rope to mark it. Any man coming by would add his own marker chime. The chimes helped scare away reindeer. He would then lift up the tree skirt and check for mushrooms before continuing on his travels. These Grandfathers would often come down the chimney, leave trades, get warm, eat something and talk to family members without the younger children waking up. Wow, were they surprised in the morning. These mushroom trees as part of the pagan winter festival, were over the years, moved inside, nailed to the floor, hung with mushrooms and later colored balls with gold chords. This was a very old tradition. Way back in the prophet Jeremiah's day. Eight hundred years before the birth of Christ. Read what God says about these trees in Jeremiah 1:10."

"Learn not the way of the heathen; and be not dismayed at the signs of heaven; for the heathen are dismayed at them. For the customs of the people are vain: for one cutteth a tree out of the forest, the work of the hands of the workman, with the axe. They deck it with silver and gold; they fasten it with nails and hammers; that it moves not"

"The Lord says in the next verse; **be not afraid of them,** and that they can **do no good!** Early Christians, when the Roman Church "made Christian" the old heathen winter festival, fought against defiling their faith. They considered combining Christian beliefs with the old pagan system a reproach to God. Christmas was a perversion; an attempt by the Angel to corrupt and destroy the Church of Jesus Christ with pagan, worldly and ancient tradition. So they moved to America to worship without the new, pagan, church mandated, government ordained, commercial Christmas."

The three women went straight back to decorating. I was not their favorite person. Isn't it sad that most people flow to the opposite of truth? Always following the broad way, the easy way the popular! Let the Word of God be true and every man a liar!

That next night, during a cool evening, we finally pulled out to the open sea. The Ark was underway once again. This is always a great feeling for us sailors; this hitting of the ocean waves. The sea was rough; choppy; with large rolling swells. It felt good; exhilarating. No dark night could dampen our spirit of enthusiasm. Late that same night, really very early the next morning, I decided that with an hour to go before our flight briefing, and the second story breezeway being shut off by bosons mates (janitors for you landlubbers), to catch a shower in the flight school head or shower. No big deal. We fancy officers often "slum it" around ship (ha-ha). But I do remember this shower; this night. As I stepped into the showers, I met a buck naked Sarah Coe as she was coming out. We squeezed sideways through the door, her and me, pausing only momentarily in passing.

"Nice ears, Sarah" I said, not thinking.

Why did you say that? I thought. I then silently scolded myself as I soaped up in the shower. I was embarrassed not by my nakedness, but by my own stupid statement. She had caught me off guard. The girl could give a man a heart attack, popping out at him like that. Through the shower door opening, I noticed I could still see her at the lockers, drying off; still "Doe" naked. She was doing that towel thing on her head that no man has ever been able to figure out. *She's not bashful,* I thought. But I was. So I turned my back to her as she walked out and I washed off.

At our flight briefing, Sarah was there. She was a qualified pilot, though not full-time on the ship's duty rotation. Joe did not let her sign-up on our flight board. He had to approve her each and every assignment. This briefing was the 'same old/same old', but they are important. Briefings always restricted our behavior; the rules of modern warfare: how low, how high, nobody cares if you die (ha-ha), where to drop fuel tanks or what type of fuel can be burned where; i.e. pollution. The environmentalists wanted to save Africa from people; nobody cared about people. For the needs of the many (the greater good), many must die (mostly Africans). This meeting was heart sickening. Sarah's long, red hair was dry now, so again she had 'no ears'. Twice during the briefing, she pulled back her hair and smiled a cute, dirty little smile my way, as if to say, "you ear gazer, you". She was playing with my head and enjoying every minute. *Shut up, Cornelius* I said. Don't play the old fool.

Early the next morning, twenty-four bug-like Boeing predator drones landed on the ship. So did another thirty men and two old black hawk choppers. These men were all American this time. All of the glass windows one level below the ship's bridge can be now found back-lit for the first time. Wow, another complete bridge just below Joe Coe! Drones would soon be taking off, like clockwork, four every three hours for the next four months. Plus, two 'eye-in-the-sky' drones; one always being on station above the ship. Drones burned the liquid hydrogen cold fuel. They did not burn up our precious aviation fuel on board. Drones would leave burdened down with fuel tanks, bombs and missiles hanging from their bellies' three hard points; always of course, coming back empty.

The top six student pilots, now only five with Harry Potter being dead, started deck landings and take-offs in B44s. We always kept a minimum of two manned patrols in the air during daylight hours. Our eight reserved B44s were now uncovered. They were duel fuel burners and could use hot or cold petrol.

The flight deck stayed busy. Our B44s only landed during daylight hours, but would take off long before dawn. Often we took flight right after midnight by using extra fuel tanks. Somewhere in Africa a war was waging. Nothing on this war was on the TV news. Nothing was ever reported. I thought about the term wars and rumors of wars; was that passage about filtered information or controlled news. The mood on ship was routine; even jolly.

The night spot on ship was called the Gospel Cafe. It was a coffee house with Christian music. Former students of a soon to be closed up Christian college in Lynchburg, Virginia played the old time gospel music. It was always a joy to visit the Gospel Cafe. Their music sounded like 'old time rock and roll' to me. Most students on ship saw life on TV as real and big government as the only answer. Everything they believed in was a lie. Yes, lies from ungodly college professors and TV producers; completely false and in reverse of obvious truth. Many students nicknamed me 'old school'.

Alcohol was served in only one place on ship; the big snack bar that my old friend Gary Litton ran. The snack-bar was one half again bigger than the Gospel Cafe and only one hundred feet away. A limit of two sixteen oz beers per day served in plastic cups was enforced by an ID badge scan. No one got by old Litton on the limit. Gary didn't like to sell alcohol, he was told to.

This war, conflict or 'mission' of our ship gave me many questions that all begged for answers. I did learn that we were not alone. That there were at least three others like us; old American aircraft carriers, remodeled and refitted to college or student service. One ship was always here on "Gumbo Station" off the east coast of Africa in a tag team fashion. We lent support to the "Dark Continent". Our students took little notice, neither of the military missions given our ship, nor of the "who or why" of our battles. Students seemed as uncaring robots or serf subjects. All of them were totally unquestioning of authority. Their blindness troubled my heart and soul. It was an affront to God and nature. What had caused this numb; and docile, youth. I loved the evenings at the ship's Gospel Cafe and the students from Lynchburg because they were still American. They still valued liberty, freedom and the Bible. No news reports had stories of a war in Africa. No mention of 'us', the Great Ark or this new private navy. Nothing of whom or what we were or 'who' was in charge. I wondered to myself, *who was paying me?* I guessed European, maybe Indian and Russian with a few Israelis sprinkled in. no answers could be found, even after much snooping around on my part. 'Follow the money' is always good advice, but my many hours of working "B" time in purchasing had not landed any fresh information. After another routine three day work cycle of flying ship protection patrol. I just could not stop myself from telling stories of 'back in the day' at my big round corner table.

The Gospel Cafe was packed that night. I took a big drink of hot French roast coffee; my own Irish version. Then I started off by going back to my youth in the now closed up, former U.S. Navy. Long before the big 'Osoma cuts'. The U.S. Navy was off this same east coast of Africa. The 'news' reports broadcasted a cover story, or 'official lie' back then that we were feeding Africans in Somalia. What a joke that was! I had been part of that operation; where the movie 'Blackhawk down' came from. What we sailors truly did in Africa during that operation is built five large airfields in remote, dry, desert locations. Our operation had nothing to do with feeding anybody. The bases we built are referred to by military logistic types as forward staging areas. When our construction was completed, we quickly abandoned them to the blowing desert sand. My old Wart Hog plane was one of only two which took part. The other plane was a rare husband and wife team. We are all still good friends. These old planes are close air support machine gunners; not fancy. Funny how smells can come back to you even years later from scenes you wish, or thought you had forgotten. Close-up war is unpleasant. I do not recommend a front row seat. War is often just like seasickness on small boats. You might think of yourself as a tough man and immune to all the blood and guts around you, but then the smell hits you in the stomach. The stench and rot of death is what puts even the so called 'tough guys' over the edge. It will send them crying; falling quickly to their knees in prayer. Yes, it's always the damn smell that gets you.

I tried to chill out and called the waiter for a free round of drinks for my many guests; all fourteen to sixteen of them. All of these students were very polite; even respectful tonight, a rare blessing. The second set of music was about to start in minutes here at the Gospel Cafe. A singer named Brenda Dole was about to come on. She was very popular. She was married to a crewman named Rodney on the ship. I took another sip of my favorite strong French roast coffee. My own special flavoring added at the table. I am after all, part Irish and also an ole Granddad (ha-ha). Then I started back to my story.

"My friends, that year the 'anti-military' party 'Clinton' had just been elected, so the first President Bush was a 'lame duck'. The coalition had ten large, private cargo ships in the Persian Gulf. These ships were loaded down with pre-fab cement airfields. One half of a full runway on each ship, now not needed for the war effort. We could have dumped the huge cement blocks into the ocean like the Russians did when they fled Cuba. Or we could deploy them somewhere close. Shipping them back to the States was out of the question. Quite reasonably enough, our military command sold Bush one on the fact that remote airstrips in Africa could be of 'use' to them in the future by just sending in troops to 'brush them off' like home plate. These prefab runways would last for years in the dry desert and this would cost little and serve us better than dumping that much cement."

The T.V. News reports, way back in my youth, were completely controlled and one hundred percent phony. I knew this from personal, first had information and knowledge. Now I feared for the state of the world and my young shipmates. They believed what they saw on T.V. news was the truth. History, science facts, Biblical truths, all education in general had become nothing but lies and political propaganda.

Really nothing has changed much for the last two hundred years. We talked about the French troops in Vietnam and the British troops in Afghanistan during the 1890's. Western men since Roman times have been sent out into the world for a couple of years in their youth to fight, kill, bomb or protect the 'poor dumb bastards' of 'underdeveloped' countries for no apparent reason or gain. No reason to stop now, I guess. Why would each generation do basically the same thing year after year, each one not knowing why they're doing it or who's in charge. But, here we go again. The fall of America seemed to slow war down very little, or none at all. No, it just made us Americans poor. I talked about the military logistical stupidity of sending large columns of troops into an 'ambush paradise' like Afghanistan. My Great-great Grandfather was shot at from behind the same stupid rock as me, now by his enemy's grandchildren. After a hundred and twenty years, what's the point? What good has it done? Why would so many different leaders of so many different western countries, over a time span of hundreds of years all send troops? To what gain? What

19

purpose? Together they've spent enough money to buy Afghanistan ten times over.

These types of thoughts depressed my spirit and soul, so I spent more and more time at the ole time hymn sing at the Gospel Cafe. These next four, long months of bombing Africa settled into a constant busy burden, but also into a cold, relaxed rhythm. We on board the Great Ark had not much a care in or for the world. We lived as a world unto ourselves. But somewhere in Africa, a real war, with real huger, terror and death, yes, a real smelly, stinking war was raging.

Sarah Coe and I both enjoyed spending off duty hours at the ship's Gospel Cafe, often sitting together; meeting by chance; half expecting the other to be there. Our odd glances, smiles and flirtations at officer's mess could not be missed. Sarah, being a young thirty-something, and me an older, over-weight fifty-nine, I didn't consider us a likely fit as a couple. Though, truly I felt like a young man again around her. She coldly brushed aside all of her many suitors. That is, all but me. And yours truly was either too scared or too 'wise' to bite. During this early time of bombing Africa, Sarah, Haley and the four gals at Coe's dinner table left on a shopping trip to Cutter; also called Dubai. Sarah was 'on assignment', doing important business for Daddy, to hear her tell it. I was ashamed at myself for missing her so much, but truly my heart ached for her return. That night at the Gospel Cafe, my spirits were downcast. Sarah was gone. Music was ok, but slow. My young students started talking about President Osoma. They talked about giving Osoma time; a chance to fix things. A young lady named Kishia, who volunteered in Haiti for ten weeks prior to college on the Ark, was an honor student; very much respected by her peers. She seemed to know little, or nothing, at all.

"Kishia" I said, "the type of misery, despair and poverty that you tried your best to fight against in Haiti is caused by only one thing. Tyrants like your damn Osoma. These men try to replace God's biblical laws with humanist, socialist or kingly dictated doctrine. This is false teaching, the ungodly Osoma even wrote a book describing himself as a communist. He often referred to himself as a Muslim. Osoma even talked about the fifty-seven states of America. Wake up Kishia! In his America you would not even be allowed in school. Why is it always the poor, dumb bastard in Haiti needing your help, who are starving to death and sick? Why not the Dominican Republic on the other side of the same, small, little island? It has to be Government, honey. That's the only difference between them.

How about North and South Korea? One is starving, one not. Wake up! Look around! Osoma is nothing new. Osoma is a carbon copy of every other humanist, socialist, fascist elite before him. Castro, Stalin, Hitler, Osoma; they're all the same! Democratic, socialist elites have been the curse of the world throughout all human history. Each one is a branch off the same evil tree."

A middle-aged professor named Tommy Mute gave me a chocolate covered toast treat like the ones Starbucks serves. He started guiding the conversation away from Osoma. My face was red and Tommy was concerned for my health. Of all things, the kids that night started talking about slavery. Young Kishia Gonzales spoke up. (Yes a different Kishia)

"My God, are you all named Kishia?' I said, thinking out loud.

"Cornelius, you are wrong", shouted Kishia. "Slavery was forced on us blacks with whips and guns"

"Yes, Kishia" I answered. "Blacks <u>were</u> sold into America by force. But force alone could not and did not keep them working in the fields. No! Not after they got here to America. Just because you learned lies and half-truths at government school, or you watched movies made about it, that fact does not change the truth. Or even make the false story plausible or even possible. In fact, what you learned is simply not so; not true; a complete fabrication."

"Let me remind you of today's lesson. Being a successful 'Lord' over others requires one to control people at the least cost. Force is a factor, a tactic, but not always the major or leading factor. Slave masters who rule by force go out of business quickly. I am speaking in a historical sense. Look at the 550 thousand modern slaves in Siberian Russia during and after World War Two. The Russian communist party slave camp system used dislocation (just like America) plus force, cruelty and starvation. Russia needed slave economic output very badly to prop up the failing central planning of communism. These Russian slave camps and communism simply went out of business. It just cost too much money to pay people to point guns; who then scare new slaves into working. Notice they did use relocation into a harsh climate to cut cost. This is necessary when attempting slavery by force. This relocation did help, but they still went out of business. What did the ancient Israelites say to Moses? The Israelites were slaves for about four hundred years, just like blacks in America. They said to Moses: 'Did you take us out here to die of thirst and starvation in this wilderness desert? We should have stayed in Egypt where we had plenty to eat.' notice also that the Egyptians failed to break the Jewish family unit; a big mistake, and costly. In Colonial America, European settlers were taming a vast wilderness of rich accessible land. American white settlers could not enslave the indigenous native Indians or use Old World European style serf methods on each other because of this close, rich, very good, productive land, the family unit and of course the Holy Bible teachings of stubborn, free men. Settlers just moved west and started their own farm or plantation. The Indians would just run off into the thick forest cover the minute the guy holding the musket turned his head. Brothers would help brothers. Indian family was never far off. The rich, gentile class planters were in a hard place to find 'workers' or 'suckers', so in desperation, they started importing blacks bought from Moslem slave traders in Africa. Soon black Africans in many states outnumbered the white settlers. Only one in ten whites could afford to own, or wanted to own, these expensive African slaves. Many settlers were servants themselves; they indentured themselves to a master to pay for the boat ride over. Also, some free blacks around New Orleans owned black slaves themselves on the sugar cane plantations. Have you ever fired an early pioneer musket? You would know. One could not hit the broad side of a barn; or another man standing fifty yards away. Your target could stand still and wave at you while giving you a free 'shot,' and then walk, not run, into the woods while you reloaded. The forest or jungle was always close by, and the fields were very long, often with one end at a river. A slave could disappear simply by not standing up straight in the crop he was working in. No, these few whites did not keep blacks 'on the plantation' with their primitive guns. What did keep blacks working in the fields of America was food plenty, relative peace, African tribal customs and yes, force. New slaves were sold from an area of Africa at war for years. Starvation, disease and suffering there was common place in Africa. Now in America, an agricultural, Roman based society, slaves lived in relative plenty, eating better than most had ever dreamed of. They preferred slavery and plenty, brought about by the white settlers free agricultural wave economy, over going back to a hunter/gather tribal lifestyle like the Indians had. They simply saw a better way of life and then began to Romanize their primitive tribal ways. This technique of worldly masters being, in secular humanist terminology, one full Toffler wave of civilization ahead of their slaves is how successful, modern slavery works. I'm sure you students have read this couple's books. Masters use the relative plenty of each next new wave. The poor dumb bastards in slavery

"What if Teddy Roosevelt had no Rough Riders in Cuba? Of what difference would it make today?"

"Would World War I ever have started if the British had still been united with America? World War I caused World War II. That's how it works. Would Hitler have even tried? During both World Wars, Germany hoped that America would not fight. Germany played with America's divided affections, but we all stayed British in the end."

"Hitler was evil, Cornelius", spoke up Tommy Rosenberg.

"Yes, he was, Tommy" I said. "The dark angel himself was Hitler's council. I'm sure of that fact. Yes, evil. He was a fascist socialist, humanist and anti-church. But so was our ally in Russia, Joseph Stalin. Our ally killed thirty million people. Five times the killing of Adolf Hitler. Death is the trademark of all democratic, socialist elites, also the banner and calling card of the dark angel. Death and rebellion against God go hand in hand. Our modern democratic, socialist party in America is the party of death. America and Mao's China are tied for the worst of the worst in all of human history. That is unless you count the Great Whore of Babylon, the Roman Church herself. I'm talking now about socialist leaders. Then, America and China are history's two worst killers by far. God will not be mocked."

Kishia started crying out loud and screaming: "That can't be true, Cornelius. My Mother is a democrat!"

"God is no respecter of persons, Kishia.'I knew you in your Mother's womb'. God said this, not me. Jesus will be our judge. Every knee shall bow. Every tongue will confess. God put his people back in the Holy land. God did not need England, and God does not need America. Our God could have used anybody. When our President Osoma stopped supporting Israel, look what happened to the old USA. We're finished. Yes, finished! Europe is trying to run the world and is united under a young German EU leader named Hein Bruch. He is a godless socialist just like Hitler. America herself voted for a fascist, humanist, Islamic socialist Osoma only sixty years after ten thousand young suckers died at Normandy, supposedly to save the world from Hitler. If they only could have seen the future and known that their own stupid, ignorant, spoiled brat grandchildren would vote for another socialist killer, with word for word Hitler's very same platform. Would they have bothered storming those cliffs? Those poor, dumb bastards in World War II died for nothing. Our freedom has been pissed away. All the graves in France are now pointless. A few poor, old men still survive, living to see the mockery of their own sacrifice."

"One thing that did happen of note in World War II was the A-bomb it was a big money maker. This bomb scared the hell out of the war merchants and ruling elites. Mature, old, powerful men now had their own butts on the line. Fear slowed down the old 'boys fighting in a field game', but not for long. Old men the world over soon used smaller low-key wars like Korea, Vietnam, Afghanistan and Sudan to keep the 'boys in the field' game alive. Always stopping the conflict before it got out of hand; meaning men over forty years old started dying. Nowadays, we mostly bomb the poor, dumb little bastards of the 'third world'. We do this for practice, sport, population control, to sell arms, to make money, and of course, to save the planet from being overrun with billions of more 'poor, dumb bastards'. Our ruling elites can always find men of low moral character, or of brain-washable will, who will kill for money. Men like you and me. We kill, or thin the herd, of unwanted population groups as defined by the elite authority in power. Men like us work for the likes of Castro, Stalin, Mao, and Osoma. You name the leader they are all cut from the same cloth. All have the same evil high priest. Guess what, children? It's not Jesus. It's not the Holy Bible. These men deal in death and lies. Not truth, life, freedom or liberty."

My many young students left the Gospel Cafe that night, off the coast of East Africa, encouraged once again to a life of military service and the Godly importance of our ship's mission. This mission of killing off all the Africans to save the world! That is the least I could do for them.

On ship, I loved to listen to the many sounds, and look out over my high deck porch railing. At my quarters, during nights and early mornings, the smell of the ocean uplifted my heart. Often a beautiful star filled sky dazzled my eyes. Lou Goodliar roomed down the deck from me, he too enjoyed the solitude. Often, we made hand gestures, for it was too far to shout. The silence was broken only by the B44s screaming off the deck and the much quieter drones coming in, and or stretching for the sky. Life was good! I enjoyed life aboard the Ark. Anyone would. Well, any sailor.

Most days of 'wartime' were lazy and uneventful. We did start making manned bombing runs to small port cities and villages. Targets were picked with care, but not by 'CARE' (ha-ha).

These targets had to be found by satellite; a house here; a dock or boat there. One target was a lone dish antenna. Two of our B44s would be lost and two more out of service by the end of our four-month long deployment at Gumbo Station.

Our longest 'feet dry' bombing run that was done with manned B44s was less than a week before the 'Big Attack' as we called it. I assumed that we, the ship I mean, had approached the shore too close to keep our bombing mission 'still night', which made it possible for the ship to be attacked. Twelve heavily loaded B44s with no cannons and no missiles, just one drop tank and two bombs on each hard point took off before midnight. Big, ugly looking cluster fire bombs, over one thousand pounds each, slowed our small, light planes. This was a 'long run' with our new hydrogen 'cold fuel' because hydrogen does not push you as far as the old 'dirty stuff' could. We were feet dry for over an hour before letting go and pulling skyward and south. Whatever we hit caused many secondary explosions. There was even some old time fireworks type anti-aircraft fire. That old gun fire didn't even start until after we were turned home; our target bright orange ablaze. I could not make out what we hit, but it was near a pretty big town. The fireworks were beautiful against the end of night mountain skyline. Of course, this night was quite different on the other side of those thin, early morning clouds, down on the killing side, on the crying side.

Young student pilot Roger Mensink was my 'wing man' that morning. We took off together; five and six behind ready deck. Only two top student pilots of our now five (Harry Potter being dead), had been picked for the long bombing mission. Later, on board ship, I commended Roger on his flying skills. We two talked that night at length, about the mission and world events.

"What's all this about, Cornelius?" Roger asked.

"What is what, Roger?" I jokingly inquired.

Roger shook his head and spoke. "You know, Sir. Our targets, who are they? Why this bombing mission. What the hell are we doing it for?"

I answered softly. "You mean who's in charge? Who are we? Who's paying us? Who's on what side?"

"Yes sir! You're old Navy like my Dad. He says we must be the United Nations or something."

I bowed my head and spoke. "Roger, I just don't know. We are not the United Nations, I'm sure of that. Roger, I believe we work for a private company with many countries owning stock. Who's paying the freight? Who's in charge? Wish I knew! That's all above my pay grade, Roger. Way above. I'm paid well and my expenses are small. My retirement is set now because of this voyage. I could go home today. I stay on to training you men for the money. Also, I love to fly! That may be wrong. I'm not proud of myself. This ship has been a good deal for me. I'm earning the highest pay of my life."

Roger was a well read, yet still young man. This was rare in his 'idiot, brain dead' supposedly 'high-tech' generation. We talked about history back through the Romans to present day. Talking into the late night, sipping red wine that his Dad had 'shipped him' at great expense. I gave him my 'each western generation sends its young people on two year missions of bombing the poor, dumb bastards of the world' speech. Roger said maybe it's in our blood. We've been doing the same thing over and over in history. Each generation asking, but not knowing the reason why. Roger then spoke my own words back to me about Afghanistan and Vietnam. One hundred years of western troops and now letting the Chinese control it all. When we look back through history and see decade after decade country after country, King after President after Queen. Why the blood? Why the money? Is there no apparent good or sane reason?

Roger started asking the 'wrong' questions, both in college and in flight briefings. Yes, Roger was, I am sure infected with my own skepticism about the worthiness and Godliness of our ship's mission.

Roger Mensink was the one and only pilot and first B44 lost during the soon upcoming 'Big Attack' by our unknown, unseen enemy. Was his loss fate? Could his B44 have gone down too fast to eject? Could small arms fire really have taken the plane down? Or was it Joe Coe's doing? Or even Chief of Staff Friday? I didn't want to think so. I kept these thoughts to my self, but I knew Roger also had them when he died.

Another grueling two full months passed by after the famous 'Big Attack' before our deployment at Gumbo Station would come to an end. Gumbo was four full months of hitting Africa hard and ugly. We grew ever so weary of war, killing, destruction and blood. I knew the time partly because of my payments 'on line' to my ex-wife Patty back in Virginia. My Patty was the true love of my life! Oh, how I missed her! Each third night when going off duty, I'd call her before heading to the ship's Gospel Cafe, where I'd often stay late. My big, round table was comfortable and relaxed. I became known as the anti-professor or old school. I was soon nick-named by the students. Old school was their favorite.

This night at my table, Billy Cash and his date, Pretty Penny, both honor students, started off conversation about Osama's economic stimulus policy. The latest being stimulus number seventeen. Their professor had a theory on his screen during class. His screen used digital chalk.

"Billy" I said. "Please listen very closely. The fear of God is the beginning of wisdom. Your professor is an ungodly fool; a blooming idiot. Just like the men who invented government stimulus. Did he talk about a sick pervert named John Maynard Keynes? Or a book called the General Theory of Money?

"No, Cornelius. He just mentioned Keynesian economic models" said Billy.

"Yes, Billy Cash" I continued. "That's old John Maynard alright. Your sick, progressive professor thinks John is a smart man. In truth, he is a pedophile pervert in full rebellion against God; a fool. I wouldn't follow his directions to the grocery store. Much less let him lead the economic policies of America. What he teaches about fiat based currency, money and banking is a perversion against the teachings of God. Just like his sick lust for sex with young boys. His economic teachings have never worked. They lead to disaster every time they are tried. When I say the old man's a pervert, I'm talking about old men raping five to ten year old boys. Really sick! Look up 'Ole John' on the web tonight and see all of his socialist, communist friends in Europe and Russia. The very type of banking system these ungodly men produced is what keeps modern slavery and serfdom flourishing in this world today. Free men, living in free republics, using real money does not allow slave camps and ungodly kingdoms to grow and prosper. So God's teaching on money, life, work, marriage and sex is always rebelled against. His Holy Bible is always hated."

"Billy, this is the basics of how the system works; how John Maynard Keynes teaching have evolved and become destructive. How he still causes pain and misery long after his death. First start off with a ruling government authority, either a socialist elite or a royal owner of a slave camp province. Note that this does not happen in a free republic. This ruler sells the agricultural or industrial wages of his captive serfs or slaves to international groups or companies. They move in and start production of products for sale in Europe or America. Any 'hard currency' will do. Let's say he takes dollars for the goods he ships. This local tyrant pays his workers in some worthless, home currency he prints in his basement, usually made with pictures of himself or his wife (ha-ha). His slaves can't buy anything worldwide because they are paid starvation wages in phony money, which is only good at the tyrant's company store. Like the old coal miner's song 'Sixteen Tons' and what do you get? You have heard horror stories about people working for wages of $2.00/month. This fiat money slave system is why. This ruler, or king, then makes profits in dollars and holds them in his bank, making him a servant of our bank and our government. Our leaders will now lend him any amount of printed dollars, even put troops in his country, to keep him in power. If his slaves do a good job, Americans are then shipped products at very cheap, high profit rates. We send this ruler fiat money i.e.; 'pictures of our favorite presidents'. If he demanded gold, we could not buy things from him very often, because we are broke. Real money speaks truth and says man's most hated word: no. so, this ruler accepts fiat money; our just printed, paper money. When this ruler comes to America for a visit, he deposits his profits of dollars in our National Bank. These deposits of his are falsely called the U.S. National Debt. His deposit slip, or 'CD' is falsely called a Treasury bond. To a bank, a deposit is a liability. That interest must be paid on. A loan is the sale of money for profit. Our U.S. Bank (privately owned) is called the Federal Reserve Bank. It lends out the slave owner's deposit for a profit, but we the taxpayers, must pay the interest on his deposit. Why? Why ask why? The people who own our Bank also control our government. Yes, America does have a King; the stock owners of the Federal Reserve Bank. Who are they? What do they hold in reserve? I don't know. Do you?"

"Phony fiat money (by government decree), or simply counterfeit money, is needed to keep the slave camps of the world open. Money must always be printed. Also, we Americans get some cheap buys at Walmart. Have you ever thought how do they do it? How can it be so cheap? Slavery, yes, simple enough, we live 'high on the hog' off the misery of enslaved, non-free people. By doing so, we will soon lose our own rights and freedom to their wealthy, world wide owners. The deposits into our National Bank made by these worldwide slave owners (or even our own fellow citizens) called treasury bills have no connection to a balanced budget whatsoever. T-bills can be sold and would be offered even during a budget surplus. Our Treasury and Fed are playing a shell game, just like the bum on a side street. Our big trading partners, are not fools, they don't want to make a deposit, in a small branch office. They know one bank controls our note. T-bills are overseen and daily managed by the 'open market committee' or "the window" as bank and money supply sees fit. The Congress of the United States does not even have the right or power to look at the king's books, much less control what is done, in his bank. Yes, our unknown king is above our laws like all true kings. Our currency is a bank note controlled by special interest groups owning the Federal Reserve Bank. Our Treasury Department and the Fed Bank can both print dollars. My question is simple. How much printed money will the market stand before collapse? When Washington spends more money than it takes in by taxes, this deficit small or large is always an inflation of the currency. This overdraft is always' printed money'! In relatively small amounts, it is not costly. This spending is always paid for by inflation or a loss of value to the currency. This money is not borrowed from anybody and it has nothing to do whatsoever with deposits made into the king's bank. Someone making a deposit does not 'make up for' overspending just because you write 'Fed' instead of Treasury on your dollar bills. Presidents Lincoln and Kennedy both tried printing treasury dollars. They did not live long after doing so. This unknown king of ours is very powerful!"

"Free men, with real money and honest banking, trade with each other openly and freely. Slaves can't buy anything. Our money with Presidents on it is really no better than what the local dictator prints in his basement. We prop up his slave camp and the slave owner is stuck with our just printed dollars. In short, counterfeit money makes possible the world's slave camps."

"There is a group of economists who call themselves the Monetarist they are the so-called competitors to the Keynesian theory. Monetarists are only better by half. The favor the Fed bank money printing and control over direct spending (printing). The socialist Keynesian men, mostly democrats, are printing money and writing checks to every wino and bum in America, trying to buy enough votes to stay in power. Both groups are perpetuating a counterfeiting scheme to enrich themselves on the backs of third world slaves; who are often children tied to machines in sweat shops."

"Slave camps have managed to sell the world over one half of its manufacturing needs. Free men can not often compete. That is why your city manhole cover says 'Made in India', your clothes say 'Made in China', and your auto parts say 'Made in Mexico'. And why America has gone out of business. Free trade is good for wealth creation, but slavery lowers demand and wealth in the end, because slaves live poor lives; they cannot buy. Slaves are poor consumers; poor customers. The foundation of our money system is and has been against the teaching of God as written in his Holy Bible. Evil men have simply 'cut the coin'. John Maynard was not a wise man. God's ways work. John Maynard's ways will lead to a fall. The ungodly democratic, socialist party of Osoma is now finding this old counterfeiting scheme collapsing around them by its own weight. Surprise! God's way works! Man's way leads to destruction! Who could have known? Billy, you've got to stand for something or you're gonna fall for anything!"

Billy Cash, tears in his eyes started to leave. "We can't talk about the Bible, Cornelius. Schools are against the Bible. People would laugh at us; ridicule us! Professors hate it. We would likely flunk our courses if we stood up for God."

"Yes, I know, Billy" I said, shaking my head. "There is no hope for America to come back. We have lost her."

Could nothing be done? Giant pictures of Osoma stood everywhere. The Bible, The Constitution and the Ten Commandments were all gone.

The next three days of flying patrol was routine. Our second 'lost' plane was from extremely heavy, small arms fire from a so called 'private ship'. The ship looked like an old U. S. Navy frigate. Ships sold for cheap when the American Navy closed up, most for less than scrap price. The rapid fall of American power and influence was frightening. What or who would replace America? The Great Ark was part of this power vacuum for sure. What would the world come to? Sink down to?

Sarah and I were sitting at my table early one evening waiting for the music to start at the Gospel Cafe. She had arrived first and waved me over as I walked by on deck. Being this early was not normal. It was very strange and out of character for her. Sarah was eating the Cafe's famous macaroni shrimp salad. I ordered pinto beans and cornbread with onions. Plus, I ate half of hers, which was our custom. A tall, lanky, Yankee, black Gospel Singer named Mike Russell (from Brooklyn) was sitting in with the house band and packing in an extra large, overflow capacity crowd at the Cafe! Mike was likable, talented and very popular on ship. He had a very different music style.

To my surprise, Captain Joe Coe joined his daughter, Sarah, and I at our table dressed in casual street clothes. Captain Coe ordered wine and fruit salad. Not from the Gospel Cafe menu, but rather his personal cook and private stock. Stage music was dialed back to two/thirds its usual volume by the wave of Joe Coe's hand. His 'man Friday' was seated with a few other fellows across the room. Friday was a balding, thin, black man, Joe's chief of staff, and, yes, Friday was his real name.

Captain Coe was blunt and to the point, as always. "I'm looking for some volunteers, Cornelius, for a landing party to India. It leaves in three days, one more duty cycle. The ship's next port of call will be the Australian International Spaceport supply harbor. We will train two semesters of college freshmen, just like we did in Brazil. I'd like to keep you as a flight instructor, Cornelius, but I need four people in India. There's a big air show coming up. Stunt flying like you did back in old days. Details will be given to you by Goldwater. Glancing to the table with Friday sitting across the Cafe, I then quickly recognized Paul Goldwater, my ex brother-in-law. This was a 'small world' moment of sucking disappointment. He was a VPI professor who married the older sister of my wife. Paul's a small, smart, girly man with tiny hands and a selfish, only child nature. He did, to his credit, have a good sense of humor.

I mentioned not my knowing of Goldwater, because I could tell Sarah was going on this assignment also and I didn't want that little squirrel Paul knocking me off the list. Knock me off he would do, as soon as he knew about me. This family feud goes way back. Just to make sure Paul didn't 'find me out', I skipped all the briefings that he called. The next three days were spent on an intense air raid bombing campaign. Multiple sorties per shift, as if to use up our bullets before Gumbo Station time drew to a close. Twelve of our predator drones had already left the Ark, I presumed to another carrier replacing us. This increased the almost frantic pace of our flight schedule, and made it easier, yes, even possible, to avoid my ex brother-in-law right up to the last minute (ha-ha).

My last bombing run at Gumbo Station was very disturbing to me. This is not good for a professional warrior. A man can't let it get too personal. We blew up a tall dam holding back a deep blue, fresh water reservoir. I could see a young couple standing on the dam overlook outside a red Isuzu pick-up truck just before my bombs hit the cement dam face just below them. My whole squad, five more B44s behind me also drilled the dam face.

These General Sherman-like methods made me sick at heart and stomach. How precious water was in this arid climate of Africa. We fly boy warriors killed thousands of Africans with our bombs. Yes we did our level best but the truth is we were small fries in the killing game. The big, and most cost effective, killers were dirty water, AIDS, starvation, disease (malaria) by insects (by stopping DDT), civil and religious wars and of course, free abortion. World leaders are depopulating Africa. For some reason or other, elite humanist, false science environmentalists have decided that Africa must be saved from humans to save the world. Killing off all the Africans has been a top world priority for over sixty years.

Our ship's first experimental use of 'Beetle Bombs' started this last week of Gumbo Station'. These 'beetles' were large and black. They could clean corpses down to clean, white bone quickly, a marvel to watch on damage assessment photos. I thought of all the pain and death inflicted on others by yours truly and men like me. All from the safe cockpit I loved so much. I tried to pray for forgiveness, but I knew I wasn't truly repentant and therefore, totally unworthy of God's gift of grace.

The next morning I would board a helicopter, saying goodbye once more to the terrible horrors and smells of war, hopefully, for the last time. My heart was no longer that of a warrior. Knowing how and when to quit was not so easy. While running across the flight deck towards my chopper, I was against the light. The tower said nothing, thank God. I jumped in and slammed the chopper door shut, even as the big bird wound up for take-off from the ship. Sitting in the back seat already was Paul Goldwater, Sarah and Unk, a loudmouthed, Ukrainian, light skinned black man nick-named the weasel' by Captain Coe. Riding shotgun was the head of aircraft maintenance, Marshall (Duck) Moore, an Irish American who was hell to work for, but a great storyteller. Who the pilot was, I still don't know. Some Boeing company guy, I believe. This masked, mystery pilot wore a complete Blackhawk weapons system helmet, but was flying a Bell cargo chopper with no weapons. I wondered, what's up with that? Who would use that big, old heavy helmet?

Paul Goldwater, across the seat from me, shook his head and said "Oh, God! It is you! Call Coe! Let me out of this damn chopper! *#*#*#*#*#*#*

"Too late, now, boss" I said with a smile. While *thinking to myself. At least that little creep Paul Goldwater was across the seat!*

Thank God for small and large blessings. And so began my great Indian adventure!

CHAPTER THREE

Lost in India

Our chopper landed on a small refueling island in the middle of the vast Indian Ocean a long seven hours later. Goldwater and I ate lunch away from the others only to trade verbal stabs with each other. Where's the love (ha-ha)? Yes, family, but neither one of us was looking forward to working together. Maybe without the evil stepsister duo, Sissy and Debbie, we two men could at least not kill each other on this trip.

"Keep your hands off of me, Paul" I shouted! Truly, we two old men (fools) nearly came to blows. Unk, Sarah and Paul each ordered a sub and a large pizza to go. 'Duck', or Marshall Moore, ordered a sub and two large pizzas with bread sticks; a deal. I thought this 'a bit much', but ordered pizza for myself, also. I guess Subway and Pizza Hut are worldwide now. This island was no more than a big sand bar in the middle of the endless, blue ocean waves. We landed in India; again, seven hours later, another island (still not mainland) and fueled again. This stop we had only a porta-potty break. Each leg of our journey was seven hours long. This transport chopper used the old fifty-five gallon drum fuel tank extension method from Vietnam that I had not seen in years. We were all cramped and cranky. By the end of this leg, I would have more respect for our strange, masked pilot. This raspy voiced Darth Vader pilot became our trusted ally, but never a friend. The mystery pilot's voice roared 'As in the days of Noah, so shall it be' painfully chilling everyone on board to the bone with fear. This dark, soggy, monsoon night was thick, wet, dreary and long. When we finally landed next to three large hangers, we had again traveled a span of seven hours. Three diminished, dusk to dawn lights, one on the front of each hangar, fought for our attention, each trying to shine through the heavy buckets of downpour. Water stood on the football field size pavement over six inches deep, which miserably soaked our footwear as we ran. The wind and constant heavy rain were unmerciful; endless. Each of us was totally spent, soaked and cranky, even Duck (haha). Each person was glad to be free of our chopper prison hell.

An Indian couple known to Goldwater, welcomed us into their simple house across the back alley from hangar one. We all plunged through their door from the storm and flood. Stopping cold, we wedged tight together inside; no room for us in the Inn. Unk, Moore and I cleaned off chairs in the front room piled high with junk and slept into the next day's afternoon. No food or drink was offered to us and by the looks and smells inside, that was a blessing. Our group of six persons, and very many large cockroaches joined the old couple in refuge from the flood. We all huddled together in their little house. Afternoon sunshine brought still no relief from the never ending rain. At 3pm, we all, (now almost dry) stood in hangar one. Unk was describing our flight plan on large, 'clean', stainless steel mechanics tables. Cold pizza never tasted so good. We tore into our boxes. All except Duck. He ate all of his food in the chopper yesterday. Nobody would show ole Duck any pizza mercy. Nobody that is, except my Sarah.

We were each to fly one new Boeing B48 to the VPI of India for the big air show. We would be joined there with others to form two groups of six; a stunt formation and team in the show. We would be at the show seven weekends in total. Then the planes would be taken apart and flown (in storage) to Thailand. At this old, formerly American base, refitting of plane's landing gear would take place to make them operational for use on the Great Ark. This whole process seemed 'complicated' and boring. Unk started talking 'Goldwater-like' during our long briefings he was not impressive; both men became overbearing butt holes. All I could think about was one Sarah Coe. She was cozy up tight beside me as we bent over flight plans during the briefing. We both only pretended to listen. Sarah was an expert at the 'one breast' back stab hug; all men know it well. Sarah used it to her great advantage. I felt like an old caged bull pawing the ground, heart pounding, hoping my embarrassing, boyish stupidity did not show. The Big Air Show was very near the VPI of India and took place in a beautiful 'high class area'. This show, for an old aviator like me, was candy store priceless. We all enjoyed flying in the show and gladly put in long hours. The first month was all practice. Unk was in charge of our stunts. Unk, four Boeing guys, four from another ship, myself, and two old, has been Indian Air Force aces made up our squadron's team. Sarah was bumped to 'alternate'. She flew only one fourth or so of the time. The Indian Air Force home team would not allow women pilots and 'Daddy Coe' was protective as to what close to ground foolishness his Sarah could be involved in with the new B48s. Unk and Sarah could often be heard screaming at each other at the top of their lungs as the old Russian 'weasel' did Daddy Coe's bidding in our flying routines. Towards me, Sarah was also hostile, cold and snobby; not like herself. Always pouting and uncaring; even more so around our comrades.

Mitch Johnston, a Boeing Vice President, would soon place orders for another three hundred B48s during this big air show. The plane was now up to seven years of production. He broke all of his sales goals. Mitch and his wife, Janet, make a good-looking, classy couple. Both were press magnets, very much at ease at black tie events. This pair was extremely popular about town. Their pictures and those of their twin daughters and sons-in laws stayed in the newspaper and on most magazine covers during the Big Air Show. I found out that they were all related to Coe's first wife, Gloria. Mitch and Janet had known all the Coe kids from childhood.

Our new B48s were not a dramatically different looking version of the B44s. No mention of a carrier version was made during the air show. Like B44s, they were light-weight and not supersonic. The B48 was almost a foot longer and five hundred pounds heavier than a 44. This weight came from an engine modification which hurt radar image a bit. It was the new plane's need of less maintenance and added thrust when using hydrogen fuel that ruled the engineering changes. Wings and tail section 'skin flex' was more 'bird like' in each generation. A one hundred mph faster dive put this plane right at the speed of sound. These planes could turn faster than the human body could endure.

"Indeed" said Mitch.

These manned versions are popular, but the unmanned versions were the main thrust of military sales worldwide. Without complex computer restrictions on flight, a B48 would kill its own pilot, snapping his neck at the first sudden turn and then making mush of his face, splashing the pilot against the inside of his helmet. When the plane landed, the flight suit would have a pilot milkshake inside. Not a pretty sight, and also bad for morale. The unmanned version was very hard to shoot down with straight flying missiles because of this bat-like flying agility.

Five large 'world class' resort hotels were close to both the college and the big Air Show. These were good times, indeed. We all received the red carpet treatment. My Sarah was constantly burning mad. She was always cold now in public; often hurtful, belligerent and stubborn (just like her Father), but little Sarah did have her warm side. Our third night in town, Sarah Coe smarted off to me in front of friends. She put on a good show with a loud, flippant goodnight. She was acting like I was siding with Unk against her. As she smarted off, she also placed a plastic room key in the left hand behind my back. This was the beginning of our 'air show honeymoon' together. I used my key and went to her that night. Without speaking, we had marathon sex, almost fighting each other in unbridled passion. Before speaking (full sentences), our bodies were spent. My old plumbing had kept up only with the help of pills. Our daily sex romps made me feel young again. Both of us enjoyed playing the part of lovers. Yes, during our month-long honeymoon together, we were both very happy. Being lovers was much more enjoyable than just being friends, and we needed to spice up our bland lives. We both wanted to live the good life. Unk started talking about 'The Stunt'. Unk said he would take the stunt himself if I was too old or didn't like the odds. I knew what he wanted. My old 'tail stall landing' like in Paris way 'back in the day'. Twelve years back, in fact.

"Unk, don't they do something new by now?" I groaned. "Do you think that old stunt would go over?"

"Old Corny, if you want it, the last stunt is yours. If you pass, then let me know now" demanded Unk, raising his voice.

I was sure from way back at the corner table talk with Joe Coe back on ship, that they wanted a tail stall landing. They just needed someone stupid enough to put their butt on the line. Yes, a glory seeking sucker to do it. Back in the day at that old Paris air show, the aviation world was all abuzz when I landed my jet in the middle of the stadium. I used a nose in the air vertical descent and then slammed to the ground with a not so gentle bounce. My plane's wheels dug so deep into the football field grass that my back has never been right since that day! I rubbed my aching back and said "Still, that stunt was very impressive 'back in the day'!"

The big air show was full of good times. In this life, I have been blessed with more than my share. Sarah and I soon grew so close that she stopped 'hiding me'. One night at her place, she popped the big question.

"I want to do the stunt" she said softly. "Oh, please, Cornelius."

"What stunt?" I asked her.

"You know" she shouted. "Your stunt, I can do it!"

"Sarah, is this about beating Haley at something?" I snapped.

"If you love me, truly love me, Cornelius, you will let me do the stunt. I've been practicing every day at ten thousand feet. I'm a great pilot. I deserve a shot. I deserve to be in the show!" She started to cry. Sarah got up from my old laptop computer and angrily stormed to her room, slamming the door behind her. She was crying pretty good; a lifetime of practice. Her act was impressive. You have to be good to impress an old fart like me. I have known some great criers in my time. Things were not looking up; we had not had our daily sex romp yet!

My heart was troubled. I did care for her 'a little bit'. Should I protect her like her Daddy or give her a shot at fame? She was a highly skilled pilot in the new B48 planes and yes, a spoiled brat! I poured myself some red wine and sat down to think. Sarah had not closed her face book. My heart was grieved by her page. She was in competition with her sisters in another race, a race to download the first Coe grandchild. All of the Coe sister's baby clocks were now being pushed forward by their younger brother's unwelcome girlfriend, Katie. No, Katie would not have the first-born Coe heir! My heart sank as I shut down the computer. I sat back in the chair, ashamed of my tears, focusing my mind on the upcoming stunt. Yes, ground effects on the flight of her plane had to be taught. Let's see, the odds of breaking something on the plane during landing, is about 50/50. Her odds of the plane flipping backwards or rolling sideways into the grandstands is about 20%. What is love all about, protection or respect? Worst, I had played the old fool, just as I had feared. Had Sarah been with me to get back at her overprotective father? Maybe she just used me for great sex, or maybe to butter me up to get her way in the stunt. I guess it could be all of the above, plus the sibling baby race. Daddy will be pissed! That's life, you old fool, get over it (ha-ha)!

The Big Air Show and our little honeymoon both were almost over. I had seen some good times for a short season. Now dark storm clouds were forming on the horizon.

A few days later the big finale came. This was the last day of the show. That day, I realized that the 'lust' Sarah and I shared was not real love at all; no, not the forever kind. Nothing like what Patty and I had. Sarah and I were just a couple of players; each playing out their cards. This world can fool you quickly; very quickly. It makes one play the fool. Now was not the time for breaking-up. This was her moment. It was time for friends to support each other. We kissed and then Sarah climbed into the cockpit with my codes and the show's tower call signs. I went over each and every step of 'the stunt' once again. Not on the simulator this time, but just talking; making believe my hand was the airplane. Sarah took off to 'fame' or 'flame'. The world would soon know. She circled in the tower pattern waiting her turn; not speaking, but using computer text with the tower. The evening sun was setting. The big air show was drawing to a close. Three large helicopters full of stunt men were thrilling the overflow stadium crowd. My plane circled the stadium slower and lower with each pass, and the, when the choppers all landed at once, Sarah came into the light right on cue. Her plane was only feet from brushing the flags and lights as the B48 dropped into the stadium. The plane's long, straight, glider-like wings seemed to reach from one end of the stadium to the other. The 'eagle reflex' set into many fans as the shadow of Sarah's plane passed over top of them. People ran, screaming and falling down in fear. Her plane's powerful jet engine wound up speed and then blasted into afterburner to break the forward and downward motion of her descent. Pulling up to a stall, Sarah balanced her plane completely motionless in the middle of the stadium, slowly backing off the throttle as fuel weight-loss tried to blast her off like a rocket. That's when I walked into Mitch Johnston's VIP press box and nodded hello to Unk and Goldwater. Unk turned and asked "Where is . . . . Damn it!" His eyes quickly focused back to my plane. Which was now Sarah's plane?

Goldwater beside me, also looking straight ahead whispered "You dumb, pervert bastard!"

We all stared at Sarah's plane as it hung motionless in the middle of the stadium, balanced seemingly forever on its powerful exhaust. Ole' Duck had designed and added to the plane a special thrust-out plate to aid the odds of the stunt. Sarah was playing it well, only now starting to fold up her wings. In just seconds, she would run out of fuel and fall the rest of the way to the ground. Sarah lingered much longer in mid-air than we could 'back in the day'. The crowd was glued to this spectacle in front of them. The Astro-turf started burning as Sarah got close. She inched down to almost touching. Then, flame out, and her B48 plane leaned forward a few degrees, falling flat onto the fifty yard line, a still smoking black hole just behind it. As the B48 hit the ground, its front landing gear crumpled so the plane seemed to bow as for her to get out. The plane's large, bubble cockpit canopy then blew off, flying high into the air; a safety regulation no-no. This was very dangerous to people in the stands. Sarah then stood on the plane for pictures. This also was against all the rules. When her flight helmet came off and that long, red hair of hers spilled out, the press stopped announcing me, and fans and the press both stormed the plane, completely overpowering fire and rescue staff. Sarah would be on every magazine cover in the world that month. A new generation of aviator was born.

"Best thing ever for the show" said Mitch Johnston. "That was pure marketing genius, Cornelius! Worth more than money could buy in free advertising!" Mitch grabbed me with a hug and grinned.

Unk, the ole' Russian weasel, was silent, holding back a smile. Goldwater had his ship phone out, looking at me with a 'got you' frown, as he frantically tried Joe's line. He wanted to be first to tell Daddy Coe, just in case Captain Coe was not watching T.V. I walked away from one lonely reporter working our high-class press box. I was quickly yesterday's news. Marshall Moore and I met in the hallway walking out. We spent the next couple of hours celebrating Sarah's triumphant closing of the air show. We were with a group of five or six friends in the lounge of our big, fancy hotel. Sarah joined us after about an hour and a half. She had been mobbed by the press. She pretended to be tired of so much attention. We hugged in the lobby and sat down for one drink. Sarah talked about almost flipping backwards twice. After her drink, she excused herself to her room. "Thank you, Cornelius, for making all this possible" she said. "I'm going to call right now. I will do what I can with, Joe. He will listen to me. Haley and I together, we will do this."

Duck and I drank one more drink by ourselves, now at the hotel bar. We both knew the hard cold facts. The odds were 50/50 that at least one of Coe's men was already here. None of us were safe. Not even from each other; or from someone unknown to us sitting in this very bar.

The next morning, our whole group took off again, plus the two Dave brothers, Bo and Don. They were two blues musicians who were close friends of Mitch and Janet Johnston. They were hitching a ride because Bo had wrecked their tour bus. These two really 'mellowed out' our flight. Think Woodstock (ha-ha)! Complete with rose colored glasses. Bo and Don were from Yorktown, Va. They were famous 'back in the day'. I still have some of their early stuff on vinyl.

For this long flight to Thailand, we flew in a small, slow cargo box plane, a puddle jumper with two old, very loud turbo-prop engines. This was a worthy 'all glory is fleeting' moment for all of us famous aviator types. We rode in cargo class (ha-ha) with stacks of air plane tires between our long, bench style wall seats. There was only one window in the side door of our plane. Old Paul Goldwater sat down between Sarah and I. Everybody in our group knew we were lovers. Paul was being his 'I'm the boss' self and an ass! Bo and Don started smoking up the cabin with the biggest blunt I'd ever seen. Unk, Sarah, Duck and I, all knowing a twelve hour flight was ahead of us, gladly joined Bo and Don's party. We all numbed the painfully loud decibels with dope and laughter. The two Indian pilots were raising hell about the smoke, but the old plane was not airtight anyway. Goldwater was fuming mad. Paul soon moved up front close to the pilots. They closed the curtain on him (ha-ha) and Paul laid his head down as far away from the rest of us as possible. Both the Indian pilots and Goldwater eventually stopped raising hell about the smoke and the 'Indian police'. We all knew that there was much more to worry about than dope and continued blunting our long flight.

I stared out 'the window' during flight as Sarah slept, and leaned on me as a pillow. I thought about 'back in the day' when Paul and I were brothers-in-law. He married the oldest (homely and stocky) sister, HEDDIE, called 'Sissy'. I married the middle, cute sister, the popular one, PATTY, and a 'big bark' Pee Wee Herman type of guy named Barnie married the hot, spoiled, angry baby sister, DEBBIE.

The Mother and Father of these three girls, and one somewhat normal son, were great, generous and God loving people. Mr. Cracker worked as a diesel mechanic all his life. Mrs. Cracker stayed home or helped in the local school cafeteria. The family lived in a small, simple home on the side of a steep hill, very close to the main 'two lane' highway. The children had a modest, but Godly and blessed childhood. The oldest and youngest sisters grew close; they were fourteen years apart in age. The middle sister Patty was their mother's favorite. The other two would have nothing to do with my Patty. All of their lives, the 'evil sister duo' has played the 'both ends against the middle' game. Both sisters hated the popular middle sister.

These Cracker girls grew up envious of their many 'middle class' neighbors who had, in their eyes, 'fine brick homes' and fancy cars. At this level of society, 'money' meant that Dad worked for the Post Office, UPS or the N&W Railroad.

Two local farmer's daughters were close school and church friends with my wife, Patty Cracker. These pretty, farmer's daughters were scorned and hated by both of Patty's sisters. They were scorned so badly that it became a source of constant embarrassment to me as a young son-in-law. The biter envy that sister one, HEDDIE, and sister three, DEBBIE, had for these two farmer's daughters with their Eigner handbags and fancy 'store bought' J.C. Penny clothes was nearly too much for the selfish, evil, 'wanna be' stepsister duo to suffer. My own young wife, Patty, in sharp contrast, worried little about social status or fancy things. Patty was popular in school and had many dates, friends and activities. She sang in church and in the school choir. She was a talented artist with a giving nature; a classic 'middle sister' personality. Patty often did the other sister's hair, their decorating, flower arrangements, etc. She had the heart of a servant. Patty was the one, of course, taking care of their Mother the night she was taken to the hospital and died. The other sisters had 'no time'. My wife's sisters spent a lifetime despising 'Momma's favorite'. For example, my Patty was not asked to be in either of her sister's weddings, while they were both in hers. Pure, cold vindictiveness ruled their lives! This evil sister duo did little or nothing in school or church, and were very much ashamed to bring school friends home and stayed angry at Patty for constantly bringing her friends and dates around the house. These girls were genuinely ashamed of their own family, of their simple home, of their Father's never come clean dirty work hands and their Mother's simple country, slang speech. Yes, this poor, selfish, step-sister "wanna be" duo was embarrassed of and by their own loving parents.

No pain this deep or grievous have I personally known or had to bear. Truly my heart has always wept for them; in soul and in spirit. This heavy burden of pain, shame, uncontrolled anger and envy has controlled them and enslaved them in misery, all the days of their lives!

The older sister, HEDDIE, called Sissy, had a crazy looking 'lazy eye' which was getting much better now with the use of store bought 'doctor medicine'. She grabbed up young Paul Goldwater in marriage before he 'went off' to school. Paul's eccentric parents never spoke to Sissy, even unto their death. She was never 'good enough' for little Paul. Sissy was wise and played her cards right. She saw Paul as her way out; her way up; her ticket to the better half side. Sissy helped put Paul through ten years of college and a doctorate degree and then became his house slave for life. That is when she started 'losing it'; a family mental disorder, or condition that the Cracker family is known for. Old Crackers reach a point when they stop bathing, shaving and or cutting their nails. They stand around urinating on themselves and mumbling nonsense. This condition starts like clockwork in their sixties and is often referred to as the curse or the HEDDIE syndrome (after Sissy's namesake). It is well known, affecting a full third of all Crackers. When Sissy started going downhill, Paul put her into the Catawba Hospital Sanitarium. This was done soon after all parents were dead. Now Paul and his equally selfish daughters have abandoned Sissy completely. No one in the family had the heart or unselfish love it takes to care for another human being. Now Paul, after his own Father's death, has proudly come out of the closet late in life, a badge of honor in his sick, academic circles. Although Sissy and I were never close, I have always despised Paul for using her so and treating her so badly. Just part of his selfish nature, I guess.

Sarah woke up and we both took a toilet break, trying not to wake the others. Bo Dave was the only one up as we sat down again. The loud drone of the turbo props made conversation difficult so hand gestures ruled our communication. Seats in the plane were of military transport or cargo design, not as of airline seats. Bo and I sat facing each other. Sarah had curled up with her back toward Bo. As Bo and I passed the dope back and forth, my reaching would cause Sarah's short skirt to 'shine' Bo. We were both cracking up laughing. Goldwater, still up front, shook his head and said 'pervert'. Bo and I laughed too loud. I tried not to look at crazy Bo Dave again to avoid laughing and stared instead out the plane's one big window once again.

The youngest sister, DEBBIE, was spoiled by her parents as best they could and was ten years younger than my wife and I. Her angry, selfish, stubborn nature even surpassed that of Paul Goldwater. At least Paul had a good sense of humor.

"I know this one is trouble" her Mother would say. Or "we can't do anything with her" or "I've got my eye on her. Fact was, neither parent could control little DEBBIE. She screamed at both her parents with little remorse or mercy throughout her youth. By her senior year in high school, she demanded a shiny red Camaro. She was used, but in good condition (the car I mean). She also demanded that she live off-campus at college (neither older sister would dare). The child-whipped parents always gave into their baby girl. Mother was already working a rare, full-time, extra job to help with the school costs. Her parents gave up a big vacation planned for years and also a trade of the family car for DEBBIE to have her every whim. Our cute little DEBBIE, of course, thought nothing of their sacrifice. For the next twenty-five years, little DEBBIE and her husband Barnie, were always slow to visit and even more quick to leave the Cracker house. This wounded her poor mother to heart. The couple would not let Mother buy Christmas or birthday gifts as she did for the rest of the family. Mother did not have taste; she bought cheap stuff; not the right brand names. All gifts had to be first approved by DEBBIE. Just before my mother-in-law died, this lonely old woman missed her grand kids so much that she would beg over the phone to be allowed to come to Greensboro for a visit. Little DEBBIE would most often say "This is not a good weekend, no, not tonight mom!" The countless times I consoled their crying Mother after she was rejected by DEBBIE and Barnie was, I suppose unknown to them. That and how close we still were during my divorce and estrangement. Yes, even right up to her Mother's death. The heartache this young brat caused her saintly Mother was shameful.

Young DEBBIE was a cute, more than pretty child. Now at fifty, her bitter continence is most disturbing to look upon. DEBBIE was 'hot' by sixteen, but was never model or prom queen beautiful. She was classic hillbilly jail-bait, a hot sizzle, a temptation; with little personality or depth. DEBBIE was usually dumped by the popular boys she dated soon after 'giving it up'. Her Mother would say to me that David, Mark or Brian (fill in the blank) had treated our poor little DEBBIE so bad! Like her older sister, she married to 'get out'. Her 'Barnie Fife' preppie looked like a great catch, never mind that he killed a friend at college; his parents drove a 'new car' a Ford LTD. With young Alfred Barney Head and DEBBIE it was love at first ride. One particular night when she was sixteen, the still young and still innocent DEBBIE spread her, I supposed, virgin flower before me. Masturbation was her specialty, an early childhood obsession. And now with years of practice under her belt, she was getting damn good at it. My seeing of her naked, spread on her bed masturbating (on the way to my shower), made her so hot that she tossed and screamed for relief. As her body arched upwards off the bed, a violent orgasm shook her frame completely. For fun, I let my towel drop, teasing her to a raging frenzy. I then continued to my shower and on to work that early morning. Back then, I had considered it an act of wisdom, or even one of chivalry, not to have taken her virginity when offered; in her moment of weakness. Only months later, her parade of boyfriends started. Her love lust, or crush on me, quickly flipped upside down into hate. There would be no more flirting or even talking much between us after that one early morning. I found out many years later that being scorned of her affection had pierced her deeper than any penis could have. Forty years later, she would have her Podifer's wife moment of revenge on me. 'No good deed goes unpunished'. That old saying is true, it seems, and goes double when you're dealing with a Cracker Head.

As our plane finally landed in Thailand, some twelve hours after taking off, I was still staring out into the darkness below. I remembered how the two sisters shamelessly conspired against my ex-wife Patty for petty, personal gain in their blessed Mother's modest estate. How they hungered all their life for 'class'; something I was born into. Though landing good paying jobs as adults, these poor Cracker sisters could never rise above the low estate of their birth. This was true simply because the two angry sisters had brought shame to their own family. Sick, class envy has scarred and shamed them their whole lives. What a sad, meaningless way this is to spend one's time here on earth. My own siblings, three boys and three girls, some of us making middle class incomes, some not, were all instilled with rich family heritage from a young age. We knew class did not come from our bank accounts, but rather the other way around. Many years ago, our Great Grandmother had helped found a small college. We are a proud family with history and heritage. Yes, we knew some powerful people, but we also knew that class was more than money. My own 'blessed' and 'easy life' always 'ate their guts out' on the better half side of the family. (A title to one of my songs) honor thy Father and Mother for the promise of a long life. God is true to his word, are you? Standing up for the few, the weak, that is class!

Truly I loved Patty's parents like my own. I was closer to them and spent more time with them, and respected them more that the selfish sister sibling duo ever did. This is a true, sad fact of their pathetic lives ruled by envy, hate and unforgiveness. The ability to pray the Lord's Prayer and mean it is all important in this world. The presence of God is where true class comes from at any level. My Father, the real Cornelius, once asked a group of businessmen bidding on government contracts to name the name of a porter or waiter in the large downtown hotel where they were all staying. How a man treats those who serve below him is good insight into his true character. Kiss-ass people are everywhere. My Father was not wealthy, but he had class in black tie or out.

Goldwater and I joked on the runway. We took a few parting stabs at each other. Sarah and I hugged; no big kiss this time. We both knew 'our summer romance' was over. Sarah got on a commercial flight meeting the 'shopping girls' from home and the ship. None of us yet knew that she had won her race and was already carrying the next Cornelius from our short, air show honeymoon. She would beat both her sisters and her brother to the Coe baby download punch by one month.

I called my ex-wife Patty back in Virginia as was my custom every few weeks or so. We talked longer this time; a very good sign. She lived back in Roanoke, in our same old house. Patty was always the love of my life. Patty kicked me out when I went middle-age crazy with a nineteen-year-old wanna-be model, but she has long forgiven me now. A truly saintly woman she is. I do count her as my wife under God. The Roanoke County divorce we both signed seems not to account for much when weighed against our vows to God and our lives together. I pray that one day she will once again receive me as her husband. A gift I truly don't deserve. Why is it that sometimes in this life we just don't know?

After a long sleep in a cheap hotel in Thailand, and now all by myself, I found myself not much fun to be with. I awaited the landing gear fix to our planes. They had been flown on a large Russian cargo plane disassembled and were not here yet.

The next days were like pulling off the fast lane on a country interstate highway, stepping out to take a leak on the side of the road, and locking yourself out of your car. Another world, just outside yours that you have now stepped into, has now become yours. Solitaire, red wine, the Holy Bible, TV movies and the road side soup vendors helped me abide the long, hot days. The third week, on the third floor of this rat and cockroach infested old hotel which was also three blocks from the old base main gate and located on Third-Street. This night would bring personal pain and terror the likes of which I had often inflicted on others, but had never experienced my self.

An explosion in the hotel lobby brought down much of the front of the building. My room was now open to the sky and street below. The force and burn from the blast downstairs left me stunned, in pain, and out of focus. Being part drunk on red wine and lying in a sturdy old metal bed with wheels was the last piece of protection that helped shield me.(in man's eyes) I stumbled out of the burning bed into a smoke filled hallway, falling down and crawling on my belly gasping for air. I now slithered like a snake down the stairs. There were many rats in this old hotel all using the same stairs I was. I then felt cool cement on my bare belly and what I believed was the metal corner of a green dumpster before I passed out.

Some weeks later, judging by the beard on my face, I awoke in still another metal bed with small metal wheels. I was the patient in six beds, with one bright bulb in a center ceiling pull string socket. I was alive! Burned on side and hurting like hell! An Indian woman nurse, with traditional scarf and nose jewel added to her nursing clothes, spoke something non-English as she reached up toward my IV drip and I was back in la-la land.

I would wake up now and again. Each time my medication would be adjusted and back out I would go. My third time awakening, I saw Unk talking to a policeman in the hallway before I blacked out again.

The seventh time I awoke, my room was different. It was dark and very quiet. There were voices and flashlights roaming outside. I got up and looked out through large, dusty plate glass windows. The power was out. I grabbed some sheets, two wool blankets, a smock, and sweat pants and put the roll over my shoulder. Was this a prison, a hospital, or maybe both? Guess I picked the right clothes; for my escape was uneventful. The gate personnel paid me no mind as I walked out. I then began walking and sleeping by the roadside. My wool blankets were my only refuge and comfort. I had wanted to throw them down to lighten my load, but I was now glad that I had not done so. As I curled up on a bank of tall grass, hearing and smelling water, but not seeing it, I was surprisingly comfortable, at ease and free. I thanked God for my life and wondered why I was back in India? This had to be India and not Thailand, or else I was losing my mind. I would later learn that twenty-six weeks had 'gone by' since the blast. The first night I slept well, but I was unaware. How often in this life we just don't know. Does our knowing, or not knowing, even matter?

In the morning, I walked down a steep ravine onto an ancient, wood covered and well worn path. There were huge trees and fancy tiles and bricks. Often the path had a hard surface, but in some places the path was only smooth-packed dirt; cool to my bare feet. The water was not fast moving, but rather gurgling out of pipes here and there into deep, clear pools. Maybe it was for irrigation, a water system or maybe a sewer system? The main road was always close by and usually above me. On this path, I met others often; one third or so were on bikes. Some carried heavy burdens, struggling on their way. Most often I was alone in solitude and beauty. Each man I passed smiled, spoke and was very polite. The women, it seemed, would rather not be spoken to. They all preferred a slight nod of the head. Watching one old man pull up a tall, straight, stemmed plant and use the long stem to wash it off in the water was fascinating. He broke off the stem, pulled off the fine hair-like roots and then ate the center part on his way. This plant, with a white, bent root was a blessing; a comfort. Truly the plant helped me survive. The third night, I arose early, awakened by many men above. A big tour bus was being towed back onto the main highway, out of the woods just above me. The men came close, shining their lights over me as they hooked up the bus. I lay quiet, not very well hidden in my trusty wool blankets. On the back of the big bus was written: THE BZ BROTHERS BLUES BAND in fancy gold letters. Soon, my still water path was indeed still again. In peace, I drifted off to sleep. Not having my Bible, I repeated the 23rd psalms over and over; always 'once more' before sleep. I was so glad Mom made me learn it by heart.

The next evening, after another day's travel, I again stopped to rest. The water path was fancy, even majestic, here, graced with many white stone arch bridges and large beautiful statues surrounded with colorful tiles. In the cove before me were two of these white stone bridges, also a bronze statue of a woman drawing water with a long, smooth vase. The kind people often make lamps or fancy whiskey bottles out of. In the deep, still water, her reflection looked like it was also drawing water. This effect was something to see. It was something to ponder over. I stared, lingering for some time, for I was worn and tired. The water then rippled her perfect reflection and a stiff cool breeze hit my face as it moved through the trees and across the still water. I remembered the words of Jesus.

Spirit is as of the wind, and like the wind has the power to show the truth. I heard a voice say **"behold"**.

Startled and awakened, I quickly hastened on my way, sorry for dozing off. Only a short way down the path, I stopped to rest again, my strength gone out of me for the day. This time I stopped on one of the beautiful, white stone bridges. Looking down into the water, I saw my bearded, scraggily, old self.

"Hello, Cornelius" I said out loud. "You look kind of rough today, old boy. No wonder the women in India will not speak to you (ha-ha)! Down in the water below me was another bridge; a perfect reflection of the one I was standing on. The God was engraved on both bridges into the large center stone at the top of each arch. This false reflection bridge was 'given away' by the word God! The word read backward? Yes, the word of God has the power to show one the truth. "Yes" I said to myself.

I drew weary again and made my bed for the night, just off and up the hill from the path. Pondering the wonderful things I had seen that day, I prayed "Lord that your servant Cornelius might see the truth." As I dozed off, I saw across the high tree tops far above me the edge of a man's little finger. As if a huge giant, much too big for this world, with his hand laid around me, was lying close by. With all the courage I could muster, I said "Speak, oh giant" and bowed. I trembled in fear as he spoke.

"Do not worship me, Cornelius! I am but your fellow servant1 give all glory and honor to God in the highest! You have learned well today! Look seeker of truth! Behold fellow servant!"

The giant knew my questions before I knew what to ask. His voice had power and authority.

"Behold! In the water! The general term BIBLE has the power to deceive in water! Look into the water, Cornelius! Always use the words HOLY BIBLE!"

Then the words flipped upside down.

"Behold, Oh servant! DEBBIE and HEDDIE are daughters in the hedge of CECIL. These are false names! They have the ability to deceive in the water!"

Again, the words turned upside down.

"Behold, oh servant! JOE COE, These are false names. The power to deceive in water is living in these names! Do not be deceived!"

Again, the words flipped upside down. Hold this page up to your bathroom mirror. Your mirror will act as the water! Words will be backwards and hard to read! Now turn your book upside down! Look in the water! A few words will be easy to read! These words have the ability to deceive in water! Their false reflection looks real!

"Be not fooled, Cornelius! Walk in faith and truth! Know you that by their works you will know them!" (Wind, Word and Works) **"Now walk! Be on your way now, oh servant! God has spared you again this night!**

"Again, you said, oh giant" I mumbled. "Thank-you, oh Giant" I said out loud as I packed up my bed. Now very much refreshed, I hustled down the still water path by moonlight. "Say hi to God, Giant! I mean say Hello!" My eyes had been opened. The words I spoke had the power to deceive in water.

"I mean, God bless you, Giant!" I knew, I just knew, that the Giant was pleased with my progress, but he was talking to someone else. Talking to God, I think; not me anymore. In the far, distant night I heard many men and dogs coming down from the main road onto the old still water path. They came crashing through the leaves and trees, coming in fast pursuit of me. If my enemy could only see the great giant that God had placed between them and me! "It sure is great to have my own giant!" I shouted.

After my seventh night of following the still water path, I was walking in the evening and heard sounds of music above. This was a church meeting? I was into the countryside now; this music sounded American. It was a Church of God missionary group. I scrambled up the steep bank as quickly as my legs could climb.

The service was both inside and outside with two sets of double doors standing open to a picnic shelter. The music swelled my heart with joy overflowing. I started rejoicing! I had heard and sang the song before in church many times! Maybe you know it, too. The song goes like this.

> Oh, magnify the Lord! For he is worthy to be praised!
> Oh, magnify the Lord! For he is worthy to be praised!
> Hosanna (clap)! Blessed be the Rock (stomp)!
> Blessed be the Rock of my salvation!
> Hosanna (clap)! Blessed be the rock (stomp)!
> Blessed be the rock of my salvation!

When the singers started singing in rounds starting with "Oh, magnify the Lord", I collapsed to my knees and prayed. I prayed "Lord, I want so much to be Holiness! Please forgive this foolish sinner and find a place for me in your kingdom. Praise God! Praise God! Praise his name!" I could not stop praising God.

A big guy named Pastor Steve and his grown daughter Jennifer, along with 'The Conner Kids', led the spirit filled service. Praise God! Fried chicken, dirty rice and pinto beans never tasted so good. Praise God! Why do I keep shouting praise God! Praise God! Those Baptists and Methodists are all right, my friend, but they ain't got nothing on these Holy Rollers! The famous Conner Kids were well known back home in Virginia. I had heard them on the radio many times before. The little ones were just babies when they started singing at the original Gospel Cafe in Roanoke, Va. I wondered if the old Cafe was still open. When I talked to Edsil, Judy and Jeraline (the grown-up Conner Family Gospel Trio, they remembered me coming to their Gospel sings years ago. They are the parents and Grandmother of the famous Conner Kids.

I blended in and cleaned up (in more ways than one) with this Church of God missionary group. They helped me call my wonderful ex-wife, Patty. True to her loving nature, she was glad to learn that I wasn't really dead as had been reported. The old hotel in Thailand had burned long, hot and to the ground. It was a complete loss. She wired me money to American Express. There was a big hotel in the next town. She was willing to send money to me even though I had missed my payments to her since the blast. Wake up, Cornelius! Who can you trust? Who loves you? What is truth?

I cashed out when the money cleared and checked into a room using my real name and Express card number, but I never went to my room. The room two doors down was checked to a man I met in the hotel lobby while waiting for the money to clear. His name was Chubby Ed."

"No" he said again "My name is Chubbie's Ed, with an S."

"Ok Chubbie's Ed." I said, somewhat confused. Ed was head of an American Christian Motorcycle Association from Philadelphia on an around the world poker run to save the Liberty Bell. The Liberty Bell was being sold at auction next month. It was hard times back in Philadelphia; the city was half empty. They had lost a lawsuit brought by the ACLU, gay pride and the Osoma administration. The city went bankrupt. It had something to do with the term brotherly love, a Jewish feast and a new mosque. The whole lawsuit sounded crazy to me. Osoma had been shot at in Philadelphia and slightly wounded by flying glass. Washington, D.C. was now a ghost town with troops around the mall protecting Osoma's family. The wrath of almighty God was turning on the Israel-hating, Bible defiling, earth worshiping, humanist, fascist, socialist voter fraud friendly Osoma administration. Talking to Ed about the fall of my beloved America was depressing as hell. I understood now more about the 'Jewish Exit' paperwork! American Jews were flooding to Israel, many thousands each month; running for their lives from Osoma. As I entered Ed's room, the maid was very courteous and obeyed my polite commands.

After a shower, a snack (some really good chili) and some new found clothes (of Ed's), I listened through the door as police, or troops, opened my door down the hall and rushed in. Through the peephole, it looked like four of them in all. Not exactly a SWAT team! How insulting! No respect! At least I knew now that I was being hunted. Yes, I was on the run, just as I had expected. I wondered just what the whole deal was. Why is it so often in this life, one doesn't even know the basics. Starting out again on foot, I now had some local currency; about twelve thousand U.S. In dollars was hidden about my body. The police were still searching my hotel. I was heading east for no other reason than stubbornness. During my hitch-hiking and walking, I met many wonderful people. I started feeling like a tourist; clothes do make the man (ha-ha). It felt good to have money. Money is empowering. I could eat at small diners. I kind of missed those soup vendors of Thailand. Some of the Indian food was very good, but one of the main spices they so often use was not my favorite. It stung my nose (ha-ha). Often rides were offered to me, but none were going very far, it seemed. I spent two nights in small bed and breakfast type places. The signs would say 'Hotel', but they were just private homes with rooms added to the sides. Most nights I was still camping with my same trusty wool blankets. I now had new sheets. My backpack was stacked high. It was real fancy with a lightweight frame. Many of the locals also carried bundles, so I figured I looked Indian. I tried my best to blend in and wore a scarf like I saw others do. Many rode mini-scooters or bikes. I was looking to buy one used, if I could. While traveling I just kept moving at my steady slow pace, always staying off the main roads.

The second 'hotel' I stayed in was modest even by local standards. It had a very small sign, so I almost missed the place. I was tired and worn out from my day's journey. The lady of the house waved me in near dusk. This behavior was very rare and bold for a woman in India. I was glad she did, for the rattle and splatter of a coming thunderstorm was upon me. I ran as quickly back to her door as my tired, old body would allow. This family had only two rooms added to their house. She put me in the room next to them. At dinner, I noticed that my plate had three helpings to their one. Her two school-age kids were very polite; their mother very strict and also a Christian. I claimed I wasn't feeling well and did not feel much like eating and retired to my room. She opened an inside door so that I didn't have to brave the storm raging outside. By not shutting the door completely, I could see the family from my bed. Just as I suspected, her two kids divided up the rest of my dinner; which, of course, had been cooked for them anyway. This woman prayed at the table; she was in some kind of distress. Her man never did show up. I slept dry and warm, 'Blessed by the Best', and thanked God for the day. I had a large print King James Holy Bible given to me by Pastor Steve's assistant, Pastor William and his wife, Cathy. We had talked for hours about the old man dying; about becoming a new creature in Christ Jesus. I wondered if I could ever be like William and Cathy. Could I really become Holiness like they were? Oh, how I longed for that type of faith! Kneeling by my bed like I saw the woman's kids do, my thoughts went back to the hotel blast. What was my life all about? Questions flooded my mind. Then the presence of the Lord filled the room. I could not speak; I could not move. I was frozen, paralyzed and still. I was aware of each section or room of the house, but I was also back at the old hotel, before the blast. I was about to say hello to the Giant, but he stepped aside and the heavens opened. I feared not speak or look toward the light! I was not worthy to be before the Lamb! My Giant bowed to his knee and was silent.

YOU ARE CORRECT, CORNELIUS! YOU WOULD HAVE DIED IN THE BLAST! MY ANGEL STOOD IN THE WAY! I HEARD YOU BY THE STILL WATER! YOU ARE MINE, CORNELIUS! I . . . AM . . . YOUR GOD!

"You mean I'm Holiness, praise God!" I wanted to jump up and down, but was not allowed to. I was held motionless at the side of the bed.

CORNELIUS!

"Yes, Lord?"

THE MONEY YOU HAVE BELONGS TO THE WOMAN! HER PRAYERS ARE THE REASON YOU ARE HERE! SHE IS MY DISCIPLE, MY FRIEND! PUT THE MONEY INTO HER HOLY BIBLE WHEN YOU TAKE LEAVE OF HER HOUSE COME MORNING THIS DO IN MY NAME, SAYEST YOUR GOD!

I understood the commands of God not just by hearing or seeing, but by both, and yet more. This was a total, peaceful understanding. "So shall it be, Lord! Your will be done on this earth as it is in heaven!" I then heard Pastor Tommy Mute, from back on the ship say "You can't out give God, Cornelius!" I wanted to put in a good word for my Giant and tell God what a good job he was doing, but my prayer was over. I was now able to get up, although barely. Becoming Holiness; hearing from God had taken all my strength. I could hardly lift the covers. Praising God would have to wait until morning. I fell asleep, knowing I was Holiness. In the morning, I jumped out of bed and cleaned up. What a day! A blessed life! A wonderful day it would be! Praise God! The woman fed me breakfast and we said our goodbyes. I felt some change in my pocket and turned my backpack sideways to squeeze back through her door, placing the coins on top of her Holy Bible. The cash was already in the book of Ruth. "A tip for your kindness" I said, tipping my hat. She smiled and said we were both 'blessed by the best'. As I headed out her door once again, I was broke in man's eyes. But now, I was Holiness and I was the richest man in the world.

I continued on my way, sleeping by the roadside and getting fewer rides. One ride I did get was in a red Isuzu pick-up truck just like the model on the dam face overlook in Africa. What a life of blood and killing I had lived! Yet, I was still allowed to become Holiness! Thank-you Jesus! The Lord's Prayer was my constant chant. The Lord had forgiven me so much! Reciting the prayer kept me in time with my walking stick.

After the seventh night, I started down a narrow country road. There was not much on this road, only fields and forest, no traffic at all. I had nothing to eat. I was not beside the still water anymore. Soon I drew weary, but pushed myself to go on. The sun was near its noonday high when I heard a car approaching from behind. This road had been deserted, I had thought. This car slowed down, but did not pass me by. A horn then sounded twice and the car pulled up beside me as I walked. It was a brand new 1964 light blue Ford Galaxy, driven by a nice looking Asian woman about my age. She shouted at me while hanging out of the car's window.

"Where you go, Joe?" I was glad to get into her car being worn out, tired and hungry. This nice Vietnamese lady glanced into the rear-view mirror and said. "You American, right? You walk like Joe. Believe me, I know."

My blending in was not that good, maybe, I could not think of anything to say. I finally spoke up, saying "You drive fast, like Mildred my old Mother-in-law did back home." One forgets just how really big these old '64 Galaxy's were, I thought to myself. I silently watched the scenery fly by as the woman kept the 'hammer down' for the next few minutes and miles. We soon approached an estate with kept grounds that would make the Queen of England blush with envy. The old, but new, 1964 Ford pulled under a covered circle entrance at some type of resort or hotel. Vintage American cars were parked around the circle. This Vietnamese lady started barking orders and checking off phones as if they were clipboards. Servants waited in line to be checked off. She told one young man to empty the circle of cars and bring in the next ones. Evidently, they rotated cars in some chosen order. A Pontiac GTO parked close to us was sported up. Not original like the others. As I walked inside, I admired it. The GTO was 'mighty fine' as my son, Shawn, back in Virginia would say.

This woman, called simply Karla or K-one by servants, walked us through the mansion and out the back courtyard into an office building; or maybe it was a hotel. Everyone we met spoke to her. She was showing me off as if she had won a prize for finding one first; 'Look, I find an American Joe'. Then in the elevator, we talked. She said "Smile for camera, Joe. Yes, you really do walk like a Joe."

On the sixth floor, K-one led me down a hallway into a large, empty room. Twenty-four flat screen TVs were placed around the walls. Each T.V. was about two hundred inches with six on each wall. All sets were tuned to American football. Each had wireless earphones hung on the wall. I started watching some games. I noticed that six sets on one wall did not have as sharp a picture as the others. All of the others looked to have the same amazing 3-d picture quality. As I walked around the room, I saw teams I had not heard of before. One game was a Harlem team playing a Portland, Oregon team. One was a Richmond, Va. team playing a Nashville, TN. team. After watching football for some time, say about forty minutes, I heard a voice from behind me.

"So, you are an American?" I turned to see a tall, young, Indian man, very well dressed, a boy, really.

"Yes" I said. "I hear it shows."

"Of course" the boy said. "What do you think of my football games? We have what you call soccer, too." He then waved away the two men standing behind him with a slight hand gesture. These men looked like nothing you'd want to play with. If you know what I mean! This young man, or boy, had power. He seemed born to it; like a King, I thought to myself.

"No, I'm not a king" he said, "Although my uncle does own this Province. I understand you were found walking up my driveway. Good for you. You picked the right road. My uncle can be a cold and stern man."

"Sir, I've been out of touch for some time now" I said. "But I don't know any of these teams, and can you read minds?"

"Yes, I can read minds, but not very well. And it is very impolite. Please accept my sincere apology" he made another hand wave, this time with a slight arm twist. "The system is off. Your thoughts are your own. You have my promise of that fact."

"My God," I whispered out loud. By his lack of expression, I knew he was telling me the truth, because I was thinking about chocking the tall lanky punk and his big tough guys did not show up again.

"My name is Jediah Emin Patel, Cornelius, of the sons of Ammond. Welcome to my home. Yes, we know your name; we have you on file. We have facial recognition software on the camera in the elevator. It is old technology now, but is still useful. So you're a pilot, one of ours even. Are you here on a rogue mission, Cornelius? My uncle's people say you are trouble. I have not yet approached him on this subject. We like to keep experienced pilots, like you on staff. We can discuss your future after dinner, if you wish. Do not be afraid for your life, Cornelius. No one, not even my uncle can reach you here. You are my guest. Welcome to the house of Patel, my friend!"

"These games are digital 3D, virtual reality" said Patel. "Not 'real games' at all. But in a sense, they are as real as you and I. If you give me four hundred hours of a football player and his stats, we can put his digital player into our system. We can even scan, or test you. Put in your skill level, body shape, size, wind, knowledge; many factors. Would you like to be in our system?"

I stopped him, saying "Not right now, thank-you."

He then mentioned his 'eighth floor' games that put one into the game from the football player point of view. Eighty percent is controlled by your own movements, size, and speed and skill level. These games were played while you wore a helmet and were suspended inside a three-ring gyro harness.

"This will be the biggest thing since sliced bread" said Jediah. "But right now, it is too expensive to bring to market. Cornelius, your heads-up flight training in the B44 used part of the same software."

Yes, that training back in Brazil had been state of the art, I had thought, and said so as we parted.

Two young Asian gals, K-21 and K-28, led me to a room in Patel's Palace. My backpack and wool blankets were already in the room. My old stuff looked out of place against the polished, marble floor. I told a fancy, uniformed man that the girls did not need to stay, but to thank Jediah very much for them.

Now, alone in my room, I thought about the football games and the Great Ark. The America I had grown up in losing power in the world. I asked God what I should do next, and thanked him for his great mercy and the many blessings in my life.

How real those football games looked, I thought to myself. They could not be distinguished from a live T.V. Broadcast. Just the sports T.V. alone would be worth billions of dollars. Teams would not have to pay make-believe players. What could men do with this type of technology? What about a newscast? Was it being done already? The Holy Bible clearly states that even the very elect will, and can, be fooled. How will I know the truth? Who are these men? How rich and powerful are they?

For the next seven weeks, I was Jediah's playmate. He would summon me to his eight floor game room and we would play like children for hours. The first day on a new game, Jediah would have the advantage. By the second or third day, I would catch up and begin to beat him often. I always tried hard to beat the tall, lanky bastard; something that was rare in his pampered, closed-off world. He respected me for that. Even loved and valued me because of it. As I got to know him, I found him even younger in age than I had first thought. Jediah Emin Patel was king of his castle, though only a boy. He could order blood and terror as easily as his morning eggs and rye toast.

At each of our formal dinners at his long fine table he would have on most evenings, at least forty, and up to one hundred people. He would stay dressed up and 'grown up' into the evening, being a true boy at play only in the mornings and only in his private game room. When time came for fencing and boxing games, I beat him quickly and easily from the beginning. He added my 'moves', as he called them, into his computer simulation and said I was invaluable (ha-ha). I told him my 'moves' were from formal lessons, topped off with living in South Chicago for a year, and then military combat training. I noticed my young friend wore a small head cap, like the ones American Jews wear ceremoniously. Also, he was supervising the construction of a new palace. This was a vast undertaking with many workmen. A large medical staff of doctors, nurses and men in waiting, constantly took measurements of Jediah. On day in the play room, while hidden from view with my game helmet off, I heard a nurse tell a doctor on the phone, "Yes, he is over one half. Part from both sides, just like the older! We don't know what will happen. He is still fourteen months from his scripture testing." I realized that my young friend, though very tall, was not even eleven years old yet.

After a seven week stay at young Patel's fine palace, and many long 'adult' talks after dinner, he offered me a job as one of his staff pilots. The depth of his general knowledge, his wide interests, was simply amazing. Jediah fluently spoke in at least five languages. It became obvious why the handlers that had 'raised him' were now becoming afraid of him. His older servants thought he was out of control. They often complained about his women. These were mostly Asian girls who attended to his every whim of sex, drink, games and food. He had absolute power over his house, even life and death, this all as a young boy.

When Jediah offered the pilot job, I gladly accepted it. We had six Lear jets; each four years old; each custom made for his personal use. His powerful uncle kept two air force type 747 planes and one 777. Jediah loved his Lear jets. With their plus size engines, we could climb in a hurry. Jediah, his uncle and ten other large estates shared a private airport. The servant's housing formed a small town in this gated community. All of which was separate from the province that his uncle owned. This province was a valley the size of the State of Massachusetts. It had one major city six large towns, and a population of over fifteen million people. Patel was seldom on his own planes. Most flights were to pick up dinner guests. No public or chartered flights ever came to his private airport. Both he and his uncle had been at the big air show in their private box, unknown and unseen. He laughed about almost buying two new B48s, but didn't like the maintenance package. Boeing had too many strings. For the next fourteen weeks, I lived in a 'pilot' house. I was in the single, or bachelor, section. Work and flying was enjoyable and I wanted for nothing. My pay stub was completely different from Ark pay. I wondered if the Great Ark and Captain Coe knew of my existence on this side of the grass (ha-ha).

About twice a week or so, I would be summoned by a servants or nurses text to come to Jediah's room where I would try to beat him at a new game. These games were played in HD virtual reality. The helmets, gizmos and suits were so real, I often could not sleep. Nightmares became common for me for the first time in my life. I grew so weary of the play, that I dreaded it. Prayer and reading the Holy Bible became a daily routine for me during this time. I declined Jediah's many offers of female companionship. His Asian girls, who were mostly from Thailand, with a few Vietnamese, and some American blondes thrown in, were often very tempting. My young friend asked if I needed virgin girls that could be properly, and lawfully, 'taken to wife' by me. I told him about my ex-wife, Patty, and being Holiness. Jediah had many questions, some of which I could not answer, during our short Bible study time together. The words 'As in the days of Noah, so shall it be. As in the days of Noah, so shall it be' tormented my soul!

Once on a Sunday evening, I was summoned to Jediah's palace by Karla, or K-one, the lady who first picked me up. I learned she was named or called Miss Connie. Karla was her title. It was after dinner, so I showed up dressed in black tie, knowing better than to offend. Jediah Patel was talking with two men and three women from something called 'Tower Watch'. Jediah wanted my input into the teachings of God JEHOVAH, these being his witnesses. I could hear myself speaking, but I did somewhat lose control of myself. A spring of speech flew out of me speaking of scriptures I had just read the night before. Test the Spirits, Jediah. Beware of false, changed names and corrupted spelling. The power to deceive in water and to deceive the Saints of God is in this root word, of Jehovah. YAHWAY is closer and much preferred. Jesus is the name above every name! No other name is given by which a man must come to God. Every spirit that does not proclaim that Christ came in the flesh and died on the cross to redeem this fallen world is not of God. The big men of Patel's drew near to me as I drove the 'Tower Watch' people through the palace and out through the front door, but Jediah stayed them with his hand. As I slammed the big front door shut behind them, I started coming back into my right mind and apologized to Jediah for my behavior. He was laughing so hard at my rampage that he could hardly stand up or control himself.

"Thank-you, Cornelius" he said. Jediah's servants then brought me red wine without me ordering. Then we talked into the night about many topics. We talked about the Holy Bible and the death of his Father. Jediah said some things as we parted about his Father that I did not understand. He said that powerful men worldwide had not known who I was, but now his uncle had my complete birth record. My file was all up to date. Much of this conversation I was not able to understand. I questioned his respect, yet hate, of his Father. His life of privilege, of early childhood power, of wealth, was not an easy one. This tall, lanky boy/man carried his own burdens, as do we all. I was glad to see that side of his life. I was proud to count Jediah Emin Patel as my friend. And very glad I did not have him as an enemy!

CHAPTER FOUR

The International Spaceport

One Thursday morning, I flew Jediah Patel to the new International Spaceport in Australia. The large harbor was under heavy construction with large cranes taking root and reaching for the sky like bean shoots. They were growing seemingly everywhere. Many thousands of Chinese workers attended to the beans, working non-stop. Our group of four Lear jets went into a holding pattern lasting twenty minutes. I saw two, old, American style aircraft carriers parked outside the port, a stirring sight against the green-blue sea. One more carrier was in port at dock. It was the Great Ark, with its big back door open to the harbor. *Won't old Joe Coe be surprised to see me!*

During the next seven weeks, I stayed at one of the eighteen new Hampton Inns near Spaceport Harbor. Another hotel opened while I was there. They all looked the same. All were owned, I believe, by the Patels.

Our four Lear jets brought six engineers apiece, plus Jediah Patel and one old man named Japeth Jones. All these men worked for Jediah's uncle. Four of these men were American and they were with me. One of these was older, He was a black engineer named Ralph Edward Low. Ralph was more laid back or 'sane' compared to the many overenthusiastic younger types, who were referred to by Ralph as the 'go-getters'. Ralph was more to my speed and liking. At least he took the time to talk. We became fast friends, more so than the others. Ralph took me on two helicopter tours of the Spaceport. Both were unbelievable; fantastic even! This was his job also he designed tours and films of the Spaceport for tourists. Ralph pushed the 'vision' to the public. People like me. Ralph's helicopter tours were not yet open to the general public. He was writing an employee handbook for the tour guide personnel. He also gave me three DVDs which he had produced about the spaceport. Or rather his company, Eagle Engineering, had produced. The plans for the Spaceport and the Space Station were so big that it all sounded like wild dreams. All about exploring, living and working throughout our solar system, and then one day going to the stars. This spaceport was over half built and was partially operational. It will be going strong by 2017. Ralph spoke into a speaker horn from the shotgun seat of the chopper.

"The Old Man does it his way! We don't need to ask why! It works and we are the world leaders. The first grand station will be built. I'm sure of it. This station and many others will be built of many rocket fuel tanks that are all the same size, each more than sixty feet wide and more than three hundred feet long. Many tanks will be put into orbit using this Spaceport system here in Australia. Others will use huge rockets and eight space shuttle type boosters to push them into orbit. Europe, Japan, China, Russia, Old USA and now Babel Iraq will all 'rocket up' supplies, fuel sections and men."

"Babel Iraq, are you serious, Ralph?" I shouted.

"Yes. Persia and the Saudi's are partners!"

"My God Ralph, as in the days of Noah, so shall it be! As in the days of Noah, so shall it be!" I said.

"Don't talk that Bible stuff around here, Cornelius. These men are serious scientists. You might insult them" Ralph replied. Under my breath I muttered "Good Lord! I'm scared for this world

Ralph interrupted me while pointing to an illustration. "This is what the Grand Station looks like! Each section, or tank, is sixty feet wide and over three hundred feet long. The cap on each end is a half sphere

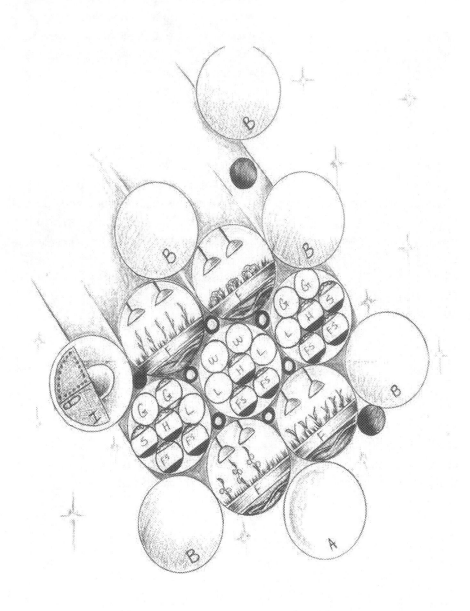

with intersecting flanges, these ends can come off in space to form round balls. The 287ft length comes from two tanks joined overlapping. Seven twenty foot wide tanks can be inside of a large sixty foot tank. It can be empty or smooth bored, depending on the use of each tank in the station. The large and small tanks both have end caps. Each tank is over 300ft. The sixty foot wide tanks come in these two types. First a smooth bore (for oceans) and the other filled by seven interior pipes (for living quarters). Each of the smaller tanks is 'almost' twenty feet wide. Twenty-six of these large tanks form a circle, also in groups of seven. They form a rotating ring in space, 7,462 feet around. A station can have many rings."

"The center 20 ft tank is always the hallway. Rings toward the outside are half full of water, with farm land on top. Some have trains hanging from above. The most protected sections are the living and working sections. Boating and fishing, even water-skiing, would be possible in the large rivers under the farms."

"Tanks are of double-walled construction and slide into each other. They are bolted and glued in place for a very strong fit. Nothing crosses the center of this huge wheel as it rotates. Space shuttles land on the interior rim. Sixty foot cap spheres are made into atomic power plant housing, extra tank storage or entrance doors for landing shuttles depending on needs. These stations are self sufficient as much as possible and placed in orbit around the Earth, the Moon, or other planets as needed or desired. These standard pieces, the rocket tanks, can be made on Earth for many years. Even many generations, depending on the effort man is willing to put into space. The U.S. Has not put a rocket section into orbit since Osoma cut the program. We can do it all by ourselves. But, it would best if the world gets motivated. The merchants of the world have mourned over America's fall.

"There have been to date, sixty-two sections of sixty foot tanks. Twenty-eight have been smooth and thirty-four have been sections of seven. Place seven straws in your hand. See how they form a perfect circle with one straw in the middle?" Ralph handed me seven straws off his visor.

"We do space launch differently here at the International Spaceport, as you know from the DVD. We start with old fashioned railroad technology. That might sound crude, but this system works wonders. The grand old man of Spaceport design, Nimrod Elam Shin, died only seven years ago. His son Japeth Jones Shin will see his Father's dream fulfilled. Soon we will have hotels throughout the solar system. Have no doubt, friend, we are on our way to the stars. To the very heavens of God! To look God in the eye! What a day that will be!" said Ralph.

"What a day that will be! You've got that right!" I groaned. "Look God in the eye? What a day? What a fool!"

"Do you have any questions?" Ralph asked.

"What's that?" I was pointing at a brochure of the Space Station. "Ralph, go back to the railroad cars, the launch system" I thought about all those Chinese workers at Spaceport and the building of the American railroads. Had anything really changed?

"Ok" said Ralph. "Here goes from the beginning. For you, Cornelius"

"Six sets of railroad tracks, straight, flat and two hundred and sixty miles long are laid in the Outback. At each end of the tracks is a Spaceport. 144 rebuilt (used) and new train engines, now totally electric, are put on each track. That is 864 engines total. Each trains electric motors have been rebuilt with the torque set for high speed. The six tracks are 130 feet wide in total. A huge moving runway is built on top of the 864 train engines, locking them together as one unit. Third rail electric is used for power. On top of the runway are two very large planes, each with the lift of seven C5As, even without the use of the moving runway. These are the large manta ray looking planes you see below. On top of each huge plane is a fat boomerang looking space shuttle craft. On top of both shuttles are two tanks. One tank is on each wing; each tank is sixty feet wide and three hundred feet long. These, of course, are the fuel tanks that become the Space Station. The two large planes, shuttles and fuel tanks taxi onto the runway and get into position. Then the fueling process takes place. Now the plane is so weighted down that it cannot take off. The Two large planes, two space shuttles and two sets of tanks are all ready to go on the same train runway."

"Six atomic power plants are running full blast making fuel and powering Australia. The power is diverted from making fuel and is put into the third rail of the Spaceport. The Spaceport runway then begins to move. Sixteen to seventeen minutes later, the space shuttles and the massive air-breathing planes are traveling at 465mph, which is their top speed. The first plane goes to full throttle and starts rolling on the train. At this speed, enough weight has been lifted off its tires and its huge jet engines are much more efficient. The assembly takes off of the train when reaching 540 mph. Four minutes later, the second assembly goes to full throttle, and it also rolls off the train at about 540 mph. These 'manta ray' looking planes climb to between 62,000 and 72,000 feet while never breaking the sound barrier. Shuttle #2 then takes off of plane #2 and plane #2 returns to the spaceport with no pilot. Shuttle #2 now hooks together with shuttle #1 which is still connected to plane #1, both using the Old Man's double hook system. After the two shuttles are hooked together as one they go to full throttle and plane #1 goes back to spaceport, also with no pilot. Shuttle #1, on the bottom is set on fast burn and is pumping fuel into shuttle #2 as they climb. At about fifty miles altitude, shuttle #1 runs out of interior fuel and drops off, leaving its two 300ft tanks on the bottom of shuttle #2. Shuttle #1 now returns to spaceport. Shuttle #2 saves its interior fuel and burns the four exterior tanks first. It gets to the space station and only then does it let go of its tanks, which will later become part of the space station, and docks with a still full interior tank. This fuel it uses when leaving the station, to slow its speed down to below 11,000 and 12,000mph, and then using 'skipping' to cool its reentry. Now its thin coating of reentry material and paint tile-like paint is enough to last through many flights without hours of costly maintenance like the thick tiles on the old American space shuttles. The fuel payload used to slow reentry is no different than any other orbit payload and could be used to put an extra-heavy load into orbit if needed. There are some layers of glue type material that is added to the exterior of the station for extra protection. This goes into orbit in tanks and is sprayed on in orbit like wrapping a spider web. Some solar panels are used for emergency back-up, but atomic power is the mainstay of space power for now. Just like on Earth." This stuff is still classified and Ralph would give no other information.

Obie Carter, retired Navy, spoke up from the back seat. "Explain again why this shuttle is so efficient that you can get into orbit with all that fuel left over."

Ralph smiled and proudly answered. "Sure Mr. Carter. As I said, it's like any other payload. But let's look at this analogy that shows why we are so efficient."

"First of all, here in Australia, we use 23% less fuel than rockets at Cape Canaveral in Florida by using the rotation of the Earth at its Equator to our best advantage. That is why we have to cut payload when running the Spaceport train back the other way. One might think that we would 'go back' and start again, and yes, it is almost a break even point, but not quite when time and money are considered. It is still to our advantage to run take-offs in both directions. Yes, with and against the roll of the Earth."

"Imagine and Indian brave hiding underwater in a stream with his bow and arrow, trying to shoot a crow as it lands on a branch high above the water. Even though he is a strong and powerful brave and uses his biggest bow, the arrow coming out of the water does not have the speed needed to kill the crow. This smart Indian finds a big rock at the bottom of the stream. When he stands on this rock, his head and shoulders come up out of the water. He waits for the crow, slowly stands up on the rock and his bow nails the crow every time. It is now not slowed down by the thick water. These big planes we use at our Spaceport, they are our 'rock' at the bottom of the stream. They lift us out of the thick atmosphere of the Earth, letting our rockets (arrows) fly faster. Couple this with the old-fashioned (running start) of our trains. Those trains let our first-class passengers arrive in space without the rough 'G-force' of a blast-off. This is a winning combination. When our first shuttle runs out of fuel and drops off and shuttle #2 goes on by itself, it is full of fuel and just getting started. It is already close to 50 miles high and going 5000 to 6000 mph. With a head start like that, we can't be beat. We have a very good safety record and our shuttles can land anywhere in the world."

We all thanked Ralph for his tour of the new International Spaceport.

That night at the Hampton Inn, I read my Bible and thanked God for allowing me to become Holiness. People don't mind one of those other faiths much. You can talk about being Baptist, Methodist, Presbyterian or even Catholic. That's all just casual talk. But if you dare talk about being Holiness and having the Joy, Peace, Presence and Power of the Holy Spirit, people run away from you. They get mad as hell. They want to fight, lie to you, test you; anything but hear the word of God. As I waited for sleep to come that night, the words of the Bible echoed in my head. **As in the days of Noah, so shall it be! As in the days of Noah, so shall it be with the coming of the Son of Man!**

The next morning, I had the opportunity to talk in private with Jediah Patel. I asked him for a leave of absence.

"Be careful, Cornelius" he said.

We shook hands then hugged instead. I had much I wanted to ask him, this young commander of men. He was as powerful as any world leader, I was sure. A lanky six-foot-eight, maybe nine, a genius; well versed on any subject. Yet still only eleven years old.

I rented a car on Patel's card, being officially on duty, ha-ha, and drove to the harbor city that supplied the Spaceport. Large cranes and Chinese workers were everywhere. At a grass strip next to a college on the edge of town and on some of the worlds most beautiful beaches, were hundreds of colorful, loud, little ultra-light planes buzzing around in seemingly slow motion and landing on the grass. Their colorful display was as a poetic shout for joy that only the foolish can afford. They brought back fond memories.

After talking a student out of his codes, I was up, up and away, heading to the Great Ark and one 'S.O.B.' Captain Joe Coe. Dead or alive, I would have my peace with him.

My flight took twenty minutes to reach the ship. Immediately after landing, I unbuckled and two student flight deck handlers came out to hook up the ultra-light to the ship's cable (storage) system. These students paid me no mind, nor did the third or the fourth. But before I got to the bridge elevator door, a crew member's face gave him away. Putting my fingers to my lips, I smiled back and keyed my code into the elevator. Yes, mine still worked (ha-ha). I was on my way to see one Captain Joe Coe. Entering the bridge, I looked around. There was no Star Trek feeling this time. In fact, the big bridge was almost empty. No Joe Coe in sight. Not even Friday was aboard. Sarah, Haley, Joe Coe and the four other women had been staying near Sydney for over thirty weeks. One of Joe's homes is there. Haley and Sarah's middle sister, Blair, lives next door year round with her husband. Both played professional basketball and volleyball, plus ran two businesses in town. It was family reunion time for the whole Coe clan. The two Johnston daughters of Mitch and Janet's had come 'down under' to visit. So had Rosemary, Frank and Dan, a Hog lady, Ann's kids and the Dave brothers. Officer Booth took for granted that I, being a family 'insider' knew all these people, so I just played along. Thomas Briton was now in charge and gave me an officer's quarter's cabin. It felt good to be back, but would this be a 'welcome' or a 'hellcome'. Would I be family or foe? It's strange, how often one just does not know. My ship phone was brought to me, a version of Apple's I-phone, but bigger with a larger battery and antenna, made for marine use. Officer Booth brought it by. David Booth was the man who first led me to this same room on my first day aboard ship.

"David, can you fill me in? What's the deal? How much do you know? I inquired.

Booth let out a slow breath of air before he began. "Sarah got married about six months ago to a pro ball player friend of Blair's husband. The couple named their new baby Aaron Benjamin Cornelius Cohen. You wouldn't know anything about that, would you, Cornelius?"

"Well, no . . ." I said.

"Captain Coe took some heat from the elders, straight from the top, Cornelius. He was not happy and almost lost his job."

"The top Elders, what are you talking about?" I asked.

Booth shook his head. "A twenty-four man committee. You truly don't know much, do you?"

I bit my lip and said "Well, David . . . . ah . . . no . . . . I don't." Booth pointed for me to sit and then he began again.

"The twenty-four elders are top or senior leaders of four hundred plus board members which represent eight thousand families world-wide. Together they own about thirty-five percent of the world's resources. Add in the next few thousand wanna-be families and you are way over fifty percent of the world's wealth. Do you get the picture? Lord's and Kings throughout history. Your boy in India, his uncle is a board Elder. The boy is not even a board member yet."

"Then they know I'm alive, David?" I interrupted.

"Yes, of course, they know, Cornelius! Now listen, Cornelius. The President of the United States might get a meeting with a board member. I said MIGHT! Nobody even knows who the Elders are for the most part. How did you get mixed up with powerful people like that as dumb as you are? No body has access to Elders. I MEAN NOBODY!" David screamed.

"David, you're a deacon in your church back home Right?" Booth nodded disturbed to be asked. "The truth is David, I'm Holiness, now." I said.

"HOLINESS?" he shouted back.

"Yes. I'm Holiness, now, David. And I have a giant that works for God with me." I cried.

"You're an idiot!" Booth proclaimed. You'll have more holes in you than you can count when Captain Coe gets back. He'll feed you to the damn giants. The worldwide publicity that Sarah got at that air show almost got Joe fired. Complete control of the news is part of the Elder's power structure. A few honest reporters can cost these people big money. That is until they disappear. Raw power, Cornelius! Real worldwide power! Don't you know who you're dealing with? The health field alone is full of bodies of bright young men with cures for disease. The Elders use disease. They profit from war and misery. They sell and kill by the thousands. How in the name of God did you ever survive? Word from Damage Assessment is that a drone from this very ship took you out, Cornelius!"

I sat down slowly and said "I thought it might be something like that. Who are these Elders again, David? Please tell me."

"Anything the Lord loves, does or has, the Dark Angel will try to copy, steal or destroy, Cornelius. Don't be fooled. The Lord has twenty-four Elders in his throne room and four beasts. Guess what? Our twenty-four elders are not of God. Ours are imitation and fake. They are the other half of a deck of cards. Wake up!"

"The Dark Angel" I asked.

Officer Booth began to calm down and he spoke softly. "I am glad you're working for the Lord now, Ole' Corny, even if you are crazy. You have been a good friend. Yes, you and I both work for the Lord, but this ship does not. It's all about the golden mean, the number 26 and the circle of fifths."

"The number 26, the golden what" I stammered.

"Yes and billiard balls stacked up on pool tables." said Officer Booth. I said nothing. I just shook my head and thought to myself. *The circle of fifths the number 26?* "Read your Bible, Cornelius. Get a math book. I can't explain all of this. It's all above your head. Take that deck of cards on your table. Stack the pairs into pairs that add up to 13, divide the kings, which have a value of 13, into two stacks, one red, and one black. Now, how many stacks are there? Oh, I haven't got time for this nonsense. This is all way above your pay grade, Corney!" Booth handed me some flight plans approved through the tower with extra fuel.

"No! I'm staying, David!" I answered. "I don't want to run! Thanks anyway. I think Sarah, Jediah, my Giant and Lord Jesus will all help me. I'm not worried about ole' Joe Coe. Joe will find me pretty hard to kill. I'm an old cockroach, just like him!"

"Cockroach, I believe! But, pretty? Give me a break!" Booth laughed, enjoying immensely my high stress level. Booth slammed the door hard as he departed.

"ASSHOLE," I swore under my breath. "Never let them see you sweat!" I said out loud. I stayed on board ship, but marked off of flight status. I did not fly 44s or 48s and worked B time in purchasing and C time in the ship's brig instead. I was helping out and waiting for the 'shoe to drop'. Would it be a 'welcome' or a 'hellcome'? I wanted to look Joe and Sarah in the eye. Have my peace with them. I didn't fly, because I would not give Captain Joe Coe the pleasure of killing me by remote control in one of his fancy planes.

Life on ship was easy and slow during this time. I moved some money around and sent the information to Patty back home. She was the only one I could trust. Even though she had thrown me out, Patty was the best thing I had in this life; my anchor. Even if these bastards do 'take me out', at least I'll know Patty and my son Shawn will be well taken care of. I also started making notes for this book during this time. It was a journal. The gospel Cafe on ship was closed for over a month for remodeling, so I didn't have my big, corner booth. I stayed to myself, mostly and tried not to talk to people on ship about being Holiness. I didn't seem to be very good at all this God stuff. When I did try to tell people how great it was being Holiness, they ran from me like the plague. Some of these same people went to other worship services or they had a church back home.

I found while working in the brig, that these twenty-eight inmates were much more willing to listen to me about being Holiness. I started to focus my 'God work' on the brig men. These sailors were being held mostly for alcohol or drugs. I started talking and visiting with them. Most would listen to my story of becoming Holiness. God's work was becoming a joy!

Then one evening, the Great Ark started out to sea, leaving out of Spaceport Harbor and heading south around Australia. Joe Coe would not be coming to his ship. His ship was going to him. I knew my confrontation with Joe was drawing near. I might end up in this very brig myself, I thought. That night at my cabin, I prayed: "Lord, that your servant might see the truth!" Before the word truth finished on my lips, I was violently taken up. My mouth was wide open screaming with fright in the spirit. I tried to speak, but was held dumb as my soul soared higher and higher, over and above this world.

"Tell him I'm human, Lord! Please! Tell him I'm human! I'm just a man!" I begged "Please slow down! Have mercy!" I saw a glimpse of myself, in my bunk, back on the Ark. And all of my childhood terrors came rushing back into my mind. I was gone, I was here, and yet, I was . . . . an inner peace then settled over me.

"Hello, giant!" I said in spirit. My Giant is too big to see when he gets this close. He becomes very confusing. He is not conformed to this world. The Giant's long arm took me from house to house. We paused just a moment at each home. **Look! Behold!** I would hear. Then his great mass would move and I would follow like a slingshot or bungee cord. Seeing was as looking through toilet paper tubes. Very clear in a small still spot, very confusing with movement. This giant was better than all of the games on Patel's palace eighth floor. My mind was not smart enough to capture it all. The flood of pictures coming at me was like being forced to drink a pitcher of water every ten seconds. Water spilled everywhere, no matter how hard I tried. Each home we entered, I saw, heard, felt and experienced people watching TV or computer screens. Not one did we find in prayer. After very many homes, I was back on my bunk in my cabin, frozen, unable to move. In my spirit, I said "Thank-you, Giant" and praised the Lord. But I was truly sick at heart and ashamed of myself. Could it have been the same giant back in my childhood? I had learned early in life never to speak of the terror. Only Grandma understood completely, she warned me, she told me straight, of the frightful wanderings of the trips. The 'going where you are not' is what I called it. Often, as a child, I would wake up unable to move. A giant force or soft massive weight was holding me down. Speaking of this 'going where you are not' would always bring you pain, misery and loneliness. People close to you would get angry; even your own mother. No one would suffer you to talk of such a shameful curse. Grandmother Juanita was right, shut-up Cornelius. Our family has problems like this. I remember one young friend. She was 'like me', except very bold. She would 'pull me out' into her stupid dreams, which I would suffer through for a while and then excuse my leave. One regular dream this girl had back in childhood was flying horses skimming across the tree tops and then landing in a small clearing by a cabin on a hill. We two would be riding two of the flying horses with my horse always being a little bit behind. Never side by side. She always had to be out front. "Please, would you just go dream by yourself" I would say. She was boring awake or asleep.

Now, once again, just as in childhood, I lay in bed paralyzed. I knew the drill. By slowly moving a small finger or toe ever so slightly, feeling would begin to flood back into my body, until I would, 'in time', be back in control again. The main thing is not to panic or get scared; or to try too hard. Even as I got dressed that morning, my heart and mind were troubled. Sure, I was glad to see my giant again, and very glad to be Holiness, but I was still terrified of my old childhood ways. I thought I had finally beaten those things; grown out of them. What would become of me? Should I war and fight against my own giant? Was it him way back in childhood? I was now somewhat confused. Why not ask him, I thought? He is your giant after all. With that simple, positive thought, I felt much relieved and was ready for my next duty cycle on the Great Ark.

Early that morning, I checked out an old-fashioned style audio/visual cart from the ship's library and rolled it down to the brig. I set it up where all the men could see the screen. The first week was always the hardest on these sailor inmates and then they would settle down. I had figured this was from the drugs and booze, but I was wrong. The men cheered and shouted as I set up. Inmates were not allowed TV or computer games in the ship's brig. The next three day cycle I worked in the ship's purchasing office. On the fourth day, my day off, I went back again to visit the brig. My TV set was still playing. I started talking to inmates about their relationships with God, prayer and Holiness. Sure enough, these inmates were just as cold and hard to talk to about God as the rest of the ship was, maybe even worse. None wanted to listen about being Holiness. I then packed up the TV cart and pushed it out towards the library. I had to lift it over each bulkhead in this part of the ship, this was quite a task. I was a hero when setting up. Now the inmates were very agitated and angry; just like 'first week inmates'. They cursed me as I rolled out. While pushing the equipment, I thought about an old man from our church during my childhood. Back then I had believed that old Mr. Snyder was being mean to his children. He would not let them have a TV in his house. Had he been truly mean? Or was he simply Holiness and knew all this way back then? That junk; silly worthless input, can block out God?

The ship stopped outside Sydney, Australia, waiting before approaching the harbor. There was no bean-shoot looking skyline of construction cranes here. Then the harbor pilots brought us through the channel. These old traditions die slow. It took hours to make our way to the cargo dock. The Ark took on and off many cargo containers, some of which we picked up at Spaceport Harbor. We were scheduled to be in Sydney for fourteen days. After seven days, Ralph from Spaceport called me on my ship phone. He sent his new video to my phone and said a DVD would not be coming out in another month. This was something about 'The Gathering'. I just said thanks.

"Cornelius, I've got a treat for you! An empty seat on a press junket to the outback!" Ralph said.

I could go for free! They had red wine! "Sign me up, old boy!"

I signed right up for the fancy press junket. We took off in the latest generation 'Osprey'. Vertical take-offs and landings from a high-class, downtown hotel rooftop.

This hotel was, of course, owned by the Patels. Twelve of us VIPs were on board, plus a guide named E. B.

This junket was all about the famous Peach Tree Preserve. Inside the plane was as of a cocktail party. We could not see the pilots. Everyone on board kept saying 'Madame Secretary, Madame Secretary'. Two women were high officials in the old Washington. Our fellow passengers glowed with excitement to meet them. Washington was empty. The American Navy had been sold for less than scrap price, but the Godless ones sucking her dry, toasted her bloody death in style, grace and snobbery. This plane could go much faster than a helicopter, but could still land straight up and down. On this long trip across the Outback this craft was needed. Even a fast chopper would still take too long; we covered a lot of territory. Our guide, E.B. Cane made fun of my old flying stunt as I boarded. He wore a collar as of a priest. (In jest) He acted very much gay. A gold chain around his neck held a locket with the earth inside on a clear ball of glass.

E.B. spoke on a large mega-horn. His sick, orally fixated, slobber reminded me of both Barnie Franks and Paul Lynn. "The Peach Tree Preserve started small and has been growing every year now with matching government funds. All land is in the flight path of returning shuttles."

I soon tuned out E.B.'s irritating Paul Lynn-like voice and didn't socialize much, except at the bar with two musicians named Mike and Greg. They were brothers and knew Bo and Don Dave and Mitch Johnston. Mitch was one of the early designers of the Osprey crafts. They also knew the whole Coe family. They had all grown up next door to the 'sissy' older brother and Sarah during Joe's first marriage. E.B. was an 'ass', so I didn't listen to half of his guide stuff. These brothers made for some interesting conversation. Each time E.B. spoke, everyone but us looked out the large windows to the outback below.

"I see them. I can see them" squealed two female New York Times reporters as Katie of TV news ran over to their window with her slave camera man in hot pursuit. Our Osprey craft flew low and slow now as E. B. Cane beat on his microphone for attention.

"The Peach Tree Preserve has shown a thirty-two percent increase in gnat population density since sonic booms were suspended at the International Spaceport just six short years ago. This great work started as a joint effort by the Young Guardians and the ACLU. It is now a textbook model for government grant environmental projects. You can all take pride in being a supporter; a lover of Captain Planet. (I mean of the planet) and one of its smallest creatures. Yes, thank-you good people for your kind human nature and your generous support of the famous 'Peach Tree Preserve'!"

I stared out the window. "I don't see any peaches. Do you, Greg?"

"No, Cornelius" he said. "The peach trees died out when farming and irrigation was outlawed. The Spider gnats eat a natural rotting indigenous cactus now."

"Spider Gnats, Greg are you kidding?" I asked.

"No, Cornelius. Look at those thick swarms or columns twirling around. That's the peach tree spider gnat!"

I looked down and said "Look at those people down there waving." Greg and Mike jumped up to look out the window and then quickly sat back down, shaking their heads.

E.B. Cane then blasted over the speaker "These new remote sensors now being dropped by our plane are solar powered and will help us count preserve population more accurately. They were a joint effort by the NAACP and a grant from Madame Secretary's department (applause). These sensors were made entirely by minority, non-Jewish, abused, gay homeless women in North America. Thank-you Madame Secretary (applause). As always, no emergency or manned vehicles are allowed to enter or trespass across the international wilderness preserve. Trespassers do so at their own risk and are breaking the law."

The two New York Times reporters and TV Katie all sat down near Mike, Greg and I. These gals were non-stop gossip.

"Did you see those people? They had kids and it was so disturbing! He was smoking a cigarette!"

"So was she, Katie! It's not the kids fault! Look at that big old gas burning SUV with a painted back fender!"

"I saw it! And that trailer had no solar cells!"

"My God, he could even have a gun!"

"A gunmen should we call the police? That blue is a Kentucky plate, Katie! Most likely those people are a coal miner's family"

"Not a coal miner? Yuck! Can you even imagine? They are so dirty! I've never even seen one this up close before, I thought Osoma got rid of coal."

"No. We had protesters working in Kentucky just last month, remember? We showed that horrible confederate flag" on the morning show.

"Yes, we put that flag on the front page!" said one reporter lady.

The other reporter shouted "You go, girl!"

"Wow, a dirty coal miner and redneck gunman that hates Mother Earth and Colored people! . . . . The poor colored people can't help it . . . ."

TV Katie started crying.

"I bet he listens to AM radio and reads the Bible" said Times reporter number two. "Did you know that there are still over 800 AM radio stations; all of them preaching hate? I'm so ashamed of being from the South!"

The other reporter spoke up "I told you Florida is different. Stop apologizing honey! You're not really southern."

"Osoma can't change everything overnight" said TV Katie. "I wish we could make him king for life! He gives me bumps and chills every time I see him" Her crossed legs began thrashing about uncontrollably.

"Oh, Katie, stop!" said reporter one, rubbing her own leg.

I waved to Mike and pulled him aside. "What are these women talking about?"

"Those people down there waving Cornelius, that Kentucky family. Those people are toast; gnat food. They will soon all die in the Outback. Many people try to cut through the preserve to find work at the International Spaceport. They hope Australia is what America used to be. They've come a long way for nothing. When America voted for . . . O." The two pretty reporter gals then snuggled up close to Mike & Greg, which changed everything!

"Those people are criminals! It is well posted! No vehicles are allowed in the preserve. We've been flying will now at 360mph for hours to get here. Nobody could walk out. Nobody could make it out." stated Greg.

"Cornelius, if this plane crashed, we would also die here" said Mike. "Nobody would save us. Wilderness and saving the Earth is more important than one family. This is war and war costs lives. You know that, Corny. Madame Secretary is doing a great work."

"Didn't you learn this in school? Or from watching TV?" questioned Greg. "The fact is, at over 15mph the gnats die when hit by car grills or windshields. That hateful, dirty, ignorant, coal mining family will now become gnat food. Yes, food for the very little ones they cared nothing about. Earth's revenge is sweet!"

Mike and Greg were playing up to the pretty female reporters and talking the politically correct line. They did get their phone and room numbers, and the reporter gals were 'hot' and 'easy'. Men will say anything for sex, I thought. This is sick. Later I was alone again with Mike.

"Ok Mike, I understand about the gals, but I missed one part about the sonic boom. Now talk some sense!"

Mike looked around to see if the coast was clear before speaking. "Sonic booms from incoming shuttles were interfering with the mating habits of the Peach Tree Spider Gnat" he said. "So the wilderness preserve was started and the Spaceport had to slow down its incoming shuttles. These gnats live for about four months. They mate often and like to sleep late."

"You're not serious, Mike!"

"Of course I'm serious, Cornelius"

E.B. Cane then blasted us again with his speaker. "Our next stop is what you've all been waiting for. Do not walk far from the craft or pick vegetation. Doing so is against the law. We will be landing soon. Disembark at your own risk. This is National Parkland, but it is not yet sacred wilderness. We landed on top of the dome rock you see on commercials for Australia. Everybody got out and looked at the view. The big rock was as hot as a blast furnace, so most of us didn't stay outside for long. Drinks were being served by E.B. Cane, but within a few minutes, only a few of us remained outside. I grabbed the whole platter of cheese sticks and two full bottles of red wine when E.B. offered and started walking away from the plane. E.B. shouted on his bullhorn.

"All aboard All aboard! I told Ralph you'd be trouble" shouted E.B. as I kept walking away.

"Pick me up on your next trip, Mr. Cane" I shouted back.

"That is against the rules, Cornelius! I will tell Ralph and file a written report" he shouted, not using his bullhorn.

I didn't look back just continued walking so dust from the take-off would not get in my wine. I sat down on a big rock with my platter of cheese sticks and dip and poured myself a fresh glass as the Osprey craft took off into the distance. I knew there were three long trips planned to the big rock today and putting up with hearing 'Madame Secretary! Madame Secretary' made me want to jump out of the damn plane.

What a great feeling it was to be all alone, in solitude, on top of the great rock. I lifted my face and hands to heaven, shutting my eyes in silent prayer. After a few minutes of sun-baked, quiet meditation, I sat back down on my rock. Opening my eyes, I saw sitting right in front of me another man also in prayer. We sat face to face on the only two rocks in sight. Momentarily, he finished praying also and then lifted his head. We stared eye to eye. Neither one of us spoke at first. Then the old timer broke the ice.

"Name's Mel . . . . cheese en sticks?" He had my cheese platter in his hand.

"Your name is Mel Cheesensticks?"

"No! My name is Mel! Do you want some cheese and dip?" He had already opened my other bottle of red wine, so Mel refreshed my glass. He had his own cup made of solid gold.

"You're not gonna try and give me a bunch of lambs, or any type of old hairy animals, are you?" questioned Mel.

"No, Sir!"

"Good! One never knows. To tell the truth I don't like lambs much. I met a young man named Abrams once. Nice fellow, but, wow, all those lambs!"

"Old man, where'd you come from? What are you doing on this rock? Nobody was up here a minute ago." I asked.

"I'm taking a break" Mel said. "I deserve one. Taking a break and talking to you. You prayed to know truth right, Cornelius?"

"Taking a break from what?" I asked. "And how did you know my name? And my . . . Oh God . . ."

Mel interrupted me. "I clean the church! That's what I do. I clean seven churches. Work hard, I do. Who am I? Let's say that I'm a friend of a friend who wants to help you."

"You're more than a janitor, aren't you, Mel?" I asked. "You know about stuff, about giants and God and being Holiness!"

"Call me what you will, Cornelius. King, High priest of Salem, the main one is not here. Neither are the others. So, yes, technically, I am in charge" he said. "But, really and truly, I am the janitor."

"Where is this church of yours, Mel? Where did the others go? When do you meet?"

"Who is in your church on Monday, Tuesday, Wednesday and Thursday? Don't you have a janitor, too" he asked.

"Sure we do" I answered.

"We meet on the Lord's day, Cornelius. Just like you! We're on a different time schedule, that's all, a different flock. What did God do when he was with the Israelites in person? He taught them to build a temple to worship him! God does not change, Cornelius! He is the same today as he always was and always will be. Our Lord is coming back here, and when that day comes, old Mel will be ready! That's what life is all about!"

"I'd like to go to your church, Mel. Where is it?"

"What did Jesus say, Cornelius? A wise man builds his house upon the rock! A wise man of his Word, he is!"

"Mel, I ask you, why don't men of science go along with and accept Gods Word.? Is God against science and learning? A preacher once told me that man should not go to the moon. Is the Space Station evil?"

"God loves learning, Cornelius! God created science! True science, true wisdom, the true church, they are always on the same page. Guess what? God already knows the answer! No, the Space station itself is not evil. It's even a good idea. But realize that Satan will try to hitch a ride. He was thrown down and imprisoned here on Earth. Also, if ungodly men build something to confront God's law with; be it the Titanic or a Space station, what happens? Read the book of Job. The angel is hitching a ride! Whatever God does, the angel will try to steal, destroy or counterfeit."

"What about this gnat preserve, Mel?" I asked. Is Madame Secretary crazy and why do most people seem to be blind to the obvious truth or . . . well . . . stupid, Mel?"

"The Fear of God is the beginning of wisdom" he replied. "She has no fear of God. These people have false religions, false gods and ungodly priests. I am a servant, as you are, Cornelius. You and I are both flesh, and both men. I am of another flock, in another season. These seasons are defined and controlled by God. Your giant is of God's world, not flesh.

He fights battles for you everyday. The scope of God is too massive, too complex for us to understand. But by His grace, God has allowed our seasons to overlap. And your giant is very nice!"

"You mean God is so powerful that each man has a giant? Wow! Who could ever fight against God?"

"What you call science is often not science at all." he explained. "Look at those gnat nuts for example. They are all false priests. They have been against space travel all along. These same false priests killed the American Space Program, Cornelius."

"How is that?"

He took another sip of wine and started again. "Do you remember the shuttle explosions and shuttles burning up on reentry?"

"Sure I do"

"That is a good example of false religion taking control away from true science. The insulating foam kept falling off the main fuel tank only AFTER NASA was forced to change the glue. The shuttle worked just fine for years with the original glue. It doesn't take a rocket scientist to figure this out. Humanist priests, an ungodly religion calling themselves environmentalists, took control. They forced NASA to stop using a powerful model airplane glue mixed with super glue and forced them to use an Elmer's "kid safe' glue instead to save the gnats in the everglades. Everybody knew the foam would fall off and very likely destroy the shuttle, but the REAL scientists were not in control anymore. False religion now rules America and lies are most often believed, false data, nonsense theories and dishonesty is the mainstream. This rebellion against God against his will, his works, his wind, and against his Holy Bible now leads America toward poverty and death!"

"You do know my giant, Mel! That sounds just like him!"

"How many times in your last century has dishonest, false science fooled everybody with fraud, lies and deceit?" Mel asked me. "Darwin proved right, the missing link found, or global warming proved with new data? Then, shortly later, in small print, the true facts are told. Both of those theories are laughably insane and believed only by false religion, not science. The false religion of humanism, or 'man is good; evolving into a god' and not needing a redeemer. Beware this is all work of the dark angel. The very words he spoke in the Garden of Eden to Eve. Cornelius, all of Psychology is false science. Their over-selling of dangerous drugs and excusing ungodliness in treating depression and the massive drugging of school kids today is just as sick as any ancient pagan, primitive culture of medicine men. Science has lost, not gained, ground in many areas. This is a crime against the congregation. Money is always spent on worthless and harmful medicine just to make the medicine men wealthy. Every ten years or so, a real, honest scientist does test these drugs, and these invented diseases. Yes, most doctors know that no anti-depression medicine ever prescribed has ever beat mild exercise for effectiveness in any double blind study. What does the Holy Bible say? Yes, that even the profit of exercise is small." Mel took off his hat and popped it with his fist! "Listen, carefully, Cornelius. You seem to focus on world leaders; remember this fact. The king is never the root. They come in pairs, always with a false front. The leader or king has a priest behind him. Very near or beside this priest hides the great angel, evil works as of a mirror; a copy of the ways of God! Let's say Moses and Aaron of God. In this world, it would be President Osoma and Pastor Wright. Always look for the hidden priest, Cornelius. We fight not against flesh and blood. Nor do we live just for our own short season. We fight against municipalities and power of a hidden, larger world. Be not fooled!"

"Mel, please, what about the number twenty-six and the circle of fifths? I don't get all that math stuff."

Mel grabbed a pen. "Time is short. I will tell you a story, Cornelius that may help you. I will have to speak fast."

"Jesus and his disciples rent a room for dinner. Judas gets there early to pay the man. He brings only thirty pieces of silver with him. A piece of sliver is worth $10.00, so he has $300.00. You like that dollar touch, don't you?" he laughed. "Being the first to get there, the man tells Judas to take a number. He is number one and the menu says $12.00 per person. The disciples were each to bring a guest to meet Jesus. Judas had figured up in his head; $144.00 for the twelve disciples and $144.00 for the guests is $288.00 plus $12.00 for Jesus, a total of thirty pieces of silver."

"Now the man tells him to pay a $1.00 cover charge each, plus the $12.00 for the meal. Judas pays the dollar cover charge for himself and is angry. He can not pay the price of the meal for himself or his guest (the devil). The disciples start arriving. Judas tells each of them how much they will owe the treasury. Add up your number and the number of your guest sitting across from you and pay that amount. Jesus, of course, pays his number also. The group piles into the room for dinner. All eager to eat with Jesus! What is the bill each disciple pays?

<u>24 23 22 21 20 19 18 17 16 15 14</u>

_____13

2   3   4   5   6   7   8   9   10   11   12

"Jesus is King, number 13. The bill is always $26.00, the center ball or sphere. Twelve disciples are the twelve points around the center. A deck of cards is a mockery, a reflection or imitation of the ways of God; the creation of God!"

"Balls, Mel? Go over that part!"

"Ok" said Mel. Mel uses seven olives left on the platter. "Take a billiard ball and set it on the pool table. Now place six around it. Just like the straws of the Space Station, these balls will always form a 'perfect' seven with one ball at perfect center. Now, cover the perfect center ball with more balls. This will take three on the top and three on the bottom. It will always take twelve balls to perfectly surround the center ball. Only one can be King! Look around your world, Cornelius. Why did they get rid of the thirteenth month in the calendar? Look at the clock, the zodiac. Don't be fooled, Cornelius! We don't have time to build the pyramids with balls. Quickly now! Add up the numbers one by one across the table. For example $2+4+2=8$ and $2+3+3=8$. Note always eight, the number for money. Now add in the bill amount; 26. When the bill is paid, the numbers now add up to seven! The perfect number! $2+4+2=8+2=10+6=16=7$. Praise God our bill has been paid, Cornelius! Remember, only one head; only one king, only one way. Goodbye for now, Cornelius. Your own season awaits you! Beware, Cornelius!"

The sound of the osprey craft coming again to the high rock could be heard in the distance. We both prayed once again. When I opened my eyes, I was once again alone. My wine and tray of cheese sticks were also gone. Thank you Lord for sending this man Mel across the seasons, so that he could teach me. I know I'm not very smart or very good, Amen. I could hear my giant laughing and saying, 'You speak the truth, Cornelius! His laughter echoed across the rock as the osprey craft landed again in a cloud of dust.

On the way back, guide E. B. Cane was an overbearing ass as usual. He tried to charge me full price for two junkets at ten thousand dollars each. We had a group of Japanese government officials on the plane this time. At least there was no 'Madame Secretary' to put up with. The Japanese did break out in a few girly man fights, so I stayed to myself.

Walking out of the big, fancy, downtown hotel in Sydney, I wondered. *Just how many hotels did Jediah Emin Patel and his uncle own did they even know?* It sure was great to stroll along the harbor. From the big hotel, I could see the Great Ark in the distance, seemingly hovering over the town. Now, I was much closer and it was hidden from my sight. Walking along the waterfront, my eyes beheld one of the most beautiful sailing yachts I'd ever seen. It was anchored beside a pier in the harbor. On its stern was written the name WINDY. That's what I need, I thought to myself. I'd sail away on the wind and forget about making things right with Joe Coe, Sarah or the Great Ark. On the big sail boat loud music was playing. A tall man with a drink in his hand was waving at me. As the cool evening harbor breeze hit me in the face, I looked up and saw the dark outline of the Great Ark in full view now. It looked too big; even out of place. Stubbornness took control. I would not run. I would not waver. I would have my peace with all of them, one way or another. I saluted First Seaman's Mate Billy Sparks as I walked up the ramp onto the Great Ark. Some days later, we slowly inched out of the narrow harbor channel, through the reef, and out into open sea. We were now loaded down with cargo containers on main and flight deck. This was a strange looking sight, but, still no sign of Captain Joe Coe.

About a half day up the coast, moving very slow the ship must have been close to, or off the coast of Coe's estate. The college students and some more eager-beaver, kiss-ass departments were up on deck in dress whites. All to salute and empress our Captain as he came back on board. News came to me by friendly crew members, not from my ship phone, computer, officer's mail or official text. Sarah, Haley, Blair and the other four women had all had enough of Joe's big boat. The Coe women were all sitting on eggs or nursing young. The nesting instinct was in full bloom in Coe-ville. The gals had all stayed home. I dressed for dinner that evening and arrived in the officer's mess 'just in time' as the bell rang with not a second to spare. I sat down across from Sarah's old seat, now taken up by Chief of Staff Friday. Old Captain Coe was polite and courteous during dinner. The roast beef was delicious. Coe toasted my return from the dead in front of all his other pilots seated at the long, head table. Unk was back. So was Duck. Both men sat at the far end of the table. Unk I very much wanted to talk to. After dinner, I made it to my cabin without any trouble. I took off my dress white top coat and headed out on a mission to find Unk, the ole' Russian weasel. Just as I opened my cabin door in flowed a red-faced Captain Coe with Friday and two other faithful disciples pushing me backwards. Joe was screaming mad and his blood vessels looked kind of funny.

"Don't think for one minute that you're family now, asshole. That kid's only thirty-three years old! You could have gotten her killed in that 'has been' old stunt of yours. Do you have any idea the hell and grief I took over my family getting that type of world-wide publicity?" He waved his disciples outside with a hand gesture. "I ought to kill you my own damn self and save the committee money. My Sarah would not give up her baby. I told her to be patient that another, more suitable man would soon be along. There is still a hit out on you, Cornelius. Not from me, but from the Elders. As soon as we reach International waters, I can legally have you shot or hung without a trial. Hanging is still not out of the question. You might get another hearing, man. How should I know? I'm just the Captain, the guy in charge around here. I don't need your kind of trouble on this ship. Don't you ever make me look that bad again? How did an idiot like you, of all people, end up with an Elder on his side? Living next door at his nephew's palace, traveling with them, that is absolutely unbelievable. My own uncle was a long term board member before he died! I'm in charge! And I've never met an Elder or his family! Hell, nobody I know has! Goldwater was right. You're more trouble than you're worth. Thank God my Sarah found another one."

"Another one," I thought to my self out loud.

"Yes, and saved me from having you as a damn son-in-law, for God's sake!" He paused, red faced.

I was silent. Then I smiled grabbed Joe's hand and shook it. "Thanks, Dad! I'll be ready for work in the morning, you and the good Lord both willing!"

There was a silent stare-down between us. It lasted less than thirty seconds, but it seemed like forever. Joe grimaced and saluted half-heartedly without speaking. As I returned his salute, he turned and slammed the door behind him. I could hear Captain Coe shouting orders at his disciples while storming up the high port walkway from my cabin.

I have a way with people, it's a gift really. To know me is to love me. Well, almost, (ha-ha) and so started my South Sea island adventure aboard the Great Ark!

CHAPTER FIVE

My South Seas Island Adventure

The famous Easter Island was the next stop for our ship. Instead of airplanes, (they were stored away or blocked in) we had cargo containers stacked everywhere. Most of these large tractor trailer size shipping containers were going to the Hawaiian Islands. The ship's crew could still get some ultra-lights above, and all of seaplanes below. The Ark carried only half the amount of students, one hundred or so elderly passengers and the 'pig tails', as I called them. These Rabbis or Holy men were given the first class women's section of the ship. I heard that the cargo containers to Hawaii paid very well and we were, after all, a private Navy. No military foolishness or waste.

The second night at sea, I had a long talk with Unk and Duck (Marshall Moore) and Steve (Suicide) Miller, his nick-name attributed to his odd tattoo art and his 'suicide' flying style. It was Unk that had stowed me away on a big Russian transport plane back to India. Unk had me arrested as a foreign John Doe drunk driver. He had been so close to the hotel blast back in Thailand that he was also burned. That fact got him pissed off enough at the company to want to help me! Sarah was living in the Coe family compound in Australia next door to Blair and the four other women. Sarah was very happy with her new husband. He was a pro ball player named Aaron B. Cohen. Their baby's name was Aaron Cornelius Cohen. No old fool could ask for much more than that, I thought. If you're 'gonna be dumb, you better be tough'. That's redneck, not the Holy Bible (ha-ha). I was glad and relieved that no B44s or B48s were being flown on this leg of the trip. To tell the truth, I was scared, uneasy and often could not sleep. It sure felt good to be Holiness. I thanked God every night. I praised the name of Jesus, our risen savior constantly.

Our job at Easter Island and two other islands in the vast blue Pacific Ocean was to build, or place, wilderness habitat living quarters for research scientists at remote locations. These habitats were steel cargo container boxes fixed up with power, lights, water and air conditioning. They used a lot of spray-on insulation. A large, tracked landing craft, of military type, was stored in the ship's big bay door at the stern. The two cabin cruisers were left behind in Australia. For Sarah and Haley, I presumed. These habitat containers had to be taken to shore one at a time. A dozen would be put on each island. Some containers were water plants, some storage. Most often two were power plants with batteries, wind and solar. We had two D9 size Cat bulldozers, two large farm tractors and four large winches for pulling trailers into position.

Building these 'camps' was hard work, much more than most of us were used to. Often dirt roads had to be cut. It was hot, time consuming and heavy work. To make things worse, Captain Joe Coe had three different groups of experts, each trying their best to run the show. Conflicts, bickering, loud arguments, strikes and Joe's temper were all daily rituals.

The first group was called the "Young Guardians of Mother Earth'. These young men were mostly worthless 'Momma's boys'. A no more pitiful excuse for afterbirth than I'd ever had seen one in my long life. They were truly unbelievable and disgusting. Just as Mel had warned me, they fancied themselves as scientists but were, in reality, a cult. An Earth witch religion in disguise. Most wore the image of Al Gorey, Castro, Osoma Mao or Islam. Not one of these pale, wimpy boys could hold a shovel or push a broom, much less drive a farm tractor or bulldozer. They were often worried sick about scraping the soil to make our access roads.

"It's dirt, Son" I would say. "Scraping it into a pile does not hurt it! Now stop crying and get back to work!"

The total lack of manhood in this bunch worried me. I asked one of the older young Guardians, a professor nick-named Cupcake, if this was a special 'short bus, retard or queer' group. Cupcake told me his campus at Berkley had a zero tolerance policy on masculine behavior. That my old school, backward, out-dated way of life was unacceptable in today's modern world. That I should get in touch with my feminine side. His young men were the 'hand-picked, cream of the crop'. All were ready to give back to Mother Earth. They were all ready to sacrifice themselves to slow down over production and pollution. They would all help Osoma change the world after this one year on the Great Ark. This older professor sat very close to me often putting his hand on my thigh. As we stood up in the hangar to disembark, I accidentally knocked professor Cupcake into the surf. Two of his boys jumped in and helped him to shore. We never spoke much after that.

Joe's second group of experts, were the 'pig tails'. They are Rabbis and 'Holy men'. Twelve were young and active workers. Another twelve were senior teachers and not allowed to work, but were still very much in charge. At a certain age, fifty I believe, one moved from the young group to the older 'has been' group. One group wore hearts, the other wore diamonds. I called them the Geezer Club and the Spades, just to piss them off (ha-ha).

These men were stern and they were often mysterious, always sticking to themselves. I would later learn that they could `see' my giant as they reacted whenever he came near. This was often in a negative, praying him away manner. I was not sure if they liked my giant or not. Mostly, my giant just stayed in the distance.

The third group was twelve working crew members, some of whom knew how to put up and wire the habitat camps. Two of these, Lou and Tommy, became close friends, often joining me at the ship's Gospel Cafe. These two were 'eggheads, but they were still old-school, like me. The fourth group was us dumb workers, drafted in to fill the gaps.

When we pulled up close to Easter Island, the natural beauty was overwhelming; even life changing. Here at the ends of the Earth, the great South Seas, the grandeur of God's creation cried out for attention. The other two islands were simply called islands number two and three. Most of our ship-bound mates living on this floating city called the Great Ark paid the islands little mind. For the small groups of us who worked on the island construction projects, we saw everything different. It was very life altering.

The first habitat camp built on Easter Island would be our easiest and fastest. It still took us over six weeks to complete. The camp had the ability to make fresh water from sea water and produced both wind and solar power. Two boxes, or trailers, were placed close to the sea ten others were in the main camp. Of these, two were power stations, four were for storage and four were for living and work space. We cut a short road. All of our trailers rolled into position on wheels. All of this work was hot and dangerous. We were working on uneven ground and coming ashore through rough surf.

About a week before we finished up at Easter Island, I got a chance to spend three days working side by side with Captain Joe Coe and the pigtail group. We worked on a special assignment on Easter Island planting trees. This was my first time of 'getting to know' Joe as a Coe-worker (ha-ha). Captain Joe would argue with the Pigtails and complain about their many requests, but he respected them and tried his best to please them. It was an honor to work with this group; if you could call it work. The Pigtails had rules. Joe and I could not do most of the work. We were too old; over fifty. Tommy Mute could work. So could young student Travis Jones, who came along to help. The leader of the pigtails was named Jehuiakim and he had no helper. Jehuiakim called Joe Coe by the name Coniah, or Sonny Boy. The other Pigtails would grin. Joe and I rode on the front of the trailer to add 'dead weight' to the trailer hitch. Tommy Mute drove the farm tractor that pulled our long, low, flat-bed trailer around the rocky grass of Easter Island. Joe and I both carried long barrel 22 pistols for shooting rabbits. We had a blast shooting Easter bunnies (ha-ha). The Young Guardians group was not allowed to help or even come with us. When they found out we were planting trees, there was a riot. Joe got so mad that he put four of them in the brig and confined the rest to their quarters under armed guard. I laughed so hard I hurt myself and I gained more respect for old 'cold as ice' Captain Coe.

The weather on Easter Island was perfect with a mild sea breeze; a day in paradise. We four and the 'Pigtails' started planting trees in a uniform pattern all across the Island. We made our own way. No road, no path; our course got very bumpy. Tommy often had to 'go slow' to keep us from falling off. Each time we stopped, twelve 'Pigtails, including Travis, would jump out and dig holes with a 'two man' turning screw. Joe and I would shoot rabbits without ever leaving the trailer. Rabbits were running all over the place. It was really very funny. I thought we might start looking for Easter eggs any minute. Each time we stopped, the Pigtails planted a different type of tree in some known order. Bashem oaks, Shitem trees, olive trees and almond trees were only some. A rabbit or a dove was placed in the hole under each tree, depending on the species of tree. A large cage of doves was on the end of our trailer. Doves were held by the Jehuiakim man, two in his left hand, and painted by bunches of leaves. Then pulling a knife, he would kill one dove and the other one would get away. Always one would escape and fly away. I told Joe that he should use both hands. Joe just shook his head.

The older Pigtails were very happy, singing loud and praising God. They danced as much as possible without falling off our crowded low-boy trailer. This day reminded me of an old-fashioned hay ride only without the hay.

Our hayride ventured onto the beach sand only a few times. We stayed mostly on the grass. The first time we drew near to the beach, the Pigtail men started pointing, praying and chanting. I was sure I had seen a glimpse of my giant in that direction right before all the commotion and unison chanting started. A large wave soon hit the beach and traveled all the way to us, washing the wheels of our trailer a few inches. I laughed and said softly "Get 'em, Giant".

Joe scolded me with a stern stare and a quiet, quick shaking of no of his frowned brow.

The statues of Easter Island were each prayed against, never to, as we passed by them while working on our tree pattern. The chanting would begin just as we approached each stone. Some were shown 'special' attention. During this three day work project, I noticed that into each hole a purple bag was emptied just after the rabbit or dove and just before the tree and prayer. Joe would not speak of this in front of the Pigtails. Later I learned it was priceless jewels, some of which were very old, having been found fifty years ago. They were 'unclean' for some reason; not to be sold or used ever again. Different jewels were put under different trees. Diamonds, for example, were put under almond trees, emeralds under olive trees. Frankincense and Myrrh trees were also planted. The fortune in jewels planted at Easter Island was as the riches of Solomon, never to be seen again. Each tree was protected from the rabbits by a small fence. Most were large enough to survive, anyway. These rabbits were a big problem. They were very much over-populated. People stopped Joe from putting rabbit poison out, but Joe did it anyway that last day. The Pigtails always got what they needed or wanted. This group was polite about God talk, but would not suffer me talking about being Holiness or teaching about Jesus. Really, I didn't know much and these rabbis knew this. They were a closed bunch and always dressed the same.

When the Great Ark pulled up beside island number two, six of us got into ultra-light crafts to scout out the rugged, rocky terrain. A couple of our sea planes joined us and we all circled the island together. This island was an impressive couple of large mountains with no apparent flat spot for our habitats. There was one small cove on the opposite side of the island from our ship. Of course Joe's experts chose the steepest, rockiest side. I saw no obvious spot to build a camp on island number two. We started out by drilling holes in the side of a steep mountain by the sea and blasting like road builders do, dropping the rocks onto the beach forming a spot to build on. After the rocks were made flat and level by our bulldozers, there was a really nice looking habitat camp. We were proud of ourselves. The explosives worked pretty well. Cables were used to pull our trailers in place. This was one very expensive trailer park. It seemed strange to be building something up instead of bombing and destroying, but at least we still got to play with explosives (ha-ha). The Pigtail group was in total control of island number two from the very beginning and they had strict, crazy rules. Only a small group of us, twelve in all not counting Joe, and the Pigtails worked on this project. We begged Joe for more help, but to no avail. Some of the students Joe picked for this detail were of little help. One of the best workers was young Travis Jones who had helped on the hay ride. I should not complain much about these youth. I could at least tell they were men, not like those weird Guardians. Our same small group put in long hours each day on island number two. No rotation; no help from the rest of the ship's crew. These many long hours working cut back on my time at the ship's Gospel Cafe, but not out completely. I loved to sing, sip and sermon at my big, round, corner table. One thing I do know for sure, all college age kids are one hundred percent ass backward stupid about everything. These students base their lives on what they have seen on TV. They think it is all true. A lifetime of government programming is often impossible to break. Talking to or teaching them was like trying to explain to a fish that it's wet. By not watching TV and very few movies or TV news, I found that I had escaped programming and still had a clear, rational mind. There seemed to be no hope for this world and its drugged masses of brainwashed youth.

On ship, we worked twelve hours on, twelve hours off for three straight days with the fourth day off. In the morning of my fourth day off, I was determined to take at least a few hours off from island number two no matter how much Captain Joe hollered. I had worked straight through my last three days off. This night I stayed late at the Gospel Cafe. Talk at my table was about the old VPI shooting massacre and now the law suits. A little student named Ali Hamill talked about VPI's failure to stop guns on campus and the lack of a warning system. Of course, the anti-professor had to weigh in. I first, as always, bought a round of drinks (coffee), to bribe my group's attention. I get a fifty percent discount off my tab at the Gospel Cafe, but don't tell anyone. It's our little secret!

"One thing for sure, kids. Anything you have heard on the national news or have been taught in class is 180% from the truth and God's word. You have been taught a deliberate deception from your anti-God professors and their masters. Don't fall for the official line. Use your own eyes, your own mind and rational thought to evaluate the facts for yourselves. Always ask yourself, what does the Holy Bible say? What does God say? Just like 9/11 and the Columbine High School massacre, the VPI shootings were caused by evil men's reaction to silly, girly-man, anti-defense, gun control laws. These anti-gun laws and campus rules are in direct rebellion against God's natural laws and the teachings of his Holy Bible. A ruling class of socialist, humanist, ungodly, wicked men are attempting to use man's way (a police state), instead of God's way of faith, freedom and family. God's way, the Holy Bible works every time it's tried. Man's silly ways always lead to destruction. Man's ways have never worked throughout all of history. I have a question for you. Norris Hall, that is the first building on the drill field coming down from the 'upper quad', or the old cadet part of the campus, am I not correct?"

Ali's boyfriend John spoke up. "Yes sir. The old Commandant of the Cadets house is the only building between, Cornelius"

"Thanks, John. That's what I thought. Self-defense is a right and a duty mandated by God to free men. As responsible citizens of a free republic, we are never to hand these rights over to any authority one hundred percent as would slaves, convicts or any other charge. Their guards have complete control and responsibility for providing for and protecting those in their care. This is not true of free men! Yes, government agencies and police can aid you, but never give any local government or school authority ownership of yourself or total responsibility for your own safety and protection. That would be an act of insanity; even blatant stupidity. No group of citizens can pay taxes high enough or hire enough police or guards to keep you safe in this world. Not even in a state prison or local jail is a man safe. How could it be done in public? Who would want to live that way, anyway? Nobody but a silly ten year old girl who depends totally on Daddy would even think that this could work."

Kishia at my table laughed and said smugly "So you would have the wild west on campus with everyone packing heat, Cornelius? That's crazy!"

"No, Kishia!" I responded. "I do realize that many of you on campus are too immature to be trusted with even a pocket knife, much less a firearm! Open up this Holy Bible to Luke 22:35-38. Note that these words are in red. Jesus, our Lord is speaking to us about personal defense and weapons. Listen, Kishia! All of you calm down. Some or most of the younger students may be too young to drive or to vote and may not qualify for a gun permit, but what about the older professors? The ROTC staff or senior students who will be active duty military in just a few short months? Some of these people must be capable of performing the basic citizenship responsibilities of a free republic. Not everybody needs to 'pack heat'. Only ten percent or less has ever applied for a VA gun carry permit. But ten percent is enough and is much better than zero. A zero weapons policy is against the teaching of Jesus. It is against the ways of God. As we read this entire scripture, remember that Jesus is talking about going away, to the cross. He will soon be leaving his disciples and Jesus plainly says NOT to be 'saps' or 'suckers' like the VPI students. Some weapons in the group will be enough, but not zero! Do NOT depend on police, a king or angels 100%. Take responsibility! The disciples obviously carried weapons when he was with them. Go ahead and read the scripture aloud.

(35) **When I sent you without purse and scrip and shoes, lacked ye anything?** Nothing, Lord, the disciples said.

(36) **But now, he that hath a purse, let him take it, and likewise his scrip; and he that hath no sword, let him sell his garment and buy one!**

(37) **For I say unto you, that this that is written must yet be accomplished in me, and he was reckoned among the transgressors; for the things concerning me have an end!**

(38) **Lord, behold-here are two swords! And he said unto them, it is enough!**

"Notice that two in twelve meets the minimum requirement of Jesus. In Virginia, less than ten percent have carry permits. At VPI, the number of people on campus who would have carry permits, if allowed by the school, would be enough to stop mass shootings on campus. Any nut job shooter would be shot himself as time went on. This, of course does not work in the zero tolerance of guns, crazy, insane world at VPI. This girly-man, God-hating, humanist, sick-o academic world is why the shooter chose this disarmed spot in the first place. Country stores in Virginia during deer season are not very often robbed by gunmen, even though most of the customers are carrying guns. Not so in crime ridden D.C. with strict gun laws. Respect and defend your rights as free men. Very soon, roadside pat-downs, searches and inspections will take away all of your liberties. Any man who will not stand up to defend his own Constitutional rights is a disgrace to his Father and Mother and an affront to the teaching of almighty God."

My young friends left my table that night having heard the truth for maybe the first time in their brain-washed lives. They just laughed and said "Good night, Old Corny". They had been taught from birth that guns are 'bad'. Police will always protect you and that God is dead. Yes, taught the ways of ungodly, foolish men.

The next morning, I walked out onto the high deck railing outside my quarters and looked out over the majestic South Seas. I stood almost one hundred feet above the waves. It always feels good to be underway, and at sea. The night was still very much dark, but the morning sunrise had just started up in all its magnificent power and glory. Professor Lou Goodliar joined me, coming out of his quarters from down the deck. We both loved the sea. Lou was a joy to argue with. He was 'know-it-all' stubborn! You know the type. Lou was a regular at my big, round, corner table. He was today preaching about the Southern Cross and a coming eclipse. I wish I'd paid closer attention, for sleep was upon me. I had been strumming my guitar last night just like a teenager, so I turned into bed. We were both glad to see island number two in the 'rearview mirror', so to speak. I started thinking about life after this voyage, this tour of duty. Maybe when back in Virginia, my lovely ex-wife Patty and I could 'try again'. God willing! How often in this life one doesn't know even the basics of life. Why then ask and seek for the vast spiritual answers of God? Look for God's ways, look to his heavens and this vast South Sea. Lord I am a fool!

Island number three was much bigger and work started off easily just like Easter Island. All of our locked up 'guardians' were turned loose on this island to run wild. Of course, this group got no work done. Their very purpose in life was to slow down production and feel superior about doing so, or to just 'get in the way'.

Just to set the record straight, that one boy who died, Peter Vault, the one who fell to his death, was none of my doing. Yes, Duck and I did laugh at the idiot boy, and we did get in some trouble and I was wrong. Death is never funny, but I will tell that story later.

The rest of Island Number Two's work crew including yours truly, were all given a much deserved break during the first few weeks on island number three. This was good, for we all felt put upon for doing number two all by ourselves. On Island Three, all of the habitat boxes came to shore quickly and right into position on trailer wheels. Work was moving fast; life was easy. We workers were all in good moods. Everybody knew that a layover in Hawaii was coming up next on this cruise. After the third week at island number three, we were sixty percent done building the camp. That morning I came ashore and walked toward Joe Coe, Duck, Friday and Unk. All of them were glancing at a set of plans and pointing up to the mountain before them. Officer Booth was serving cold beer to everyone. Our little group of workers was growing fast and not just for the cold beer. Lou Goodliar and a skinny man named Sergeant Pepper were calling out on a bullhorn. Everybody was pointing up to the rock cliffs above. By the look on duck's face, I knew that the easy part of island number three was in the past. Joe then got a call from the girls in Australia and walked away from the crowd for privacy. Joe's experts then started telling us all about the plan. Three large radio towers were to be installed on top of the mountain, two of which had to be a certain distance, or wave length, apart. All three were designed as free standing structures, but guide wires would be added because of the extremely harsh environment. Each tower would need a power station, plus two wind turbines and eight solar panels. All this had to be put up on top of the mountain and installed. Most of the pieces were too heavy for our two small choppers to lift. This mountain looked just like Stone Mountain in Georgia, except it was three times as high. The smooth dome was almost two thousand feet above the beach. People laughed and said the black rock looked just like Friday's bald head. This thin Sergeant Pepper dude who was a radio expert, used Friday's big head and a tiny toy car to explain how dangerous driving tractors and drilling equipment on the curved surface of the mountain would be. I laughed so hard, I could not stand up. This was a big job. One for Navy Sea-Bees, not for us clowns. I wondered if there were any Sea-bees left or if the famous Osoma cuts had ended them completely. Osoma showed the world that we were serious about peace. He said that the world did not have to live in fear of America anymore. Osoma disbanded all elite Navy Seal Teams and apologized for their actions. That same day, he prosecuted two 'Seal Team Six' members for beating a gay bomber in Yemen. In one year, U.S. Defense spending was cut sixty percent. Ships like the Great Ark were sold for scrap.

From the ship then landed a chopper, which were only used in emergency situations. They were too 'fuelish' for Captain Coe. Edison Oliver stayed at the controls. The Dean of our ship's college ran over to Joe. (Randy walks with a limp so the trip took a while) Coe then waved over Unk and me.

"We've got a problem" Joe shouted through his cupped hands. "Go with Leach. Figure it out. Handle it. I don't care how. Unk, you are in charge. Use of ship phones by your group is strictly forbidden. You report only to me Unk. Go, move fast!"

Unk and I were briefed by Dean Randy Leacher, a man of low stature and even lower character. He was nick-named 'the Snake' by his students. We then waved over Marshall Moore, Duck and Steve Miller (Suicide). The Dean's tongue made snake-like movements as he spoke. He was freaky, and evil.

"Gentlemen, when we left island number two, four young freshmen students, or boys, stayed behind as a stupid statement that only mischievous youngsters can think of. The four boys had all been workers on the island. They are all 19 and 20 years old and members of the same caving club back home. Evidently, the boys found something to explore on the island and could not resist. Please bring them back alive. Good luck!"

I wondered why the boys had been chosen for our work party in the first place. They seemed too immature to have been on our crew. Truly, I believe Joe Coe would have counted the boys as missing in action and forgotten all about them, but Tommy's Dad was 'somebody', whatever that means, so the boys could not simply go unaccounted for. We were out of range for chopper flights and out of range for sea planes. Unk devised a seaplane on the water refueling plan that could make the trip, using himself, Duck, Steve and myself. We would also take with us 'Doc', a nurse practitioner, who looked just like Andy Griffith on Mayberry, just in case the boys needed medical attention. We would fly to the halfway point, land on the ocean (weather permitting) and refuel. Then head back to the island. Then we would meet the planes again on the way back and refuel again to get back to the ship. We would use our drop tanks, because pouring fuel would be made much less work and give us a chance if we ended up slightly off-course. All eight planes were soon in the air after taxiing out the big back door in the stern of the ship. We all joked about how much Old Joe would bill Tommy's dad for rescuing his namesake. This was on top of the sixty thousand it cost a student to 'work' a year on the Ark.

We all landed and refueled at sea as planned. A beautiful day for it! We 'heroes' were all in a jovial mood. All glad to be out of that radio tower mess on island number three. Thank God for Joe's experts. They could have that job! Our little group seemed to have done most of the work on island two and now we were going back. We joked like fools on the old-fashioned radios and imitated truckers on a CB in a convoy. Duck brought up the student who died on island three, trying to get me laughing. Doc had been up with Duck until the refueling point, when Unk had moved him to my plane during refueling. Now I saw why; Duck was drunk! Doc now brought out the medicine bottle in my plane. I did have a slight cough. We talked and joked about that tragic day when young student Peter Vault died, trying our best to give proper respect to the dead while we sipped, skimmed and toasted our way across the blue-green ocean.

Back when we first arrived on island number three, there was one lone, tall pine tree growing on the rocky clearing that would soon become our habitat camp. The tree was tall and thin with branches only at the very top. Within minutes, a young Guardian leader, one Peter Vault, was in the top of the tree camping out. Vault was determined to save his tree from destruction by living in it. No one had as yet thought about cutting it down anyway. Peter showcased his heroism live from the top of his tree. He was a favorite on Facebook and Youtube.

Much of the island was covered with trees, but this pine tree had not had enough soil to grow old in our habitat's thin rocky soil. Peter spent the first night in his tree. The next morning at lunch his supporters were using ropes to bring up supplies to Peter. During our lunch break Peter had the attention of our entire group as his supporters slowly attempted to reach him with supplies time after time with out much success, this was a very funny site to watch!

Every one watched in horror as Peter's tree started leaning seaward until he was now hanging out over the cliff far above the rocky beach below. Then suddenly it snapped and the trees roots came out of the ground. Peter's tree slowly went over the rock cliff stopping with the root end hanging on top of the cliff. We all ran to the edge of the rocks to see if he was hurt. Down at the bottom was Peter waving back at us and standing on a big rock, he was ok! The student girl standing next to me then said,

"Look his tree saved him." The crowd all clapped and cheered. Peter, loving his tree now even more, walked over and wrapped his arms around his tree to say thank you. The heavy root end of the tree then fell outward toward the sea landing just past another big rock on the beach, and Peter Vault, Yes, he was vaulted out to sea! The crowds of people gasped, but then started clapping and cheering Peters name again when Peter waved at them from a big Rock out in the surf! The hero was victorious over death once again. Peter took a long bow, and jumped for joy! His tree was now floating away in the strong tide. Peter dove into the sea and started swimming after it, as if to save it! Halfway to his tree an Orca Killer Whale grabbed Peter and threw him high into the air, he landed like a ragdoll with a splash. Again and again the whales played with Peter Vaults limp body. Then in one big bite Peter was fish food. The crowd was solemn, quiet, and sad, all except for Duck, and I. We started laughing and could not stop. Laughter just happens. Hate crime charges were brought against Duck and me. They called it "Gay bashing" We both had to pay a fine, apologize for laughing, and now we are on record as being "perverts" If they heard us telling this story again we would be fired, and or in the brig, so please don't say anything about all this.

Our little sea planes had one single engine, and two seats. We could put one person in storage behind us (like a boy) with no problem. We cruised at low altitude, at a constant one hundred and fifteen miles per hour. Unk, Suicide, Duck, Doc, and I flew the many hours back to Island number two. Unk ran the show. He navigated, and led the way. Just a little bit off, and we would miss the island completely. These sea planes were old school and a joy to fly, no fancy computer navigation or controls. The Blue Pacific was endless and beautiful. We could smell the sea, almost as well as when on board our ship. That smell is the drug that if the truth be told has held sailors captive, forever in the sea's cold grasp. We were all as young boy scouts on a great adventure, the only difference between us and the boys we were rescuing is they had to "pay to play, and we earned "wages to work." The old playing the youth for a sucker game is fun, and often what life is all about!

Son, congratulations, you've been qualified for the loan! We did the best we could on the interest rate (ha-ha). You can now pay me three or four times what you borrowed, just send money to me each month for the next thirty years (ha-ha).

Son, we need you to go fight some bad guys, and make the world safe. We don't have much money to pay all you brave men but you can be a hero (ha-ha). This sucker instinct does not last forever so we have to fool them while we can. Old men of every tribe have been playing this game for thousands of years. These young bucks are just not wanted around the house anymore. It's hard to keep them doing chores for nothing, and they eat more than they're worth. Yes, they need to be on their way. The herd needs to be thinned out, and or new land found. A war is always the answer. Yes a war would be nice. Maybe some more land if we win, or maybe just very much less young bucks or both. Some young brides are always needed for successful older men, to make more chore doers; I mean young children. Here son, take this rifle and charge up that hill over there. We need you to kill all those people and save the world. God told me to tell you that, and good luck son! We all hope you make it back in one piece. We are all counting on you. Dinner is at six don't come back if you're wounded, blood and guts upsets the women and children. Remember a real man fights to the death son. "Doc do you hear me?" I shouted. "Are you drunk or asleep?" He stopped talking so I did also. Our endless talking and joking had worn us out. The last two hours was spent in radio silence as our little gang approached Island number Two. My mind wandered as I flew across the hours. "Women talk about people, men talk about their toys. A full one third of all speech is nothing but crap anyway, so nobody listens! Who does tell lies' the most, us bulls or the cows? Who knows? Who cares? Suicide said he was dry now after falling into the sea during refueling! I figure he's lying! Patty said she would meet me in Hawaii! I think maybe she will, I sure hope so. Doc says he has water-skied on his motorcycle twice. Now ole' Doc is pretending to be asleep . . . (Asshole) All of us guys are alligators on the radio. Big mouth, no ears, and we all talk too much when drinking".

"Wow am I tired" I yelled, and screamed out loud. "No speak the truth Cornelius . . . . You are drunk, now put that bottle away!" a voice in my head said, so I did! We landed our birds as planned, inside the one slight cove or reef around the back side of the Island. Each plane skidded up on the dry pebble beach as far as our little propellers could drive us.

We didn't bother shouting out for the boys, we just took light packs of gear and headed toward the camp that we had finished building just seven weeks before. We hiked about four thousand yards. Over, through, and across the middle and narrow part of the Rocky island.

The door was slightly ajar on habitat one. We walked lightly across the porch, then swung the door open, and looked inside. Travis (Ting) Jones, the youngest student was sitting by himself at a table booth over flowing with brown M.R.E. food packages (*meal ready to eat)* mixing up the "good stuff" into the largest bowl he could find a plastic storage tote. He stared up at us with a glaring "oh shit" and only slightly slowed the stirring of his stew mix! "I'm making dinner" said Travis, "Have some."

"Come on son, lets go!" stated Duck calmly, "Where are the others?" Marshal Moore had taught Travis Jones and one other of the boys named Malcum, in his air craft maintenance school on ship. He knew them very well.

"We can't go yet Mr. Moore" cried out Travis! "You don't know what we've found. There are artifacts, ancient Roman maybe, we're not leaving until we finish!"

Marshal Moore helped Travis up, and brought him outside. He explained to him the cost of breaking the seal on a habitat container. Ducks mouth was chewing the boy's ear off. Little Travis, was barely nineteen, with short blond hair. He looked like he was sixteen, and weighed one hundred thirty-five pounds at the most. Moore's large left hand was wrapped around the boy's right arm, half suspending Travis in mid air as he walked.

Suicide and I left the "riot act" to Duck and started checking the other habitats. Unk was on the edge of camp coming out of the South Power Station. Two habitats were still locked but their doors had obviously been "played with" yet unopened. The next was unlocked but shut. Opening it up, we found sleeping bags, and a mess but no students.

"They're at the dig" yelled Travis! His arm firmly in the grip of Duck's gorilla like hand, Duck dropped Travis onto the ground. He landed center stage between all of us Unk, Moore, Doc, Suicide, and I. While still lying sideways on the ground Travis broke the tense silence!

"Ok . . . I'll take you to them!"

Our group hiked back across the island. We were now only five hundred yards from our planes. Travis led us to a cave opening that was sixty feet wide and ten to twelve feet high. On the back wall of this round natural cave, some fifty-sixty feet deep, forming a large almost flat "front room" was a section of old powdery bricks. This brick part of the other wise natural wall was covered up with cement or mortar in stucco fashion very close in color and texture to the real surrounding back wall of the cave. I looked out of the wide cave into the sunlight and could see an obvious path, flat spot, or road. Grooves or ruts were worn into some of the rocks. This "road" leads out of the cave and parallel into the sea in the general direction of our planes. This is or was a mine I thought to myself.

The boys had opened up a five foot wide three foot high hole in the brick about five feet off of the cave floor. These bricks were old, dry, and crumbling. They were thick at the bottom and narrow at the Top. Steve and Doc went back to the planes for flashlights and rope. Moore and I looked around. Travis yelled to his buddies through the opening.

"Travis hold it right there!" bellowed Unk. "No one goes inside that cave until Steve gets back."

While standing just inside the cave, I pointed my road out to Unk. Tommy Rosenberg came out first, not because Travis had called but to fix his glasses in the sunlight. Tommy saw us, shrugged his shoulders, and sat down quietly next to Travis Jones. Five minutes later the smaller fragile slightly darker hared blond named Tony also came out, again saying nothing. Shaking his head and rubbing his eyes he sat down next to his friends. Young Malcum jumped out of the cave next. He ran over to Marshal Moore and slugged him on the arm while laughing, running around in circles fist fighting the air and waiting for his whipping. Malcum and "Duck" often played like this aboard ship. We sailors often made fun of Moore and his "Son" Malcum. The two were very close for a student and teacher. Duck was a redneck father figure; Malcum was a fatherless spoiled brat with a very light Negro complexion. Malcum continued running in circles, taunting his mentor and embarrassing his friends. Moore just smiled at him with that "I'm gonna kick your ass" smile of his. Suicide (Steve Miller) then walked up with two more packs of gear. Doc, behind him carried one more. They both piled them on the ground in front of us and said,

"Well, what's up?"

Malcum, standing still now, was trying his best to act "grown up" and said. "There's ancient stuff in there, Roman maybe."

"No man" interrupted Travis, "It has to be at least civil war . . ." His friends all shook their heads no. "Well we haven't got it figured out yet . . . . but we know this is big"

"Yea, really big" said Tommy.

"The cover of National Geographic big" declared Travis. "We're all gonna be famous man." The two boys' fist bumped in agreement. The other two just murmured and looked up to us for the next move.

We adults huddled at the wide mouth cave entrance. Most figured we might as well have a look see while we're here. Why rush back to that mountain top antenna job, anyway. The boys led us into the brick opening, all of us with better and stronger lights now. We were all eyes wide with wonder.

"This is Hebrew writing I believe Tommy" said Duck. "All three are the same word most likely, do you know any Hebrew?

"No," said Tommy!

"This middle arch center stone in the ceiling look the word or name could translate as Josh if you make a J out of that odd mark. The others we can't read but I believe they mean the same thing" said Duck.

One hundred and fifty feet into the mine were three more signs. These were more polished and much more professionally done. The one in the center we could read. This sign read Amaziah. The other two signs were vaguely similar and unknown to us, we could only guess.

"Look in here Cornelius," said Unk waving his flashlight up and down. We had walked about two hundred feet deep into the cave, the first fifty feet being the wide natural cave. This hallway was man made, cut out of the rock with the ceiling arched in the center. No other writing or signs were seen after Amaziah. We never did find the end of this mine. There were always more unexplored and or sealed up passages. In this first straight hallway we found openings on first the left, then the right each one was bricked up and then carefully stuccoed over with cement. The boys would pound on the cave walls with a large pick, sounding it out and listening for a sound change. Then they would dig out a hole and crawl through.

The ceiling was over eight feet tall at its center, but once it was somewhat taller. There was six eight or ten inches of sediment and dust lying on top of everything.

As I was walking over to the opening where Unk was, he waved his light franticly to hurry me on. Not wanting to crawl through I stuck my head flashlight and right arm into the opening. Two boys were in that room or section polishing up and brushing off. They worked as we both watched. I spoke softly to Unk, for his head was right next to mine. "Reminds you of a Gatling gun Unk except bigger. The ole' Russian weasel could only agree and nod his head.

"Look at those large spoke wagon wheels on each side of it" replied Unk.

"Wow" said Duck, standing behind us, and straining to see. The guns shone of gold and bronze, and were very fancy, not plain, simple, or crudely made.

We old sailor boys caught the gold fever bad. Maybe even worse than the younger boys. Three days and two nights later we all joined together for a big meeting to discuss our now joint effort at the dig. This is what we had found;

The artifacts were like small modern cannons. Twelve barrels each with six flat sides and a round smooth bore inside. Each barrel was five and one half feet long, always twelve of them between two large wagon wheels. A large piece of wood in the middle below the barrels hooked to an axle. Bands of metal, coated with other metals wrapped around many wooden parts. Most wooden parts when moved did not hold up very well. They looked good but could not be used or even moved. Some metal parts also crumbled, and were eaten through in spots, but they also shined with bright gold and brass. Three of these metal barrel sections we moved intact outside into the sunlight. The twelve pipes or barrels were each almost four inches thick, or across. The inside bore was just under two inches. These twelve barrels were held together as one gun by six, six pointed star mounts, all six mounts at the back half of barrel, 2+2+2. One barrel was on each side of each star. The back end of the pipe was filled in with metal another blockage was ten inches up the gun forming a back fire chamber. This back chamber had two small holes in it both about the size of a copper wire. The back chamber opened up to the main barrel with a ¾ inch whole or a little larger than Docs fishing pole handle. The center round pipe was made of an undetermined type of metal. All around it was bronze metal plated with Gold. Two different types of glass shot could be found stored in what used to be baskets on the floor. This shot was round pieces of glass or marbles. Some wooden lances shaped like cue sticks were also found. These cue sticks had no sharp end on them but had a place were metal had been on them before. A hand full of shot could easily roll down the barrel at one time. One dozen of these contraptions or guns were in each bricked up side hallway that we opened. The boys by themselves had opened two sections now four more had been opened for a total of six. Twenty two unopened sections had been sounded but unopened and marked with red mechanics rags. Less than one third of the mine known to us had yet been sounded. The group of us at the big mouth cave sat eating still another of Travis Jones mixed up stews. We sat in the sunlight all knowing that time for exploration was over. Unk needed to call Joe and make a report. The stew was not bad, Travis was praised by all.

We took a break enjoying the sunshine, and fresh air. Each looked at the three metal assemblies that we had brought out to the light. Each one of us weighed in on the facts of the find.

"These are weapons" Marshal Moore started out. "Stored here in ancient days yes even back in Old Testament Biblical time. The writings we could not read are still a mystery, but one thing is for sure. This is the work of the ancient Israelites, and some merchants from Persia. Why would anybody go to this much trouble? Why would ancient Hebrews hide weapons, and why here. Cornelius is right about one thing. This is or was a mine of some type, but what were they mining. I need to brush up on my chemistry but I believe this very pure dry limestone rock mixed with salt could be used to make sodium carbide. A coke furnace or volcanic lava combination could get hot enough to make it. Modern sodium carbide plants all use an electric ark furnace to reach the high temperature needed.

"Sodium carbide" said Unk, "That's the rocks in old miner's lamps"

"Yes replied Moore" They give off acetylene gas, which is how these guns work. I'll explain how they work in a minute but first let me tell you who built them and why he put them here. Cornelius, did you bring your Holy Bible as I asked. Moore pulled out his Bible as he spoke and I also pulled mine out of my pack.

"Second chronicles chapter 26 verse 15"

Unk, Steve, and Doc rolled with laughter! Moore went on. "The Bible talks about these weapons, about them being built and used to great effect but does not mention them again. These weapons vanish from history. The words in this mine are names. All names of Kings of Israel in those ancient days. Amaziah from this mine is father to the king who is famous for . . . . Steve interrupts laughing

"Everything is in the Bible with you two nut jobs. You've got to be joking" Moore goes on speaking, very much red faced from the teasing.

"King Uzzrah is who built these weapons. This King Uzzrah became powerful using them but then repented of making the weapons when he saw the massive death and destruction they caused. I believe the king hid the weapons away forever. Never to be used again without the blessings of God. Like our Nukes of today he took them to the ends of the earth and put them in the island that gave

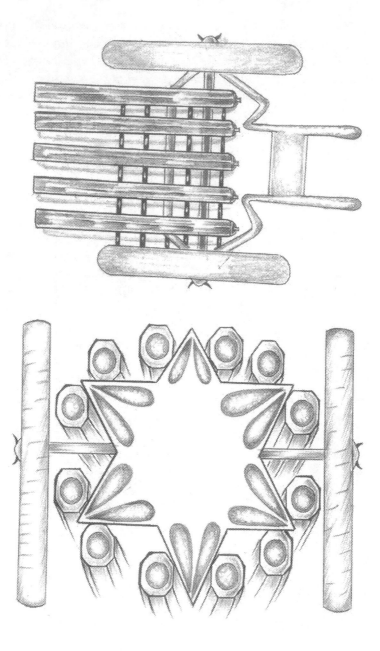

them their powerful burning rocks. As Unk and Steve started laughing uncontrollably I agreed to start reading the scripture for Duck was getting very hot about the teasing. When I read that chapter even now it gives me chills. Yes I still wonder about the secrets buried on Island Number Two.

And He (Uzziah) Made in Jerusalem engines, invented by cunning men, to be on the towers, and upon the bulwarks, to shoot arrows, and great stones with all. And his name spread far abroad! For he was marvelously helped! Till he was strong!

But when he was strong, his heart was lifted up to his destruction; for he transgressed against the Lord his God!

Duck continued, "Gentlemen I believe these weapons caused such death and destruction that they changed warfare and the fighting of brave strong men so much that this technology was hidden away. Uzzrah had one army of over 300,000 men. This king was known for building towers for military purposes in many other places.

Not just in Jerusalem. There may be thousands of these guns inside this mountain.

"You're on a roll now," shouted Steve (Suicide) as he scooped up seconds of Travis Jones plastic tote stew. Marshal Moore was fuming furious;

"Shut up Unk (laughter). Moore yelled! All ya'll sit down shut the hell up and listen!" We did just that.

These guns used on top of towers with cross fire zones would create a shocking stack of dead bodies. This would be enough to "make strong "any king and also make him want to ask for forgiveness. The same towers were likely used to make the round marble shot out of glass just as shot towers were later used to drop lead musket balls. That short reef by our planes is most likely the remains of an ancient harbor. This mine was worked for hundreds of years. Those groves in the rock, were not made by these guns, the tracks in the road are the same size as modern day train tracks (ha-ha). Man has not changed much over time.

"Mr. Moore, what would stop the marbles from rolling out the barrel when it was aimed downward from the top of a tower," asked Tony.

"Good question," answered Duck! "Just like civil was cannons cloth of some type, a wadding same as a musket solved that problem. This wadding also created more pressure for a faster projectile"

Tommy then asked . . . "Could that small little reef be the foundation of a large factory building to process raw ore into sodium carbine right her on the island, and the harbor might be out in now deeper water, it just seems like a small harbor."

Professor Moore pondered the question. This has not been ruled out, yes that could be possible. Many South Sea Islands were cut of every last tree (like Easter Island) in times past for some reason. Feeding or building a large plant with close by timber could have been the reason. It would change our view of history."

"History, I've heard enough" roared Unk. The old Ukrainian weasel shook his head. The ancient Israelites can kiss my ass. The Bible, I've heard it all now, and it is very much past my deadline to call Captain Coe. You men get the mine covered over, and that's an order he demanded.

We closed up the mine with brush. All of us were thinking that we might be coming back. Our rescue group had to stay another two nights for the surf to calm down but we did not go back into the mine. We were all warned again by Unk not to use our ship phones. Our group also made a pack with each other not to discuss or speak of our find. I thought that Doc might have used his ship phone. Doc looks like Andy Griffith his real name is Arthur Hodge from Greenville Tenn. Doc was given to calling his wife and his mother faithfully everyday. Doc started off again in my plane on the way back. No Medicine, no boys either in my plane this time, two boys had doubled up. I tried to keep a conversation up to keep myself alert. All of the boys were accounted for twice this go round (ha-ha). We triumphant rescue heroes were now on our way home with mission accomplished.

"Doc" I asked? "Ain't it funny that now, thousands of years later so called modern man would bring the next generation of new weapons (atomic bombs) here to the ends of the earth for weapons testing. For thousands of years China and India, and most Eastern leaders of civilization (and also slavery) have stayed mostly to themselves. This while Western civilization has made war with, bombed, or sent troops to every country in the world. The west has always fought to expand our way of life, our laws, and technology. Now the slow, old, slave ways, stay to them selves East is slowly winning control of the world from us. This because we have killed off each other in our many stupid wars that now the East is about to take over and rule us economically. They out number us six to one, there is just not enough of us to matter. The Bible told us to be fruitful and multiply. Guess what America. God's way always works. Who could have known?

I was getting drowsy, and started talking about the Roman West teaching Jesus in one hand and dropping bombs with the other. Ole' Doc was not much of a conversationalist, so I finally shut up. I guess he only talks to his wife and his mother. The dumb bastard fell asleep on me once again.

When we approached the refueling point the other planes from the ship were already down on the water. The sea was calm with gentle rolling swells, what a blessing. We were all gathered up by two black rubber inflatable dinghies with outboard motors. Captain Joe Coe himself was driving one, and his man Friday was driving the other. The ship's brass had come to meet us. Nothing was too good for these brave returning heroes. Unk Moore Suicide, and I were in Joe's, and the boys and Doc got in Fridays boat.

Joe backed up under the wing of his plane and cut off his motor while holding onto the wing strut to steady our dinghy. Friday pulled up beside us and cut off his motor also. Everybody figured we were due for one of Joe's crew meetings. Maybe even a rare "job well done" men speech. Friday then stepped out of his boat onto the pontoon float of the plane. When he did Joe nodded his head. Friday placed one foot on top of his boats motor and pushed off propelling his raft away from the plane, as he did so a man in commando black stepped out of the plane and started firing a semi-automatic Glock pistol with a long silencer into the boys and Docs Dinghy, so likewise did Friday. After emptying a long full clip they both reloaded. Joe, with his one free hand was pointing an identical pistol at us seated in his boat. Young Travis Jones managed to fall out of the dinghy before death. The rest died slumped over where they sat. We watched in silent horror as the other dinghy slowly sunk into the waves, motor end first. The cries and moans of death did not last long. Soon the quick jerking of the lifeless bodies gave witness to the unseen teeth below. The sharks came much too quickly to be natural. Joe had been chumming for hours. We sat quietly, awaiting our fate with three black guns with long silencers holding our complete and close attention. Joe waited enough time for full dramatic effect and then broke the silence. Those minutes, and the terrible silence of the waves is still in my nightmares.

"Gentlemen, the boys were never found, you, nor those boys found anything on any island. **Have any of you dumb sons of bitches ever seen or been to an island? Say No Sir!**

"No Sir" We all answered

"Say it again" screamed Joe

"No Sir" . . . . (silence).

"All of Doc's family and known friends some two hundred and twenty eight souls world wide were all assassinated last night. All from one stupid phone call to home Arthur Hodge made. I myself and my family, yes all of our families and friends back home will be dead within twenty four hours of any leak of this day. World wide assassins are ready, and yes we know where you and yours live. Do you dumb bastards have any questions? Do you realize the danger I've put myself and my family in this day just to save your worthless ass. I don't know? Maybe I should shoot this boat too. If any of you are brave enough to take a bullet now like a man, this will save your family for sure. This I guarantee. Also your company life insurance will pay double death by accident price" A few seconds later, true to his "handle" or nickname. The heavily tattooed Steve Miller straddled his legs far enough apart to stand up in the big rubber dinghy. With a nod from Joe, Steve was shot six times in the chest, three each from Friday and the mysterious man in black. Suicide fell stiff into the rolling Pacific. He floated for about a minute. We sat again in silence until the jerking started and unseen teeth from below pulled him under. We all then refueled and flew back to the ship. Steve's plane was set on fire by fuel and a double barreled safety flare gun. It took Friday three shots to hit the plane he was shaking like a leaf. Your first murder or killing will do that to a man. Story was that the plane crashed with "Suicide" and "Doc" both in it. The boys were never found. They were lost to rising water in deep caves on the island. It then took us another two weeks to finish Island Number Three. After that the Great Ark doubled back to Island Number Two. The cover story was to look for the lost boys, just one last time. Six of the "Pigtails" and Captain Coe took choppers back and fourth to and fro between the ship and shore Oddly enough they took buckets of cement and trials. We then lingered days longer at Island Two for no apparent reason. Then one day another six men joined us by chopper from a distant parked destroyer. The "Pigtails did not get along with these men. Two of the new comers were sent away. The Pigtails did not like these six men, but had to report to them, and were dependant on them, and had fear of them. Captain Coe and I were alone outside on the catwalk from his bridge talking.

"Pray this works Cornelius" said Captain Coe! We could see and hear the men arguing down on flight deck. They were pointing fingers and shouting as two of the men were sent away. Much of the crew, many hundreds of people were on other balcony walk ways and also watching and listening from afar. The coming of these men had been the "buzz" about the ship all morning. Captain Joe was all stirred up. He was angry, red faced, and yes it showed. This was rare.

"What is the problem" I asked very respectfully.

"Two of the six Knights that Rome sent are not even Levites. They can't help, they can't inspect they can't go to the island not even just to the camp. How could they do this to me said Joe?

"Knights, Rome, for the grace of God Joe!"

"Yes Cornelius. For the grace of God"

"What about you Joe?" I asked "You helped on the island all last week"

"I'm a Levite Cornelius, and yes ordained by Rome. At least on paper, so are you stupid. All of our team is, or was.

"You mean the boys too!"

"Yes, Cornelius" said Joe Coe. "You're not the sharpest knife in the drawer, are you Cornelius? Look, I have to call Mr. Child back. He's in Rome. Before I call these men I have to ask you, just one more time, and be swearing to God honest with me Cornelius. Where all did the boys and or your team explore on this island! Was it all inside the large mouth cave! The old mine!

"Yes Joe" I answered. "The old mine, that was it"

"So everything you explored on this island was in that one cave and nothing else? . . . .

"Nothing else Joe, give it a rest"

"No where else?" Joe asked again, while pacing.

"Yes Joe" . . . . I said . . . . no where else!"

"Ok I believe you Cornelius" said Joe. Captain Coe hesitated but then spoke softly. "Cornelius there are a few things that this Mr. Child you and I all share in common"

"What's that Joe?" I asked getting curious.

"Way back in history we were of the same tribe and also our family names have been shortened. I told my eldest daughter to be patient that another one could be found or come along.

"Patient" I shouted . . . . "You mean West Virginia cousin patient don't you Joe. Stop right there you're making me sick"

"Sarah's baby is named Aaron Benjamin Cornelius Cohen! "Kin you believe that (ha-ha)! She married a Cohen" Joe laughed and waved me out of his office back out on to the bridge railing. Then he made his phone call to Rome. The Vatican I guessed. Joe talked to two men and then hung up in a sweat. If my lip reading is any good he said, Thank you both, God Bless you and thank you again. Yes, it is done. Joe stared out his huge bridge windows and moved his thumb to an unseen app and waited.

One of the choppers on his far distant horizon then blew up. The other continued toward the distant destroyer.

Two of the six "Pigtails" had stayed behind on Island Number Two. By the serious service and praising and long goodbyes I guessed it was a stay for Life. Who got back to the destroyer? The ones who went to the island or the chopper that was sent away? I could only guess which! While I was coming down the outside stairs from the bridge, the ship's Chaplin stopped me at the bottom.

"Wow, Tommy's must be bigger than I thought. A top Vatican aide, the bishop of Jerusalem, and those four old rabbis, The Knights, did you see their mark?

"What . . . their mark Father?" I asked

"Cornelius those men are Templar Knights, They report only to the Vatican, The short guy was the bishop. Those Rabbis! I'm guessing the top Sanhedrin temple leaders, or elders.

"Are you sure father?" I asked

"Of course I'm a Priest, I know, I'm a man of God."

"Father, do you know anything about the golden mean, the number 26, or 24 elders? Father, I'm Holiness! I'm working with my giant for God, can you help me?

The Chaplin started walking hastily away. "Pray without stopping Cornelius, I'll find someone on my staff that can help you, Goodbye for now and God Bless you!"

Never talk about being Holiness to a Holy Father, or a Priest. Unless, that is you want to get rid of them (ha-ha).

That night the ship was underway again. I was back at my big round corner table at the ship's Gospel Café. My South sea island adventure was always heavy on my mind, soul and spirit. It felt good to relax as the anti-professor and discuss world events and God's word. My glassy eyed, brain washed students never had much to say. Everybody was looking forward to a month long layover in Hawaii. I was too. I called my ex-wife that night, and yes she was coming to meet me in Hawaii. Praise God, I would try to put the wonders and horrors of my South Sea Islands adventure behind me. I would find that life was not so easy.

CHAPTER SIX

— ‡ ◆ ‡ —

Honeymoon in Kauai

At my corner table tonight were Daniel and Double De from Virginia. They say Virginia is for lovers. This couple must be a state post card. They were both of strong faith, a rare and refreshing combination of people to meet on the Great Ark. They had just been "down under" visiting at the "Coeville" family get together. They knew the Dave brothers and the Johnstons. I didn't know all this tonight but I would find out later in Peal. Daniel was joking about original sin and Eve eating the apple. You all know the story. The couple talked about their home Bible study with their boys, so our focus turned to scripture.

The whole ship was talking about our up coming layover in Hawaii. Many had booked passage on this part of the Great Arks voyage just because of the Hawaii stay; Daniel and Double De were of this group. They took a few college courses but were older and more mature and here for a second honeymoon not a degree. The Ark was way behind schedule now. Hotel and tour bookings had been missed. The Ark would have to pay. This was all a big mess, and very worrisome to travelers making plans. The couple's young boys were home with grandma, and an older daughter. I ordered a round of coffee and looked at Daniel's family pictures, all while weighing in on Adam and Eve, as the anti-professor.

God teaches us in his Holy Bible that the man is the spiritual head, or leader of his house. He is ordained by God with this responsibility. The women must obey this godly calling of the man as long as he walks up right with God. The man is responsible to God, for what is done and is not done in his home. Spiritual warfare and the fighting of it, is led by the man. Each man must lead and teach his family in prayer and devotions.

A man is held responsible by God, to perform this spiritual leadership. He must properly train, and keep his family in the ways of God. His family members are not held to this same standard by God, because God made man the head. For example; if a husband allows his wife to practice witchcraft, or raise children in false teaching, worship false Gods, or if any type of child abuse takes place, then the man has sinned against God. If the man does these sane things himself; say physically emotionally, sexually, or economically abuse his own family then the wife has not sinned. This group responsibility is very serious for the man. Serious as hell! Men often sin by not doing something, by not stopping evil things from coming into his household. Let us turn to Genesis three, verses two three and four.

And the woman said! Unto the serpent! We may eat of the fruit of the trees of the garden! But of the fruit of the trees which is in the mist of the garden, God hath said, ye shall not eat of it! Neither shall ye touch it! Lest ye die!

Notice that the "woman" said, not the serpent that she would die if she touched it. God did not lie. The serpent did not lie. No! Adam lied, to his wife about what God had said. Either that or the woman is lying to the serpent as to what she was told. What did Adam say to her about what God had said to him? Let us read God telling Adam, (alone) about the tree. Eve has not been made yet. Adam being the spiritual head was to train and teach God's ways.

(15) **And the lord God took the man! And put him into the Garden of Eden, to dress it, and to keep it!**

(16) **And the Lord commanded the man saying! Of every tree of the garden thou may freely eat**

(17) **but of the tree of the knowledge of good and evil thou shall not eat of it; for in that day that thou eatest there of, thou shall surly die!**

Adam sinned by failing to teach Eve in God's word, ways and laws. Did he simply lie to her about what God had said to scare Eve away from the fruit? This before the serpent came by and exploited his lie. If not then Eve lied. Both lies came before the fruit. Adam not Eve is responsible to God for original sin. Even though both were punished for sin and all of us have been born into sin or in separation from God ever since.

Daniel and Double De seemed to agree with me, or just didn't like to argue such things. Maybe they both felt sorry for the "old man" who knows? I would have the pleasure of seeing them often during our stay at Pearl Harbor. They called their daughter from my table, the boys were fine. Who was missing who more I thought (ha-ha).

The next week the Great Ark pulled stately and slow into Pearl Harbor! It was a blessing for me to see Pearl one last time. It was very disturbing and sad to see her also. My grand old Pearl was only a shadow of her former glory. The base wasn't officially closed yet. One half had been sold. Only a few staff left to close the base up. The old U.S. flag still flew. I was glad of this but was still surprised. The Chinese were moving slow on bidding on the base, trying to lower the price. The Japanese had long ago taken over the Arizona memorial and allowed the American flag to remain in respect to the graves. A large Mosque's golden dome towered over the harbor, still surrounded by construction cranes. President Osoma had given away fifty seven construction sites, and fifty seven Billion Dollars to Islamic Leaders world wide, asking forgiveness from them for the fact that hate filled Christian Americans helped Israel survive during the resent "Islamic Spring," War of the Trumps. These extremist Christian right wing racist hate groups and Tea Party Terrorists would no longer override, and undermine American policy. This is what change looks like, American power was dead. Osoma freed this world from America and all Americans from God. Osoma apologized for not seeking out and destroying dangerous hate speech before the election, but now his swift polices would turn the tide. News and web sites were not completely censored here as in the mainland. Hawaii claimed Chinese human rights protection and so for Osoma has dared not interfere. The nightly news here was very disturbing to every American on ship. Many Jews were in the islands hoping to escape from America, by using the new Chinese human rights protection. I had thought that my retirement had been "made" by my working on the Ark. I now learned that the dollar had lost half of its value since I had been at sea. President Osoma's Chief of staff; Benedict M. Dubris was credited for this goodwill gesture to the Islamic world. Bombings in American shopping malls during the last ten months have gone down 22 percent from last year. Osoma was praised on NBC.

I got a letter from my ex-wife patty. She would be here in Pearl to meet me. Her letter had a Bill Ayer's stamp on it. Bill was on the famous Wright commission, credited for saving billions of dollars and millions of

Jobs using the new "Safety checkpoints across America" One million new police. They looked for bombers, anti-gay, hate speech Christians, and Jews trying to take "wealth" out of the country. Yes these one million police were stemming violence, and guns, many hired were good right-minded minorities. No test was given to make it fair for all. American Jews moving to Israel was a big problem. The closing of businesses in black communities made them "hardest hit" Free rent was offered to any non-Jewish minority who could or would dare open shop. Many of these shops were confiscated from tax cheat Jews trying to run out on America and steal our wealth. The Democratic Socialist party was firmly in power. Millionaires must pay more. Mothers Need Milk was the title to Bill Ayers last book. This book was all over the Oprah network. Oprah herself came out with ten million dollars to buy digital audio video books for inter city youth who had been robbed of reading skills by racist teachers. Here in Hawaii there were no road side pat downs or safety check points, as was the case on the mainland. The Red Chinese had declared the islands free of American tyranny, and Osoma was scared to act. The Bill Ayers postage stamp said "The good of the many outweighs the rights of the few" it made me sick. As we slowly docked at Pearl, I was glad that the last survivor of the attack had died. They didn't have to witness the surrender of the colors, or the foolishness of their blood sweat and tears for freedom. Still officially a state, the islands now get more money from China than from the old U. S. After the so called Walmart wars, Osoma dares not try to "take back" his home state. Now many Jews have landed here trying to get to Israel. All types of people were running from American IRS agents. One thousand Americans a day moved to both Australia, and Canada, all of which was illegal!

I was ashamed that my generation had stood by and let America fall. Not by war, but by idiot voters. People had demanded rights to food, TV, phones, healthcare, and so called jobs, all in complete safety, and freedom from responsibility. The humanist false religion and the socialist revolution elites sang sick dogma filled songs hand in hand as they pulled America down. The trash education taught in government schools that mankind was good, and was getting even smarter and wiser with each generation. That man did not need a redeemer and that resources were all in short supply. This must be true because the blessings of God were no longer to be trusted in. Big government was the only way to achieve fairness. By teaching false science and these simple lies each day they soon brought down the last free republic on earth. President Osoma caught this sick wave into power, a man who was dull minded enough to ride his own horse to its death. He was a symptom not the disease. A weed that quickly grew strong on the rotting fallen American godless corpse.

Patty had sent me a now outlawed newsletter inside her letter to me. I threw it down in anger. That big Christian College in Lynchburg had lost its case and was now closed for good. They could not pay the federal income tax bill. They had lost their tax exempt status by supporting Israel and using hate speech. Those students at the ship's Gospel Café had been so nice. I didn't know they were haters. I guess you just don't know! People can fool you! I had enjoyed their newsletters for years, but this was the last one to be printed. The sons of the old pastor who founded the school were both in jail and apologizing for losing the church buildings and property in the law suit also. The talk of a new mosque had the city of Lynchburg up in arms. Police from across the country were being sent in to quell the feared redneck hick violence. Osoma stated that he was for religious rights for all, and not just for Christians, also that some non English speaking black Muslims were not offered free books at that college. These racist extremists were the main problem, most church goers were pretty nice folks, said Osoma, but rich churches like this one in Lynchburg needed to pay more and that was only fair. After the ship docked it was great to watch all those many cargo containers leave the Ark. We would soon be able to fly again. But first a few old Navy contractors would be doing some work around the ship. A month leave was given to most of the crew. Many crew members stayed on the ship anyway because of the bad "Jewish problem". There was simply no place to stay anywhere. I don't know what the contractors in Pearl did but all four of them billed the Ark for ten to twelve million dollars apiece. This Pearl Harbor lay-over was a honeymoon period for me and my then still ex-wife Patty. We would one day drop the ex and be a family once again. Good times can still be had by saints and sinners alike even as Rome burns around you. Yes even when most people have been played for fools, "as in the days of Noah, so shall it be!"

Patty (my Tweedy) is my own hotter by half version of Goldie Hawn. Patty flew in commercial to Pearl; when she met me she had already rented a car, and we quickly sped off. This month of shore leave was the beginning of the end for years of painful divorce. Being with Tweedy again was wonderful, a true blessing. We stayed mostly on the northern island of

Kauai. That island has always been Patty's favorite, but she liked Waikiki also, she would sing and hum the song, "I'm gonna wash that man right out of my hair" and then grin at me. This girl is crazy about me, I can tell. Patty and I were allowed to stay in one of Mitch Johnston's time shares for two weeks while in Kauai. Wow what a nice place, it had five bedrooms, a great balcony and huge windows. Don't say anything to Janet Johnston about that rubber seal dish thing in the kitchen, we kind of kept it accidently when we left. It was just like old times when Patty did her Christmas shopping early at the Pearl merchant's road side tents. The grass around the tents is great for sleeping on. Men should always avoid going shopping with their wives at all cost. This rule might not be in the Bible but it is in marriage 101.

The Pearl merchants didn't have any mushrooms for me anyway (ha-ha) no Christmas spirit. Patty and I both thought about and talked about my father while we were in Kauai. My dad was the real Cornelius. Memories of him were everywhere here. This island became his second home towards the end of his life. He seemed to us, to still inhabit the island paradise he so loved. I often wonder what the old NASA scientist and the original "anti-professor" would think of today's world. Osoma would very much upset him I do believe.

My own son, Shawn T. Cornelius and his girl friend Monica joined us for twelve days of our stay during this month long layover, just as my wife and I would do when my father was still alive I guess I'm the old man now. Gods garden is always turning under don't take the flower of youth or yourself too seriously. God tells us plainly that this life is but a season, and to live life Gods way. I reminded my son and Monica to keep their heart, mind, and spirit on things eternal. We so often live for earthly garden rewards, things that God has designed to fade and die.

Our close friends Howard and Betty Janey came for a long week visit also during this month, but our time together was mostly Patty and I together by ourselves. This special time together was a much needed second honeymoon for us that helped heal our broken marriage. Short time lovers like Sarah can't really compete with the joys found in the arms of a true soul mate and life partner. Surprise, God does know what he's talking about. His way does work. Who knew this, and why has no one told modern man and all of his silly experts. I guess man just got to smart to read the Bible, much less believe it or live by Gods Holy Word.

The good life on this earth has never been better than the time we spent together on the island of Kauai. The large resorts and hotels are always spectacular and we love to visit them. Why a Hotel would ever build a lobby that is five acres in size or a swimming pool large enough to water ski in is above my pay grade. If you demand luxury or even opulence, you can find it here, but don't forget your wallet. Patty and I talked about how great our life back together in Virginia will be. The rocking chair on the front porch with my Patty sounded pretty good to this old foolish sailor. I promised her this cruise would be my last tour of duty. There would be no more Saint Augustine for me, my old friend Rosie ran the business anyway.

We drove up to the National Park at the North end of Kauai to a wide cave there that was very close beside the road. This cave reminded me of Island Number Two. Of course I didn't say anything to Patty, but I just could not help myself from taking a close look at the caves back wall.

For lunch, we stopped in a big resort hotel with a reflecting pool in the lobby. They had an all you can eat brunch special for only $99.00 dollars a person plus tax. This was cheap in the high class snob section of Kauai. One silly little local market likes to advertise itself as the most expensive grocery store in America. I do believe that they might just be right. These large world class hotels are a pleasure to visit but even Mitch and Janet's big time share suite was too grand for my taste. During our brunch, I looked at a Health Dept license on the wall, and sure enough the manager's name was Patel. I asked for the manager and told him to say hello to my friend Jediah, and mentioned the town and province in India were he lived. The hotel staff sprung into action and started treating us like the Queen of Sheba. Many servants begged for forgiveness for having brought shame to themselves for not knowing our station in life. Patty enjoyed all of this attention. We had drinks over looking the ocean. Red wine for me, and white for Patty. We talked for hours. Patty said she would help me open a Gospel Café back home, just like the one on ship with a big round corner table and everything. We dreamed of singing Gospel music again together just like we did back when we started. Maybe we could still find or invite some of the singers from that big closed down Church in Lynchburg. Our hearts ached to sing Gospel music and praise God once again. It started that very week. A flood of simple Gospel songs started pouring out of my mouth almost too fast for me to write them all down, just like songs had done in my youth. Have you ever been commode hugging drunk? Most people have at least a few times in their life. Writing music for God is just like that, when it comes, it comes and you must be ready to obey. The process is not always easy or comfortable, or convenient.

One late night on the beach, I borrowed one of those giant over-sized acoustic twelve string guitars and started to sing some of my old songs. This night begged the age old question? If you write down a song one day and then try to sing it years later and have now forgotten or changed the words have you made a "mistake" or have you just changed the song to a newer version since it was your song in the first place (ha-ha). That beautiful night on the beach will go down in the record books of my memory as a song singing, and love making classic. Men always like to recall times when we were well, at out best! Tips on beach sand removal and fancy one chop coconut opening cost extra (ha-ha) fellows. Let us face facts, sometimes the coconut does not pop open even for the best of us. The only problem with my Patty compared to "new girls" is I can't lie to her, she knows me too well. She knows when I mess up a song, and hates it when I sing the wrong part. My Patty is the best! I hope you have a lifetime women in your life my friend, a true soul mate. If you do don't ever let her go, don't be a fool like me.

On our last day of Patty's visit we were back at Pearl Harbor. Our old friends Howard and Betty Janey came in from Maui to join us again at the end, just as they had done twice before during this trip. We all still talk about the night of the big luau, even to this day. Also we met up with Daniel and Double De again. In every culture the women folk always work out the details of all of this meeting up with who and when or where. Men should never get involved in the meeting up with other couples. Leave this to the women just like the shopping. Take my word for this and don't doubt me. Everybody's favorite day on the trip was the chopper ride, but it was not mine. I tried not to talk about the Great Ark and all of my adventures. I did talk about being Holiness; first to Patty and then to Howard and Betty. They didn't run off like most but I was driving the rental car at the time with the doors locked (ha-ha). We were all old friends back through our youth. Yes through all those dumb days, and the "drug days." Howard is a little bit unstable or Zaney (ha-ha). Betty is friendly and a little bit on the quiet side. Betty is a great hugger but only if she has a chair to stand on (ha-ha). I'm sorry I did promise no more short jokes.

Our whole group went through the Arizona memorial together on Patty's last day at Pearl Harbor. That is except for my Son Shawn and his girl Monica they left for home the day before. We picked out the name of Fred Driver a relative of ours and all the pain heartache, and cold reality of war flooded in. Our vacation and honey moon was about over. We Thanked the Lord for allowing the Japanese people to buy and maintain this war memorial. Please forgive the many selfish Americans of my age group who were born with so many blessing just to throw them all away. Out in the water of the memorial I kept seeing and hearing a black dinghy sinking motor end first into the waves. Rubbing my eyes I scrubbed Doc and the boy's blood from my memory one more time. It never works for long. I looked down into the water again. No dead boys, no sharks, no words with the power to deceive! That is good! Thank God. You just married a Cracker son, you're not blood kin Cornelius, please don't go all crazy on me.

My wife Patty and our friends the Janey's got into a rental car on the dock next to the Great Ark, right on the same spot where Patty had picked me up before. My friends all headed to the airport and to a flight home. I stood on the dock alone watching them drive away. Go with them stupid don't let Patty leave, do something you fool but alas they were gone and I was too late. My old friend loneliness moved back into my heart. I looked up at the Great Ark towering over Pearl Harbor. Oh what a majestic shadow she cast. The ship makes quite an impression on "first timers" boarding I thought to myself. This was only the third time I had actually walked onto the Ark from shore. Many older passengers, most of them couples were boarding the Ark that day, their trip of a lifetime. None of these old people ever came to the ships Gospel Café I thought to myself. I should make a point of inviting them. Many of these folks could hardly get up the ramp. What are we running here an old folks home (ha-ha). We officers and pilots never saw passengers much, or most of the crew for that matter. The College also kept to themselves for the most part. We each had our own section of the big ship. We officers ate our meals in the officer's mess, and had our own quarters. The ship was even bigger now than when the old military carrier had been when she was first built. Many college buildings and housing were built on parts of the old flight deck. She could hold a lot more people if needed.

In less than three days we would return to sea. It was time for Ole' Corny to put wings on once again. There waiting for me up in my cabin, was a stack of mission orders, printed out by my own personal computer, it's an old apple lap top with an added on larger key board. Yes, I like it that way, and on real paper. I'm old and have fat fingers and can't always see or hit the numbers on these damn fancy little ship phones. Hey look! Some orders came in on paper in the pouch that is odd. I went to bed early. Paper work could wait till morning. I thought about calling Patty, but it was too early for that. I was getting as bad about phone calling wives as poor Arthur Hodge (ha-ha). Look where all that calling got Ole' Doc!

With three fingers of red wine, I looked out over the harbor from my high cabin porch balcony. Pearl Harbor . . . . Those two words meant something when I was a boy. The greatest generation they were called. Men like my dad who gave God country and family their all. They bridged the span of time from horse and buggy to man in space. Has man ever made that leap before, I wonder. They put a man on the moon without real computers, and fought for the God given freedoms of men.

Now their rich spoiled kids and grandkids have voted into power voluntarily the same old tired ungodly, anti-Jewish, fascist evil that the greatest generation had fought so hard against. History is not hard to understand, it's a record that repeats. America just like the ancient Israelites has gone "Hot-to cold" with God, now without God, from generation to generation. Could we not read? Could we not listen? These ungodly progressives started way back in the First World War, by the time of the greatest generation we were already sick. Death was not instant. The seeds of our destruction were planted the war before. How could so many be fooled? How could so many men each fail their family duties and not teach the ways of God.

Was Katie on T.V. so sweet and pretty, her skirt so short that it didn't matter the poison she spoke everyday. Osoma's democratic socialist party platform was word for word a copy of Adolf Hitler's platform in Germany. Osoma put out a book telling everyone he was a communist. Every one knew that Rev Wrights church was not a true "Christian Church" not one that preached Jesus. Why didn't Katie and her friends on T.V. tell us the truth? Why did no one sound the alarm or ring the Liberty Bell? The media was already dead to Gods word, his teaching, and the truth that's why.

We fools gave up freedoms light without a fight, without a shot. We have gone from victory to defeat, from pride to shame, from riches to rags. Young fools hating their own inheritance, hating their own success, power, and glory. "It was not fair that Americans had so much" they would say, our fathers handed us too many blessing. You fool; know you not from where your blessings come?

Osoma hates God, Freedom and America, he wants to punish her. He is a bitter man, with an even more than bitter wife. No one can hear that bitter hate speech of the black separatist movement or those Jew hating speeches of the Islamic movement for twenty years if he was not one of them himself. I have a question friend; does anyone ever shout out kill the Jews, or down with America, in your church. Wake up America! People who go to KKK meetings are members of the Klan. We have elected a monster. Osoma does not defend the constitution he openly wars against it and us. Government schools have taught the Progressive, Humanist, Communist line for many years in America. Now even racist teachings are openly used. This hatred for America has become anti-white anti-church, anti-rich and is always anti-Jewish. Sad to say most young students have been brainwashed, and agree with Osoma. Let us pick up the ways of the old world once again, they will say. A Godly Republic of free men is too heavy a burden to bear. Give us a czar, a king, let us be slaves as the rest of the world, and equal to them. Each of us to be a charge of the King and by doing so then each will be taken care of for life. My friends let us face the cruel truth! America has been lost!

I prayed myself to sleep that night, life brought so many questions. I studied up on the number 26 by taking fireball candy and making clusters of thirteen. One in the center with twelve around! Ok first I take seven fireballs. One in center with six around it, then three on top, and then three on the bottom to make a sphere. The pyramids then got a little tricky. I kept the candy in a jar on my desk to play with later. I was very proud of myself, for finally understanding some of the math of Gods universe.

The next morning Professor Lou Goodliar and I again met outside of our cabins. This time Tommy Mute was outside "Loud" Lou's cabin door with him. They invited me to hear a professor give a lecture (or preach) later that night. This man had been on the Big Island, and would be in Pearl tonight. Lou had tickets. At the lecture in a large auditorium in town many of the ships officers and crew had come to hear this professor, preacher, and author. I think Goodliar got some free tickets for bringing in so many. Lou loved Bible study he always knew more than anybody else and always got in the last word. Our auditorium was packed the seats were comfortable and the air-conditioning felt great. Many put coats and sweaters on. Our group settled in for the lecture. This professor had a long name and even a longer list of titles. He must be a very important man. He had written many history books most of them about the Civil war. Ok I know the War Between the States. He also wrote books about the Wild West. His wife Rosemary was very pretty, this man married very well. His Rosemary was a much younger, whiter, smaller, and taller version of my Rosie back in Saint Augustine. Professor Theodor Whitt (trying his hand at humor) introduced his wife as "Rose the Nose" which angered two old women in the crowd. Whitt was fond of doing Irish drinking jokes and side stories in an Irish accent. His lecture was very entertaining, and informative. His book was a run away best seller entitled "The Sons of God" by Nathaniel, Isaiah Theodor Whitt.

"Gentlemen," He bellowed. "The Holy Scriptures of God does not hide riddles for cunning men to figure out or reprocess in any way. Scripture is plain spoken and easy to understand words for life. These words come straight from almighty God. Scripture does not need a lot of long drawn out interpretation or explanation by wise professor types like me. Read it for yourself. Find your own salvation with fear and trembling. All scripture is given for and is good for both study and reproof. Jesus Christ is Lord! Say it with me again. Jesus Christ is Lord! He is the way to truth and life. No one comes to the father except through him. His word and our study tonight of it is an important thing to do. But knowing him and his will for your life and being obedient to his will is even more important than the knowing of his word. I believe in, and on the Holy Trinity and the necessity to test every spirit. Every spirit that proclaims that our Lord Jesus Christ came in the flesh, was born of a virgin, was crucified dead and buried and on that third day rose from the dead, defeated hell and the grave and that old serpent is of God. He redeemed men from sin, and all that who so ever calls upon his name, comes to him as a child, and who has a soul that is born again will be heirs with him in his mighty riches and glory. I have salvation from death, and eternal life with Christ Jesus! Do You? My friends I bring to you a history lesson tonight, a history lesson and my own theories based on ancient sand script writings and scripture. But my only obligation to you is to preach Jesus and he crucified. I love history, but studying history will not get you to heaven, but it can deepen and enrich your faith. I pray that I point you to Jesus, he is the way. Getting on your knees right now is a good start. Seek his power and knowledge in your life. Lord Jesus be glorified not myself here tonight, for the fear of God is the beginning of wisdom. For years I've heard Bible scholars speak double talk about basic biblical truths. They like to bend the Bibles simple words to suit their own small minds and narrow point of view. Men would dare to say that Israel did not really mean Israel that Babylon did not really mean Babylon, that drunk on the blood of the saints was only figurative, or one can not take the Bible at face value. Friends I've found that God's word is true, and every man is a liar! The Bible meanings are clear. God does not stutter or beat around the bush (sorry Moses). Friends I've been called a lot of things by many well meaning saints, simply because I stand on the simple word of God. I believe that when the Bible says Persia, it means Persia. When Holy Scriptures say "to the East" they mean "to the East". When it says Israel it means Israel. And guess what! When the Bible says "Sons of God" It means "Sons of God" each and every time. The meaning of "Sons of God" does not change from this verse to that verse as many so called Bible teachers pretend. Let me ask you a question brothers and sisters in Christ. What do you believe life on earth during the one thousand year Kingdom reign of Jesus on Earth will be like unto? During this time, before the New Jerusalem comes down, Lord Jesus will rule from Jerusalem. After one Thousand years, God will make everything new. Will there be honest work, trade, or justice in his court. Will there be any slavery or counterfeit money. Of course not! Jesus compared his coming again to the changing of the seasons. What do seasons do! They repeat! Will you have a job in the Lords Kingdom here on earth? Adam had a Job! Does God change his ways? "No" Will we do anything for ourselves, or others. Is this a silly question? Many people believe that God will simply zap everything during his Kingdom reign. They believe that work is not of God. This simply is not true. God is attracted to weakness, he uses us or (lets us work for him) as a gift to us. We will be full heirs with him in Glory. Humanist ungodly foolish men claiming wisdom tell us that resources are in short supply. God told us to be fruitful and multiply, that the blessings of God are beyond our human understanding. Who do you believe might just be right, God or Al Gorey and Osoma. Look into the Heavens with what we call powerful telescopes and see your answer. We can not out build, or out multiply God! The old angel Lucifer was thrown down to earth. He tries to copy and imitate. He wants to be like God, Yes to be like the most high. The Angel with the help of men was trying to reach for God way back in the times of the tower of Babel, just like the spaceport leaders say's in their brochure today. "As in the days of Noah, so shall it be. Look at our space station compared to the New Jerusalem in the Holy Bible. It's very hard to beat God when it comes to a space station isn't it? We mortals can not imagine all the wonders, the gifts and the power of almighty God. For years I've been told that the phrase "sons of God at the beginning of the Bible and the "sons of God at the end of the Bible (that we become) and the ones in the book of Job each mean different things. Why would anyone of sound mind believe or make up such nonsense. God is not given to double talk. I believe simply that when God says, "sons of God," he means "sons of God," each time he speaks it. Unless the book plainly states something different, why not believe the Book? I stand on the fact that God knows what he's talking about, even if I don't understand it all. Just who are these "sons of God?" They are clearly men of flesh and blood like you and I, who have and can mate with humans here on earth. Angels are not given in marriage we are told, and sons of God are spoken of separately from the angels in scripture. In the Bible "Sons of God" work for God and report directly to God. They are governed directly by God just as we will be in the kingdom of God here on earth. In fact we become or will be called "sons of God" ourselves. We saints become men who are in the condition of being full heirs with Christ Jesus. We will be with Christ during his thousand year reign from Jerusalem and then in the New Jerusalem when the Earth will be made new. Is the New Jerusalem heaven? Or will saints be in "the heavens" long before that during the earthly reign of Jesus. What might we be able to get done in a thousand years on earth with Jesus himself teaching and showing the way? Will Jesus be concerned, or worried about population control, or global warming? I think not! We will be living in new glorified bodies like King Jesus. Can we pretend to even imagine? Jesus stated plainly that he has many flocks; (plural) that we do not know of. Men have questioned this. I don't question the Lord. Who are we to do so? Are these unknown flocks in the same zone, or even in the same realm, are they on earth? Truth is only that they exist and we "don't know" of them. Our holy Bible states plainly that God created everything, also that the days since Adam started is about six thousand years ago, and that one day soon everything will be "made new" again. That every mountain will be moved and there will be no more sea. This New World starts and we go with Jesus all after the one thousand year reign of Jesus here on earth. Saints live in the New Jerusalem not needing the sun or the moon or stars. Is this world our first, second, or third time around, would we know? Modern science claims they have found very old bones, and fossils in the earth. Jesus speaks knowing the end of this age as the knowing of the coming of the seasons. What do seasons do? We know of course that they cycle, that they repeat. We know that the angel tries his best to imitate God. To take God's place and that he wants to go "to the heavens" as of the most high. Maybe that's what God does, this appears so. We also know that God uses his "son of God" who report back to him as they did in the book of Job. We also know that "sons of God" are of flesh, and are something other than angels. Maybe if Moses said that something flew before them that shinned like burnished brass dah, maybe it did. When Abraham said he talked to "three men" who ate with him, who were of God, and talked to him about God! Maybe Abraham was not a nut, and told the simple truth. Moses told us that no man could see God's face and live. Jesus said that God the father is a spirit to worship him we must do so in spirit and truth. Jesus was and is God made flesh. Who were these men Abraham talked to? Jesus said his kingdom was not of this world, that he came from heaven.

When God, took animal skins and made Adam and Eve clothing, did he do so by zapping or speaking them into being or was there a process? Could he have ordered his servants his angels, or his "sons of God" to make them? I do not know how God made the clothes, it does not matter. The book of Job does tell me that the "sons of God" rejoiced at God's creation, and that they took wives of earthly women. They are not angels and not Gods, but report to God. One day the Bible says that we saints become and are called "sons of God." I do know for sure that God uses weak, broken and very imperfect beings to accomplish his will. I know this because he uses me. Just like an earthly father training up and then turning over his work to his son, God must limit himself in order to give me work to do. If God has used you as a tool in this world then you know this truth already. I pray that my God allows me to work for him through out eternity, maybe by sewing some skins together for another Adam and Eve in a different flock, in a different season somewhere in his endless infinite universe. God has never needed my help, or anybody else. God backs out and empowers you and me only by limiting himself. He gives jobs over to us because he loves you and I. God has to use and employ weaker vessels than him self simply because he is the almighty. God could have zapped my lecture into your minds tonight in a moment if he wished to do so. God would have done a perfect Job, I have not, but I have done my best. Praise his Holy name My God has allowed me to speak of him, allowed me to work as his servant. This is the highest honor and blessing given to any man. Friends my point is not complicated. The sons of God in Genesis are the same ones as the sons of God we become in the end! I plan to become a "Sons of God", a joint heir in Christ! Do You? If you are here tonight and don't look forward to being sons of God then you are not a saint of God, You are not a born again Christian. You have no place in Gods coming kingdom. God has no half price ticket. We are either a full heir with Jesus or lost and without God. Yes Jesus told the truth about hell and damnation. Jesus made this point clear. Saints are not perfect, but become perfect only by being washed in the blood, and redeemed by Christ. Sons of God are not Gods, they are not perfect when they report to God they sometimes need correcting. Their work is not always easy, but they do have the peace of walking and communing with God. God of course also has angels in his heaven, God can build and use as he wishes. God has only one begotten son. Jesus Christ is a name above every name. We are adopted into Gods family. His spirit dwells in both Saints and "Sons of God". I believe God had "Sons of God" working for him back in the time of Genesis.

Many so called religious leaders laugh at me, many also condemn me and my so called aliens, or space men of the Bible. I say believe God, not me, do not limit God. Why did Jesus say to his disciples? Do not stop them from preaching just because they are not of us. If they are not against us then they are for us. How many seasons of man has there been? How many flocks are out there? How many times has God made everything new? Jesus did so much for us even during his time in the tomb. He defeated hell, and the grave. Then he ascended (in the flesh) to his father. What about these other flocks, are some of them already "Sons of God" as we will be one day. Could some of them still be in the Garden of Eden? Look into God's heaven. I do not pretend to know for sure. Will God condemn me for asking foolish questions? Suffer me the fact that Jesus may have many worlds, or flocks, that we are not alone in this universe. If the story I found in sand scrip writings be true history or be fiction or a story from hell, I know not. I am not a wise man, just a saint working out my own salvation with fear and trembling before God.

The story I discovered is one of the En's, Gods workers in Eden. These "sons of God were relatives to Enos, Enock, and Ephraim. They looked for a place, a temporary base or home. A land on earth that was separate and defendable if necessary from early man, who was now out of the Garden and separated from God. They did not want to be too far from "The City" the rock. The sight of their first landing, Jerusalem! Their time on earth was known to be ending but they had not been picked up. God would not always strive directly with man. Man now had to be redeemed. Genesis 6-3

My spirit shall not always strive with man, for he is also flesh! Yet his day shall be a hundred and twenty years!

Another group of God's early workers or "Sons of Gods" came to live and work in the South Seas, the Isles of the South Pacific. God was not pleased, he had this group leave first, and did not let them abide as long in the Earth as did the En's, up in what is now called England. The En's picked what is now the British Isles for their short season of stay (over a hundred years). These ancient workers for God were ruled by and worshiped God. They were not Gods nor were they angels. They were imperfect men who walked with God, just as you and I will be one day in the one thousand year long reign of Christ from Jerusalem. They were working for God in this realm just as angels fight battles, and work for God in the spirit plane. Some were the founders of ancient Egypt. The sons of God have boundaries and they do make mistakes. They report to God and some do better than others, this is for some reason part of God's plan. How were Pharaoh and his priests able to "keep up" with Moses and Gods plagues, against Egypt? The first four they repeated also, that was pretty good I think! What does the math of the basic pyramid shape say to us? The Great pyramid had a two fold purpose. It is or was a giant water pump. The very top was not all stone like the rest. When a fire was lit a huge siphon was started. The high water of the Nile in flood season came right up to the Sphinx. From there it was pumped to a high under ground cavern and pumped back to the sphinx during the growing season. This food supply plenty helped kick start the early Egyptian culture. The early pharaohs were En's and half breed En's and God was not happy with them The other two pyramids did not pump water they were built by later generations as a star map, much later after most decedents of the original En's were gone! If America knew and could see under the great desert of Africa, and what all is covered with sand, then they would know that God is their only keeper, and is where all blessings come from. America could be in a same like desert in a very short time.

The En's were wise to pick Ireland and England for their stay. The channel the cliffs of Dover the fall back position of Ireland with its back against the raging North Sea, still works today. England's natural defend ability has saved them in modern times just as it did in ancient wars. Yes Syria, and the Islamic world fighting Jerusalem and England both goes way back to before recorded time. History is waves of time repeating reflections of its self always coming back full circle like the circle of fifths.

Look at chapter six for the math of the pyramid, and also the six pointed Jewish star. The seven spheres in a plane (with one at center) plus the six needed to form the sphere when placed in a plane form the Jewish Star. The Jewish star stands for God becoming a man, from a perfect sphere six balls join the plane to form it. This is Gods covenant with Abraham. The math of the pyramid is of man and the Carbon Atom. Look at the simple three sided triangle, and the true four sided pyramid built of the closest stacking of spheres . . . . . *Cornelius started dozing off.*

The lecture lasted over four hours, I went to the bathroom during part of this stacking billiard balls part. I was never very good at math anyway. I have tried to read the part about the number twenty six and the golden mean squared approaching it but never getting there. I still don't understand the math. The Golden mean is about 1.614, it comes from ratios in the Bible, the Ark, the temple, etc. I didn't buy professor Whitt's book that evening but Tommy Mute did. I did buy his book later, on another island. I then would buy two in fact. I hope you are smarter than me on this math stuff, although I do get part of it. Sometimes we just don't know the basics! After the lecture I walked by myself through Pearl Harbor. I had to get away from loud Lou Goodliar for a while. I needed some solitude to keep my own sanity. I enjoyed the professors preaching, he did get me thinking but being in a crowd gives me the creeps after awhile, if you know what I mean. I strolled along the Harbor water front just taking my good sweet old time, and enjoying the fresh air. My eyes soon gazed upon one of the most beautiful sail boat yachts I'd ever seen. The type that is so big you wonder how they manage to sail her. As I drew closer oh how majestic she stood, and so close to the shore. At the pier now I could see the boats stern. The name Windy was written in fancy gold script! I stopped in my tracts. I knew this boat from Sydney! I also heard a loud voice calling "Cornelius." A tall guy smiling with a drink in his hand was waving for me to come aboard.

I walked out on the pier and up the ships gang plank where an old friend met me at the top saying "Welcome aboard Cornelius." He was Seaman's First Mate Franklin A. Donner. We were shipmates from way back in the old U.S. Navy days. Bo and Don Dave the Hogg Lady, one of the Johnston twins, and even a son of professor Whitt were all on the sail boat having a party. Franklin served very good food. Most people at the party, just like Daniel and Double De had all been at the Coe estate in Australia. They told me that Ann's kids had just left, so had Ralph from the space port! Wow! What a party, they poured lots of red wine. Bo and Don sounded great! Mike and Greg from the flight in the outback were both playing music with Bo and Don. This was crazy, I thought to myself! I know all of these people, what's the odds of that I wondered?

After partying many hours into the midmorning's night, I stumbled my way down the harbor towards the Great Ark. My mind was spinning, not only from red wine and professor Whitt's lecture, but now all those people on Frank A. Donners big sail boat. This ole' Cornelius was very glad to be off duty in the morning. I would need the time to sleep in. Partying with Bo and Don can wear a

person out. Sometimes you just don't know. Maybe life is just like the number twenty-six, maybe I would never understand all this stuff?

One full day later the Great Ark set sail leaving two months before the great name change. Pearl Harbor would be renamed the Osoma Islamic Bay Bird Refuge. I wondered if I would ever make it back this way again. The ship now carried a full crew of one thousand nine hundred and forty five seamen, plus one thousand four hundred students. Not quite a full dorm. Some like Daniel and Double De had flown home after Pearl. We did pick up some more old folks at the last minute many of them were "over flow Jews" just looking for a room. A bargain price on the trip of a lifetime looks mighty good when you are homeless; come sail on the Great Ark!

The Gospel Café student group on board was from New Mexico. Their music was called Christian Country Western. They had a lady singer; she was younger than me but not a student, she was middle age. Her husband was her manager and ran sound. She sang but also did one woman Biblical plays. This lady was a younger, more talented Christian much prettier, thinner, darker haired version of Hillary Clinton. Do not tell her I said this, she is very sensitive to any comparison to Hillary Clinton. Her stage name was simply Mia. She had a pleasant personality, and a charming nature. She was truly a treasure. Mia turned out a lot of free Christian music downloads and was very popular with long haul truckers. Her band with its singing steel guitar was very good even without her. When she joined in with them the mixture was magic. Mia's golden voice would have people standing in the doorways as they walked by on deck. Her husband David and I became close friends and could often be found sitting and talking together between music sets at the ships Gospel Café.

End of Chapter six.

CHAPTER SEVEN

Taco Station

The Great Ark approached the coast of Mexico only once. That's when a cobra chopper landed plus sixteen bug like drones. I knew we were back at war. The killing machine was about to start back up again. My heart sank at the thought of more bloodshed. Our ship held back from shore two hundred miles as if there was a magic line in the sea. Our drones patrolled the vast American southwest desert and Mexico with huge drop tanks of fuel. They were looking for many small targets. Once our prey was found they would punch hard and quick killing small and large groups of people at will. Drones used light guns based on m16 rifle ammunition not heavy cannons. No use wasting big expensive bullets on women and children.

Mexico was a land at war, of revolution, but not so for us aboard ship. There was nothing on the evening news so this war did not even exist (ha-ha). All shootings and killings that did "get out" were blamed on drug sellers. We on ship were in a world to ourselves. Often our flight sorties were slack and we pilots were growing slow and lazy, not on top of our game. Ship protection patrols by B48s or B44s were routine and uneventful. We left the "dirty work" to the robot killing planes endlessly scanning the desert. Some of the damage assessment photos and reports were so deadly bloody and shocking that any godly mans heart would get sick and revolt.

The old land owning families of Mexico's government elite had tripled their price now that America was charging per head for restitution. I guess social democrats did not need to buy any more votes. America was broke, and could not afford any more "Cats." The term "Cats" was a pop-culture street lingo, and had now turned pilot lingo for run away Mexican slaves. Some say (Central American Terminated Slave) others say (Civil Action Taco Snuff) whatever or combination of it works for you. We earned our keep during our short nine week stay at Taco Station we totaled twenty-four thousand confirmed "Cats." Captain Coe said it was over thirty thousand but many did not meet confirmation criteria, and I believe him. Joe got a plaque for his office wall from Osoma's Justice Department, not only for our high killing numbers but for our new "Beetle Bombs." Our crew had first tested the New "Beetle Bombs" in Africa. Now we had perfected this green environmentally friendly clean up technology. Bags of Beetles would multiply quickly when given a solid food source (dead flesh). Our beetles could strip dead and dying bodies laying in the desert quickly, eating one third of the bones and one half of the clothing. Bags of human only poison and fake water stations also brought us praise. These insects could destroy evidence and clean up the desert behind us thus stopping the spread of disease to innocent people or animals. American officials demanded that we burn hydrogen fuel and drop no empty tanks, so as not to spoil the desert while trying to save it! We were paid $30,000 per Cat from Mexico City plus a bonus from Washington and some states. The ship was paid over $40,000 per "Cat." No mercy was shown to run away Mexican serfs and slaves trying to escape. The "Cats" problem was seen as a Catholic Church tragedy, forced upon the Elite. The facts are that anywhere you have democratic socialist tyrants in charge the killing will follow like stink on you know what. Socialist economies always need to kill off the excess (unsold) man hours of serfs and slaves to keep themselves in business. Productivity and innovation both always die out quickly under central planning. These flourish and grow only in capitalism and free markets. The poor economic efficiency of the slave system demands the death of the most costly. When an elite group gains power and gets to decide the good of the many out weighs the cost to the few then the rights of the few are lost. Death is always the strange fruit of the Socialist Humanist tree. Death is always where ungodly men and their evil priests lead their foolish sheep. Death is the end result of rebellion against God. Leaders like Bill Ayers, Osoma, Castro, Hitler and Mao. Death is their calling card. This is business, nothing personal. Here on the Great Ark we are just the hired game wardens doing the bidding of the current elite in power.

Most of my flight time at Taco Station was spent on boring ship protection patrols. I thanked God every day that I didn't have to shoot the escaping Mexican peasants in person. I tried to put it all out of my mind; it wasn't my fault I didn't vote for Osoma! Anyway, I'm just doing my job, following orders! One popular "Beetle Bomb" video showed numerous beetles feeding on one small child's body such that it rapidly moved across the sand until it seemingly sat up against some vegetation and waved. The weight of this small body was completely picked up and covered by the large hungry black beetles feeding on it and was horrific to watch. This video kept being sent to my ship phone by other pilots with a "have you seen this one note" It made one sick to the stomach.

During one of my many Gospel Café big round corner table nights during this period I waxed words with college professor missionary and now friend Tommy Mute over strong Irish coffee. He was a joy to debate and much better than most professor eggheads. Tommy liked to say the phrase "Blessed by the Best" so often that students would shout it out when greeting him. He truly did know God. Tommy did not have much to say when Lou Goodliar was around him. He worked under "Loud Lying Lou" This was the student nickname for Lou in the college B.S. degree program. I learned that night from Professor Mute that in all of Canada and America there were only three elders on the great world committee of twenty-four. In Mexico alone there were also three elders a lopsided imbalance of power by wealthy long term province (slave camp) owners in Mexico. Professor Mute knew of two elders in England, two in the rest of Europe, One joint Japanese and Malaysian citizen, one Saudi Royal, one half Russian-Georgian citizen, Three in China, two in India (one that is Jediah's Uncle) and Mr. Child the only known Jewish Elder. Tommy guessed that the Pope might be on the list but the rest were completely unknown. The only way to gain this level of wealth in this world is Kingly tyrannical power, with government condoned slave camps lasting hundreds of years. Free men trading with each other and forming large corporations will not lead to this level of power. A Trillion dollars or two is required to start much less play or to win this game. A Billionaire is just a want to be player a millionaire is a poor small business man. Tommy Mute didn't know much about the number twenty six, or the circle of fifths. He did say something about the Golden mean, and like I said before he did know God. Tommy talked a lot about helping Africa and that the true church had not given up on Africa. Environmentalist world wide had decided that it was necessary that all Africans must die! They had to die to save the planet and all the rest of us. Osoma had sped up the African killing process much to the thrill of European Elite Socialist leaders. Africa would be a wilderness preserve and a vacation destination for the rest of the world. While talking to Tommy Mute that night I knew that my time on the Great Ark must come to an end. My life was unpleasing to God. I was glad to be holiness and knew I had to change my life. God had answered my prayers and now I could see truth but could I handle the truth? Part of me wanted to shut my eyes and turn away, but that would greave the spirit of God living within me. I was in torment. That evening my table was overflowing with students. Many did not want to hear about "Cats" some did not believe the story. The stinking blood and guts of war was unreal to them. Most would not face it; "that has nothing to do with us anyway" students would say. They could not face the ugliness of Osoma their hero because it would reflect poorly on them. Just like Hitler's Germany the big lie and Government education does work and will hide evil for a season.

Cornelius started the lesson, he spoke ever so softly.

Mexico has never been a real country at all. It has been since colonial days a huge Indian reservation, or rather sixteen separate Indian reservations or slave camps owned by eighty families of Spanish Royal and or wealthy Merchant class birth. These royal families owned and divided up everything in Mexico. Land serfs, water rights anything of value. The Royal families used gold or dollars between themselves and educated themselves to English. The serfs or "Indians" the native suckers were paid in Paso's and were always spoken to in Spanish, the Language of the poor peasant and of the slave. The Paso is a worthless "company store" currency good for buying things only in the local store owned by the Spanish Lords. The so called Mexicans worked for starvation wages while riches piled up in the Royal land owning families. This way of life is modeled after the old European serf system, very close to the cast and slave systems of India and China. The large ranches and agricultural plantations gave way to large industrial plants and shanty towns. Nothing much has changed. America was different! Notice that no large stream of immigrants flooded to Mexico. No! They had to enslave the native Indians. Yes, America was different! Here the old ways of Europe were broken down by the New Christian Education and its beliefs, where bible study was allowed, and the value of a man as equal under God. Also the cheap endless abundant close by good land and a central government that gave away land for a long time to bring immigrants in. This later became the forty acres and a mule deal that helped to break the back of serf systems in America. The land give away was short lived (as always). We should start it up again today. The central government is now the leading problem in America instead of fighting the problem. The central Government still owns most of the land in America. This is a human tragedy and a major earmark of tyranny and corrupt abuse of power. The American central Government owning land in common and then dispensing it to non-royals was one of the earliest and shortest lived communist revolutions (they always fail) in History. Yes my friends there is more than one road to serfdom. That is why freedom is so rare and so precious. Now with the Osoma government and the fall of America into a standard European style democratic socialist fascist government. Plus the end of both Catholic and independent Christian education and all basic beliefs of the teachings of God; the last hope of a free republic on earth has now sunk slowly and quietly into history. Note it was not boys fighting in a field that changed history, or killed freedom. No, it was the failure of fathers to teach the ways of God to their children. A free republic can only stand with a Bible educated free public. When Government takes over the education system the fall of freedom is at hand. All false religious teachers know this and practice it always planning on taking control by the next generation. Yes, the hand that rocks the cradle does rule the world, this is truth and it always works. This is chapter one in every ungodly worldly Lords, "How to Take Over, Hand Book" The central government should have no role in K-12 education at all. This is simply much too dangerous! In serf systems like Mexico peasants can be brainwashed easily. Remember this fact; ruling class elites know what they are doing and must claim power for minimal cost or face going out of business. If hard working Mexican slaves get undercut in price by starving Chinese slaves the Mexican elite can devalue the Paso or raise the rent (they own everything) or raise taxes or raise prices in the company store. The only way out of this endless poverty and servitude is to make a run for it and brave the harsh desert to join another system. Run to America and become an Englishmen. The sad true facts of the matter is that slavery and brainwashing from birth is so very effective that masters still control slaves after they flee. Masters often use family members still in slavery as a hook. Most people in America have no idea that Mexicans, just like the Chinese cannot freely move from one province (slave camp) to another. They are owned by the owners of that camp. The Government puts check points on all the roads to see who is going where. "Does this sound familiar Americans?": Imagine the laughs of the elite

Mexican families and the socialist democrats in Washington when the few slaves that make it through the long dangerous desert run, then take to the streets of America waving not little flags of Freedom but rather the Flag of the old slave camp owners back home that they just escaped from. These slaves refuse to give up their Spanish slave tongue. Their young men are working hard all over America and saving up not to buy a computer or a real education but to buy shiny rim wheels and fat chrome tail pipes. Even second and third generation Mexicans still act like the barefoot slum kids on the big Mexico City trash piles. Their simple eyes are still on shiny objects and worthless junk. Brown is as Brown does! "The Race," are you serious (Ha-ha). What kind of race are you Latino boys in? Your votes for Osoma have overturned the American lifeboat that was your last chance for freedom. Yes after four hundred years of poverty and Spanish tyranny, you fools voted in the masters that you just ran away from. You voted in mass to bring old style European Socialism to America; the one damn thing proven to create poverty and misery. You are "The Race" alright; the race of slaves of and by your own hand. Now Osoma has started his safety check points across America just like back home in Mexico. Now there are official government papers and police pat down and searches, just like back home in Mexico. Not to mention anti-gun laws, anti-free speech laws, and open voter fraud. Also polling place intimidations that are not prosecuted and even trained for and encouraged by and paid for by Osoma with tax money. The systematic cold blooded killing of the very old the very sick, and the very weak. The use of broad civil commitment laws, based on the testing by the priests from a false religion called Humanism. These so called doctors can imprison anyone at anytime without a trial, or even a charge. Trial by jury is so rare as to be lost to most citizens. Dare I forget all of the anti-church, anti-ten commandments, and anti-Jewish laws and of course the worship of the earth and Mother Nature? These are the buds and seeds of every socialist, communist government. Oh, I forgot the attack on marriage, morality, and the family through pornography and homosexuality. All of this has been seen before. We know what this bush grows up to be like. History has proven this fact over and over again. Ungodliness, turning against Israel, trade with slave states, counterfeiting of the currency, the hatred of individual freedom and success, love of self, the perversion of homosexuality and rebellion against God has brought down destroyed and sunk America. All the while our king Osoma has been smiling like a retard pirate as America slipped beneath the waves."

One of my young students Kishia Fernandez was having a small nervous breakdown. Hearing truth can do that to a person. It opens up eyes to dirt and can be very uncomfortable. Tommy Mute put his hand on my arm and poured me a cup of Irish coffee. We old timers stayed and talked into the night about banking and currency while the students went off to bed.

Flying patrol off Taco Station was slow paced but always enjoyable. Lord knows I love to fly these fast little hot rods of the sky. I should quit the Ark and try to break my contract but we "Patty and I" so much needed the ending or balloon bonus pay. Oddly enough I could still get the bonus if terminated, killed, or injured, but not if I quit. During these slow patrols I would leave my student wing man and drop below our hard deck to count whales. This was very much against the rules and First Officer Friday was hounding me relentlessly. His anger knew no bounds. The veins on his neck made very odd strange movements, he was really very impressive. Buzzing fishing boats and cruise ships was also great fun. An Artist friend from back home Mr. Mike Finch was painting the side of cruise ships and was very much in the news lately. I was able to find the ship and loved to buzz him as he worked painting giant pictures of Osoma. Mike had won a government grant. Osoma loved giant pictures of himself. The cruise lines were under public attack for exit paperwork violations. One ship with over six hundred Jews on it had been turned around and confiscated, Osoma said his administration saved America over one billion dollars in lost wealth just from that one ship alone. France would not let the ship fuel or dock. If France had, those sell out Jews would have gotten off Scott free. This show of force against the Jews who were causing much of America's swift economic collapse was what got Osoma elected the second and third time around. Yes that, and also the curious timing of his beloved wife's shooting. She bravely pushed her girls aside and took part of a birdshot shotgun blast in the butt by shielding her husband just ten days before the vote! The gunman was a white racist preacher who hated the poor Palestinians and all blacks. This Preacher had not allowed a popular black rapper to sing in a youth service at his church in Brooklyn. The preacher was the father of a policeman shot to death by this rapper two years earlier. No charges were ever filed even though his popular song bragged about the killing. Now this preacher's Youth Family Center named in honor of his son had been fire bombed and painted with the rappers gang symbols on the front door. The popular rapper was at a big White house dinner when this tragic attack happened. Osoma's popular wife being shot and in ICU on election day stirred white guilt so much that he was narrowly put back into office. The evil preacher gunman was shot to death in the Whitehouse vegetable garden, a lucky almost impossible shot at that distance some shot gun experts say. How this nut case ever got an official invitation is still under investigation by park police and a Justice Department task force with Barnie Frank as its heavyweight chairmen.

The very next day while on flight duty again I tried Mike Finch's cell number just before I dove on his cruise ship. I was playing around trying to force the new B48 to break the sound barrier in a steep dive; so far without success. By playing around too much I got so close to the ship that my planes anti-collision computer took over control of the plane. My back hurt like hell for days. Mike's phone picked up but he did not have connection long enough to talk. Mike is a talented artist but always falls hopelessly in love with really stupid, crazy, women. You know the type. His giant size picture looked pretty good but it is hard to tell going seven hundred miles per hour. Just like Mao, Castro, Hitler, and Stalin, Osoma loved spending public money on "Art" meaning of course giant pictures of himself. At least Anthony Weiner is not president (ha-ha). The depths of depravity and shame of all humanist socialist democrats seems bottomless endless and is always disgusting. I was glad to see Mike gaining fame and recognition for his years of hard work. My friend deserves success even if it is with government money.

Joe was getting many complaints about my fooling around. Officer Booth warned me that Friday was fuming mad but nothing was ever said. I had invested my sign up bonus and now needed that ending bonus check. I just could not manage to get myself fired, no matter how mad I got Friday. Ole' First Mate Friday often mentioned how proud it made him feel as a Black man to vote for Osoma. This was one of the greatest days of his life, he would say. Don't start Cornelius, just walk away; the man is mentally ill. I guess he picks everything in life by color! Friday the man is half and half! How could color be an issue anyway? Oh never mind; never argue with a brainwashed idiot because they don't even know that they don't know.

During this slow easy deployment off of Taco Station many of us had extra time for Holy Bible study, and also many late nights at the ships Gospel Café. Oh how I loved that country western sound with its singing steel guitar. During this time I also started having long talks with Captain Joe Coe. He wanted to retire, said he would become a minister. Joe? Are you sure about this calling? Look at your life!

"Look at yourself Cornelius" said Joe Coe "You say you want to work for God and sing Gospel Music with your girl back Home, Patty I believe is her name. Hell Cornelius the smoking gun is still in your hand Mr. Fly Boy hot shot.

That night I thought about what Joe had said and got out the fireball candy on my desk trying to figure this math stuff out. That number twenty six, what made it so special? I just could not understand the math book. I sat in solitude at my desk thinking and praying.

War is hell but my life was a world apart. Life was good on the Great Ark. We pilots flew fast planes our food and red wine was great. Holy Bible study was enjoyable and the Gospel Café was a constant comfort. On the other hand down in the desert there was a hot sweaty bloody killing floor. For these stray "Cats" those poor Mexican runaways' days were full of fear, hunger, despair and death. The killing paid well, Mexico City and Washington plus some states all paid blood money. The Mexican slums were breeding grounds that put out an enormous flood of unsold human capital each month. Mexican landlords considered them unwanted mouths to feed, not a valuable economic asset. Every Mexican "Cat" that was proved dead was worth its weight in silver at least. I thanked God I didn't have to shoot the Mexicans in person. Most people on ship gave the matter of the killing drones little or no thought. I tried not to think of the horror, the smell the Beetle Bombs. Hell their own people wanted them dead not me. Not me!

That night at the Gospel Café young student Kishia Gonzalez was back at my table. Why were so many of the young students named Kishia? This Kishia was a very pretty dark skinned girl who talked, walked and dressed like a California Valley girl" wanna be. Her date was a tall officer trainee with big white Kennedy smile and teeth. Drinks were ordered and "Old school" started up class.

Remember my friends, you have been lied to and lied to very often. Just like a mirror the truth often requires a second look and is backward from what you have been taught! Learn to think! Do not follow elite masters like sheep. For example listen to that popular add telling everybody to buy gold on the radio; there is some wisdom in buying gold but look again. Why does this man advertise to sell his gold to you? If buying gold is so smart then why is he selling? Live and die as free men and women under God. The truth is many elite ungodly leaders consider it their right to enslave you. Yes, sadly enough, this is "the way" of the world throughout all of history. This is not God's way or God's will for your life. In a free market system how many Psychologist or Psychiatrist doctors would find gain full employment per one million persons? How many have you ever freely paid for their services your self? This group of egghead nut jobs uses the government to empower themselves as the secular priesthood for and of humanism. They work very little,(they are lazy) do even less good, bill very high and pretend to tell the rest of us what is truth. When a disaster strikes a school building the so called "grief counselors" descend like locus on a town much faster than the real clean up crew does. The smell of free government money always brings these worthless flies. Money Government does not have is quickly spent for services not asked for, not needed, or wanted. This all to pay false priests who don't know what the hell their talking about anyway and often do more harm than good. Our modern day witch doctors are no better than the ones in every ancient pagan tribe. They are part of the slave system, empowered by tyranny, and a blood sucking leach on society.

The key to being a successful Lord or slave owner is to rule subjects at least cost. Successful masters of this world are very good at what they do. Beware, open your eyes. Why would run away slaves from Mexico come to America for a better life and then wave flags of the slave camp Indian reservation that they just escaped from. This is only one example of effective government education and brainwashing. One recent black conservative presidential candidate dared mention the brainwashing of blacks in America and was destroyed by the state controlled media. They simply said that he had a girl friend, and made advances toward women, and this evil man was booed off the campaign trail, the accusations never proven. Compare this to the near worship of Martin Luther King, Jack Kennedy and Bill Clinton. These three men's known and documented whores count in the hundreds. When was the last news story you heard about their sex addiction or sickness. Most Americans, much less black Americans have no idea for example that Mexican Citizens cannot move around freely with out going through check points, or that the old Soviet Union under communism used slavery just as China does today. Now safety check points have come to America! When searches at airports started here in America there should have been a revolution. Freedom must always be protected. Freedom, not safety, comes first. The words home of the brave should be taken out of our song. Americans are sheep just like the rest of the world.

Look at the history of Max a Million a nicer tyrant than the lords that followed. He was looking for help from Abraham Lincoln. This is a sad story about the deep roots of old world ways and weeds growing in Mexico. Serfdom grew up partly because the great American Southwest desert formed a natural barrier to migration. This lowered the cost of the serf "slave camp" system. Let us look now at American blacks so as not to "pick on" the Mexican peasants unfairly while we are shooting them by the thousands here at Taco Station. It just doesn't seem right.

The history of black people in America is a text book example of successful brain-washing of an underclass by their lords and masters. This brainwashing can be broken only by true, honest Christian based education. Brainwashing is kept in place by elite controlled government education and a state controlled media. Remember students; rulers of this world know what they are doing, elite groups lie on purpose to fool their charges, their suckers, or their mark just like the devil does. Let us step back and take a look. Why do modern day American blacks (since government education) always vote in robot clockwork like lockstep for the party of George Wallace and famous Klu Klux Klan leader Bird of West Va. Always voting against the party of Lincoln? Many American Blacks are very sympathetic to both communism and Islam compared to the rest of the population. Most blacks don't know their own history such as the fact that civil rights laws were passed by republican votes in congress not by socialist democrats, or that Martin Luther King was a republican and that he was spied upon constantly by government agents working for the democratic presidents in power and very likely killed by them.

With the help of the "big lie" controlled media, government controlled dumbed-down schools and greedy crooked ungodly black leaders the Negro population has been played for the fool in mass. Even today half of the black men can't read and write. This is the hard cold facts. You can fool most American blacks most of the time; this is the party motto of the democrats (sorry Lincoln). How this racist ruling elite was able to fool most blacks to vote for the democratic candidate; how these mostly uneducated people were led to disdain real education as "white" even today is a long sad story of colossal human arrogance on one side and record ignorance on the other. This has been a sad testimony to the natural gullibility of human nature and an inspiration to elite racist snobs all over the western world. European racist socialist are now so envious of the Kennedys' and their democratic party's success in controlling the "black man" that they can't stand it. They can hardly see straight.

My great, great grandfather one Doctor Bell wrote some papers for the Eugenics movement back in Virginia. The Eugenics movement was a fore runner in thought to Nazi Germany, and also gave birth to a killing machine organization unequaled in all of human history. They named it "Planned Parenthood" a big lie successful cover story for the record books. It is the world's best "big lie" to date. Their purpose was simple! Just as socialist humanist leaders always do was to kill off undesirables. This was defined as "blacks, the old, half breeds of any type, retards and the sickly. The Planned Parenthood office or (killing chamber) was always built in or convent to unwanted minority neighborhoods and most are still there today. The medical standards for these offices did not have to meet the strict standards of other medical facilities. Abortion clinics have their own laws. Free (come kill your baby) abortion services were always offered to willing poor blacks. Poor dirty little white girls had to pay, but only if the baby was a "good one." This paid for the program and kept it going. The killing chambers have been wide open and successful for many years yes killing off many blacks. Years ago it was projected that blacks would be over 20% of U.S. population by now. But now blacks are still only 13%. This was a tremendous success for elite racist democrats. The evil Democratic Party leadership is so sure of itself that it now pours tax money in to the Planned Parenthood scam speeding up the killing process. Can you imagine getting the Jews to vote for Adolf Hitler? This is how stupid American blacks have been, all because of brainwashing. The next control method was outright voter fraud and intimidation, also the undermining of black churches, and black families by free token gifts. Free muffins at school for breakfast, free surplus government bought cheese. Food stamps and or free rent a welfare check, all free but only if daddy is gone. With the Bible and family destroyed, brainwashing and slavery follows.

Owning his own business was a black mans main chance to gain middle class status in America. For many years slow steady progress was made. Basic business skills and Godly training in finance were and are still laughed at even to this day in government educated black communities. Most often the local small business in a black community is owned by other population groups. Why?

Now here comes the national Democratic Socialist party a long time minority party among working Americans with an elite Islamic, one half black Fascist socialist Osoma candidate. Could he pass the smell test? Who would take the bait? First the controlled TV news quietly brought him out on the main stage and waited. Small positive stories were passed out about a charming new leader. Up and coming they called him. The Media painted and dressed their boy Osoma at each opportunity. All negative or true venting stories were kept off the major "yes sir" air waves and channels. No stories of girl friends for Osoma! A few AM radio "hate" jocks sounded the alarm but their lonely voices soon lost the media war to the "big lie media." Osoma was black, tall and could speak or at least read clear English, just what the doctors ordered. Also he wasn't "ace of spades black" a spoon full of cream and sugar would help the medicine go down. Yes powerful men had found their candidate and money rained down from heaven. That is if Bill Ayers and Chicago Mobsters really are angels sent down by God. Well these powerful ruling elite class snobs might not be angels. They might even be ungodly and evil men but they do know their business which is lying, and not letting the truth out. They are also good fishermen and waited just right to set the hook.

Osoma was a difficult devil to hide his horns and tail obvious to any free thinking breathing not blind honest saint of God. Osoma wrote a book (that sounds oddly like his friend Bill) that said some truth! The Black Community grows as kept mushrooms cut off from sunlight and truth. Osoma was against everything that a strong black community should and did long ago stand for. What is a community organizer you ask? A government elite mushroom farmer it's that simple. Yes, Osoma was against everything that the old black community stood for and for their lowest scum. The "Rappers" and pervert black comedians with their balls in one hand and their microphone in the other are an embarrassment to black men everywhere and American culture in particular. I remember one foolish TV sports broadcast argue that the term "mother fucker" is not an offensive cuss word in the black community that black culture was "at that level" and the phrase should not send a player off the court. How low can you go is just "being black" now days thanks to Simmons and others who pump out record levels of filth into America and still expect to be treated with dignity and respect by God loving hard working people? Rappers should all lie down in and be smothered by their own waste just like Larry Flint and other rich white pornographers. They sold out standards to make a quick buck. Why do democrats love this pollution and hate God? Rap music's gutter mouth filth and lack of taste content or musical talent is well known. No! Osoma is no friend of American back culture or values. Candidate Osoma was an angry wanna be Harvard man who claimed to teach the constitution. That would be like an Islamic suicide bomber teaching Sunday school at Church! His biggest legislative achievement was a post-birth abortion bill. This was true infanticide at the state level. The unwanted baby is just set aside to die instead of giving it simple basic life saving doctors care. Osoma also supported the old black baby killing machine Planned Parenthood with increased funding. Is Osoma Islamic? Is he Black, or even American? I don't know, don't even care! I do know what he stands for and who supports him. He is supported by all Islamic and KKK Jew hating groups, the American communist party, socialist, anti-military, anti-church, anti-ten commandments, anti-gun, anti-free speech,(except pornography), anti-growth, pro-homosexual, anti-traditional marriage, anti-property rights, pro abortion, just what team is he on? Anything close to American hearts and values he is against. Osoma is no friend of American blacks. There is a core of Christian American blacks who are not in the crude hip-hop pop culture. Osoma was able to corrupt even them by giving them the pride of voting black (like First Mate Friday), his policies didn't matter. Many American blacks believed he was "one of them." Their old masters had won; freedom liberty and America had lost. Sadly almost every black citizen voted for their fellow "brother" and against freedom. This is the power of brainwashing!

Osoma like all successful democratic socialist politicians in history had his own voter fraud strong arm unit. His was called ACORN. Socialist must always do this (cheat on elections) because they know they must hide who they really are from voters. They know that no sane well informed free man would ever consider voting for them. They also believe that their way of "killing all the Jews for example" or "making all cars electric" or "not burning coal or oil" is necessary to save the world. A Socialist really does believe that their sick movement alone can "change" things for the better. They do after all know better than the ignorant dumb voters anyway. To maintain power, voter fraud by the "faithful" is always needed and encouraged. Of course some people might need to die, some rights lost, some property lost. The good of the many always out weighs the rights of the few.

Next Osoma openly supported strong take away the guns laws that targeted urban black communities and often referred to himself in public as a Muslim. When black Christians by the thousands every week were being killed by Muslims in Africa he sided with the Muslims. No help was sent from Osoma or the black churches. Blacks are fond of calling themselves Afro-Americans, but they don't stand for freedom. Osoma has dinned at the White House and shook hands with the same hands that have sent rockets into Israel and killed and beheaded many Christians in Africa. He has also dinned with radical bombers and filthy mouth cop killer rappers. Osoma has brought shame and death to us all. Through out history men have used gun control laws to control minorities, very much so the blacks and Indians here in America. No bigger fool has walked the face of this earth than Osoma himself. Black men who were hung on a tree while their family stood by helpless and out gunned are now turning over in their grave.

Can you hear the elite snob unseen leaders laughter and joy when Oprah helped their cause. Their ugly tar-baby false black candidate was gobbled up no matter the smell. They set the hook and held on. Right on the heels of decades of progress American blacks voted in mass to return to slavery; freedom was too heavy a yoke for them to bear. They were all willing to walk back through those "Massa take care of me" plantation gates. American blacks traded freedom and honest elections for a somewhat dark skinned President. They had believed the boob tube news, and their government school training. They were played the fool as easily as the newly American Mexican serfs.

Down in Mexico the eighty wealthy Royal families that run the slave camps must work on getting rid of the church. They must cut the cost of killing this stream of unsold labor force. Remember students, masters must operate at the least price to stay in business. The American military went out of business! That's why we here on the Ark have been contracted as game wardens. Yes, we kill with robot planes but we too are still expensive. The Pax-Americana world wide military bases were too much for the relative size of the American economy. The same problem as our own mother country of England had. The Mexicans must now use the American Osoma method, the "final solution" the "black solution." Mexico is producing two thousand unsold "Cats" every week; they must bring in the world wide cost control leader in killing Planned Parenthood. The problem is that young Latino slave girls are still so backward that they are scared of God and the church. These girls do not like the idea of killing their babies. The American Democratic Party is now helping the Mexican Lords take God out of their school system, and to destroy Latino families so abortion can become acceptable and popular. They point to their success with controlling the black population in America. Yes, let us get the Cats fixed, and kill off the poor dumb bastards at least cost. Only then can modern day slavery continue. I had to stop the lesson because time was getting late and also one of the young Kishia gals was getting upset again. I wondered if maybe I had said too much. If you don't like the truth I'm sorry it is what it is.

Ship life was slow with fewer sorties per day by drones and less manned flights also. In the next flight cycle I was again being a bad boy and playing around on the Job. I was convinced that the new B48 would or could go supersonic in a steep dive and maybe even in level flight. Something wasn't right. My plane was like a fast car with a governor not letting it go over 100 mph. I would turn off parts of the planes computer and dive as hard as I could. Each attempt I tried to keep the after burner on. I would get very close but could never break the speed of sound. That ship that Mike Finch was painting was way up the coast now. We were slowly moving south now. Tomorrow Mike would be out of range I thought to myself. Buzzing fishing boats was always a blast (ha-ha).

The next day I saw a Chinese Ark. An American carrier converted into a college. They were also killing serfs or "Cats" for hire. It just didn't seem right them killing our Mexicans. For some reason it bothered me. I learned from other pilots that there were three Chinese Arks. You could buy ships for cheap when Osoma shut down the Navy. Two more Arks were being built in China. These two sister ships would be the largest in the world. I remembered when Americans had pride like that.

We stopped or slowed down near the Panama Canal Zone and again local uncensored news from the states came through local radio. Sadly all web content was now completely controlled by world governments.

Riots were happening every day in the Panama Canal Zone. People were demanding to be included under the Communist Chinese human rights act just like the state of Hawaii was. Peking was slow to expand its influence too quickly. Osoma had cancelled his planned visit to Panama stating civil unrest. He was staying an extra day with his buddy in Venezuela instead. Government check points like those in America were used in Venezuela already. Panamas' leaders were seeking and demanding protection from Osoma and asking Peking for help because of the long Chinese presence in the Canal Zone.

The next human rights story that came in over the radio moved to one mile from my home in Roanoke; right near my wife Patty's house back home. A dozen prisoners from Panama had been shipped to a new regional jail in Salem Virginia. Salem prisoners were now also demanding Communist Chinese human rights protection. These demands were upsetting to hear. Could this be true? Could the local jail in my home town be worst on human rights violations than the Chinese Communist prison system? This was crazy, what lows had America sunk to under the rule of Osoma. America was once the shinning light on a hill. I found it all too much to believe but sat back in my desk chair and listened closely to the story. The inmates in my home town were making these demands.

(1) One hour outside every day!
(2) One visit per month by inmate's family.
(3) Not to be held after sentence had been served

None of these three rights were allowed in Salem Virginia. I was shocked! The Chinese hard core prisons had rights that the local jail back home did not. What had happened to my America? Change is what Osoma had said. The dollar had dropped another five percent that week.

In my minds eye there was still hope for America. I tried not to think of the problems back home. I wondered if any one I knew was in that Salem Jail. How could they keep you in jail when your sentence was up? What about the constitution. Maybe we could have one more honest election. Not all the votes could be stolen by ACORN, not everybody could be fooled by lies on TV. ACORN thugs had been paid billions in tax money to make sure that the democratic Osoma could not lose. Many people were too scared to vote. Osoma's Nation of Islam thugs ran the polling booths. Violence was encouraged by complete lack of prosecution and many military votes were not counted in the last election at all.

I remembered the election of 1960 during my youth. Even back then the democrats used voter fraud to put the gangster president Kennedy into office. He would be considered a conservative today. History tells us that Kennedy was never elected president. Nixon did win the election before Chicago voter fraud threw the close election to Kennedy. Even the TV debate was fixed that year. That smug asshole sixty minutes guy taught college kids for twenty years about how he purposely made Kennedy look good and Nixon look bad. He was openly teaching the craft of the big lie to younger generations of media mushroom farmers. Now another Chicago politician was refusing to prosecute Black Panther club swinging thugs at polling stations. Has anything really changed now except for the final bankrupting of America? Could you blame Nixon for spying on Democrats in a Hotel room years later at Watergate. What would you do if known mobsters and democrats were out to destroy you! He knew what they were capable of! Who is behind this long term effort? These people on the TV news and in congress or the local gang around Osoma are just not that smart. Who is pulling the stings? It must be something or someone evil and against God. God's word always stands up for life truth and freedom. Osoma and Humanist Democrats always stand against the Holy Bible. They always stand for death, confusion lies and increased government power. How could all basic rights be lost so quickly back in Salem Virginia? I always loved living in that little town. I guess inmates don't count for much just like so many other groups. Why should I care any way? I say throw away the key. I'm one of the good ones. Osama's thugs will never come after people like me (ha-ha). If you believe that my friend, then you are a fool! I've learned this much over the years. If men you meet are against Israel against free speech and against Christ. Then they are Democrats Islamic or Communist. This never fails! Wake up America we need to smell and face the truth. And remember; if ole' Cornelius tells you his pet chicken dips snuff. Then you look under its wing for the box (ha-ha). This is plain simple truth, deal with it.

CHAPTER EIGHT

◆◆◆

Crossing the Great Horn

During the next three day flight cycle I was summoned to Captain Joe Coe's office each day. Not the bridge but his office. This was odd it just didn't happen. Maybe I'll get fired and get out of my contract. I opened the office door that first day. Joe ignored my presence.

"Hello Joe," . . . . I said

"Yes Cornelius, come on in!" said Joe without looking up. "I have been reading Professor Whitt's book. Thought you might like to discuss some things. We have a special project coming up soon. You and I both need to be up to speed."

"Ok Joe," I answered.

"Before we start our Bible study lets clear the air Cornelius! GIVE UP ON THE SOUND BARRIER ATTEMPTS ALREADY!" Joe shouted. "You are using up too much fuel OK! And off the record you are right. B48 will or could do 1,145 miles per hour, mach 1.6 in high altitude flight. We know our planes Cornelius now quit fooling around.

"So why . . . . slow it down?" I asked

"A Boeing company selling point!" said Joe "People buy these planes because they're hydrogen powered and subsonic knuckle head."

"You mean I'm flying a war plane that's been purposely slowed down?" I answered, "I'm not sure I like that Joe!"

"You don't matter Cornelius. There will soon be a Peach tree Preserve in parts of Mexico, Texas and, Arizona. These people are serious about saving the Peach tree Gnat and saving Africa from human development. No sonic booms will be allowed. What's more important? Some old has been Navy pilot or saving a place for the lion to roar! Now shut up about it!

"Ok Joe" I said while shaking my head and thinking to myself (*The good of the many*) Joe then said

"Turn to Genesis four—verse 2 and read it Cornelius

And to Seth, to him also there was born a son; and he called his name E-nos! Then began men to call upon the name of the lord!

Joe then pointed at his blackboard and said,

"Notice—Seth and Enos are both (special) or different. Two things are very different about the Biblical birth record of Enos. First the Bible does not say that Adam knew his wife like all others before. The Bible does say a few verses later that Seth begat Enos. But does not say again (like all others before) who he begat. Also for some reason men started praising God or calling on God when Enos was born. Why Enos? Why him not others? Why the name Enos? Here is a question for you. What if there was an unnamed woman not named in the birth record. Notice that "sons of God" are never named and that they are sexual. We know that "sons of God" mated with earth women from the verse Genesis six. We also know that in the 1,000 year reign of Christ on earth that babies will be born on earth to humans and that these babies will have to come to know Christ as Lord before the coming down of the New Jerusalem. We also know that "sons of Gods are not angels, and that angels are not given in marriage and neither are saints in Heaven. The question is could Whitt be right? Could there have been a woman "Sons of God" during this time or not? Could it be just like us using the term mankind today to talk about both men and women? What do you think about all of this Cornelius?

"The Bible does not say, Joe. We don't know for sure. Sometimes we just don't know. Could a woman Sons of God have mated with the male, Seth? I don't know Joe" I answered.

Joe stood up saying, "Remember, Cornelius, God is attracted to and uses weaker vessels than himself. He must. We are here for <u>his</u> glory and Sons of God work for God. They are chosen for different jobs. They <u>are</u> the future. 'We' are washed by the blood, the King of Kings. Jesus is God made flesh. He still is in a glorified body. At the end of the Bible Cornelius where do we end up?"

I hesitated. "Do you mean us saints, or us sinners Captain Coe, maybe in Hell (Ha-ha)? You and me . . . . we?"

"We become 'sons of God', Cornelius," shouted Joe. "We are with Jesus. With him for one thousand years and yes, during this time, we are also given in marriage. When the thousand years is up, children <u>will</u> have been born. Then the New Jerusalem comes down and the earth is made new! Revelation 21v1-9"

I grinned "That's my favorite verse in the Holy Bible!"

(1.) **I saw a new heaven and a new earth: for the first heaven and the first earth were passed away; and there was no more sea.**

(2.) **I, John saw the Holy city, New Jerusalem, coming down from heaven, prepared as a bride for her husband.**

(3.) **And I heard a great voice out of heaven saying, behold, the tabernacle of God is with men, and he will dwell with them, and they shall be his people, and God himself shall be with them, and be their God.**

(4.) **And God shall wipe away all tears from their eyes; and there shall be no more death, neither sorrow, nor crying, neither shall there be any more pain: for the former things are passed away.**

(5.) **And he that sat upon the throne said, behold, I make all things new, and he said tome, write: for these words are true and faithful.**

(6.) **And he said unto me, It is done. I am Alpha and Omega, the beginning and the end. I will give unto him that is athirst of the fountain of the water of life freely.**

(7.) **He that over cometh shall inherit all things; and I will be his God, and he shall be my Son.**

Captain Coe speaks up "Yes and the New Jerusalem is huge. It's a space ship in the heavens and has been around for thousands of years, but it will be new to us. We won't need the earth, moon or sun. We will be with Jesus, doing what? Is this God's heaven? Or do we travel with Jesus?

"What did you say, Captain?" I asked.

"Turn to the book of Job, Cornelius" said Joe. Chapter 1:6 **now there was a day when the Son's of God came to present themselves before the Lord! And Satan came also among them!**

"Ok, Joe" I said.

Joe Coe then asked "What's another group of God's chosen workers that Satan also 'came along'? The disciples! Jesus told Peter to 'get yea behind me Satan! And of course, the whole, one of you is a devil'. Comment: the 'Sons of God' were not angels or the Bible would have said so. Satan hitched a ride <u>with</u> them to approach God. Also, the Sons of God <u>were</u> with God when God created the universe! Turn to Job 38:1-13. God is speaking to Job:

(1)   **Then the Lord answered Job, out of the whirlwind!**

(2)   <u>God:</u> **Who is this that darken counsel by works without knowledge**

(3)   **Gird up now thy loins like a man; for I will demand of thee and answer thou me!**

(4)   **Where wast thou when I laid the foundation of the earth? Declare, if thou hast understanding**

(5)   **Who hath laid the measure, there of, if thou knowest? Or who hath stretched the line upon it?**

(6)   **Where upon are the foundations of these fastened, or laid the cornerstone thereof?**

(7)   **When the morning stars sang together and all the Sons of God shouted for Joy?**

(8)   **Or who shut up the sea door, when it break forth as if it had issued out of the womb?**

(9)   **When I made the cloud the garment thereof and a thick darkness a swaddling hand for it!**
      And break up for it my decreed place and set bars and doors.
      And said, hither to shalt thou come, but no further and here shall the proud waves be stayed?

(10) **Hast thou commanded the morning since thy days, caused the spring to know his place**

(11) **That it might take hold of the ends of the earth that the wicked might be shaken out of it!**

Joe stood up and spoke. "Notice that the Sons of God are mentioned separate from angels. Notice that they work for God. They were to report before God. Did some do a better job than others? Why report? One would think so. One day the Bible says we will be called 'Sons of God'! Will we have a job to do, a time to report? Or do you believe we will play a harp forever and ever? These Sons of God are not perfect, they are not God. But rather with and governed by Lord Jesus. I believe God gives us important work to do because he loves us, even as an earthly father gives responsibility and work to his son."

"Yes Joe," I said, speaking up. "It's a good thing God uses men who are deeply flawed, that the gifts of God come before repentance. One could make a good argument that we are two of the world's worst, you and me"

Captain Coe laughed, "Speak for your self Cornelius."

Joe and I ended the night's Bible study with a memory verse for our next meeting; Jeremiah 33:3 and we were to repeat it. **Call unto me and I will answer thee, and show thee great and mighty things which thou knowest not (repeat).**

The Great Ark was moving south again. The Chinese needed no more help around the Canal Zone. Another Company ship was now at Taco station. The poor 'Cats' would get no rest. Both Washington and Mexico City were demanding more kills. The failing economy in America was hitting the Mexican slave camps hard. Buzz about the ship was the coming crossing of the Great Horn of the Americas where the oceans of the world come together with a clash of majesty and fury. Crossing the Great Horn is special in one's life. The ship's crew was looking forward to that day. I finished another flight roster; no whales to count. I didn't play any silly games, no cruise ships, no buzzing of fishing boats. I noticed that our flight deck was shut down. The next three day cycle was completely empty. No drones. No student training. No ship protection patrols; not even the mail plane. The Ark's flight deck was shut down. Life was easy on this big, floating college town, city or warship. We were slowing down. Also, old sailors like me could see evidence of land on the far horizon. For the second day now from the Canal Zone we were close to shore, most paid no mind. Once again, Captain Joe summoned me to his office, not to his bridge; again this was very rare for me.

I texted Joe back, "You had better have coffee or red wine! I'm missing my Gospel Cafe!"

While I walked down the starboard side of the ship, the fresh air and sea breeze were exhilarating. Even in the late evening, I could still see signs of land on the far horizon.

"Hello Cornelius," said Captain Coe.

"Hello Captain," I replied.

Instead of speaking, he tossed the big globe on his desk to me like a basketball. I then recited our memory verse.

"Excellent, Cornelius," said Joe. "Have you read the book of Isaiah?"

"Yeah sure I have Joe."

"Look at the globe!" Joe demanded.

"Ok," I said. "Well?"

"Look at it, Cornelius!" he sighed.

"Ok. What?" I said again.

"The Isles Cornelius point at the Isles!" asked Joe.

I pointed and said, "You must mean the South Seas, but some people might think of the British Isles, Joe."

"Good job" said Joe. "Read and study all of Isaiah again tonight. Then recite Jeremiah 33:3 and remember: As in the days of Noah. So shall it be. Jesus in the flesh will soon be here."

"Slow down, Joe," I answered. "Calm down!"

"Calm down? Did you notice that Osoma did not stop in Panama because of all the riots and the civil unrest?"

"Yes, I heard it on the local news," I said. "Osoma's men said it was too dangerous."

"Yes, Cornelius, that's my point," answered Joe. "Even a nobody like President Osoma has advance men. What about the 'King of Kings', the 'Lord of Lords'?" Joe lowered his voice. "I have a plane ready for us in the morning, a trainer with two seats. It is very light-weight. Only ¼ tank of fuel. I'm taking a chance on you, Cornelius! Do not speak of our trip!"

"Sure, Joe" I said, saluting. "No problem!"

"Have you finished reading Whitt's book?"

"Yeah Joe, I read most of it and some of it twice. It makes some sense. I still don't get all that math stuff" I replied.

"What did you learn about the Spaceport?" Joe asked.

"Well . . ." I paused. "What, Joe?"

"That some places on Earth, near the equator take less energy to land and take off from, Cornelius."

"Yeah, you're right, Joe"

"Why did God (when he strived with man) often appear on the tops of mountains?"

"Maybe it was for the solitude Joe." I suggested.

"Notice that Jerusalem and the great Pyramid are both very close to the center of land mass on earth. Both on a mountain, or high ground, and both have a sturdy, hard rock surface."

"Ok, Joe. Get to your point . . . keep going," I answered.

"What did God's chosen people do when they first entered the Promised Land? They killed giants, Cornelius! God helped them kill the giants! These giants were descendants of the 'Sons of Gods'. God promised the land to Abraham. God always keeps his promise. 'Sons of God' have boundaries and mission guidelines. They are not perfect like Jesus. They work for, and report to, God. I understand that you have a grown son, also Cornelius?"

"Yes Joe," I said.

"Then you know! Fathers step back, but then sometimes have to step in and correct, even fix, mistakes! Whitt spoke of two groups (that he knows) of 'Sons of God' who were on Earth and doing advance work. One group moved from Eden to the British Isles, where they stayed a short season. Ephraim is England! Note that E-nock was taken up like Jesus after his resurrection. E-nock did not die!"

"The other group of 'Sons of god' were not allowed to take root. God had them leave. They were in the South Seas or 'The Isles' and were not allowed to continue here on Earth. All part of God's promise. A promise from God is as good as life gets."

"Look at the globe, Cornelius! Pretend you are a 'Sons of God' in a large craft approaching earth from space thousands of years ago. Of course, you know all about earth. You have been here before, working for God. You know about Jerusalem, the group in England, the old Garden of Eden. And you have rules and a mission of some kind. In the great heavens you are alone with God. Satan and his Demons do <u>not</u> have the ability to space travel. But God has thrown down Satan onto this Earth. His demons even approach and fight God's angels here on Earth. You are a servant of God, not scared, but yes, on your toes; ready to be tested. Like a zookeeper approaching their charge. What happens if you fly in over the Great Northern land mass? Yes, you make a spectacle of yourself. You announce your coming. People will follow you, write about it; talk about it for thousands of years (like the star of Bethlehem). This may not be your plan. What if you don't want to announce your coming, for some reason? Maybe it's God's rules, maybe not. For some reason we don't know. No, you don't have magic or total God power over technology. You are real men in your own real spaceship who work for God. God does not zap you into an invisible butterfly or a giant pumpkin or stop time. Yes, you do pray! You are <u>not</u> a god. How would you approach Earth? You're a fighter pilot!"

162

I thought "Well, Joe, I would approach the Earth from behind the sun; always using the sun's blind spot to hide my approach through the solar system. When the position was right, I would hide behind the moon. Then again, at the right time, I would approach the Earth across the South Seas over mostly water then land on a hard, flat, landing spot on top of a mountain, near the equator to save fuel for landing and take-off."

"Yes Cornelius very good. Do you see any place like that on the globe?" asked Joe.

"Yes, right where we are now!" I answered.

"When you landed, what would be the first thing that you would do? The very first?" asked Joe, smiling. "You would worship God, Cornelius. Maybe even build a tabernacle like God taught Israelites to do when God was 'with' them in person, kind of like he is 'with' his 'Sons of God'! God does not change! Things would be done the same way God's way!"

"Do you mean they would build a church on the rock? Is that what you're saying, Joe?"

"Exactly, Cornelius"

"Now I think you may be on to something, Joe!" I said. "Have you met Mel?"

"Who,"

"Mel," I replied. Mel told me his church was in a different season!"

"I don't know any Mel, Cornelius! Listen! This one group of 'sons of God' in the South Isles had a job to do, but that job did not include 'taking root' in the Earth! God had a covenant with the Israelites. God only lets 'Sons of God' go so far. Seasons change by God's timetable. Read Isaiah 40:21. Look what unseen things God has done for Abraham. Others would have taken over. But god kept his promise! God kept his 'Sons of God' in line; including their 'giant' kids!

(21) **Have ye not known? Have ye not heard? Hath it not been told you from the beginning? Have ye not understood from the foundation of the earth?**

(22) **It is he that sitteth upon the circle of the earth, and the inhabitants thereof are as grasshoppers that stretcheth out the heavens as a curtain, and speadeth them out as a tent to dwell in!**

(23) **that bringeth the princes to nothing; he maketh the judges of the earth as vanity**

(24) Yea, they shall not be planted; yea, they shall not be sown: yea, their stock shall not take root in the earth: and he shall also blow upon them, and they shall wither, and the whirlwind shall take them away as stubble.

(25) To whom them will ye liken me, or shall I be equal? Sayeth the Holy One

(26) lift up your eyes on high, and behold who hath created these things, that bringeth out their host by number: he calleth them all by names by the greatness of his might, for that he is strong in power; not one faileth.

(27) Why sayest thou, O Jacob and speakest, O Israel, my way is hid from the Lord and my judgement is passed over from my God?

(28) Hast thou not known? Hast thou not heard that the everlasting god, the Lord, the creator of the end of the earth, faintest not or is weary? There is no searching of his understanding.

(29) He giveth power to the faint and to them that have no might be increased strength!

(30) Even the youth shall faint and be weary, and the young men shall utterly fall!

(31) But they that wait upon the Lord shall renew their strength: they shall mount up with wings as eagles: they shall not be weary; and they shall walk, not faint!

"The season of the coming of the king our lord Jesus or the king of kings is closer every day Cornelius!

As I was leaving chief of staff Friday came into Joe's office with a stack of papers.

"Wait a minute Cornelius!" said Friday, "I have to know! Island Three, Ok now how did you do it?"

"Do what Friday," I asked. Friday was fuming mad! "Ok enough already!" Friday yelled out "It was a great stunt Cornelius now out with the truth!

"Really no kidding Friday" Cornelius pleaded "What, I've not a clue about what you're talking about, I'm being serious" (Joe Coe stood at his desk shaking his head)

Friday slammed down his papers on Joe's desk and said. "The day Lou Goodliar and Sergeant Pepper briefed the crew on the radio tower construction project I flew the brass up to the top of that mountain. You, Cornelius, left for Island Number two as part of Unks rescue team that morning. Both choppers had been in the garage for maintenance until that day. On the very top center dome of that mountain the top brass found a fresh empty bottle of red wine and an empty silver tray from a big Patel Hotel in Sydney Harbor. Your fingerprints were all over them Cornelius; yes yours and some of the oddest finger-prints the ship's lab has ever seen. NOW! . . . . How the hell did you get that bottle up top? Unauthorized goof-ball flights' off of this ship is a serious offense!" First Mate Friday stared silently with his arms crossed. His hard cold eyes drilled a hole in my forehead. After a few seconds I slowly and softly spoke up.

"My friend Mel must have left them up there after cleaning one of his Churches" I shrugged! "The Island is a perfect place for a landing site." Friday waited for a more and better explanation and then slowly turned beet red.

"DAMMIT, I knew you'd say something silly and stupid. That's the lamest nonsense I've ever heard! Kiss my black ass, Cornelius. I'll catch you one fine day; you and your silly cute little games! Man up about it!" screamed Friday. Friday then slammed Joe's office door so hard that Joe's security alarm system started beeping. Joe just shook his head and grinned as he quickly rushed to cancel the security alert.

"Cornelius," said Captain Coe. "You're donna drive that man crazy! I hope I'm there to see it when he kicks your ass (ha-ha)."

Sometimes the simple truth does sound strange or stupid. Just like the Holy Bible people can't grasp it all. They think "well that can't be." Nothing is all that complicated in the end. People just think themselves more educated than they really are. The truth is they don't know that they don't know. I fell asleep in my cabin reading Jeremiah 33 verse 3.

Early the next morning just at dawn Joe and I taxied to elevator one. We were the only people moving on ship. The Great Ark was treading water against the tide just holding her place. Our brand new B48 trainer was modified just as Joe had said. We were a tight fit, single file in the cockpit yet still comfortable. We had no flight plan and our planes main electronics were all turned off. Joe had a top secret code to allow the plane to operate manually without its fancy computers. Joe said to go to ten thousand feet and look around. I was driving the ultimate sports car. The plane had so much power compared to our weight that we jumped off the flight deck.

"Do you see those mountains sticking up above the clouds?" Joe calmly asked.

"Yea, Captain Joe," . . . . I answered

"One of them is flat on Top. Fly around it, study the top of it. Ok Cornelius, I ask you, can you land us on the top of it? Tell me either way Yes or no. If it can't be done if the terrain is to rough then let me know. Don't do anything stupid but let us study the mountain. If it can be done then we want to land on top" we circled the rock peak looking for a suitable place to land our plane for some minutes."

Then I answered, "Yes I think so captain. We are loaded very light. I slowed the plane to stall speed and let her down right on the center top in a large flat spot. The top of this rock was only eight hundred feet across and its edges were a little rough. The center top was as smooth as glass. This mountain top looked like the rock that is inside the "dome of the Rock" in Jerusalem except much bigger. After landing we sat and said nothing. I was very much relieved that the landing was finished and tried not to think about our eventual take off. In our silence I studied the other mountain peaks around us. The other rock cliff peaks were similar to this one except this one looked like it had been cut off on top.

Joe got out packs and ropes while saying nothing, he just pointed his instructions. Two packs for each of us, and lots of rope. He then put one end of each rope with a hex shaped wedge nut on it into the rocks and pulled tight. Joe next studied a fancy jewel compass, then he took a few paces looked at the compass again. The third time Joe then jumped off the edge of the cliff.

"Oh no," I cried out, my heart sank. Please Lord anything but this. I was trying to decide about jumping or not and praying when a still breeze first rocked the plane and then blew me off the rock cliff edge. I hit the side of the cliff twice as I repelled down. I then heard Joe shout,

"Push off the side hard Cornelius" . . . . I did!

The next bounce Joe grabbed me into a narrow opening in the cliff face were he was already standing. We pulled our ropes down a hall way. The floor sloped upward at first but then steadily downward. No steps no doors, no lights. Joe took off his gear and then all of his clothes.

"No time to be bashful now, Cornelius," said Captain Coe, "Let us wash up and get dressed" The water was cool to wash up in but not mountain top ice cold!

"Put the robe on this way" Joe scolded me!

"Yea, Ok," I answered back grudgingly.

Joe acted like he knew stuff. He was studying a flat clear rock, the same one that I had thought was a compass before. In truth, ole' Joe acted surprised that we had made it thus far. Our robes were heavy across the shoulders with fancy thick stitching. They reminded me of an old couch with double cloth in spots, lighter material at the long bottom that was wrapped up. We were bare foot. Joe rewrapped his long robe once more as if to get it right.

"Gird yourself as of a man Cornelius, No like this then pull it tight. Wash your feet again in the shallow water and wait to dry"

As we walked the descending hallway the sound of rushing air slowly got louder and louder. The light was dim but not completely dark. A strong chimney effect from what I had guessed was a natural geothermal heat source deep in the mountain was causing an updraft through what looked like a solid gold tunnel. Air came rushing up through the floor and was sucked out again through the ceiling forming an air "doorway." Two other hallways came together here at this "door" and dim sunlight came through very small gold holes in the high peak in the ceiling. The hole in the floor across this air doorway was eighteen inches deep and about five times that wide. It was covered with round bronze looking bars about two inches apart. Behind the bars the hole looked smooth and bright shiny like gold.

"One Cubit across," said Joe crawling on the floor. "Hold onto your dress, and we will step in on the count of three, Cornelius." Stepping into darkness is very unnerving and a backwards air waterfall did not help much. We both stepped though the air door into a chamber that was completely dark. "Get out your phone and open the bible Cornelius" barked Joe. "First Kings seven, verses 32, 33, 34 &35." Joe started crawling on his elbows end to end across the floor while I read the verses. Joe was obsessed with measuring the room. I looked around in awe and wonder. The room by phone light was over forty feet wide and one hundred and sixty feet long and sixty or seventy feet high. It had a slight slope in the nearly flat floor. There were no stairs or steps just like the hallway. This room was solid gold in every direction. The air was fresh and smelled good the temperature was cool but comfortable. The acoustics were magnificent. I started singing "Oh magnify the Lord" and Joe soon joined in. We sounded like a full choir in three part harmony at least. We sang and praised God never growing weary or tired. Worship was so wonderful that we could not stop and we soon shut our eyes to our golden surroundings. The unbelievable sound of our voices praising God carried us away. We don't know how long we sang. Joe figured later that we had sung for twelve hours. When we did stop singing we prayed in silence until we burst out muttering aloud in strange tongues; able to understand each other but not ourselves.

"Turn your phone light off Cornelius!" shouted Joe,

"I thought yours was on Joe"

"No" he said, "How come it's so bright in here?"

In each corner of the room were four round gold spheres with another gold ball on top to make five. These gold balls were not noticed by us before, or they had just appeared. They did not quite touch the floor. Each sphere was about one cubit in diameter and each one would look translucent or partly clear exposing spokes as of a wheel inside of a wheel and then they would slowly turn solid gold again.

"Did you see that Joe? That's where the light is coming from," I said pointing.

"No, look up front, Cornelius, the high center wall." We both stared wide eyed in amazement. We could see an opening in the front wall a doorway into another chamber. Bright light was coming in from that other room. With the increased light our common reflection in every direction was frightening; we could see ourselves forever! A mist or steam was now in the room above us. This mist was going into the other room through this front doorway that was there one second and then a smooth solid gold wall the next. Opening and shutting in a slow heartbeat like rhythm. This mist which had formed during our worship was slowly leaving us being sucked through this "sometimes" opening in the wall. The stack of round gold spheres in each corner did the same; clear to solid back and forth and started sinking into the floor and dimming their light.

"Captain Joe," I said out loud. "I'm not worthy to go into the front light chamber! I feel too ashamed"

"I was hoping you could Cornelius. I believe the presence of God is in there."

"We dare not try, Joe, only this room is for us." Joe then nodded in agreement. Now the air above us was clear again and a feeling of loneliness and fear settled into our being. The words of Mel back in Australia came flooding to my remembrance. "The Lord inhabits the praises of his people! "Thank you Mel" I spoke aloud. You do a wonderful job cleaning the church. Yes, this tabernacle or church is very clean. I though about the temple mount; the stories of hidden chambers in God's Holy Mountain. Joe was still measuring the walls. Not me, I'm more of the sloppy fudge it type. Joe and I collapsed near the sunlight filled opening where our robes and gear were. We then held a prayer meeting and rested. We read part of first kings.

(30) And every base had four brazen wheel, and plates of brass; and the four corners there of had under setters; under the laver were under setters Molten, at the side of every addition

(31) and the mouth of it within the chamber and above was a cubit; but the mouth there of was round after the work of the base, a cubit and a half: and also upon the mouth of it were their boarders, four square, not round!

(32) And under the boarders were four wheels; and the axletrees of the wheels were joined to the base; and the height of a wheel was a cubit and half a cubit!

(33) And the work of the wheels was like the work of a chariot wheel: their axletrees, and their naves and their felloes, and their spokes were all molten.

(34) And there were four under setters to the four corners of one base: and the under setters were of the very base itself!

(35) And in the top of the base was there a round compass of half a cubit high: and on the top of the base the ledges there of and the borders there of were the same

The artist in the bible was trying to build something in the temple by description! I thought about how the spheres became translucent showing inside parts even spokes and wheels. How would I describe the tabernacle I just saw to build another?

"Let us not linger any longer now that our worship is done," said Captain Coe!

Joe first, then myself, crawled up our ropes. The early morning sunrise was still just coming up on the horizon. We had no idea that it was now days later. Joe pulled to help me up over the edge of the ledge. The weather was now frightful a roaring whirlwind as if we were under attack surrounded us. We on this high flat top mountain were formally high above the clouds. Now we were at the center eye of the storm. We sat in the plane very weary of taking off. Praying and thanking God for letting us worship in one of his ancient tabernacles. This was a Holy place that had been dedicated to God. Joe told me a story about how the ancient local Indians believed that Thunderbirds helped God create the world in six days that lasted 1,000 days each. The Indians believed that they lived on top of a high mountain way above the clouds. I thought about the day of our Lord lasting for a reign of one thousand years but just then finished my flight checklist.

The B48 fired up on its first start up sequence, the powerful roar was a welcome sound to the howling wind on the mountaintop. Our planes wings slowly stretched out sideways to their full length; as they did the wind jolted and rocked or plane as it buffeted those wings. When the dash light turned green I "popped the clutch" in back home terms. We dropped like a rock off the edge of the cliff for we were too close for take off. After dropping a few hundred feet we roared upward, as we gained speed our long wings folded back up. Joe Coe laughed and hollered.

"The Indians called them Thunderbirds Cornelius. Do you see anything around here that looks like a Thunderbird ole' Corney?"

"Just us wanna be Sons of God," I answered. Our plane was climbing vertical now, inside the raging whirlwind around us.

"Stop, Cornelius, that's an order!" Joe yelled I climbed right out of the cloud cover; as our plane peaked the top of this rollercoaster we flipped over backward for added dramatic effect. Then I was earthward bound with full after burners on.

"Sorry Joe, what did you say? The engine is so loud that I can't hear!" Joe went quiet with a stern frown look on his face. Our dive was half over, all computers were turned off. This was my only chance. Suddenly without fanfare it happened, most engine noise just vanished. We were out running our own sound. Peace at last . . . . sweet peace at last.

I pulled back on the throttle and leveled off, lowering my head in shame now for breaking the rules.

"Sorry Joe I could not hear you for a minute" The vibration and full engine noise came back as quickly as before just as I was speaking.

"You're on your own with Friday ole Corney. I warned you," said Captain Coe, "He can ground you".

We landed on the ship but then everything went black. I don't remember anything else. I woke up in medical. I could hear Captain Joe shouting and raising hell from across the hall. Friday was shouting back, yelling at Joe at the top of his lungs.

"What happened to you two, where were you? How did you end up in that trainer up on flight deck with the landing gear broken and the plane run completely out of fuel? You yourself shut the flight deck down. Boson mates found you two and brought you to sick bay. We thought you were both dead. You both have been out for three days Joe. I had to take control of the ship because you were in no condition to lead. There was also a very odd looking storm on shore; I had to move the ship! Did you take drugs or what? #*#*#*#*#*#*#* Friday then started cussing like a sailor (ha-ha). He then quickly stormed by my room shouting these three words. "STICK IT CORNELIUS!" All the while putting his arm through my open door with a one finger salute!

"Three days" I thought to my self. I then looked at the calendar and thought about just what might be involved in crossing seasons. As I got dressed I told the ship nurse helping me that I was fine because more tests had been ordered. Mel met my giant when he crossed seasons to help me I thought, why is that so? I was off duty and would have time to think later. I walked into the doorway of Joe's room across the hall paused and walked in unannounced. Joe was putting on his white dress captain's coat.

"Seen any Thunderbirds lately there Joe? I asked.

"I DO NOT WANT TO TALK ABOUT IT" Joe Coe snapped back.

"You're holiness ain't yea Joe. The sleep paralysis the giant, the whole nine yards . . . . You're just like me!"

"Get the hell out of here, Cornelius. We will not speak of this further or ever again! Do not cross me, OUT!

"Joe had learned, like me, from childhood to never speak of going were you are not. I was very confused, did we visit Mel's church the golden tabernacle in body or in spirit! I knew we had been there but things didn't line up with the facts. We did fly to the mountain, but to enter the tabernacle required Mel's help, in crossing seasons again. So how long were we gone, and how long in sick bay? I never did figure it all out! Why would people lie anyway?

Out on deck Lou Goodliar met me as I walked!

"Hello Cornelius" whispered Lou. "There was the weirdest weather on shore for the last three days. Did you see it Cornelius?"

"Do you mean the whirlwind Lou, the storm?" I replied.

"Yes, so you did see it Cornelius, the colors and the swirling clouds," said Lou.

"I had a very good view of it Lou, and yes it was wonderful!"

"I've seen a lot in my time," bellowed loud Lou but nothing like the storm of this morning, Cornelius nothing ever like it."

I slept the next day into the afternoon. It would be four days before I was returned to flight duty. I repeated Jeremiah 33 verse 3 often before dosing off from my memory now. Just like the 23 Psalm this verse would be with me forever.

Call unto me, and I will answer three, and show thee great and mighty things, which thou knowest not!

When I came out of my cabin the great horn of the Americas was upon us. Many people were out on my high deck balcony. It was crowded. For countless years sailors have talked and bragged about the great horn; where the oceans collide together in a clash of glory, tempest, and rage. Old sailors like me talked about the great horn to their grand kids. Today would be no major deal in the Great Ark. Still you don't do something like this every day. People always mark the passing. I was truly impressed once again by the roar of nature. At least fifteen hundred people came out on deck to witness or record the crossing. People were on many other balconies or perches around the ship besides mine; all persons paying due respect to the great horn and all it's furry. The waves and spray did a wonderful job of entertaining us. How blessed we were on the Great Ark. The sprinkle system came on afterward to wash us down and limit salt damage from sea spray just after the crossing. The wash system got more people wet than the horn did, but also showed due respect that day. It was great to have unlimited amounts of fresh and hot water on board. This moving city at sea had plenty of everything.

Our next stop was an island at the bottom of the South Atlantic called George; just another big rock. There was a habitat camp there like the ones we built in the South Pacific. We brought supplies fuel and also replaced a wind turbine. I met a man named Gerald Williams from UVA in Virginia. He was the one evidently in charge of making these habitats that we were placing everywhere for a company based in Canada. He was upset about UVA closing down its football team for safety concerns, a trend across the American nation spearheaded by MAIDDS, or Mothers against idiot dangerous deadly sports. UVA was a leader in this movement and was often bragged about by Osoma. Williams was on his way to Antarctica somewhere to check on extreme weather habitats. He had a lovely wife Annie with him, "what a babe" (Yes he married very well) Annie was a germ researcher and a nurse. She could smell you and tell you what sickness you had (ha-ha). She also gave me a book about the forced closing up of the football program. Some professor had proven that players had actually lost IQ during there stay in the UVA football program, and had came out of the school dumber than when they started.

This elite professor figured it was due to the violence in football. Many of these players could not even write down their name and home address, or remember the last names of all of their baby mommas. This made it hard for the school to pay these mothers their expected checks.

This nice Williams couple didn't want to argue politics or the Holy Bible much. They also knew my old Navy friend Seaman First mate Franklin A Donner. Donner had told them that I was nuts or something to that effect. They must have misunderstood, that does happen a lot at wild yacht parties you know.

The ship had orders to give Williams anything and or everything he needed or wanted. He was well known about the ship as the "Cowboy hat Guy." Williams was a good card player and took Duck, Tommy, and Obie Carter for more money than they will admit to even today. After Gerald checked out, tested and approved the George Island, an important supply and fuel point for his Antarctic trip, we parted ways. Williams headed south to the fringed cold with Annie babe to keep him warm and the ship headed north, up the west coast of Africa this time around. I was surprised when Annie gave me a big hug as they left!

"Craig just missed you at the Boat party, he says hello" said Ann, and "thanks for the free Ark tickets for Gloria, Sarah's mother. She was still alive and loved a good cruise, even though she was very old. I was a little bit tipsy that night of the big boat party so I pretended to know what Ann was talking about. Drunks and old people have to fake knowing stuff a lot. Ain't it funny, sometimes you just don't know what you don't know!

End of Chapter eight

CHAPTER NINE

❧ ⊰❁⊱ ❧

Drive by on Africa

During the evenings blowing bitter cold and rolling seas, the Ark pulled away from the George Island. I had a dentist check up that day, it was mandatory. This appointment made it necessary for me to walk by Damage Assessment or brave the blowing cold. This was the only way now to get to medical. It is always best to avoid the Damage Assessment office and the Damage Assessment personnel at all cost. They are all crazy, or simply idiot insane. I tried to sneak past the open door, but little Tony Reiker called to me and waved me into his office. This is where the really weird ones love to work. These men are the bananas in the fruit salad so to speak. Tony stood up grinning!

"Look at this Cornelius these pictures are to your cabin and your phone and in this morning's mail.

"Not more of those nasty beetle Bomb photos?" I groaned with my hands up in the air.

"No," promised Tony . . . "Captain Joe ordered these photo grids of the Ice shelf for that Williams guy; the man who wears the cowboy hat for that Antarctic trip."

Damage assessment nut jobs blow up photos on back lit boxes like doctors do x-rays. They also wear white lab coats and talk in fancy lingo or silly acronyms so nobody knows what in the hell their talking about. Just like most morticians these men are driven half crazy from the mess they have to look at every day. DAPS (Damage Assessment—photos) are often discussed by pilots, and shown in flight briefings always referring to number and grid. AMK416G20133 is the photo Tony is pointing at today. Thousands of hours of digital photos are searched by computer. So many photos are taken that most are never seen by human eyes. The very disturbing flesh eating beetle pictures were popular when new and exciting, but are old hat now. Yes the Beetle Bombs were a big environmental success story. There is some evidence that the genetically modified beetles have started cross breeding with African Locust and are eating all vegetation in sight. This has not been confirmed but could add billions more to sales if true. The poison water stations used at Taco Station have not as yet been approved by environmentalist groups for use in Africa because some lions were accidently poisoned when eating the poisoned Africans. Osoma showed this world his love of the planet earth and his faithfulness to going green by increasing the kill rate in Africa at the cost of his own family. Now he has done even more by stopping the oil companies from increasing energy supplies here in America. Poor people in South Chicago started to freeze to death in record numbers this last winter. What little money America was now allowed to spend by the World Bank Osoma spent on killing off all the Africans and thus saving the rest of the world from global warming.

"Now listen, Cornelius this is important. Osoma can't solve all the worlds' problems over night". Tony said. "Look at these circles" Tony snarled. "Nobody cares about Osoma any way no one can beat him why even try. We have found thirteen and blown them up to full size. All are very much the same. Not really true impact craters they all have a flat spot of ice in the bottom.

Cornelius pointed with his cane. "Looks like somebody's thirsty Tony!"

"What?" Tony answered!

"Tony, what if you owned a spaceship, and wanted a big drink of fresh water? Where would you go in this solar system to find a good supply? You would need clean water that is not being used with very few people around?

Tony looked at the rings in the ice once again, all with frozen flat ice at the bottom. "Ok, Cornelius, what about these odd marks in the ice all around those circles?

"Tony, what would you do if you landed a sailboat on an island after a long voyage? What would the kids do while you refreshed your water tank or went fishing? They would play there next to the boat in the sand. Don't go off too far, you would warn them strongly. Mom and Dad might even join the kids themselves.

"David Booth told me that same stupid story Cornelius, said he saw it on TV. Thanks for nothing yelled little Tony. You fancy officers always try to make fun of us. I really need and want an honest opinion for my report to Williams, not a joke off of a TV show. This is no joke! Here is a joke for you Mr. funny man Ole' Corny."

"How can a professional damage assessment scientist tell the difference between a dead Palestinian, a dead Taliban leader, or an Al-Qaeda-Hamas terrorist after a fire bomb attack (ha-ha)?" The skinny Palestinian will flame up and go out fast because they don't eat very well. The dead Taliban leader will just smoke and smolder because they sweat so much and they just pissed all over themselves when the plane flew over. But the oily head band of an Al-Qaeda or Hamas terrorist will wick up and the gas filled body will burn like a candle for days on end. They often have to be pissed out by our brave troops."

"That joke is really sick, Tony." It fits you somehow. Tony you've been in the DA bizz too long. Take a break Tony you need one, I hear Mexico is nice this time of year.

"Let me know Cornelius, I've got a report to write. Text me back yelled Tony. "That crazy old man probably does believe in UFO's," muttered Tony under his breath as I walked away.

True to form, as the ship got close to Africa, about two hundred military types came aboard along with twenty plus bug like predator drones. We started bombing again as soon as the extra drones landed. What the Hell, I mean we're in the neighborhood anyway we might as well bomb some Africans.

Some people matter in this world and some don't. Africans, they don't count for much. They are even lower than sex offenders. Not even American blacks care about poor dumb Africans. American President George Bush sent many billions to Africa trying to impress American blacks that he cared. They laughed at Bush behind his back. He thought American blacks had a heart for helping Africans. Hell no! Most blacks are ashamed of Africans. Much of the Bush African aide was mopped up by pharmaceutical companies anyway so the "kill off all the Africans" plan was not slowed down much by George. At least he slowed down the killing, at least he tried (ha-ha). The total amount of money raised in black American communities or Churches and sent to Africa each year over the last sixty years would be, on average, not enough to buy a good pair of little league baseball uniforms. Osoma himself is famous for having a brother in Africa living in a hut on twenty dollars a month. Do you think he ever sent him a card with $5 in it for Christmas? I'm sorry; I forgot the family is Islamic.

All Africans must die so that the world can be saved from global warming. The lion must be allowed a place to live; the Rhino needs grass to roam free. Africa must be saved from development. Only ungodly Democratic socialist elites have the leadership and courage necessary to make these tough decisions. We all must trust men, like Osoma, to lead! They know what is best for the world, and what is fair for us Americans. Osoma's plan to triple electric utility rates and triple gas prices to save the world is a decision based on a false religion not science. Any maniac who would stop a pipeline across America even as oil prices went through the roof killing his own friends and neighbors, and at the same time shut down the gulf oil production is a man at war with progress and a man at war with America. Stupid spoiled American crybabies elected an Islamic terrorist to their own White house. Sad but true, the problem is me and you.

We destroyed our own economy on purpose! We shut down our own power plants, coal mines and oil fields for no good reason. This government policy and raising taxes was based on the false religion of humanism. These nut jobs believe in global warming, anti-growth, anti-God and are socialist who are in truth mentally ill. "The good of the many outweighs the rights of the few" is their sick testament. In redneck back home talk; if you're gonna be dumb (without God) then you've gotta be tough. Modern America was not on a solid foundation so all of her efforts have been totally meaningless. Life is not all about us boys and girls; it's all about the cross and the one who gave us his life. The values of a false religion will always bring the strange fruit of death. God will not be mocked by a man or a nation the same. We will reap just what we have sown. The blood of innocence cries out to an all powerful God as does the blood of many Africans.

Africa will be much more valuable as an international park and wilderness preserve. A few primitive black tribes will be allowed to live (and be studied), but without interference from Western Christian mother Earth killing polluting civilizations. For the last eighty years caring environmentalist from Europe and America have tried to save (kill) Africa. But it would take a black man named Osoma to get the bloody job done. What heart, what leadership, what courage, what great intellect? A man like this comes around in history only once every two hundred years. Praise Al Gory and Harry Reed, but long live Osoma. These men together have tamed American arrogance and aggression, influence and power, and now they have saved Africa from human development and pollution. These men are now working together to bring peace to the Middle East and jobs to America. Who did we believe and trust in these matters. Did America trust these proven great men or God almighty's own Holy Bible? America decided in 2012 to vote against God. Making Osoma art and saving Africa is now the latest and biggest jobs program in history. Who needs oil gas and electricity anyway? You know friends it does gets pretty damn cold in The Windy City when that North wind blows across the lake. Can you tell me again why oil from Canada is a bad idea and why we can't build new power plants and need to shut down our old power plants? We had brown outs last year with all the old ones burning. Are you Democrats sure that God is dead, and that the Bible does not talk about Israel, Hell or these end times? Hello operator I was calling the DNC and keep getting cut off. No I don't want a DNC clinic I want to talk to the DNC. Hello, Hello! Damn it!

The Great Arks flight deck was busy once again. That second tower below Joe Coe was back in business. Our flight schedule was faster paced than at Taco Station but not as fast as on the East Coast of Africa. Sorties of drones were often of longer range off this coast so we were less effective at killing Africans. We found out that some very long distant drone bombing attacks were being carried out directly from our base in Brazil. A robot refueling bridge had been maintained for months. This new refueling bridge was much talked about by our younger pilots. All of our pilots were kept busy during these days. We had the gloves off while flying ship protection patrols. Captain Joe Coe was looking for something or somebody who could hit back. We stayed on high alert sinking anything and every thing in sight. My favorite Country Gospel music was still at the ships Gospel Café and of course I held court as the "anti-professor" every chance I could. My new young students continued to call me "old School" or "Rush." Rush was an Old AM radio talk show host who was now in civil commitment. The truth was my students needed a wise old fat fool like me to "round out" their brain washed education. Their real professors were mostly idiotic sissy narcissistic wimps like Paul Goldwater. The "PDBDKS" syndrome had taken over the world. (Poor-dumb-bastards-don't-know-shit).Conventional liberal wisdom was always one hundred percent wrong or ass backwards. My young students were completely without adult Holy Bible teaching. They were completely without wisdom. This night students were talking about the long distant bombing of Africa and the robot refueling of drones. Professor Lou Goodliar and his sidekick Tommy Mute stopped by and the coffee was flowing heavy around my big round corner booth table. I asked the students and my Christian professor friends a very simple question. Which was faster? Was it ships or planes? That is in a military logistics system. What was the break even point in cost between bombing from our beautiful base in Brazil and bombing Africa from the Great Ark? We discussed the merits of each and bounced around this silly light topic because the students seemed interested. My point in the end was that ships are faster than planes in many but not all military logistic equations. What matters most in military supply lines are not meaningless feet per second measurements but rather the all important "foot lbs per second?" The Ark carried more payload to the battle than ten thousand drones could carry and was very many more times foot lbs per second fuel cost efficient than drones in moving "stuff" to the battle. To make and maintain thousands of drones based in Brazil would cost more money in fuel. In other words we can kill off more poor dumb bastards in Africa cheaper by using the Ark than by refueling. This of course is the name of the game (Money). Yes, killing off Africans and saving the world at least cost; getting rid of the lowest producers and the most worthless and sick. How many "Made in Africa" stickers have you seen in your life? My point exactly, I rest my case. Africans don't account for much, or matter to anybody or the economy, and many of them now have AIDS. Just like the old people back home, they must be killed off to save the rest of us.

Of course world leaders of the Humanist Democratic Environmentalist Elites have much bigger killing tools than the Great Ark. These other killing tools are more effective, faster, more efficient, and much more cost effective than our bombs. These proven killers are dirty water, taking away DDT, AIDS, the Islamic sword, ethnic warfare, the closing of farmland, government controlled education, and Planned Parenthood abortion mills and pills. American Democrats would soon have their international park. Africa would be a people free zone where the religion of "Mother Earth Worship" would reign supreme. This false religion has many priests and high officials. They are recognized, respected and obeyed the world over.

This false religion makes claims of knowledge and scientific truth, but nothing is further from the truth.

These elite ruling class modern day witch doctors call themselves Doctors and Psychiatrists. They are truly false ungodly priests, and medicine men; no different from any ancient pagan tribe. Throughout all of human history this fact always stays true and cuts across all types of societies and governments. The official "High Priest" of that particular group is the one that the civil authorities use to test charges or prisoners in life and death questions. This is the Kings highest law, and the official God of his reign. In Virginia Humanism is the official state religion and Psychiatrist, and environmentalists, have set themselves up as humanist false priests. Counseling by the government priest is (always) the answer to any problem, and is always part of the sentence of most crimes. Mother Earth and saving her is always the trump card while God and his Holy word is laughed at and hated. Who tests the charges, the prisoners, and who can put them into civil commitment (life in prison) with out offense, without jury, without charge in your state. Do you know? Do you care? Will they ever come after you? Will you ever be forced to go to counseling for not believing correctly?

During this "drive by" of Africa we dropped many of our new Beetle Bombs now combined into a one drop or one bomb package. We still had no approval for our poison water products from environmentalist groups. No point spoiling Africa while trying to save it from humans.

We lingered off the West coast of Africa all the while killing as many unwanted, unneeded, surplus humans as we could. Stopping or slowing all over production just like the guardians of Mother Earth at Berkley talked about in the South Seas. At least I didn't have to hear that irritating voice, or put up with that wimp "Cup Cake!"

I had hoped the ship might stop by the water desert of Brazil but alas we did not. My old girl Josie had probably dumped me by now anyway and found another sailor boy. I guess I could have maybe called her by now and I did forget her damn Christmas card. Oh well, thoughts of buzzing around those sand dunes did bring back great memories of Brazil. That watery desert landscape was beautiful yet eerie and amazing; and straight across the pond from the great desert sands of Africa.

Be careful what you wish for, I would get my sand dunes alright, not in Brazil but in the great Sahara Desert. Mostly our manned planes worked ship protection patrols. The defense of the ships air space was our prime responsibility. We did "bomb up" a half dozen or so times during this second African campaign, each time using our new B48s to good effect. One bombing run was a one hundred percent feet wet attack on a large marina. Three others were also mostly in the coastal area or feet wet targets, only two went deep into the mainland like most drone attacks did. Only these two could be called real feet dry bombing runs. At the first marina attack two gun boat military like looking craft were parked in a marina containing fifty or sixty sailboats and motor sports boats. Six B48's made short work of the whole mess. Fiber glass sailing boats fly apart like confetti when hit by modern military shock wave producing munitions. Every thing was gone, docks outbuildings even part of the shore line. Tony sent me some extra pictures. One village or town destroyed by manned bombers was a Y in the river spread out over a wide area it reminded me of Pittsburg back home. By switching to crude cluster fire bombs instead on high punch weapons we were able to take out many "Non-Sambo" targets. This is called "rooting." These non-Sambo's or "Women" pay double price a bonus just started this year. We pilots finally got a small little piece of the action. Elite environmentalist priests were now swimming in blood money. Al Gory announced the largest public land expansion in the history of the planet in Africa. He was funding the non-Sambo's bonus, or (save Africa man boy only strike). Joe was getting bonus after bonus from the Beetle Bomb Company owned by George Soretoes who was some Greek-American campaign supporter of Osama. The other major bombing hit by manned planes was a long feet dry attack by only three planes. This one bombing run would blight my flying career and bring me professional embarrassment. This long lonely sortie was the beginning of the end of my fly boy days. On this bombing run we did not have to refuel. We put on drop tanks and lighted our bomb load. This was for sure not a massive target in size. We hung one mini bunker buster on each plane. These are for cracking and breaking not burning. We three pilots took off before dawn. Two top student pilots who were about to turn pro and myself.

I keyed in the target zone on my personal computer as we sped in low across the desert sand. This use of the World Wide Web is highly against our rules and pilot protocol. I had never done this before in my life. Air defense was not a concern and briefing on the target had been short and vague. I wanted to know just who or what I was hitting. We flew in low over endless miles of sand now in bright daylight sunshine. Satellite web photos showed three Fuller (not the dome) but Mushroom houses. Three spaceship looking mushroom houses on thick center pole stems, with cables from the top to hold them in place. These three houses were set all by themselves just outside a very small oasis green spot in the middle of the vast desert waves of sand. My heart and spirit was not into bombing these beautiful homes. I wondered who it was that lived there and I had always respected Dr. Fuller. A war raged in my soul as we approached the target; as team leader and center plane I called out the signals. Just a split second before the target computer lock tone I manually jogged my plane to the left which caused the students plane on my left's anti-collision system to override his controls and forced him left also. Both of our seven hundred pound bombs hit left of target and did little or no damage. The plane on my right, "Mark Howard" stayed true to programming and took out the house on the right and slightly damaging the center house. The house on left was left standing (no joke) with no damage. Calvin Young the student on left was raising hell and justly so. Mark Howard the student on my right said not a word neither did I; as flight leader I gave commands over the computer. After giving Young time to vent I ordered radio silence by keying it in. My report would not be a fun one to write. I had failed to do my job. I had let the Young pilots down (ha-ha) (still no joke); as a teacher and a highly trained well paid professional that's just not accepted. I wondered though, had this foolishness saved a life? Would the cost to me on this one be worth it? I lost some respect and ranking in the tight group of my pilot peers. These elite fly boys who lived a privileged life on ship, even when compared to other officers. A man has to do what a man has to do. He must be true to himself and God and then face the consequences. Not Joe Coe or any other official briefed me or scolded me, or took me to task about "My Miss." I was sure Friday was happy to investigate the big miss and put nasty notes in my personnel file. The miss was the topic of gossip throughout the ships crew and a deep embarrassment to me around my colleagues. Sambo Station was coming to a close. I was glad to be rid of it. I told myself never again. I was washed up, no longer a warrior no longer did I have the heart for it. "Thank you Lord" I said for allowing me to work in your church; "thank you Lord" for not giving up on me when I was chief among all sinners.

End of Chapter

CHAPTER TEN

Docked in Portugal

Two weeks later we pulled near the Azores. The Great Ark took on a load of aviation fuel, the old expensive stuff; and then parked outside of a Harbor in Portugal while waiting on a dock that was way behind. We were on hold, just taking life easy. The whole ship needed a brake after a season of war, this bloody killing field of Africa called "Sambo Station."

One particular end of shift cycle evening during this time Lou Goodliar the radio tower expert and Tommy Mute joined my table with some very disturbing information. Both men were professors at the ships college yet both still oddly and officially Christian. Sometimes I get up to twelve students packed into my big round corner booth but this evening Lou Goodliar, Tommy Mute and a drummer named Rodney seemed to fill it up. They're all big spread out types like me. Goodliar opened up conversation after eating with,

"Some say you missed that target on purpose Cornelius! Is there anything to that talk?"

"Why would I do something stupid like that Goodliar?" No students were around. Lou looked at Tommy Mute then Rodney as if to say, should we do this? After a pause Goodliar started up again. "Cornelius, I watched you come aboard ship back at Pearl Harbor with a group of elderly passengers? Do you remember that day?"

"Sure," I said.

"Cornelius, have you ever seen passengers or elderly people get on the Ark before?"

"Yes I believe so, in Brazil," I answered. "Why do you ask?"

"Well, Cornelius, have you ever seen any elderly passengers get off this ship?"

"No Lou . . . I haven't noticed!"

"Let me ask you Cornelius, have you ever seen any elderly passengers on ship during a cruise, or at any time while at sea?"

"Well no, I haven't Lou," I said. "These old people stay to themselves. I'm not sure they're even allowed on the main deck or flight deck. I don't believe that they are!"

"Wake up, Cornelius!" stuttered Lou in a rough whisper shout! "Open your eyes man! You haven't seen them on walk-ways, cat-walks, snack bar, medical, balconies or pharmacy because they're not here. You have shut your eyes to the obvious truth. You have looked the other way and lived your own little pathetic life in your own little protected world. You, Cornelius, are just like the retard Osoma voters you like to rail on and on about. Many people are apolitical and do not cast wise informed votes but you also have been selfish close minded and unwilling to face the obvious ugly truth. Truth is painful, it hurts and you would rather not look at your own failings."

Lou sat down his coffee and hung his head in silence. "The truth is this ship is a death camp a concentration camp. Those old people are fish food soon after we put to sea! One half of them are Jewish Cornelius, you and I are both of German families, we have become our grandfathers, we have become who and we hated."

"Goodliar things just can't be that bad, cheer up," I smiled. "You must be mistaken. This whole death camp story sounds crazy. Why would they get on ship if this story was true? Who puts them on board ship and why?"

"They are picked out by computers in the personnel dept Cornelius. Many world governments pay bounty per head for each one eliminated. These people are killed and their property stolen," cried out Tommy Mute in a coarse whisper. Lou laid his hand on Tommy's arm interrupting;

"Cornelius, they are picked out by computers in the personnel dept. Democratic socialist and communist governments pay per head. They are required by the simple laws of mathematics to kill off their most costly citizens and their least productive. Elite leaders must do this constant killing to keep their slow, crude inefficient government planned economic systems alive. This or go to work and or do without themselves. This of course is not even considered. They simply have no choice, Cornelius. To be a socialist is to be a murderer, for there is no new wealth to pull from. Osoma is not a terrible, evil man, he does mean well on a simple level, but he is ungodly and without the wisdom of Gods teaching. You know all of this is true."

"Let me put it this way," said Lou. These old people are just not worth having around in a country with socialized medicine and social security payments. Also, these old geezers vote the "wrong way" and are often strong in their faith and independent in their personal opinions. Often they are Christian or Jewish and use older out-law hate speech terms to describe modern day perverts.

"Cornelius these death camps are bigger than you might imagine," broke in Tommy Mute, and it's not just old people! Governments around the world are looking into certain families. This search has something to do with one hundred-forty-four thousand young Jewish boys and their families. Have you ever heard of Snuffer Wagons Cornelius?

"Snuffer Wagons?" I answered,

"Later Tommy," Hold up on that snuffer stuff," demanded Loud Lou! "First things first, let us not jump ahead."

"Do you men have any proof of this death camp talk or is this all just a rumor," I asked.

Lou reached behind Tommy Mute and handed me a piece of paper from Rodney and said. "Here are some maintenance door codes, only Boson mates in brown jump suits have them, Cornelius. Rodney here has a brown suit in his quarters that will fit you. Rodney Dole will stand on the breezeway corner deck and give hand signals. Tommy and I both have a shore phone they work fine here in the harbor. We will be your look outs. Be sure not to face the camera on flight deck by the drink machines, it does have facial recognition software connected to it. Take your time Cornelius and check this out for yourself."

"Cornelius, this is how the death camp system on the ship works or how it operates" explained Rodney. Our friend Rodney was a great sailor and a drummer and also hopelessly henpecked. He was famous for being thrown in the ships brig every three months at bonus time for drugs or alcohol. He was married to one of the band singers at the ships Gospel café. She had a habit of throwing him out and then begging him back when she got lonely. The couple was in a constant state of either breaking up or making up. They would be constantly kissing or kicking, and or slurping or slapping each other which wore on the nerves of everyone around them. Rodney drew on a napkin and said. "The bottom two front sections or the part before the college dorms eighty-eight cabins in all, these are the killing chambers," explained Rodney. As he drew I sat holding my head in my hands. "Oh Lord," I started to speak!

"Just listen, Cornelius," interrupted Loud Lou. "Do not go into those rooms that would alert security. Motion sensitive lighting and cameras are installed. These codes will get you into the maintenance hallway between and below the killing floor rooms. Both showers, two in each room have bullet proof, soundproof, electric locking shower doors. These showers can dispense a deadly gas and the floor then opens up and the shower flushes it's self with hundreds of gallons of scalding hot water. A large fiberglass tube leads to a huge bus size garbage grinder in the bottom of the ship. The bodies are fish food never to be seen heard or thought of ever again. A clean up staff consisting of only two sailors then empty the rooms of luggage into an incinerator and then those ashes too are flushed at sea. Those old and unwanted people are now history, saving governments millions in social security payments, knee replacements, hip replacements, diabetic shots, all types of medical costs housing and food plus they take the family estates. This is big business. The world governments can't collect enough tax money. The good of the many always outweighs the rights of the few when it comes to big government providing everything in life. You do the math son and see for yourself, it has to be that way.

I went to the maintenance door. I made double sure not to face that camera on deck. Tommy, Rodney and Lou kept watch. Sure enough large fiberglass tubes leading down from the rooms above to somewhere below; two becoming one from each shower were plainly visible. Could this be true I thought? Could the Worlds governments like Osoma and that guy in Germany who promise everything in the world to the poor? Could they have let their mouth over load their wallet by promising everything would be free. How could their stupid citizens believe all the lies? The ignorant uneducated people are successfully and easily controlled world wide. Slavery is common place Freedom is rare. Free men need Bible based independent schools to remain free, this is truth! Today's leaders are just as bad as the ones we studied in history. Well of course they are! Why would any one believe that men have changed and are better now than they used to be? Oh yes, I pondered and thought to myself; in the humanist religion or man becoming or evolving into a god. That's what they believe. That man is getting better and smarter and does not need a redeemer. Modern man does not need Jesus or to be bought with his blood. That's what is taught in government schools, just as did Stalin, Hitler, Castro, and Mao. What is this death camp evil I have become part of? Shooting Mexicans by the thousands with robot planes could I guess be argued even worst than death camps, but the "Mexicans" like our own Indians and the Africans never did really count. All were worthless people living worthless lives just like Osoma's brother. These old people were real people who could read and write and speak clearly. They passed college boards, got married for life, washed their hands, prayed to God, played and made musical instruments loved their children, invented, manufactured, wrote poetry, worked hard, took showers, owned homes, used deodorant, and sailed ships. These people were just like me, even my very own. Back in my room changing clothes I thought about life and death and my heart grew heavy.

"God is no respecter of persons I heard the scriptures say! God's way is family and church not an all powerful king or state. God's way works"

The Humanist false religion leads to socialist government leaders like Osoma which is man's way and against God! Elite socialist leaders put government in charge of everything to destroy and pervert the family and the church. They teach the goodness of mankind and worship Mother Earth. They think themselves as wise but have no fear of or faith in almighty God. The fear of God is the beginning of wisdom.

The hard cold truth of a mans life here on this earth is that for our first twelve years and our last twelve years of life only our family will suffer us enough to keep or want us around. During these years we are a net cost or basically more trouble than we are worth. When government is given the job of taking care of us through taxes they always start killing us off. Let me explain why. Walk up to any young couple in your town and show them the picture of an old woman living in that same city town or province. Tell them you are looking for someone to adopt the old woman and agree to have $150 a week taken out of their paycheck or the old woman will have to die. How many young couples would sign up? Now go door to door showing pictures and asking people to pay child support each week. How much money will you get? Now you the king or leader has told all the old people and all the kids and all the sick and all the retards that you the king will write them all checks each month and take care of them forever. What happens when the money runs short, can you place a heavy tax on each young hard working couple? You guessed it; the good of the many outweighs the rights of the few. Those silly little promises that were told to gain power don't amount to much. The blood starts to flow like a river. This is truth and has been true for the last six thousand years and guess what, it's still true today. God knows what he's talking about and his way of family and church works. Man's way of putting big government in charge, always with an elite ruling class and high taxes always fails! Who knew? Who could have guessed? That God could have been right all along and that Al Gory, Castro, Osoma, Barnie Frank, and Hillary could have been wrong. It's just amazing I mean who would have thought.

I met my friends back at the Gospel Café at near closing time just as we had planned and Tommy Mute asked me point blank! "Cornelius, my Uncle Bob and his wife Alice are getting on board this ship in Portugal. I plan to get them off the Ark before she sets sail. I want to save them both, are you with us? That's all I need to know? Will you help me?"

"I nodded yes without speaking!"

Two volunteer ladies Peanut and Linda were filling in and waiting to close up the Gospel Café early that night. Peanut had been counting money for the last half hour or so, as a hint for us to leave. The guest gospel singer that night was named Bobby String. He was booked by my friend Lou Goodliar. Most people had left early. Bobby had effectively cleared the room with his high twang cat like voice. The two women were very much put out with the low crowd and not getting much attention. They had fluttered and frowned all evening telling patrons how much work they both did.

I walked back to my cabin alone, very much perplexed and down in spirit. The famous Gospel Café is just not the same when those two women fill in. They seem to talk about themselves nonstop. I guess the regular workers like Julie and Betty deserve some time off everybody does. Why do people run from truth, from holiness? Why get all crabby like those two volunteers, and bring everybody's spirit down? Why does Loud Lou always have to have the first and last word in every conversation? Why ask why? God will turn you inside out and humble you, becoming holiness will show you truth. People do not like to admit that they are sinners and need Jesus and need to change. Just like my friend "Loud Lou" those volunteer women wanted the focus on them not Jesus! The regular crew at the Gospel Café has never told me about all the work they do, or gone on and on about their own personal problems, nor had they ever wanted to close early. They worked as servants to a higher cause. They were not too good to clean the bathroom or sweep the floor. Jesus said it best in Mark 9:35

And he sat down, and called the twelve, and saith unto them, if any man desires to be first, the same shall be last of all, and servant of all.

The Lord does not play, he will not be mocked. How did things get so bad here on ship and also back in America. The answer is simple, sin. Men in rebellion against God, and man's pride!

We finally docked in Portugal and supplies sailors on leave, girl friends, freight, passengers went on and off the Great Ark. The dock was a mad house of activity. This dock was much too small for a ship the size of the Ark and there was not any wonder why they had gotten behind.

While walking down the water front alone many prayers and thoughts came rushing through my mind. My heart grieved for peace. I needed to get away from all this madness and maybe not ever come back. Soon I walked upon a familiar sight! My eyes gazed upon the most beautiful large sailboat I'd ever seen. This fancy yacht had graceful lines as of a woman and Yes I knew it! Sure enough the name **Windy** was on the stern and a dancing Pig was over hanging the bow. The boat was empty now no loud party tonight. Windy belonged to my old Navy buddy Seamen's First mate Franklin, A Donner. I saw her in Sydney, and in Pearl Harbor was good to see a familiar face. "Hello Pig" I said out loud. They must have gone through the Panama Canal and beat the Ark here. This sailboat was over two hundred feet and had all the extras. I shouted out loud once more, the pig spoke up and said.

"Come back later please" and it danced a gig. If this talking pig seems rather odd than you just don't know Frank. I thought nothing of it. His boat was truly empty now but maybe I'd see him in town. I walked up the steep hill into town and sat down at the first restaurant or watering hole I came to. The neon sign said simply "Bar and Grill." I needed time to think eat and drink. I wanted to be left alone and to be anywhere except on the Great Ark. What about quitting, my bonus, my retirement, my wife Patty. I must have lonely sailor written on my forehead for shortly after I sat down the owner of the bar a lady named Aspasia Hoeabit sat down at my table and tried to sell herself to me for the night. I wasn't much interested. Her light but pronounced mustache didn't help much. I played that old country song "Where I Come From its Cornbread and Chicken" three times on the jute box that night. She and I bargained off and on throughout the evening. Hoeabit would sit down make me an offer and I would make a counter offer. I got her down to $14 and a kiss before she finally left me alone (Ha-ha). Must be hard times in the women's crotch market here in Portugal! Hoeabit said she had a sister in Brazil named Josie that lived near some sand dunes. No I didn't ask. I didn't really want to know, I mean really, what are the odds?

Late into the evening my old Navy buddy Franklin Donner came bursting through the door and started buying me drinks. We talked into the night laughing it up like college age fools. Frank's wife was asleep (passed out) in their room at the big Hotel Casino up the street. Frank wanted to talk to the Hoeabit lady about something but Aspasia Hoeabit avoided Frank all night. With the spirit of drink full in me I finally said "Franklin brother let me lend you some advice. Get on that beautiful Windy of yours and sail away. Forget about this lady Hoeabit and in a New York accent I said it again "forget about it" I put down a $14 tip as Franklin had paid my bill. Franklin said that he and his Hog lady were going to "The Gathering" and they that were so proud to be invited. I had no idea what he was talking about. When leaving the bar we found the bottom of the hill filled with police cars and flashing lights.

Catholic Priests were being arrested during anti-abortion demonstrations and prayer. My friend Franklin Donner warned me "Go around Cornelius" he said. "Don't let them scan your face. The locals have warned me. I don't know what it's all about Cornelius but innocent people do disappear. Those patty wagons are called snuffers. The people with the scanners are psychology student volunteers or specially trained police. This has something to do with young Jewish boys and their family heritage or tribe and reporting all births to Denmark. Many people are Israelites but not all claim to be Jews. Most do not even know the name of their own great grandfather and grand mother. The DNA tests and facial scanners are said to require very powerful computers. It's like trying to count the sand on the world's beaches. I remembered those silly questions that Rosie back in Saint Augustine had asked me. What if I was part Jewish or part black, what should it matter to those thugs from ACORN? God gave man marriage and family it is his way. Those who are in rebellion against God will always fight against his ways and laws and try to destroy family. You will know them by their fruits, their works. Be not fooled Cornelius test the spirits that they are of God. In my long walk I was "not so much alone" any more and felt much better, Praise God.

That evening at the Gospel Café four cadet students (two with their dates) joined me. All four men were from our elite fly boy group of college students. We talked into the evening about the old abandoned "skunk works" manufacturing facility, UFOS, old war planes, NASA's mission being changed by Osoma, the shuttle program having been destroyed by environmentalist and bloated administration cost. Then they all wanted to talk about the sick shameful shallow pitiful ungodly 9/11 memorial service. These men were a joy to fly with and very informed. We had a great evening discussing world events. This bunch was a few grades ahead of most other students. We ended up on the subject of taxes. Young James Goodlatter pulled out a picture of all the members of congress on the front steps. All four had been congressional pages last summer and his father was a congressman. The boys talked about a flat tax, and that their daddies all paid 50% in taxes and what an outrage that was. They were very much against labor unions and belonged to a group called the Young Rich Republicans. I told them, "You boys are very refreshing, and are at least half right on most subjects but be careful young republicans for you also have been lied to and fooled. You are still one half ass backwards wrong about everything. Look at this group of congressmen in this picture notice they are mostly older not younger men and also lawyers. The truth is none of them pay any taxes at all. If your Goodlatter daddy makes $160,000 a year salary at 50% tax rate that means he would have taken the job for $80,000 if we did away with the tax. It would make no difference to him this is just a numbers game. All of your fathers are union men of the worst kind, the most powerful union there is "Lawyers." Much of their pay comes directly from government. Your daddy is just as guilty of destroying America as the rest of the unions. All of them are sucking the Government treasury dry. Truth is none of these government sucking public union types at any level pay any income tax at all. We should make them tax exempt and lower their pay and stop playing the game. Every other roadside billboard sign in America is about getting signed up on government disability or group medical law suite scams. The Lawyer in each disability claim bills the government $6,000 for every wino and bum they sign up just for filling out the stupid government forms. The doctors and lawyers are bankrupting the system. Government subsidy of lazy liars, lawyers, and loony bin priest or so called doctors is the biggest abuse of power in America. In a free market we would need only one half of the lawyers, one half of the government workers, and college professors and philologists. There is no real need or honest demand for most of these lazy worthless men anyway! They do nothing to create wealth or better our society at all. There would be no college degrees in silly worthless subjects, and much less fake "do nothing" jobs in Government. The bottom 50% of wage earners is called menial or low skilled labor it is not taxed much because the law makers and those men in power are high consumers of menial labor and know that they themselves would be paying the bill. These men not only don't want to tax labor at this lower end but always try to subsidize it; thus using government money to lower their own personal cost. This is the true reason for many of our stupid government programs and also the driving force behind allowing illegal immigration. A government ruling class of elites always needs an underclass for cheap labor. They need to get cheap menial labor to live life to its fullest. Paying honest wages to free men is not to the elite's best interest. If a man's business idea or model can't turn a profit unless he can find men willing to work all day for near nothing (this is called slavery). Then what good is his stupid business plan anyway. The great Steve Jobs has today over 300,000 Chinese slaves working twelve hour plus days, living at the factory, and making $17 dollars a day. This is not the free market at work. These slaves are not free to leave, many committed suicide to get world attention and press. In a true free market business men like this would go out of business. I have as a free man had the opportunity to turn down many job offers because they would not pay the rate I demanded. I have never been unemployed for very long. If you have not been offered jobs by others in your field without ever applying for them then you need to strengthen your skill set no matter what level you are now in. False crony capitalism Fascism communism and slavery is against the ways of God. Why would powerful lawyer types vote to raise the cost of all the labor they buy every day? Look up the owners of any local franchise business, half will be lawyers flush with cash and influence who dabble in business on the side. This large pool of subsidized low end workers many of which are wino bums and drug users is were Osoma gets his voting base and his cheap rent a mobs, brown shirt units and voter fraud units. His occupy Wall Street Mobs are paid thugs of the Democratic Party. Osoma and his party should be hung for gross treason against our constitution.

The fact that all these bums get a small check from the Federal government keeps these men available and keeps their wages down. They also get more back in taxes from the IRS than what they paid in. This very progressive tax system comes straight from Karl Marks but take a closer look. The lowest paid wages in America are not enough for a worker to sustain or feed themselves. These low end workers would not take the low pay unless the big socialist state paid part of their upkeep. Watch these men being picked up for work at very low rates. The small government check is enough to buy their vote and keep them in the "cash only" economy but not enough to live on. Almost every bum in America works a small limited amount at low wages. Each wino knows how much he is allowed to make without losing his check and would always rather work for cash. Half of these bums would move on or dry out without a government check to depend on. Mostly these government checks support illegal drug use, cigarettes, and alcohol in short all of the Osoma voters that are not lawyers, school teachers, and government workers. Most government programs do the exact opposite of what they say they are supposed to do. Poor people are better off in a free economy rather than a big government one because low end wages are suppressed by government programs. A good example of this is migrant farm workers (Mexican slaves) being offered off season government checks, and healthcare to keep them there in shanty towns instead of moving on. Growers could not keep enough workers around at low pay so they used government tax money to subsidize their workers. In a free economy farm work would have to pay more, in a free market the bottom end menial labor cost would go up and benefit poor people more than all government programs.

We Americans have slowly lost all of our personal freedoms during the last sixty years and have slowly sunk into the mud of government. We are becoming just like the rest of the world, and we will soon be as poor as they are. At our present high level of government cost changing the tax collection method will not save us. If we could cut the flat rate back to 10% or less it might work. Tax rates this high on menial labor or a sales tax (fair tax) or consumption tax higher than 15% would just distort economic behavior as people circumvented the tax. This would bring about the end of cash as we know it. All buying and selling would require the mark of the beast to successfully collect the high tax rate. The holy Bible will be found true my friends and every man found a liar. God does know what he's talking about, listen to him, read his word. My young rich republican friends had to leave early still long before closing time. They were nice young men but two of them were angry with me for talking about their Goodlatter daddy. The other two men had hot dates with two girls named Kishia from the ships drama department. These two took their ties off and unbuttoned their shirts revealing two save the whales go green pink t-shirts with an attached AIDS ribbon, and Osoma poster. I was quite impressed yes there was still hope for these young men. They were getting ready to play the bulls and cows mating game and they knew how to impress silly, mindless (easy) liberal women. Why does much of life have to be so phony? The whole game was pointless from the beginning, because the gals were most likely being phony too (ha-ha). I finished up my last coffee sitting by myself and thought about being young again. I was so glad to be old. I have had a wonderful life; truly I've been blessed by the best!

Old men like me in every state legislature have passed a lot of silly laws about sex, mostly to protect their "perfect" little angel granddaughters and to keep their wives happy or at least off their backs. These old men have now forgotten all about being young and shot full of raging hormones. Most of the old men have failed to raise their families in Biblical teaching and do not want to face truth. The cold, hard, truth is that women have been taught not to value their virginity but rather to hate and despise it. In our sick society both marriage and virginity is ridiculed and their perfect little angel granddaughters are mostly vile sluts given over to raging lust, sexual depravity and self love. Each sad young woman is a mirror reflection of our sick, perverted, ungodly, popular culture. God's truth is always rebelled against by wickedness and sin, and sexual transmitted diseases now ruin many young people's lives. We should have never told young Christian girls not to marry and to first screw around for ten or fifteen years. This is against the ways and teaching of God. Do not try to change the Bible to fit your own desire for society. Surprise! God does know what he's talking about and he speaks plainly in his Holy word. We had better listen!

CHAPTER ELEVEN

Iceland and the Volcano

By the evening of our seventh night in Portugal it was time to leave. Tommy Mute's great Uncle and Aunt Bob and Alice Paxton did board the Great Ark just in time. Tommy did not meet them or give away his family connection. Down on main deck our mail plane had been in the garage during harbor stay. This plane was a two prop straight winged old box, with long range and light payload. We planned to use it to save the Paxtons. Early that morning our little team ran around the ship like mice in a grocery store. Before Marshall Moore "head of aircraft maintenance" came to work, we four brave mice led Bob and Alice Paxton to the mail plane and hid them in the baggage compartment. We also mailed their belongings to Ireland so our mail plane would be on track to go there first. A pilot friend one Scott Womack a retired Major living in Ireland would be on the tarmac when the plane landed. Old Marshal Moore or "Duck" always came to work early, but this morning he was very early so I spoke to him in a quiet, stern, and sober voice.

"Duck you never saw us, don't even ask. This is Island Number two serious this is life and death."

Thank God for men you can trust in a pinch. Yes godly men or honor among thieves whatever works. From the gym-or "fitness center" railing I watched the old mail plane come up elevator one and park just off the edge of our flight line. Hours passed, and still we were all watching the plane and pretending not to. When the plane did take off three hours later we all breathed a sigh of relief from distant parts of the ship. I had almost pushed Tommy Mute into that mail plane with Bob and Alice, but did not. I should have known better and trusted my instincts. Only one day later professor Tommy Mute disappeared. Our ships computers had caught up with his family connection to Bob and Alice Paxton. We all feared the worst. Lou and I waved to each other on the deck outside our cabins but we didn't dare hang out together. It seemed we had not yet been found out. Each day now when in sight of the front killing floor cabins I could not stop myself from glancing eerily at the closed doors for any signs of life. What duty to these others did I have? Those men who were not family? Those men who didn't matter? What did I owe them? Should I mutiny the ship, rebel against leadership maybe confront and shoot my old friend Captain Joe Coe. When younger we baby boomer Americans looked down on Germans of World War II age; those Germans that did nothing and looked the other way during the holocaust. Judge not, less you too are judged my friends. I had now become what I despised. I was now just like the frightened Americans back home, too much of a coward to stand up for the rights of the minority.

American road side and airport searches were not constitutional but nobody stood up for freedom. Now there was road side pat downs at "safety" check points and huge prison camps were built all over the country. The local jail inmates of my home town of Salem Virginia were asking for the same rights as Communist Chinese prison camps! The local new jail is bigger than the Salem downtown business district and had no outside yard for inmates at all. By design no inmates would ever be outside to see the light of day ever again and no real visits by family were allowed to save money. Complete lack of sunshine and vitamin D is deadly to humans because men are not moles. Yes it was true that Communist Chinese prisons gave inmates more rights than the local drunk tank in Salem Virginia. Osoma had not prosecuted thousands of counts of voter fraud. Blatant and openly filmed voter intimidation by Black Panther thugs was applauded. Billions were paid to his "brown shirt" street gang ACORN. The laws and rights of free men are laughed at by power drunk low class hoodlums while many lawyers in high paid "fake jobs" sucked the government dry. Why stand up to tyranny in government? This monster was growing bigger every day, why should you? Why should your family take a bullet to stand up for freedom; for the right to vote in honest elections, for the constitution? Take your paycheck and shut up! People who stand up for the Holy Bible or the constitution are hated and laughed at. The Democratic Party criminal gangs will never come after me. I'm one of the loyal, one of the good ones. I even drive an electric car! I'm one that counts. Hell I still watch Oprah show reruns and cry right along with her. I even recycle and don't eat red meat.

Sometimes you do know and you pretend that you don't know or see. You simply look the other way because it's easy. Standing up for freedom, being hated, taking a bullet, fighting tyranny, fighting against Osoma and his thugs is hard. A brave man is one who stands alone and obeys God like Christ did. One who stands for the rights of the few against the popular crowd? The home of the brave is gone forever. American men have been found not worthy, all of them to shy to stand for the few.

After seven cycles of flight duty or twenty eight days the Ark pulled into Iceland but did not dock. On the way we delayed and took our sweet good time spending ten days off the coast of England where we transferred many college professors by helicopter. Ship defense was at a low level and nothing much was going on. When we arrived in Iceland we again picked up some more professor types. All of these new professors were volcanic rock nuts. The same "save the earth" nut jobs as all the dishonest "Global warming" so called environmentalist. They all are required to sing the same "America is wrong Song" to make the big easy government money. True science has nothing whatever to do with their work. There is not a brave or honest man among their ranks. Save us from hair spray, cow farts, air conditioning, motor cars, and farm tractors they shout. Please outlaw the smoking of cigarettes, and the burning of coal and oil and all cars should be electric and expensive forcing most poor slobs (like you) to ride the bus. All of these ideas stem from false science and mentally ill priests unable to see God's truth when they stare it in the face. This false religion bunch wouldn't know a basic science fact if it bit them on the ass.

About one hundred little electric cars were unloaded in Iceland and four tractor trailer loads of freight, all done by ferry. I think Joe was too cheap to dock. Nothing much was going on except the Volcano.

The volcano was wonderful grand and majestic to behold. It had been cooking again now for some months. The heat column reaching skyward and east ward was so large that it caused a mild constant breeze. This mountain put out more air pollution every two hours than all the cars in Europe did in a year. Many hours were spent watching the mountain. Its majesty made you feel small and weak, and not in control of this world. It was awesome and humbling to see a tiny piece of God's power reflected in his creation. That is if you are not a mentally ill humanist earth worshiping environmentalist nut case trying to save the world from deodorant spray and air-conditioning.

Lou and I had heavy hearts about our friend Tommy Mute. We started talking again at the Gospel Café but still did not associate together around ship. To tell the truth, we were scared for our lives. We knew facial recognition software was used on ship and that computers tracked and recorded our movements. Lou was always a pleasure to discuss politics, Holy Bible, and economics with because he was always only half right at best. While still in the harbor at Iceland three more flight cycles later, Lou Goodliar and I were again seated together at the Gospel Café. Lou pushed me a napkin with" Mutes not dead" written on it in very neat script. I smiled, a weight lifted off my shoulders. I crumpled up the napkin and soaked up coffee with it.

That night I'm sure Lou disagreed with my anti-professor speech just to make things look good. The students brought up slavery and the civil War again that night. I pointed out the facts that ancient Ethiopians had light skin European slaves. How brainwashing of the young by government, Church, or home is effective and powerful.

This fact is true be it false teaching, or the ways of God. The hand that rocks the cradle does rule the world and the family; never give this God given right and responsibility to the state.

Mid morning the next day sixteen or eighteen grad students came aboard, all were volcano watchers. Captain Coe asked me to test a new ultra light plane by signing up these students and filing a report. Flying was dangerous in these cold waters next to the huge volcano. The small open planes required flight suits in this weather. Both the flight suits and the planes were manufactured by a Swiss company. These planes worked well with our ships "cable" storage system and flew ten mph faster in level flight. Joe bought thirty six of them. I would never get the chance to fly them again. Our group of student aviators used in part the powerful updrafts from the mountain to soar to dangerous heights. Flight was dangerous here because the planes did not have enough fuel to fight their way back to the ship. I spent my time waving students and shouting "head back now" but many did not listen. My friend Lou was with a group of students that ended up landing on volcano rocks. Six planes were brought back by harbor ferry unable to take off again after landing. I just wasn't into hot rocks and cold weather. The air around this mountain was "brass monkey cold" so I did not go back up again. I also warned Friday to shut down the student fliers. Not until one of the new planes burnt up on hot lava rocks did Friday finally shut the lightweights down. I sent a report off to Joe about the ultra lights "needed increase in fuel capacity and bigger tires." I made my report short and sweet. My mind was on those famous hot tubs in town. I planned to enjoy a little global warming for myself. I signed up on computer to use a sea plane as a taxi into town. Very little shore leave was allowed here in Iceland but not so for us special high class pilots (ha-ha). When I got downstairs I found that many of my pilot buddies had the same idea and were in sea planes in line ahead of me. Every plane was loaded crammed full of pilots all thinking like me; a few beers and the famous hot tubs in town. We pilots were a spoiled lot and used our privileges to the max. There was no shame or care in any of us. I waited through line and slowly came up to the dock and release port in the bottom of the ship. The cable system gave me a green light and I was ready to taxi out. Just at the time of release Lou opened the door of my plane and jumped in. This is against the rules, I was past the green light and also released. The cable system operator then had to run out, and reset the line and his computer. James Kiesler was on dock line duty that night and he angrily waved me out of the way. James gave me the "I should have known it was you" head shake and screamed again for me to keep moving while he walked back to his controls. Looking over at Lou I saw I saw that he was upset dirty, and half frozen to death. Burnt plastic odor filled the cabin.

"What is that smell?" I asked."

Lou was tired and put out. He had melted the soles of his expensive, made in China, boots on those hot lava rocks. The wind in the small open planes was very cold and sucked the heat out of a person very quickly. On the ships deck it was now ten degrees and the little planes were miserable even with a flight suit. Lou for once sat quiet.

"Lou," I said, "I don't mind drinking with a preacher professor if you don't mind drinking with a watering hole Holiness!"

We taxied out of the stern of the ship into the dark harbor, our landing lights worked only fair as headlights. We did not fly but rather skimmed or boated across the harbor."

"Are volcanic rocks hot, Big Lou?

"Yes, hot as hell," he replied, as we splashed our way through the large harbor. Tommy Mute then sat up behind us awakened by Lou Goodliar's large left hand. The plane bounced on the water throwing the half asleep

Tommy Mute back down. We three were laughing and off to a night on the town. Hot tub here we come.

Lou Goodliar did have a (hidden) agenda as always. He let me down my customary two beers during dinner and then suggested we forgo the hot tubs to join with Brother Whitt again. I was a hard sell. The two men bribed me with two more rounds of beer. Lou wanted to buy more books (one for Bob and Alice Paxton and one for his wife.) Little did we know that night that those E-books many months later would cost all three of Lou's friends their lives? Lou Goodliar's friendship was their undoing. Yes, some friends are like that. It's always about them, at the cost of everyone around them.

Professor author and preacher Nathaniel Isaiah Theodore Whitt was still on his book tour and in Iceland this weekend only.

"What's this Whitt guy doing touring with the ship?" I complained loudly as I paid the tip. We all finished eating and started walking up the street. Five blocks up a hill was the auditorium where Whitt was speaking. The sharp wind was bitter cold. We all rested in the lobby gasping for breath, our hearts pounding, and our faces numb from the cold. Professor Whitt was well underway and no one was collecting tickets at the door, so we walked in without paying. That was the highpoint of the evening for me. Whitt was speculating about the Great Pyramid being pre Noah's Flood and the works of the "Sons of God." I bought a book for myself this time still trying to figure out the number twenty-six. The most special number there is. Old Professor Whitt is right about one thing. I do want to be an heir with Jesus Christ and adopted into the family of God, to become one of the "Sons of God" one day. Yes, I want to be a joint heir with the king of kings, nothing else is important in this world. Professor Whitt talked again about Billiard balls and then the number twenty-six. Also about the fact that the numbers nine and six were both modeled after the two thumbs of a man's hands. He placed one ball on the pool table just like before then put six around it and then six again forming the Hebrew Star. God becoming flesh, the covenant with Abraham, and the twelve disciples with Jesus at center. I started to understand the reflection of God in Math when he demonstrated the circle of fifths and the overtone series. He then, like before, took the six balls of the Hebrew star and put three on top and three on the bottom forming a sphere. The closest stacking of spheres always in groups of thirteen twelve points around one center. He then started doing pyramids and the Carbon atom, the number 666, then the golden mean and I was lost again. I never was good at math. The golden mean squared a deck of cards and the number twenty-six. (Soon it all started to run together.)

Only one king can be at the table for a double mined man is unstable in all his ways. Look in the mirror, do not be fooled. Remember the fear of God is the beginning of wisdom. Time is short in this life. The change of season is upon us. Study thyself to be approved before God. Study his word. Secondary is math proofs and study. Notice his word has twenty-six letters a reflection of God an overtone.

Test the spirits, seek out your own salvation with fear and trembling. Even the elect can be fooled. As in the days of Noah, so shall it be . . .

"Cornelius wake up," said Tommy Mute shaking me violently, "The lecture is over."

"As in the days of Noah, so shall it be, as in the days of Noah so shall it be" plagued my mind as we walked out of the auditorium.

Goodliar and I left Tommy Mute in Iceland. We gave him all the cash that we had.

"Don't worry about me," Tommy Mute said. "I'll stop by Ireland first and then move onto my mission in Africa after a few short weeks. It's much too dangerous to enter America. The three of us had shared information between us on the world wide snuffer wagons that president Osoma and EU leaders had deployed. No place was safe for Jews and terror was spreading Worldwide. We said our Goodbyes. Tommy Mute paid cash for an upstairs room and Lou and I started up the sea plane. I shouted at Lou above the engine noise.

"Lou, I didn't know that Tommy Mute lived in Africa. I've heard about the killing of Christians, the killing of white farmers, the AIDS epidemic. I thought the world had given up on Africa. The Global warming people have targeted all Africans for death! Doesn't Tommy Mute know a lost cause when he sees one? Both the Church and Islam the (east and the west) have held a holy book in one hand and a bomb or chains in the other killing off or enslaving all the Africans for hundreds of years. Do we save them, then kill them or kill them to save them or does it matter?"

"The true church, like Tommy won't give up," said Lou, "Only the nations will. Leaders like Osama, and of course the Great Whore on Babylon herself."

"What did you say?" I asked.

"Remember this, Cornelius," replied Lou. "Wherever the flock of God is, there you will find the lion also. Wherever God is and whatever God does the angel is not far off. He is always on the hunt to kill, steal, or destroy. He is the dark cards in the mirror trying to copy God. The angel wants to be as the most high. Look at the letters on your cap. Pull down your visor say left hand right hand." We pulled into the ships big back door and docked even as we were talking!

"So you are saying it's my fault, Brother Lou?

"Look in the mirror again, Cornelius!" said Lou as he got out of the plane. I think Lou pretended to know more than he really did.

"See yeah, Cornelius," Lou shouted, as he jumped onto the dock and waved goodbye.

Alone now I thought to myself. Between being Holiness, my giant, Whit's book, this ship, being a drunk, Captain Coe and this fellow Goodliar; it ain't no wonder I'm going nuts. Goodliar sounds good at first but always leaves something missing in the end. Sometimes you just don't know and you have to go with your gut.

After a full days rest I was back at my big round Corner table at the ship's Gospel Café. Two students had a copy of the New York Times and were talking about the need to raise taxes before America defaulted on its debt. These two young students were sitting together both of them were named Kishia. One ordered an expensive fancy whipped chocolate coffee. The table filled up and the anti-professor weighed in on taxes and debt!

"Kishia," I asked, "That's a large fancy drink you ordered. Why did you buy one?"

"I love chocolate, Cornelius, and I made a good grade on my test so I deserved it" she giggled.

"I scored a high grade too," the other Kishia laughed, "but I don't have money to burn. My daddy's not rich like fancy pants here".

"That's our lesson for today," I replied. "Note she desired the drink and she had the cash, so she demanded it. Nobody forced her. That is the simple key to understanding economics; the buyer always pays. Every one of us makes choices of buying and selling every day; this fact is simple and always true so remember "Only buyers pay." This is true when it comes to taxes or coffee or Newspapers. Kishia number one's boyfriend, Jim Roberts, sat down with us and explained how hard he worked cutting grass last summer. Jim boasted that he would never pay that much for a fancy coffee drink. He said that rich people like Kishia's father should pay more in taxes to help out America.

"Jim, how much did you charge for cutting grass?" I asked.

"Some lawns were very small so I charged only $10," said Jim. "Others I got paid up to sixty dollars each."

"Did you pay income taxes on your grass money?"

"No, cash money only," laughed young Jim.

"I see here in the paper that President Osoma has hired more IRS agents to catch tax cheaters like your self Jim. What would you do if he made you pay taxes?"

"That wouldn't be fair," said Jim, "I'm not rich!" the grass might not even be worth cutting if I had to pay tax, Cornelius."

"What if you were cutting my grass for $10 and I told you that all I could pay you was $5. Would you still do my grass?"

"Do you know how much gas costs since Osoma has been elected, Cornelius? I can't afford to start my mower for $5. I'm sorry."

"That is my whole point, Jim. The reason I have to pay a young man back home $10 to cut my grass is because he won't do it for five or six dollars. This is how income taxes work. If Osoma hired enough agents and charged you 50% tax on cutting grass what would you do? Would you then cut a yard for only $5? No! I would have to pay you $20. Osoma would take his $10 and you would still get your $10. This is true because you won't do it for $5. The same is true for "fancy pants" father in his work. "The Buyer always pays." Most income tax is really a sales tax on labor and causes unemployment. Some people will not pay the $20 cost of getting their grass cut and so less young men like you, will be cutting grass, others will complain and pay to cut less often."

"Her daddy does income tax returns. He runs a big company and owns some stock in Ford Motor Company. He is on TV doing advertisements everyday about doing taxes. My father drives a big rig truck. He "works" for a living. My father says he pays too much in taxes and it's just not fair, and that Fancy Pants father should pay more."

"This simply is not true," I answered. "If you increase taxes on "Fancy Pants" (Kishia's) father he will "pass on the cost" to people getting their taxes done and double his price. Your father the truck driver is the same. If his boss calls him on the phone and says; I have a run to Chicago for you tonight it pays the driver your usual $100 but Osoma has taken half of your money so will you do it now for only fifty. "What would your father say then Jim?"

"I'm not driving all night to Chicago for only fifty bucks, give the run to somebody else. No one is forced to drive a truck, and no one is forced to do other peoples taxes for them. They do work only when the price is right and someone is willing to pay. Jim's father's boss would have to pay $200 and increase the freight rate charge to get a truck driver to take it. When the freight rate goes up then less trucks will be on the road because some freight will not be worth shipping. Note taxes cause unemployment, and the buyer, only the buyer always pays".

"We must raise taxes on the rich, Cornelius," cried out Kishia number two. "We must raise taxes to save America before we default on our debt." Fancy pants father makes money off of his Ford stock also, and only pays capital gains tax. It's just not fair." Kishia, people who buy stock are part owners of a company, Ford has thousands of different owners; the small dividends paid per share to stock holders has all ready been taxed many times before. The Ford Motor Company pays income taxes at 35% on earnings, and then the owners pay 15% again if they share in that profit, and after tax income was used to buy or invest in the stock in the first place. Taxing them more would only raise the price of Ford products or put them out of business. "Let me tell you students a story that will help you understand the world economy. A simple story about a small island named America and its king that became very powerful after the world war. America was a small Island in the middle of the sea rich with forest and farmland and blessed by God. Good King Washington ruled over the fifty families who lived there. He was a Godly, just, and honest ruler. The King owned one half of the land ran the only bank and ran the only store (king-mart) where everybody shopped. He also owned a gold mine which made him fifty coins a day. The king kept taxes very low. His people worked hard and the store was always full of wonderful goods to buy and his people were in happy days.

One day another king came to visit who had a large ship and a kingdom far away. This Eastern King offered to sell King Washington shoes to put in his store for only $2 a pair. Since he sold shoes for $35 dollars a pair, King Washington was delighted. King Washington had nothing to sell the visiting king (at least not much.) He bought the shoes and sold them in his store for eight dollars a pair and made lots of money. The cheap shoes were very popular and the people of America praised the good king. The shoes flew off the shelves and he ordered another ship load. Everyone was happy except the five families who used to make shoes on the island. They all went out of business they could not make shoes that cheap. The many Eastern kings from China and India used slave labor. They were evil kings who did not pay honest free market wages, they had so many slaves they wanted some dead anyway.

The next King to stop by had a load of cars for sale for only $200 each. King Washington was delighted he could sell cars for $800 a piece at King-Mart, make a fortune and save his citizens money. The cars on the Island cost $1,500 each back then. Again everybody was happy except the ten families who made cars on the island. They all went out of business. The king needed some office workers and also needed sailors for his new Navy so he hired the people who went out of business to work for him. He had his New Navy sail around the island and they looked very impressive. His office workers were very happy because they only worked four hours a day and could retire after a few years and do nothing. The king did have one main problem. He was running out of gold coins, because each time another king came by and he paid them in gold his pile of gold got smaller. The next time a ship came by the good king would be out of gold money! He had to do something different.

The king printed up paper money that was redeemable for gold at his bank and put the little Gold he had left out where his people could see it, and said his Gold mine was doing very well. His subjects trusted the king and this worked great, but he still didn't have gold to pay the next king that stopped bye. The king had his Navy drive around the world on tour and drop bombs on people. They looked very impressive. The good King Washington had promised his people many things to stay in power. He took in $3,000 a month in taxes but was spending more than that each month. The king kept this a secret and pretended to have gold in his bank. When his old friend the King with the shoes came by again, this Eastern king agreed to accept payment for the shoes in the new paper money. This made things much easier on King Washington. Everyone the World over trusted the good king Washington and most people were now his office workers, and his New Navy looked really nice. Good King Washington printed paper money and sent it all over the world and the world shipped him anything he wanted. The Eastern Kings now had huge stacks of his paper money and each time a ship would come by they would come ashore and make a deposit in the Kings bank. Not in gold but in his new paper money. The good king always bought more stuff than he sold to the Eastern Kings and the Kings kept depositing money in his bank. All of these deposits the king had to pay interest on. The good king pretended that when an Eastern King made a deposit that it made up for his over spending at home, so he just used the money they deposited. This of course is simply not true. The Kings "overspending" was done with all new printed money. So were his overseas spending sprees for junk for his wife, and also the money he spent for his Navy. The good King Washington ran the most successful counterfeiting ring in history. In the year 1971 the king had to admit to everyone that he was out of gold and now for fifty years his money has gone down in value each year. This is called Inflation of the Currency or printing money.

Each year now since, King Washington prints more money to make up for the dollars loss in value. Each time someone deposits money in his bank the king must pay them interest on their money. The many evil kings of the world supported him, because they had so much of his phony money on deposit that they could now lose everything. The slaves in these other kingdoms could not afford to buy anything because being slaves they were not paid. King Washington kept hiring the people on his Island that the slave camps put out of business, and his Navy looked very good. He was very proud. Now almost everybody on his Island worked for him doing or producing nothing of real value. He even paid his pretty wife $350,000 a year to be a public relations officer at his college. Then he told his bank to loan money to his family and friends, even if they could not pay it back and ordered his people to shut down all of the coal mines, the oil wells and the smoke stacks. He then wrote checks to all the drunks and bums to keep them happy. He, the wise king, now believed that the earth would soon come to an end because his people in America had life too good and that this had to change. The King said that his people in America made too much smoke cooking out in the back yard and breathed too much of the world's air. They should become slaves, like everybody else in the world, to make things fair. They should all get by on less food and not drive big, fancy cars. Yes, King Washington was crazy even certifiably insane, but nobody would dare say anything about this crazy new religion of his because he had a rare skin condition that darkened his complexion so much that everyone felt sorry for him. No one would admit that he was a stupid babbling fool who followed a false religion. Soon the King Washington turned against God, the Holy Bible and God's chosen people. He passed laws that men could marry men, that killing babies was now legal and that only his thugs could carry guns, that not liking him was a hate crime, that all cars had to be very small and electric and gasoline prices had to be very high. He wanted to punish his people and make them change their ways because they were just too rich and had lives to good and would not let dark people like him win on TV game shows. His people were and had been blessed by God, but the king got rid of God in his schools and on his money. The king told his America that they were not a Christian country and then double crossed Israel. He would not even talk to their prime minister when he came to visit. It didn't take long before his kingdom was forgotten his people were all dead and his Island was filled by desert sand."

"Tell us who King Washington is in real life Cornelius, we love stories," said both Kishia's in duet high pitched voices.

"That's enough of my story for now," I said, as I mixed up some flavoring in my strong French roast coffee, before continuing again.

"Free trade with honest money between free men is God's way. Printing counterfeit money and slavery is the way of man. The Holy Bible calls it "cutting the coin." Who could have guessed? God knew what he was talking about? So did some idiot named Thomas Jefferson but Osoma was smarter and knew better than God.

The Holy Bible was right all along! Who knew? Many honest kings have been tempted to "cut the coin" before in history and many have. The truth is a small amount of money printing might even be good for a kingdom as mild inflation is less destructive to wealth creation than deflation. But a tyrant (like a drunk) can not stop. A drunk can function for a while and not stumble. A little bit of red wine is even good for you the Bible says. Yes God is a loving and forgiving God but in the end God will not be mocked.

America gave up all pretence to honest money in 1971 (just a few short years ago). America has also turned against God during this time. The US Government has grown drunk on power ever since. Why say no to anything or anybody? We have a money printing machine. The price of over spending and printing money is always paid for by the loss of currency value or inflation. This cost is paid by all the Kings citizens and everyone else holding bank note dollars, not by adding up all the deposits to the bank and calling it our national debt. This is a made up story and it is simply not true. Truly the private owners of the Federal Reserve Bank owe interest payments on deposits made to their bank, not the Kings treasury. We gave them the privilege, right, and power to print a bank note which is used as our national currency. That does not mean we pay the interest on any deposit made. All deficit spending is printed money. It does not matter if we write Treasury bill or Federal Reserve note, or greenback on the top of it. With our 100% fiat money no bank reserve is used. A reserve of what? Cash (ha-ha).Please let me be plain! When someone makes a deposit in the Federal Reserve Bank by purchasing what we falsely label a Treasury bill this does not mean that the bank is owed money by the taxpayers. This is a shell game just like the Democrats and the Republicans. One half the Republicans are fake and really siding with the Progressives and Socialist. Our Federal Reserve fronts itself as a true national bank, and then prints money and wants to charge citizens interest on it while the ink is still wet. This system is due for an overhaul. How did this come about? Out of necessity!

The sad truth is a free republic can not tax the people of New York and spend the money in Germany. Then tax New York again and spend it in Japan. Many client states since World War II have tried to work with us and become great allies but the sad truth is our world wide military Pax-Americana empire cost must be paid with printed money because we do not tax them. We have today the same problem that our mother country Great Briton had with us. The cost of empire is only the beginning. Our trade deficit and budget deficit is a one two punch adding to our dizzy counterfeiting madness. We are paying most Americans not to work or to work at worthless government jobs as councilors, and advisors. Our department of education is a joke and all departments need to be cut by at least 50% but that's another matter for another day.

The model America is presently following based on printing money is not stable and is against the laws of God, his Holy Bible and simple math. The "ship of state" is not on a strong Godly Foundation and will not survive history. The pressure of our demise and fall will lead us toward a one world government and a lost of all our liberty."

The students left my table that evening, each one still calling for higher taxes. Each one still wanted to soak the rich, and each one hoped to work for the government and have full retirement after twenty five years of long coffee breaks, longer vacations from doing little or nothing.

End of Chapter

CHAPTER TWELVE

The Gathering

We on board the Great Ark believed that we were heading towards the Big Apple. We were steaming the usual Atlantic crossing route as liners have done for years. Unknown to us yet the ship had turned southeast that night instead of southwest.

A tall lanky older black Gospel singer named Mike Russell had flown from his home in Brooklyn to catch the Ark in Iceland. Mike came aboard the evening we departed and was there early waiting for me that night at the ships Gospel Café. This visit was now one of an old friend. Mr. Russell was not on the music schedule for another five days or so. Mike had pulled up a chair and turned it around backwards as was his custom or maybe it was to match his hat (Ha-ha). Tonight Mike was down hearted. Worry showed heavy on his face. I greeted my old friend with Number six (24-26) you may know it by heart.

The Lord bless thee, and keep thee, the lord make his face shine upon thee and keep thee, **the Lord lift up his countenance upon thee, and give thee peace!**

After our hugs, hellos, and a bowl of hot chili, Mike got straight to the point!

"Cornelius some friends in Brooklyn have come to me for help. Things are very bad! Yes, very bad. My friends believe that because of my hit songs twenty-five years ago and the little bit of TV I do, that I'm someone who can help them (a leader a strong man). Truth is I'm none of these things."

"Come on Russell give this a rest, you started out as a boxer remember? Sing us one of your old songs, singing will cheer you up. How about singing "Operator" I've always liked."

(Mike-interrupts) "Now listen up, Cornelius! That's not my song anyway, now just listen! Snuffers, Cornelius; in Brooklyn every night, they call them "snuffers." (*Mike having a breakdown crying*)

"Don't sit out there on that chair brother Mike slide yo` black ass in this booth so we can talk"

Brother Mike leaned over the table giving me three quick lightning fast left jabs to my face with sound effects for comic relief. He mumbled something about "hillbilly cracker." Mike and I have always played around with each other, we are both old fighters but he doesn't know about my wife's Cracker family, at least I thought not (ha-ha). I held up two fingers and volunteer worker Kathy Daily knew what to bring, she could see me clearly across the near empty Gospel Café! Kathy sent Julie with two full pots of strong French Roast Coffee. Both pots would be dry twice before Mike and I stopped talking that night. (So would my personal container of Irish flavoring).

"Cornelius, I know first hand of four "Snuffer" vehicles in operation. I have seen them myself and I know one place where they go with the bodies. My friends took me and showed me! I would not have believed them otherwise. We took pictures inside and out. There is another one in New Jersey I've only heard of. Politicians brag about the crime rate and drug use going down year after year but my God, Cornelius, what's this world coming to? I heard this stuff started to stop sex offenders and then grew over time.

"Slow down Mike, stay calm and start at the beginning" He nodded.

"Ok," Mike said taking a knuckle breaking stretch.

"A "Snuffer" is a police paddy wagon. It looks like any other Paddy wagon, but it never has any unit numbers on it, just the word, "Police." It holds up to fifteen or twenty people. Police scan your face then they know which Paddy wagon to put you in. Many honest police think they are relocation wagons. Cornelius the truth is these people are never seen again. Police pick up street people, drunks, bums, anyone without papers, prostitutes, punks, drug dealers, just about anybody. The streets are cleaned up quick. Police are looking for members of different families often only part Jewish, often from western European background. My Preacher said they are looking to kill the one hundred and forty-four thousand before the advance team leaders get here."

"What did you say, Mike? Did you say advance team leaders? Do you mean angels?

"No, Cornelius," said Mike. Two flesh and blood men, two witnesses, two men who come here and are working for Jesus! These "Snuffers" are trying to stop the people of the book, trying to stop the Bible prophecy from coming true. These young male babies and their mothers are targeted. They are looking for tribes and families scanning and then DNA is how this is done. Cornelius, my preacher could explain it much better but he's gone. He disappeared. Yes, we fear the worst. He said finding the right mothers to kill was equal in difficulty as a math and computer problem, to counting the sands on the beach, or stars in the heavens, many colleges are helping.

"This is how "Snuffers" work, Cornelius," said Mike continuing. "As the wagon travels the exhaust fumes are pumped into the back of the paddy wagon. No arrest, no judge, no trail, just a computer face scan. The good of the many out weighs the rights of the few. They kill all of them, Cornelius, just as Pastor Thomas they are simply never seen again. The paddy wagon pulls through two automatic doors and parks on a tipper. The wheels are grabbed by the machine and the paddy wagon tilts 90% like, a drawbridge. Then a big hose is hooked to the backend and the doors come open for an automatic wash cycle with hundreds of gallons of steaming scalding hot water. The bodies` dead or alive, all slide down a big fiberglass tube to a garbage grinder the size of a city bus. I know you don't believe me Cornelius but I've been off drugs for years"

"Stop Mike, I do believe you! In fact did the large fiberglass tubes have clear plastic high pressure hot water lines wrapped around them to add more water to the flush?"

"Yes," said Mike Russell

"They are made in Germany, Mike, old traditions die hard, so do many modern day Jews it seems. History does repeat itself! Those people are fish food right?

"We believe so, Cornelius. Yes, we believe so."

"My friends asked me to help them also, Brother Mike! People refuse to believe that Osoma is just as bad as the entire Democratic Socialist Humanist, known ungodly killers throughout history. Truth is they all grow from the same plant and the same seed, the same weed. We all know what it looks like when it grows up, and it's not pretty. This evil is not just the godless leaders fault. The public itself is half to blame. These voters want to be taken care of forever, and willingly hand themselves over to earthly kings forsaking the ways and blessings of God. Only your family loves you enough to be a care giver for long. Young or old, God's way works every time and man's way leads to blood and killing every time. This is always true. As corn has tassels, the Socialist Humanist weed has class and race envy, hate, warfare and always kills, kills and kills. God will not be mocked, not by Osoma or by America.

Look at this old article from the former Hill and Dale College before taxes shut them down and Osoma turned it into a federal prison. They say some of the professors never left and now never will (Ha-ha). Just like Osoma closed that big school in Lynchburg Virginia, and the Heritage Foundation. They were on Osoma's hate speech hit list early in his second term as president."

"Cornelius, you can't blame Osoma for everything! He does care about us brothers, yes including you fool. Yes, I know you're family, just look at your hands Nigger! That was not Osoma! That was the Department of Education that Czar Barnie something. Government had to keep standards. Hill and Dale was an old "Cracker school" with divisive hate speech! They taught stuff like the civil war was not about slavery. Osoma's leadership is the only thing good about America. He's even got the Islamic brothers helping out the black communities."

"Oh Mike," I said, "Where do I begin?"

"Mike, with all due respect both of those schools were shut down by Osoma to control information and education per the Communist Manifesto Handbook for ruling Socialist Elites. Just like old Karl Marks taught them to. Remember much of what you have been taught is a lie and is backwards from truth, just like a reflection in a mirror. For example, do you think Osoma cares about homeless people? You just told me about the snuffers. Remember back when conservatives were in power? Every day you saw a story about poor, dumb, homeless people and the economy was booming. Now with the second great depression and the serious bankruptcy of America how many stories about homeless people have you seen on the TV news? . . . Why not? . . . . It's like they don't exist! They are lying to you Brother Mike!

Now listen to this article, in this old newsletter. It says that 78% of the residents of New York City get some type of check from the City, State,

Port Authority, or Federal government, or they are students, minors or non-citizens. These are people on Social Security, retired teachers, cops, and firemen, or those working now and people on welfare in jail, the list is endless. There's simply not enough left to be taxed to pay all the people getting checks. Government raised taxes and then borrowed and now every level of government is broke. What else can they do but thin out the ranks of the most costly, the most useless, the least wanted, the ugly ones, the stupid ones even the black ones, or the Jewish ones. We have to decide some way of picking out which ones to kill. That old saying is completely true. When they came for the (fill in the blank) I did nothing when they came for the next and so on. That old saying is not a joke. This is truly how socialism works and that is just what people voted for in your boy Osoma! Mike, it matters not what color our leader is but rather what his relationship with God is. We fight not against flesh and blood, but against powers and municipalities in high places and spiritual wickedness. Osoma is simply against the Holy Bible and the ways of almighty God." Mike and I talked a few more times during the cruise but when he left for Dublin he was still paranoid, fearing for his life and still supporting Osoma.

Three days cruise from Iceland, Lou Goodliar and myself were both standing on the high deck railing outside our cabins. It was obvious to both of us that we would not be going to the Big Apple. The Ark was moving south by southeast. Lou was pointing franticly at the sun and waving at me from down port deck. The ship was moving very slowly, very much not in a hurry, making only about four knots. This was just enough to keep us stable in the water. As an old sailor I knew we were tuning our ETA to meet or miss somebody or something, and by the looks of things it must be somebody important.

Our ship's paint crew was always staffed by about eighteen men, all on daylight shift. Every day of every voyage they were painting in at least two places around the ship. On the bottom of the ship and up to just past the water line were round robot painter scrubbers. These amazing little robots are called "crabs." Every twelve hours or so, the "crabs" would move around to a new location. At this time the ship would slow down to below four knots for about six minutes. This slow down was called "crabbing" We had now been in a long term crabbing mode for some reason. 400 plus seamen were added to our paint crew, and the cleaning crew was doubled. The whole ship was cleaning and polishing every thing in sight. The ole' gal was putting on makeup and eye shadow for somebody, but who I wondered? Dress white inspections were held by all departments. We also practiced very difficult military stuff, (ha-ha), like standing still in a straight line for the first time for most students.

We pilots and officers always dressed for dinner. Each man had his "best" coat and pants (or two) and our more worn everyday pair. We officers also had inspections and practiced our spit shine and brass polish. Yes, we were all getting ship shape. Groups of student flyers practiced formation flying at slow, low to ground, salute speeds. Many younger pilots had to be passed off on three major formation flying skills. We pilots drilled the squads of beginner, pro, near pro, and student flyers. Everyone was working hard long extra shifts as the Ark sailed at crabbing speed, while killing time to make ourselves look pretty. When we approached the rock of Gibraltar all flight operations stopped. The Great Ark slowly and majestically steamed into the Mediterranean Sea. All activity on ship was soon radically different from normal. A wave of excitement filled the ship. No flights, no destination on computer, nothing on our phones, no briefings. Rumors ran wild. The crew didn't know what to believe. More drill, more painting was ordered. Our work pace drew to a high fever pitch. The main deck "where planes are stored" shone like new money. Another carrier was behind us, another was south of us. We continued moving, painting and polishing nonstop. Three weeks after Gibraltar, the ship ran into the Island of Cyprus. I mean we "ran into" the Island of Cyprus. This is crazy I thought to myself. Just ahead of us was a rock face full of sea birds with waves breaking against the cliffs. We were just right of center from a volcano shaped mountain and parked much too close for a ship this size. I had never seen anything like this before. Our crew came out on deck to have a "look see." The old US Navy never did anything like this. We anchored down hard with extra lines like I'd never seen a battle carrier do. All of the ships older model B44s (sixteen of them) had flown off two days before to a land base and were practicing for "The Gathering." Old guard pilots like me were sitting this one out. "Praise God!" Our remaining aircraft were parked on the flight deck or crammed into garage space. Our planes looked good, but we could not fly. On our left and on our right was parked other Ark type carriers. Each one pulled in close to us and anchored down hard. Three ships in a row with the Great Ark at center. We were very close together. Flags, banners, grand-stands decorated our flight deck. On the left or north side of this Volcano were three more old American carriers parked just as ourselves.

Three in a row close up to the rock face. In the center was open water. At the center front face of the volcano were parked still another three carriers. These three were set back from the cliffs a little bit more than the length of a carrier. Nine Air craft carriers were parked around the open water at the center of this high rock face mountain. High up on the cliff was an overhanging stage and podium. Above that was a long white column building or hotel stretching across the side of the mountain. We sailors were so close to the cliffs that an echo formed as men shouted. Pyramid shaped laser boxes containing powerful speakers were placed on deck. One could hear clearly from any place on ship. High on the cliffs in front of the long white buildings grand stands were being constructed. Flags and lights were everywhere. Excitement was building as people formed this big party called "The Gathering." I remembered now what Franklin A Donner had said. He and Wendy were going to "The Gathering" and they were so proud to have been invited. This was a big deal this Gathering, but nothing was on the news about it at all, nothing on the radio. I watched the file that Ralph from the Space Port sent me and it chilled me to the bone! How could a party of this size be secret?

There were many private yachts covering the sea like lilies on a pond. Security was handed over to four destroyers (that I could see). These ships stayed on the distant horizon. No planes or helicopters flew inside of this "no fly zone" inside of the destroyers except for show planes. After six days of preparation and practice "The Gathering" came to life that Friday evening. At mid afternoon people started boarding the Great Ark by ferry. Each ferry docked into the large sea door at stern. The main deck (below) was now a large dinning room with white tablecloths. The flight deck was now grandstands. Porta-Johns were everywhere, so were beer gardens and snack bars. Casual business is what they called the dress for ticket holders; dress whites were the order of the day for crew. Bridges or walkways were placed between ships that were parked side by side. Fifteen thousand people (at least) came onto the Ark that day. There was to have been over three hundred thousand people at "The Gathering." Tickets to this affair started at twenty thousand dollars a piece and went up. Just before dusk our student flyers that had been practicing for days started circling overhead sixteen from each of the nine carriers for 144 planes in total. They flew slowly with wings stretched out straight like sea birds. On the belly center hard point of each plane was a large fuel tank and a laser box. These laser light boxes were being were being controlled by computer. Laser light and sound would blast between the boxes on the ships and shore and planes. Like soaring Eagles the planes flew circling above us. The laser show was very impressive. Not even choppers flew inside the destroyer ring "show" planes only! Some of the crew said that "The Gathering" was a show to out do "Al-Quds Day" (the further most Mosque) or Jerusalem Day put on by the Islamic World. We would outdo the Moslems big time (we had bathrooms Ha-ha). Yes, the Islamic World is "Quadded" alright! Islam got the notion that Mohammad flew away to heaven on a winged horse from the spot of the dome of the Rock! This notion was just the Devil himself day dreaming of course. Big stupid lies are always fun to make up in any in any culture. The bigger the lie the better and then repeat it often. I guess that one is just as good as those 72 virgins. We (the West) are just as stupid with our classic "National Debt" lie. It is very hard to beat a really good "big lie." Ask Satan he is the father of them all.

During that evening the big show roared and flashed all around us. Holy Bible verses filled my mind to overflowing often knocking me to my knees like a hammer. I prayed without stopping but could not concentrate or very well stand, or walk a straight line. "**Oh how I loved thee oh Jerusalem-I will make Jerusalem a stone among the nations—Bones trodden down until the time of the Gentiles is full filled!** Verses echoed in my head!

I was constantly miserable and ill-tempered. The planes and light show was incredible. They soared up and down, back and forth, as if leaves in a whirlwind. Our planes anti-collision system and maneuverability was entertaining and put to good effect, it was truly a wondrous spectacle to behold. All heads pointed skyward in wonder, "oohs" and "aahs" were common. When the laser show intensified and images were projected onto the cliffs and into the air, people cheered. Holograms formed in smoke and everyone stood in constant awe of the show. The planes above looked as of the inside of a Christmas tree or a giant whirlwind of light and sound. The sound of the speakers was loud enough to "rock your bones," with lows so low you could not hear but rather felt the music. Real fireworks also sent shockwaves of sound that could seemingly knock a person down. Many speakers spoke from the platform and it was obvious that this "Gathering" was about one thing "Jerusalem."

This show tonight was only a warm up, a practice run or prelude to the big event Saturday night!

I stood on a railing with Captain Joe Coe and Lou Goodliar. How strange it was to see them together. Many of the other officers stood inside and outside the Great Arks main Bridge in cocktail fashion. These seats were now priceless at "The Gathering" Joe only allowed officers. We all watched the fancy show of glitter and lights and just like a Christmas tree most were fooled. The dark angel is an angel of light that knows his craft. I was sick inside, and stayed constantly in prayer, this "Gathering was not for me.

Speakers spoke about Jerusalem but not much about Jesus. This show was all about not letting the Islamic world overtake Jerusalem. They spoke about God's Holy Mountain and protecting it at all cost. This sounded good to many 'untrained ears" but to one with holiness ears this "Gathering" was a fright, and a heavy burden. I could tell that some Saints felt as I did but most of my shipmates were taken in by the glitter. This was a sick perversion of our Lord Jesus that tried to kill our spirit. The people on ship were drunk, not only with drink, but with evil!

Yes, each speaker spoke of protecting the city of peace but also then stated they were fair. They talked about the rights of non-Jews and of helping the Palestinians. Many stated that the Jew could not use the Holy Bible to justify a claim to the Holy Mountain! They called it an "International City."

"What Bible did they read," I shouted out loud!

Speakers at the big podium really wanted to take Jerusalem for themselves, and save it from Islam and Jews both the same. They spoke lies and double speech and sounded like Democrats on political campaign parade always divisive, untruthful, vengeful and ungodly. They were preachers, but were not working for Jesus. Some speakers came very close to true preaching, but still stood as liars in the end, yes even Goodliars.

These speakers filled me with disgust and fear. I thought about the bloody crusades going on for years and the big light shows Hitler used in his Socialist Party Rallies in old Germany. Bible verses continued to flood my mind and I wished Jesus would return or just turn my giant lose. One is all it would take. God could just say the word, but he instead takes insults from evil men. God was today still giving sinful men a chance! What love is like Jesus! I looked around for my giant, but he was nowhere to be seen. I wondered how many giants Jesus had working for him. If these men could only see, they'd run to the mountains and hide. God has a master plan. God has his own schedule, "to everything there is a season."

Joe and Lou went into Joe's office, talking loud and, or arguing and I joined them. Friday nights show was now about half over and much of us could not stand it any longer. When I walked in Leo Pugh was wound up. He was preaching to Joe, Unk, Duck, Booth, Lou and Chief of staff Friday (who was asleep on Joe's couch). Excuse me make that drunk on the couch. Yes, both Friday's show and officer Friday were now one half gone (haha).

The lights in the office were turned off but enough light flashed in through the windows to see clearly. Lou and Unk got in a few words here and there, but Leo was on a preaching role! Joe tried his best to console and calm down the old preacher back into the party spirit, but to no avail. "The Gathering" had gotten Leo (an old Radio preacher) mad and fired up for God, which raised my spirit!

"You will know them by their fruits" roared, Leo Pugh slamming his fist down on Joe's desk. "The angel comes to kill and destroy. He always leaves a river of blood and always tries to replace God. To take over what God loves. What does a modern Catholic Priest say? Your sins are forgiven, that is God's place not mans! What about Islam? It is a heretic religion of the sword of lies, of mans blood, mans laws. Why that nutcase, pedophile, pervert Mohamed never even came close to Jerusalem. Further most Mosques my ass, there was no Mosque in Jerusalem, not yet back in his day, much less flying off on a winged horse. Death misery and lies are the signs and fruits, the calling card of the angel not of Jesus. The Jews are God's chosen people and his instrument in this world, no matter what Rome or Mecca says or does about it! Today or in the very last day, during the coming time of Jacob's trouble Gods Word will stand. The bloody history of Rome, the Crusades, the Inquisition with fifty million dead, the holy wars of Islam these are all fruits of Satan. The Golden Head of Babylon has awakened. The great statue, that profit Daniel warned us about, is coming to life here in these last days of grace. The Jewel of God cuts it to pieces (Jesus). This is how it must and will be. This Great Whore of Babylon, drunk with the Blood of the Saints. The King (Banker) will be in Babylon again. Now watch world wealth pour in after the Iraq war. His whore is Rome, and she is us! Yes, the merchants of the earth will weep for us and our former glory from their slave camps. Open your eyes we are in Cyprus for God's sake, the jumping off point for the crusades, the Vatican's Unholy Wars. (Leo slammed his fist down again). Joe pushed his chair back and was uncomfortable with old Leo's stare and spitting breath

(Ha-ha). Joe turned toward me to lighten the moment! While raising his arms in a self defensive gesture!

"Cornelius, tell us what you think" . . . . There was a moment of awkward silence.

"Blood of the Saints," I stammered. "I'm still trying to figure out the number twenty-six, the Levites, my giant, and being Holiness."

Joe Coe jumped in with yet another question. "What do you think might be hidden on Island number two Cornelius, besides old ancient guns?"

"Are you drunk sir, you're talking out of your head, and this ship wasn't named after Noah's Ark, was it?"

A simple "No," was all Captain Coe said.

"Oh my," I muttered slowly sitting down. Lou Goodliar then took Joe's painting of the last supper and took it off the wall. He then walked over to a large mirror and held the edge of the painting up to it and asked,

"How many men are in this picture now Cornelius?

"Twenty-six," I said softly.

"Which one is the real and true church?" asked Lou! "Which ones are the true disciples of God? What does the angel do in this world? He wants to be as God! He is a counterfeit God! What does Satan Say in Isaiah 12?

"I will ascend above the heights of the clouds: I will be like the most high!"

Leo Pugh then started up preaching again, "In this world the dark angel tries to fool and deceive the nations, mix up man and cause confusion. The angel is very good at his craft, and most men do get fooled, and don't realize it until it's too late. Few find truth or salvation so ministers must have a heart for the lost and their eternal damnation!

The worldly way is not God's way. Wide is the path to destruction and narrow is the path to heaven. This is always true. Look at the river of sick secular music in this world. The great hymns of the church and Gospel music is not the broad road or stream in this world. Satan was thrown down into this world and denied heaven and access to God almighty. God in his mercy has given even Satan and his rebellious fellow angels a season to live, just as he does with rebellious sinful men. Satan's war is against God. He and his demons try to use men and "Sons of God" alike. They even caused a split and rebellion in Heaven but God will be victorious! God has told us that victory has been won! The old angel that old serpent has been defeated by Christ. Note that the serpent did not crawl on his belly across the ground before his success in the garden and that reptiles once ruled this world but now they do not. Man started out here on Earth in Satan's prison in a protected garden. Have you asked yourself protection from what?

Captain Joe Coe tossed me his globe again. My Holy Bible lesson continued even as the evil "Gathering" waged outside. Joe pointed to the top of the globe.

"Say King of the North" Joe shouted

"King of the North," we all answered. Joe then pointed to Jerusalem!

"Say City of peace," he demanded

"City of Peace," we all answered. Joe ran his finger down the Globe and said,

"Say King of the South." We all answered.

"Look outside at the Gathering, Cornelius! Do you see anything that looks like a whirlwind? How many ships? Do we conquer and pass over these days.

Leo Pugh stepped back into our discussion again very much calmer now and teacher like then before with his loud preaching.

"The king of the North is much stronger and comes first into the glorious land or into Jerusalem in time of peace to "protect," but of course the covenant is broken. The North betrays the Jews. Note that the North also does not regard the natural desire of Women. (They have turned over to a reprobate mind set or turned homosexual). Men will be in strong rebellion against God! Read all of Daniel and Isaiah tonight, Cornelius, and let us all read together Daniel 11-40 right now;

(40) **And at the time of the end! Shall the king of the South push at him; and the king of the north shall come against him like a whirlwind, with chariots, and with horsemen and with many ships; and he shall overflow and pass over**

(40) **He shall enter also into the glorious land and many countries shall be over thrown; but these shall escape out of his hand, even Edom and Moab and the chief of the children of Ammon!**

(45) And he shall plant the tabernacles of his palace between the seas in the glorious Holy Mountain: yet he shall to his end! And none shall help him!"

I then shouted out almost unable to control myself! "Between the Seas Joe," just like in South Amer . . . .

"No Cornelius!" shouted Joe!

"But tabernacles is plural Joe" I answered

"I said, No, Cornelius, now shut up," so I did!

Leo started his calm teacher voice again, very much tired of Joe and I interrupting his lesson. "Yes the North comes in peace invited by the Israelites. The Catholic Church is not all bad or 100% evil, part of the true Church does still work for God even today. Just like the disciples in the mirror both good and bad are present. Some godly Catholic leaders still remain, and of course some followers. Look at the men in this room, you for example Cornelius. You claim to be Holiness? Look at yourself, you are covered in blood and drunk with power and you're not even anybody important. Imagine having real power, how would God's profit describe you men; drunk with the blood of the Saints is an honest appraisal of your leaders don't you think? The day of the Lord draws near. The birth pains of this creation cries out to his coming presence. These often flawed but faithful workers on God's advance team are not perfect as he is. They are not bullet proof or all powerful or all knowing. No, they are flawed, but in a relationship with Jesus, just like true saints of the Church. You know not the power of faith at all! This might be a let down or a shock for some but just look at the last 100 plus years, the quickening of this age is at hand just as the Bible told us. "As in the days of Noah, so shall it be." Gentlemen they are back, the Sons of God are back, and they are not teaching anyone how to build an Ark this go round. They are preparing the way for the Kingdom of God, the changing of a season. The Israelites have bigger friends than the ole US of America. God keeps his word and the nations are toast. There is no hope for fools like Osoma to win. He has put us all in danger and judgement.

These "Sons of God" came from the safe haven of God's Heaven and into the danger zone, or this prison called earth on missions for God. Both angels and Sons of God come into this realm (or this world of ours) as warriors and prison guards. Satan and his demons can not travel the heavens as God does but he can "hitch a ride" to approach God. God's angels must often fight when they are sent to answer prayers. Just like when Jesus walked this earth in the flesh Satan came among the disciples and tried to deceive them. Satan is in jail here. Man was made for the garden, but then turned out for a season. When the Sons of God come here Satan is free to try to deceive them too. He is not bound, as he will be, during the reign of Jesus here on earth. During this time we saints will become sons of God and the one only begotten Son of God, Jesus, will rule for a season from Jerusalem. When the Sons of God show up the game of the ages is on. Satan knows his clock is ticking. Sons of God must work with the church "as it is," not as it will be. Soon the two witnesses and then Jesus himself in the flesh will be back in this realm. Now they must deal with the counterfeit half of the church just as men do, Jesus has not yet separated out the goats, has not yet sat in judgement or sifted the wheat. Here on earth there is sin. Sons of God are not Devine like Jesus. God will tell Jesus when to get his Church and when to end this season. Only Jesus is able or worthy to open the seals and to give orders to the angels to finish this battle. "As in the days of Noah, so shall it be with the coming of the son of man."

That night back in my cabin on ship I looked up the number twenty-six on the web, and played with billiard balls. Doctor Fuller it read, the closest stacking of spheres. This Fuller math guy talked about spheres made out of triangles made from his spheres, like that big ball at Disney World. I wish I could understand this math stuff but I was too lazy to work out the problems. (I wish I could play the guitar better but I don't practice my scales either). This same lazy way of life stops people from bible study, and growing close to God. People become satisfied with their own miserable state and don't hunger for anything better. If you, my friend, no longer hunger after God, if you don't pray everyday for a closer walk with Jesus, then start afresh today with Bible study and prayer and worship. Anyway this Fuller math guy invented those Mushroom shaped houses we bombed in the desert, or missed in the desert. Sometimes you just don't know. I played some solitaire attacking cards by 13 from the bottom of a Christmas tree triangle. You know the game. I put the kings together and split them into two stacks one red one black this made 26 stacks I grew drowsy and was thinking to myself while half asleep . . . . *The trees on Easter Island we were planting and the disciples have a heart for god, and we saints are covered by the blood. The diamond is a priest Aaron's rod sprouted an almond tree, The king his priest, What do we buy women? Diamonds! God has twenty four elders in Heaven around his thrown, one King of kings and four beasts, four corners of the earth! Pyramids have square bottoms, my God does not change, city built four square, what did he do the last time the seasons changed as in the days of Noah so shall it be, so shall it be.*

I sat up in my bed. I realized what that old Preacher Leo had said. They're back! The Sons of God they're back, my God! My spirit will not always dwell with man, but will again. Mel's church was just like the Israelites in the wilderness, it shown before them like burnished brass. Jesus is not a spirit he is coming in the flesh just as he went away. How does a real flesh and blood man who is God Travel to earth? I just don't know. Could he use his Sons of God? Does he transform himself? The scripture says no, that in like manner he will return. I jumped out of bed and poured three fingers of red wine! Praise God for a glimpse of understanding. God uses angels and he also uses Sons of God and Saints. God knows that the Jews are about to be double-crossed, and God made a covenant with Abraham. God keeps his word. My God comes right on time and he never changes. What he did before he will do again. My giant does not need a spaceship; neither do angels, nor are they given in marriage. Jesus is the king of kings God's only begotten son! Sons of God are not God or God's. Sons of God are joint heirs with Jesus in all of his riches and glory. They work for and report to Jesus.

Jerusalem has become a stone among the nations. Jesus is the stone not made by human hands that breaks up the statue of Babylon! Daniel told the king "You are the king of all earthy kings you are the head of Gold. God almighty works this stuff out no matter what man does. A great shaking is coming. This ole' World is toast. Good night giant. Even so Lord, please come quickly! Being Holiness means we don't have to worry about this failing world, because you are invested in a city. I'm going to a City where the lame can walk. Praise God! I'm going to a city where the dumb can talk! Praise God! I fell asleep feeling much better and praising, and worshiping God.

In the morning the day was lazy and hung over. At our Bible study nobody showed up. Lou Goodliar was supposed to teach, I could not find him. People on ship were short tempered. Old friends snapped at each other. It was like the after Christmas blahs times ten. This hang over was not from drink but rather one of sinking spirit. The ship's brig was now over flowing onto the deck above it requiring extra guards. Just days ago the brig had been emptied by Captain Coe to increase the painting and cleaning crews. There was an electricity of excitement in the air but no peace. It was like waiting in line all night in the rain for tickets to a rock concert tired and not trusting of the others in line. Fights and arguments were breaking out all over. That evening the sun started setting, as people finished eating, and our planes were in the air early doing their stunts. The blinding lasers soon started shooting holograms changing color and type. Yes, the curtain was going up on the greatest show on earth!

The music started first, then a long line of preachers and clergy with more music in between. None of the speakers or preachers spoke for very long. All were so honored to be here, to be able to mention their church or ministry. Of course they thanked everybody on staff for great work, and for making all of this possible (their success). We were all surprised when Lou Goodliar spoke for about five minutes; he spoke about how many services he had done last year and that he didn't take money and that his back and legs hurt, but God kept him going to save the lost and forgotten people of the world. God was mentioned by a few of the speakers, Jesus was mentioned twice, but the main topic was saving Jerusalem from Islam. The King of England was the first "Big" speaker. I don't think the old queen would have come. She was still alive but to feeble to rule. Mostly the king was there to introduce the young new head of the European Union. This young German politician came out of nowhere just a few years before, just like Osoma had. This capacity crowd was ready for red meat by this time and the young prime minister started throwing it to them. His name was Baron Frank Zia Von Cuttenberg the III. Only twenty-eight years old. He spoke for forty-five minutes and had the crowd screaming for more. He had been a long time friend of the Arabs, but he was now willing to die to protect Gods Holy Mountain. (Even willing to work together and live side by side with the Jews). No Rabbis spoke that Saturday night but there was one famous Jewish woman singer who had always been anti-war. The `good of the many outweighs the rights of the few` was in her phony over produced popular song.

Pictures of the Vatican and our Holy Father started being projected on the cliffs and the music got even louder! Smoke music and mirrors told the story. The Dope himself was going to speak next to close the big show called "The Gathering." Three-D laser holy holograms and color changing combinations of real fireworks all dazzled the crowd. They had amazingly saved some special effects until this very end! The Dopes image was giant size and real time on the cliffs. Our Holy Father took many minutes to make his way through the massive crowds. Most like American Vice President Warner bowed and kissed his ring. Osoma was afraid to come. He wanted to show support and brotherhood to Hamas, Al Qaeda, and the Taliban (*but only the non-violent political wings of these groups of course*). As the Dope neared his high Podium music was at a fever pitch but some people started pointing. The sea in front center of the mountain had started bubbling and soon rolled into a hard boil. The Dope spoke of God's Holy Mountain as the center of the world. The International City of Peace! About taking a stand for God! The Dope officially forgave the Jews one more time for the crucifixion of Jesus. Yes, he was saddling up the Cavalry, to Calvary (ha-ha). (I'm sorry God). While the Dope was speaking a large white gold sphere broke the surface of the sea directly below and in front of his podium. The sea boiled so hard that waves splashed against the ships moving them under our feet. Four more huge spheres came out of the water all at once directly under the first top center ball. All of the spheres were of the same size gold yet white and still sometimes clear. These spheres were as the ones in the Holy Tabernacle of the high mountain in South America except these were very massive. The size and proximity of these spheres above us, plus the crushing sound of rushing water paralyzed the crowd. Many thousands fainted, and hundreds fell off the edge of the flight deck into the boiling sea. The last or bottom sphere was at the center under the middle four just like the one on top. All six gold spheres moved together as one slowly headed skyward in front of us. They towered over us. These six balls were, I guessed, larger in mass all together than all nine carriers. They made their way through the center of our circling whirlwind of planes. The sound was so loud! The six spheres were so blinding bright and then (nothing). Total blackness, total silence, fell like a thick blanket. The crowd was startled with fear and was quiet for thirty seconds. You could not see your hand in front of your face, our bones ached. One group of people who were all barefoot, glowed with light, their skin radiated energy. This lasted a few days. The plants in the beer gardens glowed as of with fire for about a day. The power was completely out. Twenty percent of the crowd had passed out. A pitter-patter sound then started in the darkness and then increased. It was raining dead birds and light debris, mostly dead birds. The birds stacked up across the many flight decks and the sea in between. I didn't know there were that many birds in God's heaven. All but three planes started up their engines again and managed to stay in the Air. The scared exodus of people that followed was a disaster.

People jumped and pushed their way, many got hurt or killed. Joe Coe did not suffer the crowd any type of service, care or first aide. "Get on the ferry and off of my ship," He ordered. Have a nice day but don't ever come back." Power was restored in about ten minutes. Within the hour all of our guests were gone. Dead or alive they were off Joe's big boat. How many bodies hit the water still alive no one knows? We lost sixty-six crew members. All of them went unceremoniously into the water also, along with anything else on deck! Porta-johns, grandstands, dead birds, live or dead bodies, if it was on deck it went splash! What a mess the sea was. Why is it that environmentalist nut jobs always make the biggest mess and live life as slobs? I did not see the early morning mess still in hanger deck (I slept in). But I did hear all about it. That night before making it to my cabin I met and talked to Marshal "Duck" Moore. "What was that thing we just saw?" I asked Duck, "a trick of some kind?"

"Was a damn good trick if it was one," said Duck, not wanting to stop or talk.

Lou Goodliar, who was also heading to his cabin, shouted, "Yes, I think you said it right Duck, a damn good one!"

I poured some red wine, prayed, and crawled into bed. Just like many others, I went absent and did not answer my ship phone. Something had sucked all the strength out of me and the rest of the crew the same. The ship was shut down, and most people were just completely worn out. Two student crew members were glowing and just like the other group they had been barefoot (among other things). This young couple caused so much trouble that Joe had the two locked up in Medical for days to observe them. The next days and weeks brought not a word on TV news or press about "The Gathering" but soon a few internet blogs in the Arab world were ablaze with strange reports and pictures. The Great Satan was the theme. Most web sights in the world were completely filtered and controlled. Osoma had passed the Truth, Fairness, and Equality of Standards Act helping web disadvantaged groups such as Palestinians, homosexuals, minority women, Latinos,' Blacks, Moslems and AIDS patients, gain much needed web presence and radio air time being unfairly taken up my white Christians. He also stopped all the hate speech coming from anti-government extremists and selfish greedy corporations who cared only for their stockholders. The good of the many must be maintained, some men are natural born gifted leaders. These men just like our fathers look out for everybody and must have the power to act quickly to protect us all. Selfish pursuit of profit can no longer be tolerated or allowed, not now with scarce resources staring us in the face. Nancy, a student from Dearborn, Michigan, had to have her parents "Put down" or "mercy murdered" this morning. She was whining about it all over ship; she was going to appeal the medical boards ruling decision but did not because she wanted a journalism career. She could not afford to have an appeal on her record. In journalism she could make such a difference in the world by becoming the face of stopping over-production and greed. Osoma health care computers used Science and Counseling, not Income and Wealth to decide care decisions and not blind faith. She knew her parents' death was best for the world, but she still loved the old farm. She didn't even know her family was wealthy. Her parents must have hidden away the money until she left for school thinking to live it up in their old age. She knew the computers were fair and that her parents' death would let six more people live, and that many of them were poor blind Palestinians with AIDS and without fathers or teeth.

A group of us sat down at my big round corner booth table at the same time that evening and started talking about "The Gathering." Three days had passed and we were still in sight of Cyprus. Captain Coe was still in meetings on the Island. The total lack of "mainstream" press coverage or even any strong internet chatter about "The Gathering" was an unbelievable mystery to me. Leo Pugh the older professor I had met in Joe's office stopped by and explained that nothing spreads faster than a secret. Also, this Gathering had a target audience for its message. This audience was not the vast pool of worldwide, brainwashed, government-educated, drone serfs. No, these could be brought in at anytime. Now was still too soon for the masses, the idiot sheep who still watched TV news, wrestling, game shows, soap operas and American Idol. In short, all of the "dead above the neck," and "give me" Osoma voters. Many of the target audience had been in attendance. The leaders and "wanna be" leaders just below the "Somebody's" of this world. These leaders (both East and West) are the only ones who really matter anyway. In the Islamic culture the hapless pawns will be ready as will the noble Knights and the rest of the players when the final crusade does come. The leaders of Persia, Damascus, Turkey, all the "Stands" Cutter, the Saudi Royal Family, and Egypt, these types were the real target of "The Gathering" and mission accomplished was declared by the West.

The last crusade did not start with this Gathering but the push of the South will soon come. The king of the North will ride into the glorious land to protect it. The time of this age or season is drawing to a close. Jesus explained that we will not know the day or the hour but that we can know the season. "These times they are a changing"

"I thought Bob Dylan said that" spoke up Duck!

"Yes, Duck, you're right I just threw that in for old hippies like you and Cornelius to see if you were awake" said Pugh as he cleaned his glasses.

"Real funny Pugh, real funny" I spoke up, while still finishing up my corn bread and pinto beans.

Leo Pugh does an old AM and shortwave radio show that is broadcasted from the ship, working from his home by satellite. He is retired now and comes on ship about a one month a year. Mostly he's home taking care of his lovely wife Shirley Temple Pugh!

"Pugh, I wonder if I've ever bombed any of your listeners while you were still talking to them" (ha-ha)?

"Would be just like you, Cornelius," Pugh answered.

I thought about my own words about a bomb in one hand and a Bible in the other, the word Christ on my hat, the disciples in the mirror, the ability to deceive in water. I paused then spoke up again!

"Where is the true Church?" I asked Pugh. "Why does God still use the Dope if he's just going to cause another bloody crusade? Why did he build up the nation of Islam, this strange one of 167th old false God of Ali?"

"He didn't fire Judas before the fact did he?" said Leo. "No, Jesus did not give up on Peter, and he still uses you Cornelius. The Gifts of God come before repentance! I hear you are Holiness! That's not the man I used to know! The gifts of god are not about you they are all about him. Jesus could use anybody."

"Leo Pugh and the others waited for my response. I hung my head in silence and in shame! Then I prayed to be allowed to work for the Lord for all the days of my life."

End of Chapter

CHAPTER THIRTEEN

Becka Comes to Bermuda

The next morning the Great Ark was still in the Mediterranean Sea but now fast under way making at least ten knots to the west. I stood outside my cabin, on a high deck railing, looking out over the sea. There was no sign of all the stuff and "stiffs" we had dumped overboard. The flight deck was still shut down but not for long. Our older model B44s never did come back to the ship, but most of their pilots did. Those planes were sold to some country or some body. I skipped that mornings' flight briefing (just to piss Friday off). We are still shut down Friday "give it a rest" I was busy breathing in the sights and smells of the sea. Always good for an old sailors soul and spirit!

I heard Johnny Cash singing "Ring of Fire" up ahead of us from the sea below. Johnny was getting closer and louder. A crowd had formed on the edge of the flight deck watching something below and cheering. There was a flame, and then Johnny Cash sang again. The Great Ark was slowly catching up to, and passing, the most beautiful sailboat yacht I'd ever seen. One with great lines, yes, as of a woman. The music played once again and was coming in very loud now. The trumpets sounded fantastic. I cheered along with the crowd. It was Seaman First Mate Franklin A. Donner pulling along side us. He had four monkeys on swings up in the rigging of his sailboat playing basketball. His monkeys wore white T-shirts, two with red letters named John and Paul, and two in black letters named Ben and Dick. The number six and the word Rome was on the front of each shirt. The four were as playing cards, the four suits in design. At the center flat cabin roof top of Franklins boat was a pyramid laser box stolen from "The Gathering." Each time the monkeys would score a basket Johnny Cash would sing, the Pig would dance, and the rim would flame

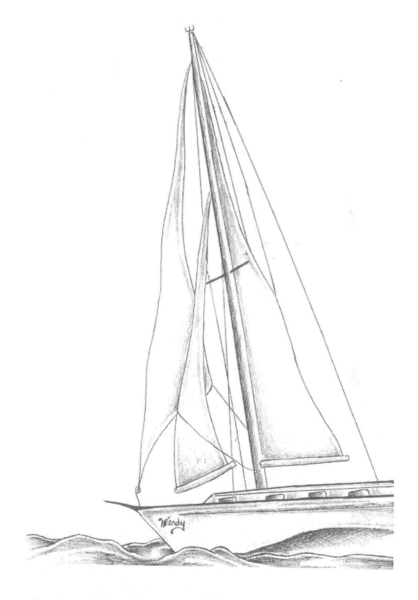

up, and a banana would pop out of the squealing pig on the ships bow. The monkeys were quick doing flips and robbing each other of both basketballs and bananas. Franklin and Windy stood together waving. Bo and Don Dave were sitting at a table on deck watching two ladies fish off the stern. Both men were half asleep and wearing large Mexican hats. They were leaning hard on golf clubs with both hands as if to help them sit up straight. At the end of a long rope, hooked to the back of Franklin's big sailboat was a small lifeboat being pulled behind? The lifeboat was half filled with golf balls and what looked like a very much bruised up Steven Hawkins with a "green" flag, duck taped to his wheelchair. His chair was then handcuffed to a very red and battered Jane Fonda sun bathing behind him. Instead of a small sail this little boat had a large poster of John Lennon dressed like Jesus with bonus points written on top. My friends are a little odd sometimes, they are hard to explain. Sometimes you just don't know.

The Ark was slowly cruising to Bermuda, times were again fun loving and easy. We would soon be going to Virginia (at least that's what the computer navigator said). Praise God! Tell my Patty I'm on the way home. Ship protection patrols started but were often done by drones. We could all use a break after "the Gathering. James Kessler head of the "Boson mates" (or janitors) sometimes called "Bozo" from his hair do, (or lack of hair to do with); stopped by my big corner table. He was complaining that everything was dumped on his crew during and after "The big Gathering" with no help during post cleanup from other departments. He did have a point; we all got the ship ready, and we all pitched in and made the mess. After his venting nobody cared. What is the point, James, just man up and take the hit, because nobody cares. He continued on his way complaining again to each person he saw. He reminded me of Peanut and her complaining. We all know people like this who talk about fairness all the time, the poor thing has been offended in life. Try your best not to be a constant complainer or searcher for fairness because this is all crap. In the end no one cares, or even gives a damn, about your pitiful, stupid problems, even the ones who like or love you.

That night hundreds of undergraduates from all over Europe joined the Great Ark. Tuition now was eighty-five thousand dollars. It had gone down in price from last years cost of sixty thousand because of the bottomless Osoma dollar. Osoma's narrow views, slowness of whit, and his burning desire to be accepted by his slum, Ghetto, rapper, thug cronies and his elite academic wanna "bees" had brought shame and disgrace to America. His endless apologies for American greatness, and his illegal pandering to crocked cronies by the billions of dollars was not even hidden from public record. No the U.S. Treasury and white house silver was raided both the same as a no pride low class street thug would do. One of the least qualified American Presidents in history, he was the hidden from view affirmative action nightmare from hell. Hiding his overriding stupidity took a hard working loyal staff and a go team spirit from the press. Some white house guests got so concerned that they presumed he had been the victim of a stroke or heart attack and worried about the government collapsing. Osoma once got lost on the white house grounds on his way to a beer summit and often did or should have canceled a speech if his teleprompter broke. He was mentally incapable of even high school level debate, without his ear piece.

This night four of the "New kids" on ship joined my table and all praised Osoma. All four had signed up to "give back" by planting trees for a year. This for the good fight against global warming and to save mankind before it was all too late. It was high time for the anti-professor to shine the light on a repeat lesson of "fighting the forest".

"Have any of you students ever flown over or driven across Virginia, West Va. Carolina, Kentucky, Tennessee, Alabama, or Georgia? I suggest you get in a small plane and fly all day, look around as long as you can afford or stand! Fly anywhere up and down the coast this side of the Mississippi where most Americans live. A vast forest and jungle you will see. Grazing land has been allowed to "go back" to forest because of low farm prices. Many farms of yesteryear have grown back to wilderness again and yes some are now suburbs. The forest is expanding year after year at a steady rate. The truth is Americans have been "fighting the forest" for hundreds of years now and we are losing! The damn forest is over taking us. Now whom do you think planted all those new trees? A bunch of "go green" idiot college kids like you! Hell no! God did! God uses critters, birds, and the wind and guess what? God knows what he's doing. Have any of you young saps ever owned a piece of property or been responsible for one? (None had) To grow a wilderness or forest all you have to do is just do nothing. All property in Virginia back home grows up at a rate of three to four feet a year. Just like a man's beard if you "let it go to seed" or without cutting, his beard will soon show. God designed the forest to plant itself. Whatever planting you kids do will not make much difference except to maybe a paper company creating pine thickets. Planting a tree can be a joy, so can watching it grow up, but all that "plant a tree to save the world" crap is bogus. Your yard is a planed deforested garden spot with controlled tree growth and the problem is always too many trees. You don't have to plant them. Even in big city parks like Central Park in New York City, stopping trees from growing and cutting back, or cutting down trees amounts to most of the work not planting more trees. Workmen spend most of their time killing trees, not planting trees. Too many damn trees, is always the problem for mankind because men do not like the forest. Go out in the woods and look around, see if anybody else is there. Duh, why are you all by yourself? People say they love the forest but they do not like the forest. People never spend much time in the woods; at least not 99.9 percent. How much time out of your life have you spent in the woods and or forest, since you were born? Hell most people won't walk through tall grass much less a forest thicket. The truth is we are falling behind in fighting the forest ever since we killed off the Indians. The Indians killed off trees much faster than us silly white men. Thousands of men go to work every day just in my home state of Virginia alone all trying to kill and cut back trees. They have even resorted to modern day chemical warfare against the forest and the forest is still overtaking us. Trees are a crop in some places, a very good renewable resource. That is probably who has fooled you into working for nothing. As a forest worker you may not be very skilled or productive so nothing might be a good price for your work. Kishia, please stop this save the world, Captain Planet, nonsense. He is a cartoon just as dumb and silly as Bugs Bunny. You have believed a lie. It's time now to grow up and get over it. Please don't base your life on a cartoon. Grow up and answer me please? Is your name really Kishia? Or is this some kind of sick joke? . . . . Ok then Kishia it is!

Every day back home brave men "fight the forest" (the power company, the railroad, farmers, homeowners, state roadway workers, lumber jacks), some men even use big robot tree cutters and we are still losing. Clearing forest is hard work and expensive. People are lazy and the trees are simply taking over; some mountain roads have been closed and given to the forest, too costly to keep cleared.

(Young Kishia started crying and getting upset).

"This just can't be true Cornelius I love trees!" shouted Kishia. "I want to give back to the trees for helping me breathe!"

"Yes, Kishia" I answered, "I also love trees, and trees do need CO_2 to breathe so you help them in Gods cycle everyday. The more CO_2 in the air, the more trees like it and the faster they grow. This all works the same way with the green algae in the world's seas. Your know it all professors have convinced Osoma that CO2 is a pollutant that should be taxed. CO2 is what trees breathe, what humans expire and is part of earths design and cycle. Does that sound sane to you Kishia?

"Cornelius, our class needs and loves the trees and the earth just like the Indians did. The white man is evil and no good," cried out Kishia!

"Yes, save the trees, "said Kishia." This was a different and slightly fatter Kishia with a small dream catcher in her hair.

"Oh Lord," I said out Loud! And looked to the other two girls sitting there . . . . "You two are not named?"

"No, we are not named Kishia, Cornelius. We are Clarishia and Clarissa, we're sisters and both studying and majoring in Islamic food and dance, but we love trees too."

"Everything you girls have been taught and believe in has been a fabrication, a complete lie. The truth is that there are more trees, and more deer now than when the Indians ran things in America. What you have been taught is reversed from truth. It is nothing but false science, false history based on false Gods. I gave you some good advice to fly in a plane and look at the forest yourself; this is important. Always check it out yourself if possible. Have you kids ever been to an Indian reservation? Well I have! What a pile of trash, what a mess!

"That's because of the evil white man, Cornelius," Kishia said crying. "Killing us and making us learn English and Jesus."

"Yes, it's white men who caused the big black ghetto slums and high crime rates not the poor colored people" chimed in the two sisters. "Those rich Republicans who don't pay their fair share in taxes and greedy corporations who have polluted the air and water."

"Yes, I know the drill" said Cornelius. But the historic truth is simply that no primitive tribes and most other civilizations have not successfully competed with Roman based civilizations. When the cultures clash the others always "Romanize" and are glad to do so. Do you know how primitive pagan American (Indians) lived back home in my native Virginia. No iron, no written language, only oral tradition and history, a hunter gatherer society with small garden patches? Indians in Virginia lived on waterways, which were also their sewers. They had few if any beasts of burden like horses, and no kept vineyards, or real roads. The ancient people in the Bible did better than these Indian clowns. The water was their main highways. Indian tribes often fought battles for the land between head waters of steams. This land was called a "carry." At a carry point canoes and rafts would have to be carried to the next close stream. Controlling this crossing point would control the whole land area, so often this is where they lived. Fighting or wars between the tribes centered like today on how many stupid young bucks each tribe could produce. Meaning how strong the tribal king was and how much growing in territory or wars of growth were needed.

Have you ever shot a real primitive, made in the woods, bow and arrow? This was not a long range weapon, it was not much better than a spear or a blowgun. Have you ever carried deer through the woods for miles, or chased them down after shooting them with a modern bow that was a near miss shot (none had).

Virginia Indians used nets and spears for fishing, made canoes out of bark. They also made rafts and lived in a wood and dirt lodge. It was comfortable. In shallow mountain streams Indians used Mountain Laurel to poison the water to stun fish, a very successful method! Around my home in Roanoke or "salt lick" the method of hunting was forest fires. Indians would paddle up stream, often in a river cut back, or hike into the forest against the wind and then spread out in a line and start a forest or grass fire. All animals in the burn zone would run away from the fire and into the stream or river where the whole tribe would be waiting with spears bows and arrows to kill anything that ran out and put them on rafts. Getting the catch home was easy by simply coasting back down the river or stream. No walking or dragging game miles through the underbrush. After the hunt the fires were left to fend for themselves. Often the next moons hunt would paddle past the fires from the hunt before. These fires sometimes burned for many months. Hiding in the woods and sneaking up on game types of hunting was used but was not as successful as burning down the woods because their many weapons were just not that good. The early settlers' musket is now famous for being a near worthless scatter gun, but let us face cold hard facts, almost anything is better than the sharpened end of a stick or even a chipped flint rock. The Indians were primitive simple hunters and were not very skilled ones at that. The natural forest fires and all the stupid Indian hunting fires kept the woods in check or (burnt down). Yes, wild fires would burn continually for miles and months at a time. The early settlers also lived by the waterways and simply plowed up and fenced the old burning grounds (I mean hunting grounds). White men stopped the forest fire burning method of hunting because of his belief in private property and also burning down everything was against the values of civilized man. Primitive man is always nasty and crude (a high level of pollution and a low level of morals) this is the sad truth worldwide. Everything you have been taught about the noble savage is the opposite from truth or a plain simple lie. You have been taught lies on purpose. This is not an honest difference of opinion. Your professors have an agenda and are in rebellion against God. When the burning stopped settlers built many types of fire brakes with their roads, railroads, dams, and even cleared plowed fields. The forest slowly came back and has never looked back. Many suburban housing tracks today have too many trees creating a fire hazard. Yes, the trees are back and all it took was killing off all the stupid Indians. We love the forest back home in Virginia, but let us face truth, most people do not like forest and most towns have laws against it. If you want to grow a forest just stop cutting your grass, or maybe just the back yard; it will grow three feet a year every year forever and so will the bugs and critters. If you kids plant trees even many thousands of trees you will not hurt anything, but remember, trees would have come up anyway if you had not. Go plant some trees, get outside and enjoy yourself. But do not believe what you are told. This constant repudiation of and apology for western culture is a false religion. One example of this is Osoma asking NASA to help the Arabs and other cultures not to feel like the pitiful losers that they really are. Asking you to give back to mother earth by not using air conditioning, not driving a car, not using a computer, not using the net, or living like the Indians, living like the Islamists or the Africans, none of this is sane behavior. There is nothing wrong with winning, we are the best. Don't be ashamed of winning. There are good reasons why inventions are born here, and why Americans hold their heads up straight. Take pride in being the world leaders, stand up for personal freedom, and God given rights! Now repeat after me! THE WEST IS THE BEST, say it again!

THE WEST IS THE BEST. Don't be shy!" Many students looked around the room much too embarrassed to make such a statement. Maybe I should ask them to say the West was the best, the West was the best, but I was too proud and now ashamed to ask for that.

"Saving the world from Judeo-Christian values and Western Culture is all bull crap, and a lie. Surprise, God plants more trees everyday than man has planted in all of history. Surprise, free men worship God and invent technology (The-West) Surprise, Islam, Eastern slave states, African tribes, and European serfdom socialism, and communism, slow technology, innovation and the middle class. Surprise, Islam and or socialism brings slavery, poverty, and death and is always anti-Bible, and anti-Jewish. Why is American republic so precious? Why is Freedom so rare?"

My Café table college students all filed out from my table that night still talking about making a difference and saving the world by planting trees. These students did not fear or search for God. They claimed a guilt free moral high ground. A claim to caring and "giving back" to the society or state, to being one of the "good" ones; people who helped conserve "mother earth" who did not plant or weave for profit of self or family, but rather for the "greater good." Of course tithing, true love, God's grace, salvation, hard work, freedom, personal responsibility, individual excellence and personal Bible knowledge is all foreign and unknown to them. In their brainwashed view none had ever loved mother earth like "real" American Indians. No one can hope to ascend to pure "Indian level" not even blacks can join that league, this must be born to. Evil Western or White or Jewish men can only dream of Indian "purity" and must constantly show remorse for inventing the iron horse, killing the open range buffalo, starting farms and ranches killing off the savages, and growing evil amounts of wealth using the concept of private property, and free enterprise. Most of my government school brainwashed students claimed a vague sick humanist "goodness" by not eating meat and being a true believer of many big and small lies. The humanist priests granted this sick "goodness" to some and denied and shamed non-true believers in turn. This old carrot and stick method is time tested and has been put to good use by all mushroom farmers and false priests! Here are some examples: Hunters are hateful, guns are bad, farmers are stupid, fathers are not needed, God and bible is just for kids, no need to fear God, America's unfair, (we have too much) Communism in its pure form is a good idea, pure capitalism is evil, and Osoma is a great leader! Young Saps planting saplings that's the way it should be I guess. Jesus pointed his early Church toward the west first for a reason. Friends thank God for your roots and honor your father and mother each day for the promise of long life. Often times many kids or young adults just don't know what they don't know. That's why they act so stupid.

As the ship neared Bermuda word came through the grapevine that the Great Ark needed major dry dock time. The ship would go to Newport News Ship Building and Dry Dock Company, in Newport Port News (now owned by the Communist Chinese Army). The ship would be there for a full year. This service was needed by order of the "nuke's" who lived like trolls in the dungeon bottom of our ship, (men like Paul Goldwater). I'm coming home Patty, I'm on the way home to Virginia. My contract will run out and I'll retire to our front porch and sing old Gospel songs with you forever. Praise God, Praise God, and Praise God!

Only three days later a call of "General Quarters" rang throughout the ship. We ran to our battle stations. A full strike force took off at 0400 that morning. Each of the sixteen B48s took off with full drop tanks, cannons, and a full bomb load. We also used the six drones we had on board. Our strike force attacked tiny fuel storage facilities on a very small rock island, consisting of 55-gallon drums covered only with camouflage netting, and also a ship that was bigger than a gunboat, but still smaller than most coast guard cutters. We blasted the ship and the island then dropped some sonar buoys, and then headed the many hundreds of miles back to ship. My old Navy buddy Gary Litton met me on port deck smiling from ear to ear just after our strike force landed.

"Hello Cornelius," shouted Gary. "I hear your Indian buddy Jediah Emin Patel and his new football sports net work is in Bermuda. He is breaking worldwide broadcast records. Just his internet channels alone out does all of the major networks combined. Now over broadcast stations he beats them all again. Turn on your phone, Cornelius, this is the same guy right? Or at least his company! Gary held up his phone and tried to get me to look at it. They don't mention him by name but I could tell from talking to you that it must be him. You can get all forty of his TV channels, even here in Bermuda."

"Thanks Gary, I'll check it out," I answered "That does sound like Patel and I'm not surprised that they don't publicize his name or photo." Gary walked away still pointing to his ship phone screen even as he sent me the details he started talking with and it to showing another pilot.

After approval from Bermuda, we embarked for shore, many hundreds at a time using barge like harbor boats ferries. We could not dock or use any ultra-light planes on Bermuda because island officials had very many rules and even more paperwork. The Ark anchored only six hundred yards from shore. One old British destroyer and a big destroyer sized yacht pulled ship protection duty for us by patrolling the sea. It was R&R time for many of us. Word was that "Becka" was in Bermuda for the whole weekend shooting movies and video's and would do a concert! All of my college age kids had downloads of "Becka." The hottest selling name and face in all of music history. Nothing in show business as big as "Becka" had come along in the modern era or at least in the last fifty years. Students often chanted, "Becka, Becka, Becka" at the top of their lungs at the ship's Gospel Café to make the band play her songs. This world wide "Becka" craze was now only two years old. Her fame started when she was only eleven years old. Now she is described as twice Madonna, three times Disney, and bigger than country music. She's about the same age as Jediah and even bigger in some ways (ha-ha). When I told some students at the Gospel Café one night that I knew the Great Becka personally, they found it hard to believe. Many of them also wore her clothing line and could not imagine the "old school" anti-professor ever being in the same crowd. She was very "IN" and I was not! I found Becka hard to believe myself back then and still do sometimes. I laugh at her videos all the time today.

In the lobby of a large resort hotel Jediah stopped his entourage, waved his security, and we shook hands, and then hugged. He locked me down with a one arm hug that picked me up off the floor, and shocked the workers at the hotel. "That boy could kill somebody by accident with a hug like that" I thought to myself. He looked to have gained five or six inches and two hundred pounds! I understood the fear of his handlers now for the first time. Jediah looked to be five years older. Four of his Asian girls tried to make me jealous, something they are very good at. Jediah called them down and sent them away. Yes, Jediah was different looking, his face was shocking even. One of his girls was one of the two I had refused back at his palace and she did not seem happy. Jediah and I talked in passing and I promised him faithfully to stop by his place soon after the "Becka" show ended. Patel not only owned this big resort but he had a private resort or home adjacent to this one which was "not for the public." I learned that South of France, Kauai, England, Williamsburg, Va. and the Black sea were just some of the places that Patel could "go public" without being seen by the public. I wanted to ask him about his father. I promised him once more that I would see him after the show.

In the big ball room of the 'Public" main hotel, the band was warming up, and testing out the stage. "Becka" was not there, she was under close heavy security at all times. It was much too dangerous for her to be in public. On stage were some dancers and the original Gospel Café Band from the mountains of Virginia. I have all of their old CD's back home and I know every member. Tommy Turner was still singing and leading the band. I had figured him to be dead by now. He must be old as dirt but he looked great. I got Jackie Robers autograph to prove to the people on ship that I did really know her. The Durrett family were all still with the band; Buddy, Dorothy, and Joey. My old friend Buddy had just become the most successful song writer in the history of recorded music with a little help from "Becka!" Buddy's top one hundred Gospel songs download had been number one for over ten years now. When Joey came in the public entrance he was mobbed by young gals from the ship. Joey unaware that the public had arrived was quickly cornered. This was a funny scene but Joey soon got back on his feet and started signing autographs. Both generations of Kovacks were there also, I looked around for my old friend Chuck, his wife Christina said he had lingered in the casino trying to lose his pocket money, but kept winning instead. Chuck was the original Dobro player in the band and also "Becka's" dad. His family has cut many music CD's in their own studio including one nasty Rap video of the Osoma daughters, that was too sick to even name here, but paid very well. His older daughter named Summer had much success in Nashville, but now his daughter "Becka" was in a world wide class all by herself. I had hopped that the spoiled little "Becka" had not "gotten worse" for all the wear and attention of fame, but I feared there was little hope. "Becka" was always a hardheaded child before her fame she was just a little tot back then. The last time I saw her she was only five. "Becka" started singing every weekend night at the original Gospel Café the day she turned one year old; before she could even walk or talk much. "Becka" was in charge of the little Café gospel singing spot by the time she was two, or so she thought. No wonder she became a singer, she was born to it. Yes Becka was only five years old the last time I saw her. I asked her mother if she might still remember me, and Christina said "sure." I wasn't so sure it had been years! Tonight in Bermuda the old Gospel Café Band was going to open up the show for "Becka" and even back her up in some numbers at her request. Each of them would be featured solo to this "older" crowd here in Bermuda. Security slowly tightened up as band practice started. This ball room could seat five to six thousand people. One thousand five hundred had come ashore off of the Great Ark. The show was now over sold and that might be a problem for security. The ballroom had two sides facing the ocean and beach. These walls were surrounded by a patio about the size of two football fields built on the sand. Three double sets of French Doors on each side opened onto this brick patio with hundreds of cement benches and small shade trees. This made a good over flow area.

Students on ship found it hard to believe that old Corney, the anti-professor, was a personal friend of the popular young "Becka." We seemed to be from two worlds apart. The little Becka I knew was a wild headstrong, healthy, too cute four and five year old brat that beat up on her eight year old brother and told her parents what to do. She was famous for throwing her toys across the Café floor and or onto the stage.

"Back in the day" before Jackie quit the band for the first time, I was a regular at the old Gospel Café. I even sat in with the band playing rhythm guitar many nights. In those early days Gary Litton ran sound. He was my witness if the kid has forgotten me. She might make me out a liar (ha-ha). The band made a recorded live CD for me of my songs. I never sold any but I still keep one on my wall back home. Looking around I saw Linda Howell, Ronnie Howells wife and went over to say Hello, and yes, Ronnie married very well!

"Where's Ronnie?" I asked as I walked up to Linda.

"Right here," shouted Ronnie from the sound booth and "you stay away from my wife you old cuss."

Ronnie had a great since of humor and was known in Gospel music as the "Words greatest drummer". Ronnie waved me back towards the sound booth. He was sitting in the sound booth at the back wall of the auditorium with Gary Litton, Rodney Dole, plus a Becka sound technician that now had more help than he wanted or needed. Ronnie said he wasn't playing tonight, too much like work. He and Linda were enjoying Bermuda and taking life easy, not spending time coming to rehearsals or keeping a schedule. He had more money than God anyway, said Ronnie and laughed.

"I let Becka's road drummer play tonight said Ronnie! Jackie Robers liked to have her old friend, Ronnie, in the sound room whenever he wasn't playing drums, so this poor sound man was stuck with all of us.

Ronnie leaned over and gave me a proper warning, "If Jackie or Tom calls me up to sing and play a set of songs be ready. You will be called next. Have two songs ready off of your old album, Cornelius!"

Not thinking that Jackie might do something like call me up to sing I started getting nervous and kept going over old song lyrics in my head so I didn't talk much.

When the crowd stood up we could still see over peoples heads while sitting down in the sound booth. Ronnie was telling me "Howell" good he was doing after open heart surgery (ha-ha).He said my wife stopped by the Gospel Café now and then but not often, and that the old place was still open and that he only made it there occasionally. My Patty always did like to sing with others more than singing solo. He and Linda didn't make it much any more because of his health neither did Big Al, and Helen (famous singers from the old days). Then Ronnie asked me if I was still playing music anywhere?

"No Ronnie" I answered. I don't have much time to play Gospel music anymore, I've been busy bombing Africans, and shooting run away Mexicans, important save the world type stuff. All the while helping my giant work for God and becoming holiness. It's been a hard job but somebody has to do it. Not much fun really, but it does pay the bills, and I got to see the "Dope" but not in person."

"We always knew you'd be doing something for the Lord Cornelius" said Linda. "Yes Cornelius said Ronnie we both always knew!" It sure was great to talk to my old friend Ronnie and catch up on things; as we were talking they started introducing him.

"Ronnie it's been years since I sang my old songs" I complained. Ronnie walked down the isle and played a set with Jackie and the Band and then just as he had said, Tommy "D" Tuner started introducing me. Wow, what a set up! Not like the old days. I didn't have to try to play guitar and Jackie had the words of my old songs come up on a heads up display screen just below my sight. That's money talking for yah! My cat could have sung those songs.

I sang "Little White Church" and then "Preacher Steve," and ended up with "To Fly up, Get down. I sounded pretty good that night I thought!" On each of my old songs Ronnie played also and then we both sat back down. Jackie had never let being a big star go to her head. I prayed that the young "Becka" was handling the pressure well. What a joy it was to have friends who will share the limelight and still admit they know you after they've become rich and famous. Often it's the other way around in life; if you have some trouble many friends dump you like a hot potato. Sometimes you just don't know.

Becka had watched her older sister Summer become a recording star first. When her mother Christina joined Summer on stage people said they sounded like "The Jugs" an old mother and daughter duet from my childhood. Summer and Christina, although very successful were both still mere mortals. This wild crazy star world that "Becka" was now living in was different, and even bigger than fame. Jackie texted me and said that

I had done alright on my songs. I wondered how she sent that text while she was playing on stage.

By the time Summer and Christina came out to sing Ronnie and I were both seated back in the sound booth, by the time they finished I thought to myself, "*this crowd had already gotten their money's worth.*" Summer was first then her mother, then both and on their last big hit song "Becka" was singing with them in live shadow from behind a screen and the crowd was going crazy. The shouting soon started, then the feet stomping began, Becka! Becka! Becka! The youngsters' in the audience chanted! First Dorothy and Buddy, and Joey Durrett, and then Jackie and then Tommy "D" Turner all did songs off their best selling CDs. Then the background lighting began to change and CO2 smoke started pouring from back stage. This was "Becka's" trade mark entrance. The theme song of Becka's new TV chat show started playing. Her show was already twice as popular as the old Oprah show. Young girls in the audience started fainting, many fans in the crowd started moving forward and a line of shielded police rushed in across the bottom of the stage. The music and lights dimmed as the orchestra pit started rising up slowly with a huge red parade type drum at center; every one figured that "Becka" was about to break out of that drum. Becka started all her concerts with a prayer from off stage through her wireless microphone. The prayer ended and the smoke was thick as fire works sparkled. Just as the Band struck its first note a shockwave jolted the building. It felt like the whole Bermuda Island had been moved six inches to the left. Glass showered the large ballroom. For the first few seconds the youngsters kept shouting Becka! Becka! Becka! Thinking this blast was part of the show.

Gary Litton, Rodney Dole and I knew all to well what it was; the sharp shock wave produced from modern military ordinance. We grabbed Linda and Ronnie and threw them down violently to the floor. Glass rained down on us! After a very short time we all peaked out from behind the sound room wall.

"Becka" had been still inside the drum and was unhurt, her mother Christina was on stage left playing fiddle and was hit hard. Becka saw her mother standing and bleeding on stage as she jumped out of the big red drum. Becka then ran towards her catching Christina just as she slumped to the floor. Becka then jumped back onto the Orchestra pit that was now starting on its way back down with her bleeding mother Christina in her arms. They both landed on top of the grand piano; as they hit Becka's knee buckled with the force of the landing causing her to fall to one knee. Just then as Becka looked up holding her bleeding mother limp in her arms a photographer took a picture of the pair on top of the piano.` This picture became the photograph of the decade. Becka was already bigger than the Beatles, Michel Jackson and Elvis. She now became a world wide idol figure to young girls across many cultures. This one image on stamps, posters, billboards, coins, and magazines covers made this photographer a billionaire and Becka a God! In worldly eyes that is, the most known person on planet earth. This was all done with Gospel music at a time when God, Jesus and the Bible were often hated, unwanted and unpopular.

We stared out over the sound booth wall still not moving from our knees, people were in a state of panic everywhere. It was dark inside and out, but plain to see in the moonlight that the great Ark had been attacked. The ship had thick black smoke pouring out of a hole in its starboard side (the side facing us in the ballroom). All of the windows and doors, in the ball room facing the ocean and some parts of the walls were now gone giving us an unobstructed view of the Great Ark burning against the clear moonlit sky.

People at the "Becka" show were steadily pouring out onto the brick patio and beach. Many were trying to stop the bleeding from big and small cuts. Blood ran "tomato topping thick" forming a glass and ceiling tile pizza that covered the floor. "Crying, loud hysterical" people and also "still frozen quietly dying" or statue people as I called them were both everywhere to be found in abundance. About four hundred were dead quickly, four hundred more would die before help came, slightly less than nine-hundred would die in total. Two thousand people were treated, the rest of us were unhurt. Two ladies from "purchasing" lay headless in the doorway. I told police their names and title, I could tell them apart from their smell. One of them had smoked cigarettes, and one smoked those cheap little cigars. Their bodies lay for some time because emergency personnel worked on the living first. Joe Coe paced back and forth in the edge of the beach sand, his ship phone glued to his ear but going unanswered. Joe, by being off of his ship as it burned close by in front of him was fast going crazy or mad. About fifteen hundred of his students and crew had come to shore with him most were also in the sand watching her burn. Out of a hole in the side of the Ark pumped a huge black plume of smoke reaching skyward as of a volcano. EMT and hotel medical staff started arriving about twenty minutes after the blast the first ones on the scene were doctors and nurses from Patels palace next door. I had met them before in India. The Gospel Café band was rushed away by security. In all this confusion I almost forgot my appointment with Jediah Patel.

I walked across the sand toward the other resort or Jediah's Bermuda home next door and was soon knocked down to the ground with my face in the sand by security personnel wearing military body armor and holding M16 rifles. No Business suites here in the sand (ha-ha). My face was in the sand before I could raise my hands and that grinding boot on my neck was not fooling around. I stated my appointment and I still had a Patel employee ID card in my wallet. Even so they still scanned my face, waved me with a wand and patted me down. One led the way while one held me at gunpoint with my hands on top of my head.

On a large porch, just before the next security check point were two more guards were waiting inside. A voice from the dark patio to my right said,

"Hello Joe" It was Connie that sweet Vietnamese lady from India! Glancing right I could see the glow of her cigarette brighten. She waved the guards and I sat down at her table. The guards left us alone. We talked about twenty minutes. I thought about taking up smoking again. Her cigarette smelled very good, like "back in the day." These were real cigarettes, not "fire-safety" cigarettes like all those made in America today.

"America used to make the best cigarette, the best car, the best music and the best rockets in the world" said Connie. "Your government had a better idea and well not so much now, Joe. In fact you guys really suck, do you remember that idiot black guy back at Super Bowl Forty six! Every year there is another low class rapper with another how low can you go stunt, or a nipple ring. The whole world is laughing at Ghetto America, don't you have any pride left at all, letting the lowest scum you can find define your image on TV world wide. My daddy was American, and also part black and I'm ashamed to speak of America now days. How could people so proud fall so low so quickly? You should be ashamed Cornelius! (You sound racist Connie I said)

Those same two big guys from Patels palace in India came downstairs and ended my conversation with Connie by walking me up to see Jediah. Both of these men were in expensive business suits. One waited outside the office with me and one went through the huge wooden double doors. Being inside a Patel home always makes a man feel small, the steps, the doors, hallways, ceiling, and railings are built to a massive scale. Starring eye to eye with door knobs is creepy. While waiting outside the door I thought about Jediah's new house being built in India, right next door to another just like here in Bermuda. Could his daddy be of normal size and his sons be large I contemplated.

The big doors swung open "Hello Cornelius, we have much to discuss," roared my old friend. "This has been quite a night so far. I love the excitement! It is good for ones digestion just like your red wine (ha-ha). His voice was low and powerful even when he laughed, not much like a young boy anymore. As we talked one of his Asian girls poured my glass, then he nodded and she retired into another room.

"Personal things first, Cornelius," said Jediah. "We must speak of personal things first." Jediah slowed his speech. "Every man has his castle. Cornelius, you were completely safe in my palace even when hunted by my uncle. We, the house of Patel including my uncle, did our best. Cornelius please know this, we both did our best. You are counted as a friend so I wanted to tell you about all this in person. In Virginia your own people lay in wait for you with papers. My uncle has old agreements with your commonwealth. We must honor them. Your life is not in danger and it is a small and old matter concerning a woman. Your own family claims that you have shamed them. You may be jailed, or fined or both! The Prince of your Province seeks you! Some advice Cornelius! Do not ask for rights from your Philadelphia constitution jury! This Prince will crush you in anger! Beware the courts in your Province of Virginia are his to do with as he wishes! This has been true since your man Woodrow Wilson sold Virginia years ago. Cornelius your charges come from a woman thirty-five years ago, she said you did not have sex with her but shamed her. This woman's sister knows a citizen who has the ear of a board member, who is the Prince of Virginia. I'm sorry Cornelius you could run of course. You know you are always welcome back in India at any time."

"Thank you, Jediah, but I won't run, and I've always suspected that the governor was not in charge back home!"

Jediah then took a phone call but he had no phone. He gestured me out to the balcony, and I obeyed. I walked out onto his third floor balcony into the night. I could see the Ark plainly leaning to its port side or out to sea. The hole in her starboard side was plainly visible in the star light. Smoke was of very much less volume as it poured out of the hole, I guessed less than ten percent of what it had been. After some minutes Jediah then joined me on the balcony, still talking to more than one person on a phone. I could not hear or see.

"Yes, I do see her. She's in plain sight, so Friday says he can save her. Ok! If I think she's worth it. Ok, then, Friday! Good job, do continue for now and give an update to my man Winston every twelve hours on your progress. You are in Charge Friday, be on time. Yes, I will be talking to Joe Coe, don't worry just do your job."

Friday had evidently saved the ship. That is if he could get her to New Port News leaning as she was. The ships lean was almost twelve degrees to port. Many things on board ship were being dumped into the sea. The nose biting smells of petroleum jet fuel being dumped off the Ark burned our noses on shore. The smell was very strong on Jediah's balcony. Joe's Chief of staff First mate Friday had acted very quickly and had shut off the bulk head doors and purposely started flooding the Port side of the ship even as the missile was about to hit the ship. Shutting those doors and starting those powerful pumps condemned six hundred and sixty six men to death without a chance to get out, but lifted the damaged side out of the water far enough to save the ship. A rocket, a very fast skim the surface torpedo had been fired from near the middle of the harbor. This unprotected side was easy prey. Our protection was down. This was the same type of rocket that just missed us in the "big attack" off of Gumbo Station.

"Joe would have saved those people Jediah" I said softly as we stared out to sea together in silence. "I think Joe would have evacuated every one on ship to Bermuda and then run her aground to try to save the ship".

"Joe is not in the clear yet, neither are you, Cornelius. Those crewmen died to save the ship. They had to die for the greater good," said Patel, "not really believing it himself."

"Whenever some don't count, whenever some are flushed as worthless, God is not glorified, God is not honored. God is no respecter of persons Jediah"

"I hear your wise counsel old friend but do not push your holiness on me this night, because you are still on trial and I have much more to say to you, much more."

"He can only carry one, Cornelius," said Jediah.

"He . . . . Who, one, and what?" I stammered?

"The one you missed. The one you left in the desert. His mothers home really. It has been in the family from before this season. We have owned that land for over five thousand years Cornelius, one day I will see under that sand! One RU118 Russian now Persian skim torpedo missile, a Chinese diesel submarine, one missile is all she can carry.

"So you know him," this man in the submarine?"

"Yes, Cornelius, I know him well. He is my older brother. His name is Phinehas Emin Patel. He uses a non English older spelling of Pudahuel, for our name. He's the one who killed our father. Phinehas seeks my life too Cornelius, one of us will have to die. The blood of our father Phinehas took to save us both. I do owe him that much, but after my scripture reading and lessons are over, it will be game on between us. Our Father knew not of us for many years, when he found our mother out, he was ashamed of us both. He had known and given seed to a woman of Adam, Yes, he had been tricked. You are not the only son who has shamed family my friend. I am one that is between seasons Cornelius. My father has brought shame, I do not belong here Cornelius pray your holiness prayers for me.

Phinehas is the king of Africa. We and my uncle also, are of the "sons of Oman" He calls himself the "King of the South, Cornelius.

"The King of the South, Oh my God," I whispered as a cold chill hit the room.

"Listen, Cornelius, my brother is three years older than me, some say he's ten feet tall but I know better he's only about nine foot six, and weights about five hundred and fifty pounds. It's him or me in the end Cornelius. I will have to kill him. It's him or me. Our lives are on a collision course to death. I play him every day on the computer. I can beat him now at least part of the time thanks to your help Cornelius. I'll be ready one day, ready to face him, yes I will! "My big brother has a friend, who helps him, a missionary named Tommy Mute."

"Oh Lord," I groaned!

"Yes, your friend gets around. I asked you once before, are you on a rouge mission Cornelius? Your friend, Tommy Mute came here to Bermuda with my brother Phinehas. They evidently laid in wait before the Ark arrived! You also have another rebel friend, another trader Cornelius!" Patel turned toward the sea and pointed. One guard turned on a powerful spot light that shown down on the sand below us straight out from our balcony. Two men had Lou Goodliar hands bound behind his back, on his knees praying in the sand.

My heart leaped, "No, Jediah" I shouted!"

One guard put a revolver to my head also, and one grabbed my arms from behind. With a nod from Jediah my friend Lou Goodliar was shot once point blank range in the right temple as he prayed. His limp body falling face down in the sand! Jediah then took my ship phone away from me. "Pray that your phone does not get a call from Tommy Mute, also my friend!"

Jediah then held up his palm as if taking an oath, and turned and spoke directly to my face. "Cornelius Captain Coe and all of his senior officers, including yourself, and all who are on this island will board my private yacht and go with me in the morning. You are all under house arrest. We will follow the Ark to Newport News. Friday is in charge of the Ark. I will find out who is a trader, and who is not. You will be all kept in basic comfort as befitting a gentleman. That will be all. I will see you in the morning. These men will show you to your quarters! "Send in Joe Coe" shouted Jediah. "No not you Cornelius, the guards. My phone is in my teeth. It will be on the market when the time is right."

As the guards led me out I met Captain Joe Coe coming in. He was not happy to see me or to be second in line. Joe had his ship phone turned up on loud speaker; some of the crew Friday had locked in the Port side dungeon were still alive and still begging for rescue from Captain Coe. The desperate men and women's loud screaming for help filled Jediah's large fancy office. I slowed even as the guards pushed me out the door. I could hear two young Kishia's from my table crying out to Joe for help. They begged for mercy not to Jesus, but to Joe Coe, their trusted head master who had failed them. Men will always fail you in the end, God will not. I wish I had taught them better, and had taught them to trust in King Jesus, not in earthly Kings, Captains, or Presidents. Today they were on the list; today they were the ones who did not count! Sometimes you do know, and you are just powerless. You are too little, too late, to the fight.

CHAPTER FOURTEEN

❖

The Sargasso Sea

Jediah Emin Patel's yacht was a US Navy destroyer converted to luxury use. It had a helicopter pad at stern and six motor boats hung on each side as life boats. These motor boats looked like small PT boats. Instead of military gray this ship was egg shell white and gleaming with plated polished stainless steel, she was redesigned inside and out. Still the old destroyers form was obvious to any old Navy hand or sailor.

The next morning we boarded the Patel Yacht early along with his crew and were taken to more than adequate quarters. After we were all aboard we looked around and I counted the group. We stayed under constant armed guard confined to the third floor rooms of one section of the ship. We were free to move around from room to room in our little section, and were fed and treated well, just like Jediah had said. Joe Coe, two of his women, Marshal Moore, Unk, Thomas Britton, James Kessler, Roger Clark, Gary Litton, Big Jim, Rodney Dole, myself and a male nurse from medical, that was our group.

We were all in party mode, although prisoners, we all tried to make the best of our situation. A case of red wine was sent with each evening meal. Our group wanted for nothing except honest information, honest work, and freedom. We were just like most Americans back home; fat, lazy, and stupid. The guys started amusing themselves with all types of silly behavior, jokes and songs, trying to lighten the mood. The Great Ark limped in front of us slowly making its way to Newport News. Patel's yacht stayed back keeping an eye on her and offering some protection, or I suppose some help if she was to roll over and sink. The Ark was moving slow always facing into the swells, if possible. We had nothing to do except watch the sea and drink red wine.

My ole' friend Joe Coe was not a happy camper. Our ship phones had been all confiscated and we were all prisoners. Joe still had to bark orders at somebody constantly so we tried to console, or to stay away from Joe as much as possible. Joe was one miserable soul. Joe was like a spoiled brat kid being forced to watch his younger brother play with his favorite toy. Friday having his ship was killing him. On the first early morning the Ark started pulling ahead of Patel. Marshal Moore and I were standing outside our rooms drinking red wine, eating egg rolls, playing trash can basketball and arguing about once saved always saved. No one else in our group would stay up or play keep up with us because we are the two undisputed world champions of drunk and dunk trashcan basketball, and Bible knowledge. Joe kept muttering to himself saying "You eat my guts out" under his breath, and wanting to play rummy, but we were all to wise to play cards with Captain Joe.

The Ark was more stable now. Friday had been patching up the hole and had pushed everything overboard that was not nailed down, gaining him many precious inches above the holes water line. We could see sparks from welders at night, as Fridays' crew tried to save the ship. Telling Joe what a great Job Friday was doing was a hoot! You could watch his blood pressure rise (ha-ha), as he turned red. A temporary patch was important for the Ark, because with any seas she could easily sink or roll with all hands on board.

Marshal Moore "Duck" had a little too much red wine. When the Ark kept pulling away from us Duck started leaning over the railing and shouting at the engine room and the ships bridge. "Hey boys, give her some gas you dummy, the Ark is getting away! Hey, you up there give her some gas," I said. The bridge seemed to listen to duck the first time but soon we were losing ground again. Duck then fell over the ships railing, but was still holding on and slowly flipped onto the deck below completely passed out. Our guards seemed to pay him no mind, and we were all glad to get some sleep. Joe and I went down the stairs about mid morning, and drug Duck back upstairs. This is not something you want to do everyday. Dragging Duck around is not pleasant, nor was this our first time at this chore.

After another hour or so of holding our own with the Ark, we slowed down again until we stopped dead in the water. The ship was quiet and still. All vibrations from the ship's motors had ceased all movement, all breeze, and all waves had completely stopped. We were motionless in the water. The Great Ark slowly disappeared into the distance. Emergency power came on, no hot food, no cold food, no air-conditioning, not much lighting. We were not passengers, not crew. We were prisoners, powerless and uninformed. We only could guess what was happening. For hours we sat motionless at sea. The ocean was covered with a thick mat of floating seaweed as far as the eye could see. The air was still, no wind, the sea stunk. Unk waved us over to the Starboard side railing to see past the ship's main bridge. Our group watched as two men were led to the chopper pad, no it would be four men. They were lined up at the stern of our ship and shot by firing squad. Their bodies made an eerie thud-splash combination sound because the seaweed was so thick. In the dead silence we could hear conversation from afar up the ship. We all strained to hear in the stillness. We were in the Sargasso Sea, the trash dump of the Atlantic. The wind was calm and smells of every type were ripe. Rotten odor smothered us like a blanket. The ship was out of fuel, or out of good fuel. Our tanks had been drained or laced with chemicals that had shut down the motors. The ship's motors might even be shot, a complete loss. This was sabotage, done traders, those men that were executed at the stern chopper pad. Tension grew on ship and conditions were not good, no flush toilets, and not much food. Conditions could not have been much better for Patel and the crew. Moore cracked a joke about money talking.

"You know he's never been without power before!" Unk called a meeting with the latest overheard news from the guards. From the high life to starvation, boy can things really change fast when you run out of oil. Our fall was like hitting the wall, or like America electing Osoma who hated oil companies (ha-ha). Yes we were just like Osoma's America, no oil, no oil pipeline, and SOL.

"Ok, listen up," said Unk "this is what we just heard. A ship from Portsmouth is coming after us. It does not leave until tomorrow. Patel's little chopper does not have the range to make it to shore, and neither do these speed boats because they use gas motors not diesel. An ocean going chopper is coming from Langley to pick up Patel. Langley is closing in about six months but they still have two choppers. We will have to wait maybe for days so conserve water and food. With about an hour of daylight left we heard Jediah's big chopper approaching in the distance. Our group ran to watch the action. We were outside already, because it was very hot and smelly in our cabins and bathrooms. Even before the big chopper landed, a group of people lined up to board each one bending forward against the down blast. None of them were tall enough to be Jediah Patel. Just like a big wise buck he had sent his doe's into the chopper pad clearing before him (ha-ha). This chopper reminded me of the one President Clinton used. It was old green and bulky looking. Before the steps popped out for the people to board two men stepped in front of the chopper and emptied Ak47 rifles into the front windshield. Another man emptied his rifle into the engine compartment from the side. The chopper now sat in silence like a large dead green bug on the back of our ship. Smoke was pouring from its engine compartment vents. The ship was still and quiet again but not for long. Like pop corn the sound of sporadic gunfire echoed throughout the ship. Our group, a little aft of center took cover not knowing which group if any was on our side. We were only spectators to the battle on ship. Many different caliber and types of weapons rang out and about the old destroyer. Twelve men had taken position around the center bridge. They had firing position covering the top deck. Our guards were still there but had taken to hiding behind the stairs and drink machines on deck. We kept a low profile looking through the round holes in the railing but not standing up. Heavy fighting lasted only a few minutes then back again to the endless silence. The men in the tower now had the advantage. Jediah if he was still alive must be in a bad way and holding position below deck. The men in the tower had the whole ship pinned down.

We prisoners stayed mostly outside our rooms for fresh air and low to the floor, trying to keep out of sight. We had been without food now for about ten hours, and we were hungry. Our railing was metal with round holes cut in it. Mostly our backs were up against the wall. On the deck below our cabins were swollen dead bodies which had become too nasty for most to abide. We opened our last case of red wine. Even the non-drinkers were sipping now. It was drink or die. Our little group of prisoners were now only war weary spectators to the battles on ship and things did not look good for my old friend and jailer, Jediah Patel.

When the sun started its first hint of coming up the next morning the standoff on ship had not changed. Sanitary conditions went from bad to worse, and lack of fresh water was a big problem. If not for our supply of red wine we would have all died. The big green bug chopper lay silent on the pad, and the tower men still ruled the deck. The air was quiet and thick with the smell of death. Bodies lay both on deck and on the thick seaweed pad that covered the water. Six motor boats hung on each side of the ship looking to all like the only way out no matter their short range. Joe called a meeting, but just as his meeting started all hell started breaking loose on the starboard side of ship. Our three guards were shot or gone. The fighting was intense. This would be "the big one." We peaked over and through the starboard railing at the action below. Armed men were boarding the ship from the starboard side, the men boarding were in alliance with the men in the tower. Down on sea level next to Patel's yacht was a flat top Chinese made submarine, with men standing on it pointing rocket propelled grenades and rifles up at us while others came over the side. These men cleared the ship shooting anyone who didn't surrender. We got on our knees outside with our hands on our heads, and sure enough young black soldiers soon found us. The sound of gunfire and tear gas could be heard through out the ship. The one crew member nurse and the two women were hiding in a room, and not out in the open on their knees with us. These were Joe's personal attendants and nurse. A young soldier panicked and open fire on the room spraying a full clip of automatic weapons fire. Our ears and hearts rang out. All three died in a messy blood and guts on the walls scene. The type you will see in your minds eye for eternity. Very soon our little group and everybody else on board (not shot yet) were led downstairs by the troops of the winning side. I never knew the names of Joe's personal assistants (those who had just been gunned down). As the soldiers marched us past their open cabin door ole' cold Joe bawled uncontrollably. Just as we topped the outside stairs the main attraction blasted off from the submarine below grabbing my attention and sight. This was a damn funny looking sight.

"Chariot of Fire," Unk said from behind me!

There was a rocket man coming straight up before us from the water. I had paused slightly looking at this spectacle. A rifle butt smashed into my back pushing me down to the next landing on the stairs. I got the message quick! Duck laughed at me as I looked back. We spoke not a word as we were led downstairs except in silent prayer. This odd flying "Chariot" had six pairs of bottles, six rocket nozzles and just enough frame to hold it up. A huge figure wearing an oven glove or mitten type of robe was driving. He stepped in he was not strapped in like a rocket belt. The blast from his "chariot" was very considerable even deadly. The deck was thick with sailors. His fancy rocket blasted a hole in the crowd.

We were all about to meet the "King of the South" his real name Phinehas Emin Pedahel or (Patel). The words "Sons of Ammon" were written in Gold thread throughout his mitten glove garment. I learned later that it was almost impossible to kill a man wearing this type of garment. It shielded infrared heat, was fireproof, bullet proof, and radiation proof. The King's troops were all on one knee as so were we. Duck was slow getting down on his knee and he got some rifle butt encouragement to the back of his neck. It was my turn to laugh (ha-ha). I learned the first time. The young man who had shot the three up stairs was sitting beside me shaking and quivering uncontrollably he looked to be twelve years old and mumbled in French. I prayed with him for a short few seconds I think he understood. The King stepped out of his chariot and pulled back his heavy hood. He then stepped out of his silly looking quilt mitten robe. Holding his robe at arms length he girlishly let it drop. The thick robe fell on James Kessler and one of the king's own guards, neither man got up for some minutes the weight of his garment pinning the men to the deck.

This "King of the South" was a light skinned black man very close to ten feet tall. He wore boots and a bicycle type helmet making him look eleven feet tall. I'm good at judging these things because of my old boxing days. This King was a lean muscular seven hundred to eight hundred pounds. His head was large, in proportion correctly to what a ten foot size man should be. The king was the size of any three or four normal men with hands that looked like he could palm a small car.

Now with his mitten off he stood before us in silk, with light weight bulletproof armor in patches. Bare arms neck and thighs. His garments were fancy, with purple, gold and brass buckles. I guessed his arms and neck were both about forty to forty-five inches around.

The king's sword hung across his back (a long saber). He pulled out the sword and pointed it straight to the sky with both hands. He spoke something and the crowd cheered. His troops and three white robed priests shouted.

"Sons of Ammon! Sons of Ammon! Sons of Ammon!" He then brought down his long blade sword and held it straight out before him. With the length of his sword and his long arms he towered directly over all of us and I'm sure could have killed any man in the crowd at will. His servants, sailors, and we prisoners cowered before him in fear. Marshal Moore was still a little drunk and was bowing very close to me; he whispered in a low quiet voice.

"That's got to be the biggest Ni . . ." before that fool Duck could get the "N" word out I back handed him across the mouth!

"Shut up Duck don't you even think that stupid?

With the King's nod his three priests brought Jediah to court before him. Jediah did not bow, or whimper. The young Jediah stood strong before his older brother. The three priests had a cup. Jediah was made to drink it. All three priests now walked back to the side leaving Jediah alone before the King. The giant King Phinehas Emin Patel laid his sword blade across Jediah's shoulder like he was teeing up his head like a golf ball. The king then said two words unknown to me. He said the words again louder. I was sure that he was about to chop Jediah's head off. Jediah said nothing. The King said the same words again. Still there was silence. The three priests backed up again. They poured out the rest of the cup and then pulled back their hoods and garments reviling what looked like the doctors staff with snakes wrapped around it. They then bowed and departed. The king and crowd started singing a word I did know, and he put away his sword. The word halleluiah was then repeated over and over. The King picked up Jediah at arms length his seven foot ten inch frame dangled in the air like a child. Phinehas Emin Patel then hugged Jediah to his chest and then placed him down beside him and said.

"BEHOLD! FLESH OF MY FATHER, BONE OF MY BONE," The crowd roared with approval! The king leaned over and said something to Jediah and then Jediah pointed straight at me.

"Cornelius," He said.

"Oh shit!" I cried out. My heart jumped a beat! Troops quickly brought my comrades and me, before the giant king. The King again drew his sword as we all bowed before him. Jediah was still standing by his right side. The king placed his sword on our shoulders one by one and said two words. These were two different words from what he had said before.

"Thank you, old soldier, fellow warrior and friend. You have taught my brother well. Thank you for the lives of my family and of our mother, you will not be tested by the priests this day. You served and answered to an eternal God that day in the desert, not you're Northern King or his committee of earthly elders. A greater giant than I also stays my sword this day. Your blood will not be on the house of Patel. You will remain under guard as long as the battle rages.

Tommy Mute came up and gave me a warm embrace. "Welcome to the struggle, Cornelius," he said. Tommy and I talked about five minutes later on that evening. I told him about Lou dying face down in the sand. Just like Joe earlier, Tommy had nothing to say. He was speechless but his eyes, dripping with tears said it all.

Sixty or so crew members of Jediah's Yacht did not fare as well as us lowly prisoners. These men were tested by the priests using a test of "Eli." Two priests brushed something on the chest of the men using hyssop, thus marking the men. Then they filed past a priest named Abiathar and were divided into two groups. One line went to dinner and was now part of the loyal crew and one line went to a firing squad at the edge of ship and they were promptly shot, their bodies hitting the thick seaweed ocean below. Our group was led back to our same third floor prison. One of the old guards was back the others were now all dead. I watched the priest Abiathar dividing the men by looking at their chest, yes looking on the outside. I thought to myself "only Jesus knows the true heart of a man." In every tribe of man one group is the "go to" experts on truth, and all matters of life and death. Back home in Virginia these high priests are called Doctors or Psychiatrist, thus making humanist paganism the official "go to" religion of Virginia. Who or what do your leaders "go to" or trust "who you gonna call?" Should we ever give civil authority, kingly power over free men at all? Who does the testing, who makes up the test, are they scientist or false priests? Psychiatrists have no claim to hard, pure, or even serious science. They are always reduced to playing games with statistics and making up new names for old conditions. They operate in a pagan pop culture of false science, and lies where silly fads are the norm; all or most patients have the latest bull shit condition such as Bi-Polar or Attention Deficit. Young (over active) boys are drugged to make them (almost as good as girls)! Are we are to believe that 50% of young men in many schools now have a chemical imbalance in their brain that needs fixing by these quacks? These modern day witch doctors always over medicate, over bill, and have pushed more people to ruin and death each month than the whole lot of them has helped in all of human history. That is the true science facts. They simply do more harm than good. This is obvious to see in all open and honest double blind medical studies and publications. Most of the students who study this crap in college take the course for the "easy, lazy A" to raise their grade point average, only hopeless losers and worthless bums stay in this field. None of them should be taken seriously, much less given the power to decide another mans fate.

Within hours the large motors of the old destroyer class yacht were humming again. We were all fed well. Jediah's loyal servants brought us a hot meal and a case of red wine. We were jailed just as before, trying to make the best of our lot. The time was still way before noon and the king was now in control of the ship. He had taken over the master suite and Jediah's Asian women and made First Mate Cory the new Captain. Our group was busy cleaning up blood and guts and dead bodies. It felt good to be underway again and leaving the nasty Sargasso Sea behind. All the bloody mess did not depress us much, it didn't seem to matter. After we all worked as a group on cleanup we gathered again in Joe's Cabin. Joe was making drawings and maps around a small table and as soon as every one was present and settled down Joe started!

"Unk, you had a good view of how many 55-gallon drums of fuel were brought on board from the submarine. Now how many total barrels came aboard?"

"At least twenty Joe, but no more than twenty five I kept a close eye" said Unk.

"Yes they must have had a supply very close" said Joe. "Maybe he met another small vessel?"

Marshal Moore spoke up, "that amount of fuel will only push a crate this big but so far."

"Yes," said Joe," That's my point. We are heading west, we are going after the Ark to finish her off, now what do you think Friday will . . ."

"RRRaaaaRRrrrrrrrrr"

As Joe spoke the tell tale horn like blast of a Phalanx guns fifty caliber rounds blasted through the quiet afternoon from an automatic air defense system on top of the ship. We ran outside to see a predator drone hit the sea in flames in close proximity of the ship.

"Looks like Friday knows now," said Unk.

"Joe, where do you figure that drone came from?" asked Duck.

"Not from the Ark, Duck" replied Joe. "Most likely that drone came from Langley Air Force base if it's still open. Friday was using it to scope out the threat.

"Yes, said Unk, "I don't guess these people have been answering the phone much lately in the bridge."

"What will the Ark do, Joe," I asked Joe Coe who was still scribbling on his paper!

"Gentlemen, we must get off this tub and fast. The King made a big mistake leaving that Phalanx system on. Friday will blow us out of the water for sure, and quick. His first set of missiles will hit us in minutes. They have slightly longer range than the French missiles that this yacht carries. Friday will fire first to save and use that advantage. Yes, I'm sure Friday will fire on us. We must make a dash up the deck right now and at least try to bet in those motor boats, some of us just might make it. Look down the port side. That's what the King and his men are doing already. Marshal Moore spoke up, everybody listened!

"The Ark is listing twelve degrees to port so she can't get any plane off her deck except maybe an ultra-light craft or two!"

"Shut up and listen," Joe said, "All of you! The Ark is only 100 miles ahead of us, Friday sees us on radar, on drone footage and by satellite, he has already fired on us and we will soon be hit. Our only chance is to charge up the deck and get off this boat. Look, I trained Friday, the man has killed hundreds of his own men to save that ole' tub already. I figure he must have hit the bulkhead door locks even before that missile ever hit the ship!"

"That sounds like John Wayne stuff," scoffed Unk! As if to accent Joe's point, the first missile hit our starboard deck just up the ship and below us knocking us all to the floor and ringing our ears as the cabin floor flexed from the blast! "That's six minutes early, Joe," I mean Roster T, LET'S RIDE, shouted Unk."

"Stay down, not yet," shouted Coe, "They will come in sets of two!" Just then the other missile hit taking out all six motor boats on the starboard side.

"We have two minutes or less," shouted Joe as our group jumped straight over the third floor railing to the deck below, broken bones, or sprained ankles were of no concern at this point! The stairs and our guards below were blown sway by the first blast anyhow! We robbed a few rifles from dead crew members on deck. One sailor begged "Duck" to shoot him. His legless and handless body was bleeding on the deck. Duck turned his head, and shot him once in the face. Like John Wayne, we ran up the port side of the ship, our two guns blazing what little they could. Unk manned a boat launcher as James Kessler covered him with fire from deck. Some of us jumped head first into the hanging boat. Duck fired his last bullets, and jumped in feet first. Unk was cranking away and shouting jump, jump! James Kessler was hit first, and he fell into the boat, then Unk was showered with bullets from the side, he kept cranking even unto his death. We hit the water with a jolt. Unk must have hit the release button. Gary Litton fell down in the boat breaking a leg as we hit the water. Bullets rang out from above and hit Thomas Briton and our boats motor in the same burst. Big Jim was hit by another quick automatic mussel flash blasting down from the deck above. Our boat scrapped the side of the old destroyer for some seconds nearly capsizing us. Rodney Dole kicked the ship to free us, and was knocked out cold. He quickly disappeared into the raging water. We then bounced clear into the waves and darkness. Two missiles blasted off from the yacht above us on their way to the Ark. Their bright flair lit up the night. Then within seconds the Yacht was hit yet again by a volley from the Ark. In the flare of the missiles we saw that another boat was down in the water with us. The old destroyer was in bad shape, and on fire at mid ship, but was still standing up straight in the water. We heard Jediah's small little chopper take off the backend of his yacht before its fire and light disappeared into the night. We were quickly absorbed into the waves of blackness, quiet and solitude. Duck was trying to get the boat started while Joe was at the controls. Moore had been hit slightly on the fore arm and was bleeding, but being the head mechanic he considered it his job to fix the motor. Shooting automatic rifles at them is not good for motors or men. We sat in the roller coaster darkness praising God that we unbelievably had made it off that ship alive!

"Do you see that other boat?" said Joe.

'No," I answered! The ocean swells limited our vision, so did the low cloud cover and the loud concussions of the incoming shells had made us all deaf. We could not for some time communicate very well by voice. When Duck got the motor sputtering along using his gum in a vacuum line we all felt it more than heard it. We raised our arms in victory and praise. After an hour the bell ring in our heads subsided enough for us to talk.

"Patel took his chopper southwest" Litton said. "To a submarine I would guess," said duck. I wrapped up Ducks arm with part of James Kessler's clothes. Joe said about two words, crossed himself and James went overboard. Next Joe put his hand to Big Jim Calkins neck smacked him around a few times and then Jim, like James went overboard. Duck was sleeping and Joe grabbed him.

"Help me with this one, Cornelius I can't pick him up! Moore then smacked Joe in the face giving him a bloody nose, not thinking throwing him overboard was all that funny. Joe went back to the front seat without saying a word, and knowing he was in the wrong. During that night we argued about compass readings, what little stars we could see and listened to Thomas Briton moan and cry from his gunshot wounds. By early daylight it was a relief and pleasure for Joe to throw the dead body of "crybaby" Briton overboard.

"Are there anymore of you gonna die anyway crybabies on this damn boat?" announced Joe! "I need some sleep!"

The King of the South had the same obvious plan for the motor boats as we did and his crew had been in the process of loading up supplies and fuel into them when the missiles hit! We had some extra five gallon plastic and one gallon metal containers of gas, only one gallon of water. These motor boats were old mini-PT boats with 454 gas motors that were fast and fun, but did not have much range like diesel motors would. Our motor was sputtering and poorly running because of age and gunshot damage.

After heading west all night we could see the other boat behind us about two hundred yards back. The other boat must have heard us get ours started and then followed us all night. We wondered if it was friend or foe. We kept an eye on the boat behind. It seemed to be one lone man doing the driving. By full light the boat behind was racing towards us, and obviously on fire and smoking badly. We had not the power to out run it and I soon recognized the lone driver. It was Tommy Mute. He pulled up beside us and handed over a five gallon container of gas, and then jumped into our boat holding a half-full box of red wine and a quart of oil. Within thirty seconds Tommy was passed out drunk in between the seats of our boat. He had been driving all night with nothing to drink but red wine. Joe and Duck started sighting the sun and arguing about our course. Gary Litton with his broken leg suffered in silence. At least he didn't whine like Briton. We wrapped up his leg as best we could. Tommy Mute came to in about two hours. His gas had long since been dumped into the near empty tank. His half case of wine and quart of motor oil could have been just what we needed to survive, praise God! When Tommy Mute woke up that morning he told us that the King himself had thrown him in the boat while Jediah cranked it down. The two of them had pushed the ole big Green chopper off the pad and into the ocean with their bare hands. "The King had let us escape, he told his men to hold their fire as we ran up the deck. They had you in their sights, Cornelius, and did not shoot!" Too bad they shot half of us before the word got out," said Joe. That sounds like some of the clowns that work for me." Our group gave a toast to Unk, James Kessler, Rodney Dole, Big slim Jim, and crybaby Thomas Briton. Only God knows the truth of who and why of life and death.

CHAPTER FIFTEEN

***

Welcome to Virginia

"Land ho!" shouted Joe Coe. I stood up to "see" (ha-ha), and fell backward hitting the motor compartment very much hurting my back and smashing my old friend Gary Litton. The boat had hit a wave just right to push me backward. We were in surf praise God. I just stayed down and opened the last bottle of red wine. Gary and I lying down passed the bottle between us as the others were standing shouting for joy. We two needed more medication anyway. A hard thud into the sand told the whole story, the others all jumped out getting their feet wet. I stepped onto the hood and dropped onto dry sand, the last third of the wine bottle still in my hand. Duck, jealous of my consumption rate grabbed the bottle and started chugging. The others shouted "go, go, go, go," in idiot college kid drinking fashion until the bottle was empty. When the cheering stopped Duck took the bottle and smashed it against the hull of the old fiberglass boat. This did not break the bottle but put a dent and hole in the fiberglass instead. After three "Moore" attempts Duck could not break the bottle so he tossed it into the back of our boat where it shattered into little pieces. Duck burped very loud and raised his hands in victory and we all fell into the dry soft sand in laughter and celebration. The motor sputtered, there was silence as we all listened, and then broke out laughing again. The boats motor had just cut off, she had given her all and "Moore" to get us safely to shore. Praise God!

Our group picked ourselves up and started walking north up the beach. We could see trees and a building in the distance so we kept in that direction. No other buildings were in sight. There was a little white church in the trees with a white hard packed unpaved parking lot. Before we

got there cars started pulling up, two then two more then one. It was Sunday morning and people were arriving at Church. We cut straight in to get off the soft beach sand. The hard ground was a comfort to our stride. Tommy Mute was ahead of all of us, Gary Litton and I pulled up the rear, while Duck and Joe walked together in the middle. By the time all of our ragged group got to the church there were now nine cars, that's everybody Pastor Woods then stated. The old Pastor welcomed us warmly.

Our five was a ragged looking beat up bunch. We stayed in the bathrooms and tried to suck his water fountain dry for some time before joining the service. The people in the church spoke a heavy slang speech that was very hard to understand at first but they sang songs kind of normal. It was hard to figure. The Pastor was a very old frail man who spoke in a soft but clear English voice (no slang twang like the others). We all sat together except Tommy Mute. He paced back and forth in the back of the church and did his daily exercises, and shouted praise God. I thought he might be holiness like me, but I didn't know about exercising in church. Sometimes you just don't know what you don't know.

I think the old pastor was glad to see a bunch of sinners like us stop by. The piano was very old but the young lady piano player was not. She was about ten I would guess. We sang many old hymns three of which kind of sounded the same I'm sure. It was a joy to sing and praise the Lord. The little old man never did preach and we just kept on singing. The four of us sitting together sounded like a Southern Gospel Quartet. We sounded good. I was very impressed! I didn't know my shipmates could sing that well, praise God what a good time we had singing. The whole congregation said they admired our singing. Just when I thought the old preacher was going to speak a tall man with a cowboy hat on came bursting through the oak church doors and started apologizing for being late. His group set up electronic equipment computers, lights, even a flat screen TV. They must be high-tech/ /red necks (ha-ha). There wasn't much on TV just still pictures, words and stuff but I wanted to look at the singers anyway. These singers did a great job, but the cowboy would always play tapes of other people singing the same song when his singers started singing to drown his own singers out. I thought this was very silly and impolite of him but I didn't say anything about it. The Cowboy didn't have a name people just called him Cow Man. I sat next to his wife and didn't know what to call her. You just can't call a nice Christian Lady "Cow Woman," not with a straight face. When Cow Man told the congregation that they had been held up by a traffic jam and that a big aircraft carrier had almost hit the bridge, Joe started sobbing uncontrollably! His baby was still alive! Joe bowed his head and shouted.

"Thank you Lord, thank you Lord," over and over again. Tommy Mute kept doing his exercises in the back of the church until he got so tired that he passed out cold in the middle of the floor. A big guy named Jack looked at Tommy and said he was alright. Jack's wife was the lead singer of the Cowboys. She was very pretty and wore a bigger cowboy hat than Cowman did. A long haired man ran camera and another man came with them named Norris who everybody liked for some reason. Cowman left one of his boots on the table in the back so I took off one of mine also and put it beside his. He must have appreciated this very much, because he tipped me $15 dollars for doing so. Being a world traveler, I'm very sensitive to other peoples' ways and customs. You never know, they might even be Episcopalians or some weird, queer faith like that. I had a sister in-law once who made you take off both boots at her front door! Our little ragged group hung our heads and begged for forgiveness, except for Tommy Mute, he was still out cold in the floor. This Cowman fellow spoke with authority about spiritual authority. I was worried about my friend Tommy, so as the sermon started I took a quick glance back. Cowman didn't seem to even notice Tommy. He was not concerned at all. The man was impressive but cold as ice. Romans 13 (1-8)

(1) **Let every soul be subject unto the higher powers, for there is no power but of God; the power that be pre ordained of God!**

(2) **Who so ever there fore resisteth the power resisteth the ordinance of God: and they that resist shall receive to themselves damnation!**

(3) **For rulers are not a terror to good works, but to the evil, wilt thou not be afraid of the power? Do that which is good, and thou shalt have praise of the same!**

(4) **For he is the minister of God, to thee for good. But if thou do that which is evil, be afraid; for he beareth not the sword in vain, for he is the minister of God, a revenger to execute wrath upon him that doeth evil**

(5) **Where fore ye must needs be subject, not only for wrath, but also for conscience sake**

(6) **For this cause pay ye tribute also; for they are God's ministers, attending continually upon this very thing**

(7) **Render therefore to all their dues; tribute to whom tribute is due; custom to whom custom; fear to whom fear; honor to whom honor.**

Hebrew one (1-3)

Who being the brightness of his glory, and the express image of his person and up holding all things by the word of his power, when he had by himself purged our sins, sat down on the right hand of the majesty on high;

Isaiah 14 (12-19)

(12) How art thou fallen from heaven, oh Lucifer, son of the morning! How art thou cut down to the ground, which did'st weaken the nations

(13) For thou hast said in thine heart, I will ascend into heaven, I will exalt my throne above the star's of God; I will sit also upon the mount of the congregation, in the sides of the north!

(14) I will ascend above the heights of the clouds; I will be like the most high!

Mathew 26 (62, 63, 64)

(62) And the high priest arose, and said unto him, answerest thou nothing? What is it which these witness against thee! But

(63) Jesus held his peace and the high priest answered and said unto him, I adjure three by the living God, that thou tell us whether thou be Christ, the son of God.

(64) Jesus saith unto him, thou hast said; never the less I say unto you, here after shall ye see the son of man sitting on the right hand of power, and coming in the clouds of heaven!

"Wow! What a great service," I said as I shook Cowboys hand and thanked the old pastor once again. We didn't see any cows, but it didn't seem to matter. They all looked good in their fancy cowboy hats. Our whole group hitched a ride in the Cowboy van. Big Jack drove and his pretty singer wife named Angie rode shotgun. Angie had big eyes and a creamy spellbinding voice that almost drove Duck crazy. He bought fifty of her CDs. Angie said most of the time she just gave them away to spread the gospel. The Cowboy group also had a big pick up truck pulling a horse trailer. Our group all fit into the vehicles with no problem. We took a small ferry to the mainland and I was pretty sure that the old ferry driver waited for us to arrive which was nice since they only ran twice a day. Then I saw it! "Welcome to Virginia" the sign that always gives me goose bumps and that once (long ago) stood for something grand. Yes, the sign said I was home. We were on the Eastern Shore. Cowman had planned to pick up a pony in his horse trailer for Angie's mother to ride when they got back home. She was too short to mount up on a regular size horse but the deal fell through at the last minute. Something about new state regulations at nursing homes about cats, rabbits, birds, horses and Mexicans. Angie was upset about not getting the pony for her mom, but she didn't need any more Mexicans.

After a quick lunch at a roadside Diner our group was on the main road and reached the long bay bridge in about an hour and a half. Once over the water we could see the Great Ark out in the channel. The Ark was being helped by many tugs. Soon the traffic came to a stop once again. We all got out of the van to stretch and Joe jumped up in the pick up truck shouting and pointing to the far horizon. Coming into clear view was a cloud of smoke. It was Captain Cory in Jediah's yacht. He was still trying to sink the Great Ark. Bug like drones were diving out of the clouds like wasps, stinging the old destroyer the best they could. "Cory's going to ram the Ark," shouted Captain Coe. The bridge was now lined with people watching this epic battle. Just like the Monitor and the Merrimack these two old ships could not finish each other off. The Great Ark was like a tired old wrestler reaching for the safe corner of Hampton Roads, the place where she was born! Jediah's Captain Cory was just as stubborn as Joe's First Mate Friday. Both were pursuing each other unto death for fame, fortune, and glory. As we watched the old destroyer rolled belly side up and the thick, rolling, black smoke was quickly snuffed out. Like a peaceful swimming whale the old destroyer without notice or fanfare submitted quietly to the still waves of death! Yes, Friday had done it. The Ark had crossed the highway. The Great Ark would live again. People were raising hell behind us now for the traffic had gone on in front and was some ways down the road. Back in the van Angie gave her red-faced stubborn and now mad husband a kind facial expression but knew better than to speak. Tommy Mute who had lost it during the church service so bad that we had all feared that he was dead, was now praising God and shouting "Blessed by the Best" He would be shouting for many hours of the drive back to Salem. Tommy might be Holiness I thought. He never mentioned any giants so I wasn't really sure. On the long bridge I stared out the wide side window of the van. I was sitting in the back with Gary

Litton. Gary was pretending to be asleep so that I would not talk so much, he's had years of practice at doing that and has gotten pretty damn good at it. Out in the bay past the bridge posts rushing by my window I saw the most beautiful sail boat yacht I'd ever seen. On the back or stern were three men asleep. Two women drove the big Captains wheel on its bridge. Daniel and Double De stood waving to a fishing boat from Port railing! Hey, look there they go, that's Franklin's boat. They soon dropped out of sight and I lay my head back down. Sometimes you just don't know?

That evening I was standing at the front door of my house or really now my ex-wife's house. The cowboy van rode off into the evening sunset. I knocked on the door and Patty answered!

"Do I live here?" I asked?" How many of life's basic important questions you just don't know. Patty grabbed me and pulled me inside. "Welcome home honey," she said. That evening and night was spent in each others arms! Not cold marathon sex but real love making. We so much enjoyed spending time together, as only lifetime partners can really, fully understand.

In the morning we headed for the Cracker Barrel for breakfast. This is a long time old family tradition at my home comings, but no relation to Patty's family (ha-ha). After breakfast Patty reached into her purse and handed me a summons from Roanoke County.

"Cornelius, honey you've been indicted. I'm sorry. This is about my sister. Don't worry, Cornelius, she filed charges on me also down in North Carolina. I did beat all of her silly made up charges, but it cost thousands of dollars and many trips back and forth going to court. Cornelius, I showed my North Carolina Lawyer your case and she laughed out loud. She said only a commonwealth state would ever bring up silly charges like yours, that my sister plainly said that you two did not have sex and that her thirty five year old allegation would not have been taken seriously! My lawyer also said that Virginia was famous for poorly written sex laws because so many lawyers from state schools were incompetent and backward.

"Oh! I see, maybe those lawyers went to UVA and played football. I did hear something about that! Patty Honey please tell me what did Debbie Cracker Head, your little sister charge you with?"

"Stalking," answered Patty, "and trying to kill her dog, and bring harm to her minor children. It was simply crazy and mean and evil, Cornelius! I haven't been to my sister's house in over seventeen years, that can't be stalking?"

"Sounds bad, Patty, I thought your sister's three boys were all big tough football players in college, how did you manage to scare them, and the dog, (ha-ha), is that the same dog you would dog sit for at your mothers when Debbie and Barnie would go on trips and vacations (ha-ha). That dog likes me more than it does Barnie. Your mother always did say so. That dog was a very good judge of character, just like your mother (ha-ha)."

"Stop laughing and making fun, Cornelius, this is serious. Both of my sisters are cracking up and poor little Debbie is only in her fifties. She has lost all touch with reality, honey. She filed charges on you and me both the same week after I would not sign my mother's estate settlement paperwork!

"Your mother had money?" I thought that was settled years ago." "No, Cornelius, they have been dragging their feet, the old house has sat empty for years. Our family is the shame of the community. The grass is six foot high, nobody cuts it much and my brothers and sisters argue about everything. Little sister Debbie has stolen all of mother's jewelry from the house and of course I told you I gave her what mother had at the hospital, she said at the time she would have it cleaned! Barnie rented a truck, and hauled away all of Daddy's garage tools, the welders, air compressors all that stuff in Daddy's shop. They wanted me off of the executors list because I was so sick all the time so I trusted them and signed away most of my legal rights and power. I tried to go along and stop some of the arguing but now they have given me nothing at all. I trusted them Cornelius, and now my sisters and brothers have turned on me. They all changed when Momma and Daddy was not around to keep the peace. My momma and Daddy were people of faith they would be so ashamed of them. All I asked them for was one of the four Bibles one of momma's many rings, and a piece of Daddies old military uniform Cornelius. They will not talk to me, or even give me copies of family pictures over the web. This is not about the money. I guess they just hate me. I'm so sad because I love them so much. They will not even let me in the Church, not even for my uncle's funeral! Debbie filed charges on you Honey, she said you were naked in front of her but did not have sex with her when she was sixteen."

"Well, honey, she's right about the not having sex part. I'm sure I would have remembered that."

"That was almost forty years ago, can she really file charges against you now, honey?"

"We live in the commonwealth of Virginia my dear we are not like all the rest of the fifty states. I have looked into this some. Did you know that the laws in Virginia are famous for being poorly written? Salem is a backward hick town and few powerful families run it. There is no justice here Patty or honest Judges! Do you remember that crooked Salem Judge Uncle Allen had fired for me during our divorce? That Judge was a friend of your brothers. I wish that Allen and Dad were both alive now but I guess I'm on my own on this one. I'll talk to the police in the morning and see what's up."

The next day I came home from the magistrate office and my Lawyer to tell Patty the news! "Honey I talked to the police and my Lawyer! The magistrate let me out without bond to get my affairs in order before I go to court and to jail! I will not have a trial."

"Jail," Patty said (crying).

"Yes dear, the court date has been moved up. Court is now set for in the morning. Our lawyer said the only way he could get me out of life in prison without parole was to take a deal offered by the prosecutor and go to jail for six months. If I don't take the deal and demand a jury trial then we would spend all of our retirement money and you could even lose the house and I would likely be put away using the new civil commitment laws of Virginia and would never get out. Almost nobody ever gets out of civil commitment in Virginia and it only takes one offense on a list of twenty-eight different charges. They said that if I didn't "play ball" and take the plea that they could keep me in jail anyway for six months just waiting on a court date so there was no reason to be a smartass and try to claim constitutional rights. I was deemed a danger to society even though I was sixty years old and had a clean spotless record and had run a public charity in the town for over ten years.

"Did you say in the morning, Cornelius? Go to jail? Did I hear you right honey? The sentence for not having sex with my Cracker Head sister here in Virginia is life in prison? How could this be? Lots of boys have not had sex with my sister? At least I would think so. I mean she's been living down in Carolina for years."

"I'm sorry, honey. I have to take the crooked deal they offered me. This has nothing to do with truth, or justice only power, hate, and money. I would not spend all of your money on me, not at our age. I don't think we can fight them and win. The laws in Virginia have changed since back in 1975, and 1978, but not for me. The two top sex case lawyers advised me not to try to fight Salem. Do not try to prove the fine line argument of innocence or guilt that it would be impossible. In Virginia the law was so broad, and obviously written to confuse for the express purpose of empowering dirty local officials, and that fighting for justice was not possible. In fact I could be convicted (and was) of having carnal knowledge of a minor with no claim of any type of sex. I remembered what Jediah Emin Patel had said about the Prince of Virginia and signed the plea deal. There was no evidence against me except my own statement to the police. The next morning I walked into the courtroom and after a quick five minute plea bargain hearing I walked out in shackles. An old man of sixty with a lifetime clean record not even a parking ticket now a felon in trouble forever with the law. Patty cried as I was led away, my friends shouted "We love you, Cornelius"

Paul Goldwater was smiling like a possum, as were the evil Cracker Sisters. I was not allowed to say goodbye or hug my wife. In the holding cell I remembered what the giant had said. "Don't be fooled Cornelius, these are false names with the power to deceive in water. DEBBIE, HEDDIE, in the hedge of CECIL, a double effect. My plaintiff sister-in-law DEBBIE was fifty years old, with long thin blonde fair, five foot seven, and ninety two pounds. Her brand new capped, "too white" for real teeth shining like new money. It does not take a doctor to see a classic anorexic female with teeth destroyed by stomach acid standing before you. Anyone who saw her immediately had compassion for her deep sunken AIDS patient type face. How could a person who obviously could not see truth in the mirror each morning still be found capable of recognizing the truthful witness about herself from thirty-five or forty years before? Not filing charges after all these years until her parents are both dead and she was in a selfish fit or rage in an angry estate fight with her sister! Was the judge Sam or Randy his prosecutor really that blind or where both dirty pawns directed from above?

Hold previous page up to your bathroom mirror (water) now turn it upside down! The names you still find easy to read have the power to deceive in water.

I next sat in a holding cell awaiting transport to the big new regional jail in Salem Virginia, or WVRJ for short. These next six months in jail would be harder on my wife Patty, than me I thought. I was finally back, but now gone again just when she needed and wanted me. In the holding cell with me was a tall young man named Jim.

"Maybe I should have fought them and not taken the plea agreement," I told Jim. "I feel so dirty, and cheap like taking a dive or something. Maybe I could have beaten them in court. Goldwater, Sissy from Catawba Hospital, all the Crackers! I'd hate to be the next one sitting on that court bench (ha-ha)." The tall young man named Jim held up his hand and shook his head side to side before speaking!

"No, you did right Cornelius! Don't try to fight Salem, learn from me! I demanded a trial! The girl was sixteen years old! I just got thirty years and have spent over forty-five thousand dollars! My lawyer says I may never get out!"

"Wow, Jim, thirty years what did you do have sex with her, rape her or hurt the poor girl."

"No," said Jim, "nothing like as that! I think they shoot you on the spot if you have sex with a sixteen year old here in Salem. This woman looked older to me and I was a fool. She had talked about having an abortion two years ago to a woman friend of mine and I took from hearing about the abortion that she was more than a kid I didn't figure she was fourteen and having an abortion. At trial she didn't look like a hooker anymore but like a little school girl. I was not so much ashamed of touching her crotch as I was accused, I admitted that I did touch her crotch, but ashamed for being such a fool.

"So you didn't have sex with your victim either. Jim, are you telling me the truth? This is so crazy! Thirty years! The value of a female crotch is much higher here in Virginia. In Portugal it's down to fourteen dollars (ha-ha).

"Look, Cornelius," said Jim, "What can you expect this state is actually named after a female crotch."

"Jim, as dumb as that statement sounds, I'll have to admit you do have a point. I was told "only in Virginia by very many top lawyers!"

"Likewise, they said that to me also," said Jim. "Cornelius, they laughed as I was taken away, "Thirty Years" It's not like we had sex, or I raped her! She came to my house, she wanted sex, I was the one who stopped, I was the gentleman who did not have sex with the little tramp, most any boy her age in my position would have jumped at the chance but now I'm the bad guy, because I touched her nasty crotch before I threw her out, and then told the truth about it."

"I know the feeling big Jim, really that's no joke!"

"Cornelius, do you know where they are going to take us? Well, do you know?

"To Jail," I answered

"Not just any local Jail, Cornelius, that big new jail in Salem, the one that's been in the news. The prisoners in that jail have been demanding the same rights as Communist Chinese prisoners," said Jim.

"Is that really asking a lot I said, here in America? I mean come on really, the Communist Chinese have rights?

This is the land of the free, the home of the brave, Jim."

"The home of free food stamps and the free cell phone," said Jim. "But rights under Osoma well not so much. The right to another 100 free minutes means more to most than the right to vote in honest elections. Virginia is not like all of the other states, Cornelius. They don't have to let you out of jail when your sentence is up! All sex offenders or anyone, really, can get life in prison on their first offense. You are tested by the State of Virginia's high priest and then they decide your fate. These priests all live high off the fat of the land. The state pays $140,000 per each so called pervert convict like you and me that they can lock up. All prisoners out on probation are forced to pay for "counseling" if they ever are let out. The system is built by and for the support of worthless Doctors at huge expense to tax payers and has no known benefit to the public. You will be tested by these high priests, and then they decide your fate. To cover their own butts the high priests put everyone away for life to protect the public and to make them selves rich. You get no trial, no jury, no charge, just life in prison. The doctors or priests use statistics and group you with others to prove you are dangerous. Many people show up at the Salem Jail only after their lawful sentence is up somewhere else. They have no real legal or constitutional right to hold any of these men. Even in Communist China the officials would have to make up false charges, or set men free, in Salem Virginia under Osoma your sentence is just the beginning. Men are held without charge Cornelius. The constitution is dead now officially in Virginia. This was tried here first as a test, and also to control Washington DC, that is the sad cold truth."

"This all sounds very bad brother Jim!"

"There's more, Cornelius! In this Salem Jail you will never see the light of day again, and there are no visits allowed like in all state prisons. In China each prisoner is allowed one visit per month by his family members.' In the big new Salem jail no visits are allowed to save money.

Only phone visits are allowed in Salem, not even wave through the glass visits are allowed.

"Ok, Jim, I'm listening, keep talking please go on."

"Prisoners never go outside in Salem Virginia, and all the skylights are painted over. In Communist China each prisoner is allowed one hour outside each day. No one is ever allowed outside at all at the Salem Jail. There is no outside court at all built into the design of the facility. We know the importance of sunshine and that vitamin D is necessary for human life. What Salem, is doing is a worst crime than what most of the fools they lockup have done. I'd rather see some dumb pervert dropping his pants next to every stop sign in the state then I would to pay one hundred thousand dollars a piece for quack doctors to get rich by supposedly counseling the poor dumb pervert bastard. Surprise, your little girl has seen a penis anyway, at school. Half the retards on stage are doing about the same damn thing; grabbing their balls and cussing, and we put them on the air during the Super Bowl"

"Jim, is it really as bad as you say? I'm not so sure about all those stop sign perverts, will some of them be women? (ha-ha). Salem seems like such a nice town, could our local jail really be worst on human rights than prisons in Communist China? I just don't want to believe that!

"Well, Cornelius, that's the facts, what's your story," asked the tall young man?

"Jim, I simply told the police the whole truth without a lawyer present. I was guilty of a misdemeanor of exposure when I let my towel drop back in the 1970s. They had me on that, but then they charged me with a felony and made me plea to it using their big stick and club the new civil commitment laws in Virginia. Life in prison without parole can be the result of any sexual allegation made in the State of Virginia. My lawyer said that almost nobody ever gets out of civil Commitment here in Virginia. The politicians will soon have absolute power to imprison their enemies. The good of the many is always more important than the rights of the few. This power to lock up people at will, without charge, is very dangerous. Men are locked up not for crimes, but for what someone thinks they might do in the future. Doctors and lawyers make millions of dollars each month off the tax payers for doing nothing much more than sending out the bill. Could this power be abused? What do you think (ha-ha)? When US attorneys could not lock up the Wikileaks founder on any "true" or "real" charges, what was the first thing they did to try to shut him up? Of course! They made up some sex charges and threw him in jail. Some poor innocent women have been victimized by this evil man. This works all the time. I have found in life that women play the Bulls and Cows game as good as or even better than most men. If there are any poor innocent women being victimized sexually in the western world then they must be on drugs or very young, and most of those deserve what they get. I just don't believe honest sexual abuse is all that common. That is unless you let angry feminist gender haters define the terms of the debate, and gender correctness along with political correctness rule.

Most young girls lean how to control men very early, and most of the perverts I know of have been very weak men."

"Jim, we do not have to trash the United States constitution to protect Virginians from perverts, as Virginia law makers evidently believe. If you give government officials that much power, it will be abused by men like Osoma. Look what happens to his political opponents with out the power of the state in his hand. When the good of the many is decided by an elite few then all freedom is soon lost. Churches are told to give abortion pills, The Boy Scouts are told to have gay leaders, oil and coal companies are told not to drill or dig and America slides into the mud of history no better than any other loser pagan kingdom."

Jim didn't fall asleep during my rant in the holding cell and we became friends during my stay in jail. I do not believe he will ever get out. So feel safe that your half a million dollars paid to Virginia, "witch doctors" for just Jim alone has been well spent in the end. The ruling elite always suck the wealth out of society through the straw of Government. Free, brave, godly men have to stand up and say "hell no, lets cut every thing by half" at least once every generation, or just like the forest the government will take over everything in our lives.

When I got to the big regional jail in Salem I was locked in solitary confinement for the first nine days, just a bunk and me. I was not allowed to shower or shave. The eighth night I was awakened one and one half hours after lights out or in the middle of the RIM sleep cycle to have my sex offender picture taken and to be fingerprinted. When you look through sex offender photos and see how sick we all look, know that this same method must be standard issue. This is how police get us worst of the worst to look our worst as we should. After my sex offender photo was taken I was allowed to shower and shave each day. All of the guards were polite and professional, even friendly at times. The big new building was kept clean. Most all meat was processed and turkey based, presumably to make inmates drowsy. No real coffee, no fresh fruit, no salads, no juice was ever served to me during my six month stay. Our food was mostly bread and potatoes and water in some noodle form, a very cost effective kitchen. I would guess a net cost of less than one dollar per meal. I would like to thank all of the officers that befriended me and those who did not take my writing pens from me during those months (they are weapons). I walked down a long hallway to my jail cell carrying my mattress in front of me and what did I see? There in the jail in Pod C was Captain Joe Coe, playing cards with James Kessler, Duck, Unk, Suicide, they were all still alive and in the regional Jail? Briton, Roger Mensink, the boys from the Island? "Welcome back old school" shouted Mike Fitch? "What is this you boys are all dead?" No Cornelius!

"Don't you remember" said Travis Jones, "the guards' double tasered you, you've been in the hole for weeks. We all thought you might be dead!"

"Yeah, Cornelius the guards said you were out of it! Remember the song you taught us! Yea the song said Cory! You said we could all work for the lord even in this jail"

The inmates started singing the old song that Cornelius had taught them. An old Negro spiritual he learned as a boy on the Delta.

"I'm a soldier in the army of the Lord. I'm a soldier in the Army" More and more inmates joined in and the singing got louder and louder. Some inmates started standing up on their seats and dancing!

"LOCK DOWN, LOCK DOWN" shouted the guards over the loud speakers! Shielded guards stacked up in the hallway at the Pod door waiting to rush the Pod and shut down the day room as soon as the door buzzer sounded. The guards soon rushed in Pod C stopping the song once again. The inmates who were once singing at the top of their lungs were quiet again and back in their locked cells. Cornelius and two others were tasered and all three dragged out unconscious with a guard under each arm. Joe Coe shouted from his cell at the top of his lungs

"Taser me" Come on "Taser me" He knew Cornelius was back having adventures on the Great Ark.

I looked out over my cabin railing gripping it with all my strength just to stand up. The sea breeze and salt air felt good and refreshingly cool on my face. I was gazing at the most beautiful sailboat I'd ever seen with lines as of a woman! Hey, I know those guys!

"See you all in the funny papers"

The End

For now

Best regards
T.C. Driver

Stay tuned for the real life Tom in the next few pages.

THE SONG THAT CORNELIUS SANG WITH HIS FELLOW INMATES

I'm a soldier . . . In the Army of the Lord
I'm a soldier . . . . In the Army!
Well I went to the river . . . . Water was so cold
It chilled the body . . . but not the soul!
Well I went ah little bit farther, and what did I see
The angels of the lord coming down for me!

(Chorus)

Well I went to the Warden, begged mercy on me
He shook his head what will be will be
I went a little bit farther the hangman smiled with glee
This rope that I'm tying boy, we'll test with thee

(Chorus)

Well I went to the Chaplin . . . Sir Will you pray for me!
He said one is cursed who hangs on a tree!
I begged for forgiveness . . . . as he slammed my cell. You lived for evil
boy . . . . Now rot in Hell!

(Chorus)

Well I went to the Lord Jesus . . . . fell down on my knees
Lord do you have a place . . . for a sinner boy like me!
He said come unto me son your faith has set you free
Forever my riches in glory . . . . You will see!

(Chorus)
Repeat first verse

WORD FROM THE AUTHOR

Thank you for reading The Great Ark, my first attempt at writing. I wrote this book by hand while an inmate at the regional jail in Salem Virginia! I am a felon and a registered sex offender now, per my plea agreement with the circuit court of Roanoke County where my wife Patty and I have both lived and worked for forty years! Normally I sing and write simple gospel songs but since I had six months in jail and the band at the famous Gospel Café had enough songs anyway. Why not spend the time writing? I was alarmed to find out that most of my fellow inmates at the jail had already finished serving their due court appointed sentence, or were being held in jail without bond while waiting before trail. Yes most men in Pod C were being held without any legal charge at all, completely against the laws and constitution of these United States! I had never cared or thought much about the new jail. Why should I. I was one of the good, law abiding, citizens! This book is dedicated to up holding and protecting the constitution of the United States by ending the illegal Civil Commitment laws in Virginia. Yes, I was guilty of a misdemeanor and my six months in jail was completely legal and fair, but let us stand together against abuse of power and the rights of every American!

The Great Ark is fiction. Any resemblance to real persons living or dead is unintended unknown and unwanted. If you believe yourself or someone you know is in this book, you are mistaken because you are not! The Great Ark is a work of fiction, not a true story about my life! That's my story and I'm sticking to it. You have my word! Of course as I just said I am a Felon, a convict and a very dangerous sex offender, so really what's my word worth! My word and twelve dollars will buy you six local phone calls at the regional jail with a dollar to spare. You can then spend 80 cents for a jail Ramen noodle soup the same kind that sells for 15 cents at Walmart (ha-ha).

Ten years ago I founded a local public charity called the Gospel Café here in Roanoke Virginia. You are invited to drop by for a visit and listen to the Gospel Café Band any Friday or Saturday night. That's open microphone sing time. Café Bible College is Thursday night at six and our Sunday Chapel service is 2-4 Pm. Look us up on the web at starcitygospelcafe, or Gospel Café at Roanoke. Be forewarned, I will be there and I am known to be a very dangerous criminal! Ask anybody, enter at your own risk, and think twice before you dare bring your kids. Please join me at my big round corner table, and meet the anti-professor face to face!

(I'm sorry at sixty years old I get confused easily, that anti-professor stuff is just in the book) Sometimes you just don't know (ha-ha).

In the Great Arks pages are many Holy Bible verses! Remember always my friends that the word of God will stand when this world is on fire! All works of fiction like mine will not. Study to find thyself approved, seek your own salvation with fear and trembling and test the spirits that they are of God!

I like to imagine who the "Sons of God" were or are! My understanding or thoughts are just that, my thoughts. Believe me I don't know and I know I don't know. Be not fooled by any man, myself included. If some wise man tells you he does know these answers, than he's a bigger fool than even I. The fear of God is the begging of wisdom! Salvation is of the heart. Do not miss salvation by eighteen inches. One does not have to figure out the universe or every verse of the Holy Bible to be saved, born again and a full heir to the kingdom of Jesus Christ our risen Lord! God will reveal his glory and his ways to us in his time, not ours. My rightness or wrongness in pondering about the details and works of Gods universe does not gain me extra points or separate me from my Lord. We saints stand, live and work in and by faith not our personal understanding. Preaching Jesus Christ our Lord has come in the flesh was born of a virgin and him crucified dead and buried is all important but I am not. Jesus was lifted up on the cross at Calvary to redeem all men from sin, and draw all men to him. Our Lord Jesus defeated hell and the grave and death and gave us salvation as a gift to us, yes those who love him, and serve him. We serve a living Lord! Be not concerned with men's words but be not ignorant of God's teaching. Lean not upon your own understanding but read and study to strengthen your faith and then stand firm in your faith. God's will is even more important than God's word or study and our knowing of it! God's way is not fully known to man but it will be in the future. Praise God he calls us friend and has given us the Holy Scripture! Walk in faith, occupy, trust, and obey for the battle and victory is truly of the Lord and not of man.

A special thanks to all of my friends at the Gospel Café during this trying time of my incarceration and the writing of this book. Thank you for being a true friend when it cost you something! For being tireless workers for the Lord! Truly I'm a blessed man in this world and the next to have you all as partners! We are all "blessed by the best" Thank you to my loving wife Patty, my life partner and soul mate. Pray we may spend what time God grants us in this life together for better or worse, sickness or health, for rich or poor. Thank you for putting up with me these many years. Thank you also to my son Shawn who has taken on many extra responsibilities and duties around the house and around the charity building during my absence. Thank you for your life of serving God, I'm very proud of you son!

To all of my friends, loved ones, detractors and accusers I would like to apologize, and also beg forgiveness for failing you, and or causing any hurt or pain in your life. Please remember that all things work together for good for those who love the Lord! We fight not against flesh and blood but against spiritual wickedness in high places! The battle is of the Lord and it is won! Yes, it matters little the judgments of man, even of Roanoke County Judges! Though these men are Godley empowered, and I have obeyed them as is their due; know that no decree of a judge, just like works of fiction, or trinkets of earthly estates will stand. Only our personal relationship with Jesus and his court will matter in eternity! Forever is a long time! Being able to say the Lord's Prayer and really mean it is all important! I pray that each of my friends and foes alike have the joy of a close daily walk with our Lord Jesus Christ! You are all loved by him and he in me the same! I count you as all equal brothers and sisters in Christ! Please hold no unforgiveness in your heart to my account. Life on this side of the grass is too short for that. I pray you are all "blessed by the best"

T.C. Driver

OUR CIVIL COMMITMENT LAWS IN VIRGINIA

M y fellow citizens it is now time to change or repeal all recently passed civil commitment laws in Virginia! Let us stand together and take this green evil stick from our spoiled child's sticky fingers less that she might soon attack us all. She has grown so powerful under these laws that by attacking us she could thus slay all personal rights nay even unto taking our very lives. Virginia's recently passed civil commitment laws are against the ways and teaching of almighty God and against the laws of our free republic. Our rights even for the most hated among us are more important than layers of false security afforded by a police state. If a man be competent to take punitive punishment and is able to prevail and perform his just sentence and his sentence is then lawfully completed let us be done with him. Our society's just and lawful revenge, yes justice has been satisfied. No longer should he be kept as a public charge! Not one day, not even one hour! If you my fellow self rightist citizens maintain fear, or hate or unforgivenes yet burning in your soul, let it be yours and not that of God's just civil ministers! Dream up another charge if you like or let other inmates slay him by giving tribute to a dirty deputy of your own like mind. You could bring false witness, putting his blood on you and your family. Anything is better and much preferred over our current civil commitment laws. These stupid laws give our civil authority the kingly power to incarcerate at will, without law, without due process, without trial, without charges, without jury, without offense! Our Virginia law makers must be crazy. This ancient type of kingly power is always accomplished through testing of the charge by the various tribes official high priest. This type of unconstitutional abusive power should never be turned over to the civil authorities' of a free republic!

Virginia civil authorities have both a glorious, and also a dirty filthy past full of abuse of power and crimes against God. Yes, our beautiful state has a heritage as the birthplace of freedom and many great presidents but is also the home of a history of flagrant abuse of power and one not so great even shameful president Woodrow Wilson. From the birthplace of slavery in the new world in 1607, to a strong hold of the eugenics movement with untold horrors practiced in state hospitals by sick witch doctor physiatrists, to laws of Jim Crow segregation, the crooked machine politics of the Byrd years, and redistricting fraud you name it we have it made in Virginia. Our proud state is now today back in the history books. She stands alone of all the fifty states with unconstitutional and abusive civil commitment laws.

Yes, Richmond is now the world leader, the proud worst of the worst in all of the American Nation. They are embarrassing us Virginians once again! Since 1998 Virginia has run a completely unconstitutional justice system. We did alright for hundreds of years without these stupid and dangerous laws and we do not need them now. The men in our general assembly in charge of this constitutional blasphemy should each and everyone be all now put into the civil commitment prisons their own selves. Hanging is too good for them! Our leader's total and known contempt for the just laws of a free republic can be shown yes, even show-cased by its recent traffic laws. Special enormous fines were imposed on groups of citizens depending on where they lived! A lowly Virginia domestic serf would pay big fines, out of state people "who may be somebody" and may even have a lawyer would pay low or no fines. This total contempt for equal treatment of citizens before the law or to simple blind justice is on public display in Virginia for everyone to see! Even a dummy old retired truck driver like me could smell a breach of the constitution in these laws. The same is true with Virginia's civil commitment laws. This contempt for equality before the law goes way back to our roots in Virginia law even into our simple traffic safety laws and codes. I remember laughing out loud while sitting at a desk at the DMV years ago while studying for a test to drive a bus in Virginia. The Virginia code still says today that it is against the law for people on your bus to sit in the floor, or isle, or sit in unattached lawn chairs or to stand everybody must have a real seat; unless the people on the bus were migrant farm workers, "read Mexicans" they did not matter. Our safety laws did not apply to migrant farm workers (ha-ha) they officially do not count for much here in Virginia. Our masters in Richmond and Washington are not stupid. They are lawyers who understand completely when they trample all over your rights. No, they are in rebellion against God and think we are not watching! It's them or us, it's that simple. We must as free men each stand up for the rights of the few against the tyranny of the state, even men we disagree with or who are themselves disagreeable to us. If we fail to stand up for our rights we will soon find ourselves on the terrorist hit list and all of our freedoms gone. Liberty is more precious that a false state of security through a police state, this is the message of history. It we continue down this road to serfdom and slavery we will lose America. Do not give up on even small freedoms even if they seem not worth standing up for. Safety check points, road side police pat downs the ole "show me your papers" will be next. Patrick Henry and George Madison and George Washington and Thomas Jefferson would all be ashamed of us. We have shamed ourselves by not attending to citizenship duties! Our progressive hicks in Richmond are no better than the fat Georgia sheriffs arresting speeders to pick peaches for local growers, the ole "pick or pay' game they are famous for. Ours is much more serious! Only naïve young uneducated women, or brain washed girly men would seek absolute personal safety and or total security by giving the kings guard dogs absolute power! Let us put an end to our recently passed civil commitment laws and put an end to another chapter of Richmond's abuse of power. Shame on us if we pass this evil on to our kids in the name of protecting them!

T.C. Driver